Fire and Steel

The Cor Chronicles
Vol. II

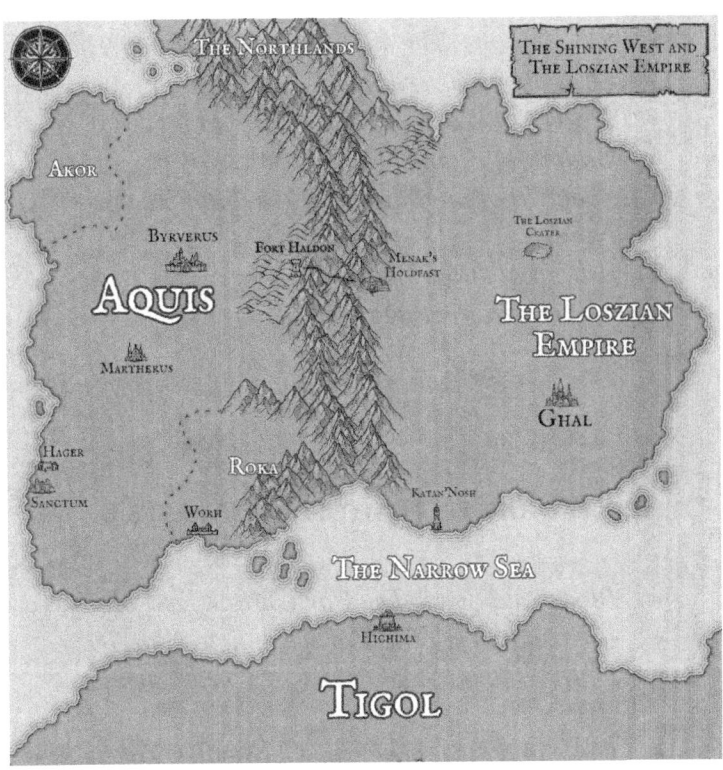

UPCOMING NOVELS BY MARTIN V. PARECE II

- *The Oathbreaker's Daughter (Book 1 of The Dragonknight Trilogy)*
- *Wolves of War – A John Hartman Novel*
- *Bound By Flame (The Chronicle of Thyss)**
- *Spectres of the Black Sun – A John Hartman Novel*
- *Advent of Judgement*
- *The Horizon's Edge*

OTHER WORKS BY MARTIN V. PARECE II

- *Blood and Steel (The Cor Chronicles Vol. I)**
- *Fire and Steel (The Cor Chronicles Vol. II)**
- *Darkness and Steel (The Cor Chronicles Vol. III)**
- *Gods and Steel (The Cor Chronicles Vol. IV)**
- *Blood Betrayal (The Cor Chronicles Vol. V)**
- *Blood Loss (The Chronicle of Rael)**
- *Tendrils in the Dark – Eight Tales of Horror*

*Denotes a novel of Rumedia.

Fire and Steel

The Cor Chronicles Vol. II

By

Martin V. Parece II

ISBN-10 : 147811357X
ISBN-13 : 978-1478113577

Copyright 2024. Martin Parece and Parece Publishing. www.martinparece.com

Cover Art by Jan-Michael Barlow. www.janmichaelbarlow.com

All Rights Reserved.

This book is a work of fiction. Any names, characters, places, or events are solely the author's imagination and used fictionally. Any resemblance to anyone, anything, or anyplace is purely coincidental.

Any scanning, uploading or distribution of this book or any part of its contents is theft of the author's intellectual property. Please consider this before pirating copyrighted materials – independent content creators work hard to bring expression for the enjoyment of all and the enrichment of our culture.

I dedicate this one to my father, who has given me more than I can ever repay.

And my wife, without whose support I would never have finished.

Prologue

The world of Rumedia has seen several human civilizations come and go over millennia. Our history dates back only three thousand years, and we have little knowledge of what came before us. As Chronicler, the gods have gifted me with the sight of everything that Their people have seen, but it is known that before our gods arose, there were other pantheons. We do not know what happened to them, nor do we know what happened to their peoples, only to say that their civilizations apparently crumbled and disappeared with the loss of their gods. Sometimes, we find signs of these peoples in the forms of ancient writings, tombs, or even entire buildings that they left behind. Sometimes, we find amazing artifacts that give us clues as to the strength of their powers.

Men rule this world now, and I believe that men ruled it for thousands of years before I became Chronicler. But men are not the only denizens. There are other beings and creatures in Rumedia, and most of them can only be found in the dark and deep places of the world. What purpose they serve, I cannot say, as they serve no gods that we know, and they do not entangle themselves in the workings of men.

One such race of creatures are known as the Grek, and they live inside the volcanic mountains of the continent of Dulkur with an average lifespan of eight hundred years. Grek live in the great heat produced by the magma of these mountains, and they pay it no mind, breathing sulfuric fumes as easy as men breathe fresh air. They are typically larger than men, even Loszians, standing an average of eight feet in height, and they have lanky, bony legs and arms to match that hang nearly to their knees. A Grek's skin is as rough as tanned leather, colored in mottled grays, browns, and greens, and to gaze on a Grek's face would remind one of a bullfrog with its great eyes and lack of ears, excluding that the protruding lower jaw is full of sharp teeth.

While the Grek live deep underground and inside the volcanic mountains, it is not unknown for one to come to the surface on occasion. They can live for a short while in the open air before having to return to their own sulfuric climes. Carnivores by nature, the Grek find human flesh to be particularly tasty, though they have learned it dangerous to seek human prey too often. Their biology is wholly foreign to ours, allowing them to go large spans of time, perhaps even decades without a meal, which is advantageous to them as the primary food source a Grek tends to be another Grek.

Fortunately for the Grek, the imperative to mate generally exceeds the need to eat. Otherwise, it would be unlikely for the species to survive for long, and as might be expected from a species of cannibals, Grek do not make quality parents. The males mate and immediately leave the females when sated, and the females birth and care for their children only in the disinterested way of a child who is forced to do chores. They raise their spawn only until the young can walk on their own, and then the mothers abandon them to their own devices. As far as their cannibalism is concerned, the Grek seem to avoid killing their own immediate blood relations but do nothing to stop another Grek from eating their offspring.

Around two hundred A.C. by the Western calendar, a Grek was born who came to call himself Feghul. Unremarkable for his species in appearance, his mother abandoned him and his sister shortly before they turned the age of four. As Grek are concerned, this is still a very young age, and Feghul and his sister had only just begun to walk and learn what was edible and what was not. Unfortunately, Feghul's sister met her end in the mouth of an adolescent Grek, who, his hunger sated, left Feghul alone in the dark caves. Feghul did not mourn his sister, since such emotions are somewhat beyond the Grek's comprehension, and he continued about his life such as it was.

Feghul was nearly twenty, not even to budding adolescence in Grek terms, when he first ventured outside of the mountain caves in which he lived. Deep in one of the caves, he warmed himself by a magma pool when he scented something on the air the likes of which he had never before encountered. A sweet odor was carried by a slight draft of fetid, non-sulfuric air, and though the current of what we would consider fresh air was repulsive to Feghul, it was the new scent that caught his attention. He followed it through labyrinthine caves miles deep into the mountains. The smell and the air current on which it was carried continued to grow stronger as he made his way out of the depths. Eventually, he reached a point where the sulfuric air of his home was all but gone, leaving him with the distasteful air of the world above and outside the caves, but the unknown scent drew him onward.

The caves eventually ended, opening to the outside world, and Feghul had to shield his eyes from the bright sunlight that threatened to blind him. The cave's mouth overlooked a lush green jungle, full of large leafy plants and trees, the likes of which Feghul had never seen, since such things obviously do not grow in his subterranean home. As he sniffed the air and looked about, he saw the source of the smell that drew him from so deep. Perhaps a mile away and well below the mountain, a clearing containing a human village carved a clearing in the jungle.

The thing was alien to him, as he had no idea what to make of thatched huts or the near black skinned inhabitants that he could see milling about their tasks. Extremely curious in a way little different from a human child, Feghul carefully made his way down the mountainside, hiding behind the rocks so as not to be seen by any of the humans. Following his nose, he entered the jungle, though he was loath at first to touch any of the dense green growth. Such things did not exist in his underground world, and he feared them at first. Feghul learned that the plants would do nothing to harm him, and he eventually came to ignore them completely as he approached the village.

The jungle ended abruptly at the clearing in which Feghul could see a large number of huts with human beings moving around the area, all involved in some chore or another. The round huts were made of dried mud with thatched roofs, and the rear of the huts faced the jungle foliage. A few feet away and behind one of these huts, Feghul saw a small child who played completely alone. It should be noted that Feghul did not recognize the child as such, except that he knew that this human was much smaller than the others, and he seemed to have an innate sense that this being was somehow like him, at least in age if in no other way.

Feghul edged around the clearing, staying out of sight of any human adults, until the child was directly in front of him. He was not stealthy in the dense jungle foliage, and the child had stopped playing to look in his direction. The child, female he was sure from her smell, did not move or shout to one of the larger humans; she merely sat there and waited expectantly. Certain she could see him, Feghul stood, nearly five feet tall, and shambled out of the foliage to stand only a few feet from the child. She was ugly to his eye and small at just over half his height, and she sat quietly in consideration of him, her hands holding a tiny cloth figure.

"*Cazak thon dak tos?*" came a sound from an opening that he assumed to be the girl's mouth.

It should be said that the Grek have no language of their own, so Feghul had no concept of speech as communication. He sat down on his haunches and scratched the side of his face, staring at the little girl. She stared back at him and repeated her question, which of course received no answer from the Grek. She held out the cloth figure with one hand towards Feghul, and when he made no move to take it, she stood up, walked over to him and sat down next to him. She placed the doll in his clawed hands, and he had never felt anything so soft against his rough skin before.

"*Hagat tosh walik Kytha*," she said, and he could only look at the doll and then back at the girl without comprehension.

She took the doll from him and moved to sit right in front of him, mere inches away. She continued to speak and played with the doll in front of him, trying to include him in whatever game she was involved in. The little girl would occasionally laugh, and Feghul, after hearing the sound several times, endeavored to duplicate it. His laugh was a terrible sound to hear, like two rough stones being grated together from within his chest, but the small girl accepted it for what it was. Every time she laughed Feghul would try to mimic the sound. They played in this way for the better part of an hour.

However, the little girl's mother realized that her daughter was no longer where she was supposed to be, and the woman began a search of the small village, ending with her coming around the backside of the hut. Seeing her daughter sitting with the disgusting creature, a monster of unknown origin, the woman loosed a terrifying scream. The little girl and Feghul both started to their feet with the suddenness of the sound, and Feghul backed away from the girl, her doll still in his hand at that moment. The woman continued to scream, bringing warriors running with axes, clubs, and spears, but the little girl did not understand and tried to calm her mother. The men arrived and surrounded Feghul, shouting at him and threatening him with their brandished weapons, and Feghul did not understand their angry voices and gestures.

The men had not enclosed him completely, and Feghul turned and charged back into the jungle. The men were shocked into not following him for just a moment, and he could hear the little girl behind him wailing as she shouted, "Kytha! Kytha!" Feghul ran as fast as he could through the dense foliage, and the warriors followed him closely. When he reached the mountain, it was easier for him to outdistance the men, as climbing the rocky incline came naturally to him. He disappeared into a cave and hid himself deep within the mountain. After a short time, the men realized that the cave was in fact only one in a system of caves within the volcano, and realizing the impossibility of tracking the Grek, they called off the hunt.

It is possible that Feghul was closer to being human than any of his kind, for he sat quietly in that cave for hours simply staring at the doll he had taken from the girl. As years passed, he would look at the doll and long to return to the girl and listen to the sounds she made that he did not understand. One day, Feghul decided that he would return to the village and find the closest thing to a friend that any Grek had ever known.

It was night when he climbed back down to the village, following the scents in the air to one particular hut. While he was not the stealthiest of creatures, he remembered that the males of the village had shouted at him and tried to hurt him with their weapons, so he moved as quietly as he could manage. The village was larger than he remembered it, and the scent led him to a hut close to the village perimeter.

Entering, he found two figures asleep on the ground. A large male lay there with his limbs intertwined around a smaller female form. The scent was unmistakably that of the girl, but this female was much larger than he remembered and looked very much like the screaming woman he had seen. Then he noticed, cuddled in the crook of her arm, a third tiny creature that made odd soft sounds.

Now it should be said that the Grek are not entirely stupid creatures, but their perceptions of time are extremely distorted compared to ours. When one lives hundreds of years and is still a child at the age of forty, albeit a six foot tall child, the concept that a small child can grow to adulthood in less than twenty years is entirely beyond a Grek's understanding. It had been long enough for the girl to grow and have a child of her own since Feghul had run from the village's warriors, but to his mind it seemed only to be just the other day.

He hunched over the sleeping forms and extended one of his clawed fingers to run it down the exposed arm of the sleeping woman. His manner was extremely gentle, just like many small children have done to their own parents in the middle of the night. Unfortunately, Feghul comprehended neither his own strength, nor the ease with which he could harm a human being, and his claw carved away several inches of the woman's brown flesh.

She bolted upright screaming frantically and clutching the wound, the jostling motion of which disturbed the baby and set him to screaming. The man with her immediately attacked Feghul, attempting to grapple with him, but Feghul's strength was terrible when compared to a human's even at his young age. He tossed the man like a large version of the doll in his hand across the hut, and he crashed into the back wall and fell still to the ground. The woman continued to scream, and Feghul could hear that the rest of the village was beginning to wake due to the commotion. Frightened that men would again come and try to hurt him, he dropped the cloth doll and charged from the village back to his mountain home. It was only after her husband was roused and she was sure that he would be well that she looked at what the creature had left in her hut, and as a wise woman bandaged her wounded, she vaguely remembered a childhood friend from long ago that had never returned to play with her again.

In his caves, Feghul lamented and screamed his fury, pounding his clawed fists against stone. He was furious and confused that she did not realize who he was and even more furious that he had dropped the one thing by which he had to remember her. For a moment during his raging and mourning, the Grek became nearly human, having experienced two very powerful emotions, but he collapsed into the depth of his sadness for a time. Feghul never again ventured outside of the caves, except to occasionally eat a hapless human who was unfortunate enough to be on the mountainside.

The Grek have a relatively instinctual existence, but Feghul always seemed slightly different than others of his species. He had thoughts and inclinations that went beyond the mere instinct of self preservation, food, and mating. One thing that always stayed in his consciousness was the use of weapons by the warriors in the village below. He even had one, a curved sword that he had taken from a man who became his meal. The weapon intrigued him, but he found that his own claws and fists were far more dangerous. The sword did have one advantage though, and that was adding length to his attacks.

Feghul spent the next three hundred years of his life attempting to make similar weapons. His volcanic home had no shortage of raw materials with which he could experiment, and he found that the raw heat of the magma pools nearby could heat metals to make them malleable. He learned how to shape them once heated and how to make them sharp. Feghul determined that iron was harder to heat and work than metals like copper but was substantially stronger and could be made to be much sharper. Unfortunately, none of these metals could make a weapon that proved to be more effective than his claws.

Perhaps it was pure chance, or perhaps Hykan or some other god of which we have no knowledge guided him, but Feghul one day stumbled upon an underground lake when exploring one of the higher sets of caves. Daylight poured through a huge opening in the mountain dozens of feet overhead and reflected off the surface of the lake's calm waters. Deep in the water at one end of the lake, a green gleam unlike anything he had ever seen caught Feghul's eye. He sat on his haunches next to the lake's edge staring at the green light that shined from below.

Simply put, the Grek do not swim. In fact, they do not even need water to survive, unlike most creatures; as I said, their biology is completely foreign to us. Immensely strong, the Grek are extremely dense of bone and muscle, and to enter water means that they simply sink to the bottom. Feghul's first attempt at entering the lake did not go well; as he walked into its depths, his weight keeping him firmly on the lake's bottom, the foul wetness of it poured into his open mouth and made him choke. He clambered up onto the lakeshore, coughing and hacking up the lake water.

After several more attempts, Feghul learned to close his mouth and hold his breath as he simply walked on the bottom of the lake. As he approached the source of the reflecting green light, he could make out the shape of a small boulder. Upon closer inspection, Feghul realized it was made of stone, but had a vein of a bizarre greenish metal running through it. It was heavy and well settled into the lake's bottom, but after returning to the surface several times for breath, Feghul eventually hefted the object out of the lake's depths and onto the shore.

Most of the Grek are pure wanderers, but Feghul had a favorite haunt near a large lava pool. The Grek are not impervious to such things, but they do find a brief wallow in lava quite relaxing. He carried the find back to his lair to spend several days inspecting it at great length. He used his primitive tools and brute strength to break away the excess stone and rock until he was left with only the green metal, and it was stronger than any metal he had yet seen in the mountain depths, even iron.

To be certain, Feghul was an extraordinary example of the race of Grek, certainly more intelligent, with some ability of rational thought, and he even showed signs of emotion at points of his life. But what force or intelligence guided his clawed hands through the next steps will forever be a mystery. Using the hellish heat of the magma pools, Feghul softened the alien metal to workability. It would not melt but became very soft so that he could shape it into a blade. Feghul had once loved a curved sword, a bronze scimitar that he had taken off of a human warrior, but he had accidentally broken it on the hide of another Grek. He worked the green metal into a similar shape and even fitted the new blade with the same guard, an irregularly shaped hexagon. The metal still glowing, Feghul sharpened the sword's outer edge to a razor that he somehow knew would cut nearly anything with little effort and retain its vorpal edge forever.

Feghul, a member of a savage and unintelligent race of creatures, had crafted a sword that even the greatest masters from Tigol would envy and covet. He doted on the blade, showing it great affection, and in return the sword sang to him whenever he wished. It was more than a prideful trophy, however; he used it in combat with the occasional Grek or human he encountered, extending his reach to a truly vicious distance. Feghul exulted in the death he caused with his blade.

It was one day deep in his cave that he scented something sweet that he had not smelled in perhaps a century. The lovely smell of supple human flesh wafted through the air currents into his lair, and he was amazed that he had not noticed it sooner, for it was close. He puzzled over this as no human had ever entered the caves this deeply, as they could not seem to survive the heat, and the air was toxic to them, and as it came closer, it became quite apparent to him that the smell was that of a female, reminding him of the girl child turned to woman long ago.

Whoever she was, she tried very hard to approach as quietly as possible, but Feghul's ears were keen to pick up any sound not natural to the caves. She was most definitely heading toward his lair, and she could not be far away. The fact the human was willing to just walk so deeply into the caves made Feghul cautious, and taking his scimitar, he lowered himself into the lava pool. The cave floor sloped gently into the magma, which allowed him to keep his head and the scimitar out of the molten rock. Someone approaching from the far side of his cave would only see his eyes and the top of his head if they were able to distinguish him from the cave itself at all.

Feghul did not have to wait long before the woman came down the cave tunnel leading to his lair. She was beautiful with the bronze skin and golden hair of the nobility of Dulkur, but this fact was completely lost on the Grek. She wore clothes, as Feghul had seen other humans do, and was clad in a shimmering black material that clung tightly to her form. Her feet were protected from the hot stone floor of the cave by soft soled sandals held to her feet by silk laces that wrapped around her calves and shins. She strode into his cave with a swagger that a human would have recognized as confidence, if not arrogance. When she entered his abode, she came to a halt and surveyed the interior intently, her eyes washing over Feghul briefly. The woman smiled slightly as she moved toward and fondled the implements Feghul used to make his weapon. She then turned and looked directly at the Grek in his hiding place.

That she saw him was plain enough, and Feghul jumped to his feet, his rough hide steaming in the slightly cooler air from the extreme heat of the lava pool. He held his scimitar in one clawed hand, and the woman's eyes rested on the beautiful weapon. Her smile widened as her eyes narrowed, and Feghul knew suddenly that she had come to take his possession from him.

He roared in anger and charged the human. A mere twenty feet separated the two figures, and knowing her life was in immediate danger, the woman extended her left hand in front of her. Blue flame shot from her fingertips and washed over the Grek, who stopped suddenly in the unexpected attack. The fire was extremely hot, but no worse than the heat of the lava, which he enjoyed bathing in from time to time. Realizing that she could not harm him, he began to approach her slowly, relishing with every step the violence he was about to inflict upon this trespasser. He laughed, the sound a horrible mimicry of the little girl's from long ago.

Feghul was an oddity for his race to be certain; in addition to creating his scimitar. He was capable of some emotion and thought beyond basic survival instincts, but even this Grek could not have been prepared for what happened next. He could not have known that while Hykan was this sorceress' patron god, she had some ability to call on power from the other three elemental gods, nor would such knowledge have helped him.

The woman backed toward the mouth of the tunnel that opened into Feghul's cave and crossed her arms violently in front of her as if they would protect her from his impending attack, and she muttered some words that he could neither hear, nor understand if he had. He stopped his approach, hearing a sound build from behind her in the tunnel. It was a low rumble that built slowly to a roar, and the cave began to vibrate with some oncoming force.

Having so little experience with it, Feghul did not recognize the sound of rushing water. The woman dove to one side, covering her head with her arms, as gigantic plume of water exploded from the tunnel and impacted the Grek with impressive force. Though he did not fall to the cave floor, it did force him back a step or two. It was appallingly cold, and under its rushing roar, hissing emanated as it sizzled away upon striking the cave, Feghul's hide, and the lava pool beyond. As the frigid water impacted his body, the opposing elemental forces of extreme heat born of fire and lava and unnaturally cold water cancelled each other out violently. Intensely hot steam filled the cave, but it was not this that ended the Grek. His hide, his protection from all things that would harm him, grew stiff and rigid. As the flow of water ended, he realized that he could not move, and a sound little different from the cracking of glass sounded in the now frighteningly quiet cave. Feghul looked with instinctual horror as his now tight hide pulled itself in opposing directions, cracks forming all along its surface arrayed like a spider's web. He had one last thought, to get back to the safety and comfort of the lava pool, and it was that final effort he placed on his muscles that wrought his end. What little control he had caused a great twitch in his legs, and though they did not move from where he stood, it caused his entire torso to wheel and fall off balance to the ground. As Feghul's body impacted, there was a great shatter, and he came apart in every direction as if his body had always been made of brittle stone or glass.

All that was left of Feghul was his forearm and clawed hand still wrapped around the hilt of his scimitar. The woman stood from her position on the floor, brushing imaginary dirt off her black silk clothing. She casually strode to the severed claw holding the sword, the only part of Feghul that was spared, and picked it up by the creature's forearm. She carefully took hold of the sword by its odd guard and uncurled the claws from around its hilt to let the hand and forearm fall to the cave floor. She held the scimitar by its hilt with her right hand and marveled that a creature such as Feghul could make such a beautiful and lethal weapon. She could feel its strength adding to her own, and she knew it would amplify her sorcery as well as be deadly in its own right. The golden haired woman of Dulkur whispered a prayer of thanks to Hykan, Elemental God of Fire, before turning and leaving the cave behind.

1.

Cor stared incredulously as Thyss related how she came by her blade. Hykan, God of Fire and her patron god, had imparted a vision unto her of the scimitar and where it might be found, showing her how a monster named Feghul came to construct the weapon. Cor had of course seen visions of and through his own apparently enchanted weapons and armor, and it was becoming quite clear to him that these items had their own intelligence and will. It seemed that these artifacts always found their way to someone who could make the best use of their power, one way or the other.

Cor rode his brilliant, golden palomino named Kelli, and he rode ready for battle excluding his helm, which stayed conveniently clipped to his saddle should he need to don it quickly. The helm, round and large with no apparent visor, would have covered the entirety of his head and neck, hiding the long and unkempt near black hair of a Westerner and the gray skin of a Dahken. His face appeared strong and angular, as if a solid jaw, strong chin, and cheekbones were chiseled from stone by an artisan of the greatest skill. Cor wore the hauberk and legguards he had retrieved from Noth's catacombs; the match pieces to his helm, they too were apparently made of gleaming black steel. The hauberk was actually two solid pieces of plate armor, a front and a back that buckled together under the arms. They were wrought in the form of a heavily muscled torso, and the torso they protected was not quite as developed but no less strong. The legguards were made of several pieces of black plate held together by chain, and a pair of plate sabatons and chain gauntlets, both of which he had taken from

Taraq'nok's armory, rounded out his ensemble. This left most of his upper and fore arms unprotected, the deathly pallor of his kind for all to see.

Soulmourn and Ebonwing hung ever present at his sides. Soulmourn, the single edged longsword he had taken from Lord Dahken Rena's tomb, reflected purple in sunlight, and Cor was still uncertain as to what kind of metal from which it was made. He had never sharpened it once, and he was certain that neither had Rena. Yet the blade always remained undamaged, unscratched, and free from rust, even as it punched through steel armor. The crosspiece was unadorned and led to a hilt that was leather wrapped for the top hand and plain steel for the bottom. A pommel, wrought of steel in the form of a miniature, fantastic skull completed the hilt.

Cor always held Ebonwing in his left hand while in battle, and he always thought that the fetish had some power of which he was unaware. He felt it course through him every time he fought. Ebonwing had been a symbol for kings and queens of some ancient world long past, and Cor was certain they had left part of themselves within it to make sure the talisman never left the sword for long. The thing was evil looking at nearly a foot long with a leather wrapped handle made of ebony. A bleached white skull, perfectly human in appearance if one overlooked that it was the size of a cat's skull, adorned its head, and two tiny black batwings attached to its neck right below the skull. However, Cor never had any reason to suspect an evil nature about the thing, despite its truly wicked appearance.

After she related her tale, Cor told Thyss of how he came to own his own weapons. She did not stare in wonder at him, as he did when she told her tale, but he could see flickers of interest spark within her eyes when he related the battle with the giant spider. He described the building in which he found Ebonwing in detail, both inside and out, and this brought several questions from Thyss as she tried to understand what magic was at use in its construction. At this, Cor regressed back to the vision Soulmourn had granted him, reciting both weapons' history as well as he could remember it. Thyss merely nodded at this in understanding but made no further comment.

They rode at the head of a ragged band of mostly children, and as such, they had to stop regularly. The children simply were not prepared for the hardships of a journey, and the weather turning colder as autumn deepened did not help matters. Cor worried about the infant almost constantly, and at times he could hear the babe crying from behind him. The wet nurse had chosen to accompany the group as she had no family of her own, and the baby needed someone to care for him. And beyond that, nothing other than continued slavery awaited her should she stay.

Cor did not fear pursuit; in fact, he knew it was inevitable. Emperor Nadav would send someone, likely a small, swift moving force to Taraq'nok's castle, and of course, the slaves and overseers that the group left behind would point the pursuers in the right direction. But Cor knew, that even with swift horses, the emperor's trackers were a good ten days behind, if Taraq'nok's statement as to the distance of Ghal was accurate. He estimated that, if they could not pick up their pace, it would take five days to reach the Loszian side of the Spine, and there he would somehow have to face Lord Menak.

Cor endeavored to puzzle through this problem, but he could not come up with a clear or obvious solution. When they stopped for the night, the group huddled closely together for warmth, as both he and Thyss thought it a bad idea to light a fire. Cor strayed from the others and walked alone in the dark some distance from the meager camp. There was no chance that Menak would simply allow Cor and his refugees to pass the gate into the mountains. Despite Menak's apparent wish to avoid Loszian politics, he would not miss such a chance at glory – the killing of over two dozen Dahken. Also, to allow them to pass would no doubt forfeit his own life, and if Cor was certain of one thing, it was that the Loszians value their personal survival over all else. Cor heard quiet footsteps approaching from behind, and he stopped his slow pacing.

"What are you doing, Dahken Cor?" came Thyss' voice, almost a whisper.

"I don't know how I am going to get these people through Menak's garrison," he answered, turning to face her.

"Oh, I think your only course is plain," she said, still approaching. He could see that one corner of her mouth was slightly upturned in a knowing smile. "You are going to have to kill the Loszians."

"There are hundreds of them – warriors, crossbowmen, and a necromancer. What chance do I have?" he asked. Even as he put forth the question, he could feel the urge to spill blood grow within him in response to Thyss' suggestion. Cor suspected from where the urge came, and he pushed it away for now. The time would come.

"Perhaps you should have considered that before setting out in this direction," she answered him. "But you have me, and I will not be conquered by Loszian worms. Somehow, I am sure they burn as well as anybody."

Cor continued to work on the problem over the course of the next day. He could admit to himself that he was no master tactician, and in fact, his actual experience in combat was somewhat limited. But so far, he had been outnumbered in every battle he had fought against men, and he prevailed in all of them. Surprise and a quick first strike were no small advantage in any of his victories, and he would need to rely on them again here. His only chance was to come at the garrison at night; the few guards and pickets about would be protecting from an attack from the other side of the wall, not from behind. Perhaps, if he struck quickly enough, he could get his Dahken to the other side and into the Spine before the Loszians even knew what was happening. Something told him it was foolish, but he saw few options.

"Well of course," Thyss said. "Even I am not so suicidal as to attempt a direct attack in the middle of the day. We will need to scout their positions. If we know precisely where Menak's men are posted, your gambit just may succeed."

"I know something about sailing, farming, and fighting, but I don't know anything about scouting," Cor retorted darkly.

"It's simple. You must get close enough to see them, and if they see you, you're dead," Thyss responded, and she laughed heartily at the disdainful look on Cor's face. "Leave it to me, Dahken Cor."

The group traveled better this day than they had yesterday, crossing more miles in the same amount of time. It impressed Cor how well this group, mostly children, had adapted to this new hardship, and he wondered if it had something to do with most of them being slave stock. He estimated that they would be within a few miles of the Loszian fort by the end of their fourth day. Thyss would then go ahead alone to glean what information she could, and they would spend the next day formulating the specifics of their attack. Cor did not sleep well.

Queen Erella of Aquis had been here before she was sure, but it seemed to have been long ago. She stood on a massive plain, populated with plush, knee high grass that stretched in all directions as far as the eye could see. Massive mountains adorned one horizon, but she could not judge in what direction of the compass they were. The sun overhead was completely obscured by massive, stone gray clouds. She remembered it had been a dream long ago that she had seen this place, and it occurred to her that she dreamed again.

As Queen Erella looked across the plain, she knew she would see the black armored warrior with his sword and fetish. He wore steel plate legguards, the plates connected by chain links, a hauberk of solid plate, and a bulbous black helm, all of which gleamed even in the subdued light. This time, Dahken Cor did not stand alone, but with over a score of other armored warriors. She knew they were a formidable fighting force, and she could feel their strength and power emanating toward her. But somehow, she knew this was not so, for the rise of a group of Dahken warriors had not yet happened.

From the direction of the mountains came a massive and frightening host. Thousands upon thousands of marching feet stamped the ground as an incredible army marched towards the Dahken band. The front lines of this army were the walking dead, those corpses that the horrible Loszian necromancy had forced to rise again and do their master's bidding. Queen Erella shuddered both in revulsion and anger at the desecration the Loszians wrought upon the dead.

Behind them came live foot soldiers, the first ranks of which were a downtrodden lot, dirty and wretchedly thin. They wore no armor; in fact, few wore clothing of any sort, and they carried crude wood clubs for weapons. Then came the true soldiers. There were two ranks of armored professionals wearing black chain mail and plate armor, and they carried their swords, axes, and maces in ways that one was certain they knew how to use them. Immediately behind these men-at-arms was a line of armored crossbowmen. These weapons had less range than the West's longbows but were feared for their ability to punch holes into armor, where arrows from bows had to find weak points and joints. They also required less flexibility of movement, allowing their users to wear heavier armor.

Riding chariots, the robed figures of Loszian necromancers brought up the rear. They were all long of limb, tall figures, none shorter than perhaps six feet and many as tall as seven or more. All Loszian necromancers are lords of some level in the empire, and most wore dark colored silk robes carrying seals, crests, and other emblems of their rank and title. Each Loszian seemed to have his own small group of soldiers surrounding him or her, a personal guard to protect their lord from direct attack. Though this was not a likely scenario, as they were in the rear of the army, far from where the battle would take place. It occurred to Queen Erella that these elite guards protected their masters from the treachery of fellow Loszians, rather than the army's foes.

The great army marched onward, a huge dark mass that seemed to engulf the grassy plain as it inexorably closed the distance to the Dahken. The army stopped short of the Dahken only a few hundred feet away, and the corpses, slaves, and soldiers began to spread out on either flank. They thinned and stretched the ranks in either direction, slowly forming a circle around the Dahken until the small group of warriors was fully enclosed by the forces of darkness. The scene held still for several long moments before the Dahken drew their weapons and arrayed themselves in their own circle, defiantly waiting for the impending attack.

The risen came first. The innermost circle of the Loszian host shambled its way without haste for the Dahken. No other Loszian soldier or slave moved a muscle as the corpses waded into the ring of defenders. They were no match for the warriors as the Dahken hacked through bone, sinew, and flesh to bring down body after body. At times, it appeared the mass of corpses might overwhelm the Dahken, but the blood warriors would suddenly surge to regain their place. If a Dahken went down, it was only a matter of moments before he or she were again standing to the fight. Hills, and then small mountains, of bodies stacked around the Dahken's defensive ring as the Loszians power over the walking corpses was broken one by one by Dahken sword blows. A horn blew, and the remaining risen, now reduced to half their original number, pulled back from the Dahken and returned to their original positions at the front of the army.

Erella could see the soldiers shifting ranks forward and back, though she could not see the purpose of these movements at first. It seemed somewhat random until the crossbowmen created a layer directly behind the walking corpses. They positioned themselves so that they could see between the risen and fire their crossbows. Then, the crossbowmen with the walking corpses in front slowly closed the distance between themselves and the Dahken, no doubt to reach the range at which their crossbows would do optimum damage. Erella surmised that the walking dead would provide cover to the crossbowmen should an errant bolt miss its target and cross the field to hit a friend.

The concentric rings of lifeless animated corpses and crossbowmen stopped only a few dozen feet from the Dahken. The scene held still and silent for an eternal moment before a single shout went up from within the Loszian army. A loud "twang" erupted as hundreds, if not thousands, of crossbows loosed their quarrel simultaneously, and steel tipped death shot like gossamer at the armored Dahken. An enormous wall of orange fire exploded around the Dahken, consuming the rain of crossbow bolts as quickly they were fired and then was extinguished. The Loszian crossbowmen were momentarily stunned into inaction, and it took several shouted orders and whip lashings from officers for them to shake off their shock and begin reloading. Even from her hilltop, it was difficult to see due to the massive number of people surrounding the Dahken, but Erella thought she saw an unarmored woman with golden hair in the middle of the Dahken's defensive ring.

The Loszians, their focus returned to the task at hand reloaded their crossbows and prepared to fire. Orders were shouted, but from her position some distance off, Queen Erella could not make out exactly what was said. Another order was shouted, immediately followed by the twang of crossbows, but Erella could see that only perhaps a third of the quarrels had been loosed. Again, a wall of fire sprouted from the ground to protect the Dahken, incinerating the bolts in flight. The flame's roar obscured the sound of more crossbows being fired, but Erella could see an almost constant barrage assaulting the wall of flames. The Loszians fired their crossbows in groups, which allowed time to reload but kept a constant pressure on the Dahken's magical protection. She idly wondered where the Dahken had found such power, but she also knew it wouldn't matter much longer. In only a few minutes, the wall of flames lost volume and became thin and translucent. Erella knew that without help, the Dahken would soon be at the mercy of the Loszians.

It was with that thought that Queen Erella of Aquis awoke in her plush bed. She thought back to the last time she had such a dream; then it had been more like a nightmare. She had bolted upright in bed, covered in sweat, and she could feel the presence of her god in the room. This time, she was calm and serene, and while she could not feel Garod, Erella knew he had brought her this vision. And strangely, she was fairly certain as to what it meant.

The aged queen arose from her bed and clothed herself in a thick, warm robe to conceal the simple shift in which she had gone to sleep. Wrapping the robe about her body, she then stepped into a pair of soft slippers that she kept at her bedside. She crossed the room to her door with a smooth grace that for her apparent age would have amazed an onlooker. Of course, she was actually much older than she appeared, and she appeared ancient.

Normally, she would have asked one of her chamber guards to find Palius, who would most likely be asleep in his own chamber and bring him to her. But this time, she felt it better to go to him. She exited her chambers, motioning for the guards to stay at her door so that she may cross the palace alone with her thoughts. She crossed paths with several guards on her way, and they would all straighten quite suddenly upon seeing her approach. Even those who already stood at a perfectly erect posture found a way to stand more so.

Even though he was Queen Erella's most trusted advisor, Palius' chambers, like most in the castle, stood unguarded. The old man requested it to be so, having said on many occasions that he would not be so presumptuous as to believe he was as important as his queen. She soundlessly opened the door and slipped in, allowing only a small lance of flickering orange torchlight to penetrate the dark interior. Palius' first chamber was his study and office, and the queen quietly glided through a portal to her right that led to his bedchamber. Autumn had been unseasonably cold so far, and a fire burned to one side, warming the room and bathing it in a bouncing light.

Palius lay asleep in his bed as she expected. Erella could hear his breathing across the room, and it was labored and raspy. The man had grown old quickly in the last few years, developing a bend in his back, and his beard and hair were thinning. But there were other signs as well. Palius' hands shook slightly, but almost constantly, and he had begun to cough lightly now and again. Queen Erella knew that as autumn turned to winter and the cold deepened, Palius would continue to worsen. As she approached his bedside, she could see a slight black ring, a dark halo, wrapping his chest, and she knew there was nothing she could do for him. It was simply that his time approached, and she wondered if her path would always be so clear without his sharp mind at her disposal. She lightly sat on the bed next to him, and his eyes fluttered open.

"My Queen, what brings you here in the middle of the night? You give your subjects cause to gossip about us," he said to her, sliding backward to sit up against the headboard.

"My subjects," Erella responded with a soft laugh, "know that my heart is Garod's alone."

"It is true, but why did you not send for me? I would have come to you, as always."

Queen Erella looked away at the fire briefly before turning her gaze back to Palius. She was careful to keep her eyes on his face, and not the cloud she could see growing around his chest.

"I needed the exercise, such as it was," she answered him.

"My Queen is a true daughter of Garod, and as such, she is a terrible liar. What is amiss, Majesty?"

She closed her eyes with a soft sigh, willing the memory of the dream back to the forefront of her mind. She related it completely, with every minute detail from start to finish. Palius listened impassively, and when she finished, he closed his eyes and tipped his head slightly to one side, pinching the bridge of his nose with his left hand. She waited patiently for a few moments before he opened his eyes and asked one simple question.

"What does it mean?"

"It means," said Queen Erella of Aquis slowly, "that Dahken Cor has found what he was looking for in the Loszian Empire, and now he needs our help lest he be destroyed."

2.

Thom had been the commander of Aquis' garrison force at Fort Haldon for nearly five months. He performed this duty half of every year, being one of Aquis most experienced garrison commanders. In late spring, he would leave his wife and children to keep his home safe from Loszian invaders, not that any had ever invaded since he began the duty twelve years ago, but he trusted few to do the job should the Loszians decide to. He grew tired, as his time for this year was nearly up, and he knew it would be any day that a message was brought to him detailing the departure of he and his men.

When one of his soldiers woke him before dawn with a message brought by a rider, it was not what he expected. As ordered by the Queen Herself, he was to send a quick moving force through the mountains to the Loszian fort with all haste. They must arrive quickly and unseen. The force will wait until the right moment and then attack the Loszians at range. Unfortunately, the orders did not explain when the "right moment" would be, but only that it would be clear. The message contained one final piece of information – they would likely be saving the life of Dahken Cor, the strange man that passed his gates somewhat recently.

To any other soldier, this set of orders would seem utterly ridiculous and impossible. Many lesser commanders would have griped, sending a message back to their superiors saying that such a mission could not be accomplished, and in so doing, they would have missed the window for its undertaking. But Thom was not a lesser commander. He was an experienced soldier, scout, ranger, and scavenger, and above all else, he was a great patriot. If these orders indeed came from the queen, he would risk his own life and the lives of everyone under his command in the execution of them.

Commander Thom jumped to his feet and strode to the large table he kept in his quarters, upon which he unrolled the large and detailed map of the pass connecting Aquis and Losz through the Spine. He was a tall thin man, but strong, his body wiry from the rigors of archery. Approaching middle age, his straight brown hair that he kept restrained in a neat ponytail had streaks of gray. His face was lined with the concerns of a commander of men, but also from the smiles and laughter his children gave him.

Thom made some quick calculations and reviewed a mental roster of all of the men under his command. He would head this task himself and bring ten of his best scouts and archers. They would travel on foot, packed lightly, and he was sure that they could reach the Loszian wall by noon of the next day if they stopped to rest for only one hour. It would be grueling, but these men were used to this kind of work. The Loszians would have spies in and around the pass, just as he did. Normally, these spies ignored each other as a form of professional courtesy, but now they would have to be eliminated as Thom and his men moved. Approaching the Loszian wall unseen would be another tricky part, but Thom had never once failed his country.

Cor halted the group for lunch on the fourth day and announced that they would be staying there for a time. The weather had warmed a bit, and he allowed the group to relax and rest their rears. The plains had turned to rolling grassy foothills, making the ride a bit rougher, especially for the young and inexperienced. Cor explained to the group they were very near the Loszian fort that they would have to pass through to reach the mountains. He and Thyss would formulate a very strict plan, and it would require everyone to do exactly as they were told when they were told lest they all be killed. Cor should have anticipated that this would lead the smaller children to crying, and he realized that he would have to heap large amounts of responsibility on the adolescents when the time came. For now, he allowed them to simply rest, and eventually the younger children took to playing as children do while the elder Dahken watched or slept.

Over the past few days, Cor had endeavored to learn the names of all those he led to gods knew what. They were but children. Even the oldest of them, Keth and Geoff, were only barely younger than Cor himself, two boys just entering manhood. There were also two other young teenagers, a boy and a girl named Celdon and Marya, but the rest were all ten years of age and younger. They had gravitated to each other based on common age group, which was not surprising, and Cor had to remind himself that he was not much older than any of them.

As evening approached, Cor became restless. He had no desire to put Thyss in harm's way, but he had no idea how to scout the Loszians. Beyond the fact that if something happened to her, getting the Dahken out of Losz seemed suddenly impossible, something about the idea of losing her troubled him. It felt as if a great mailed fist crushed and twisted his stomach and intestines, and simply put, he did not care for it at all. He recognized it as similar to the sensation he used to have when he thought back to his mother's murder only a few years ago, and he wondered what he would do to a Loszian, or anyone else, who dared to harm Thyss. He sat brooding as he overlooked the Dahken, and his thoughts wandered to the coming fight as the sun reached the horizon.

"It is almost time, Dahken Cor," said Thyss, sitting down beside him.

"Are you sure you can do this?" he asked her without looking up.

"You doubt me?" Her response was more of a sneer than a question, and Cor looked up to see her eyes narrowed dangerously at him.

"No, I wouldn't dare do that. I," he paused not sure what to say. "I just don't want you to get hurt."

"Do not fear for me, Dahken Cor. They will not even know I watch them."

Thyss abruptly stood up and stepped a few paces away from the encampment. She quickly shrugged off all her clothing, handing it and her beautiful scimitar to Cor, who stood open mouthed at her sudden action and lack of modesty. Thyss' body was thin and tone, her muscles strong as bands of iron, but it was also lithe and supple, able to bend when necessary. She had the hard, trained body of a warrior mixed with the luscious body of a seductress, and the effect was like nothing Cor had ever felt. Many of the older boys stared openly at the exotic, beautiful and very naked woman who stood in front of them, and the younger boys giggled, though they were not sure why. Cor forced them to redirect their attention by turning and making it clear with his expression that their gazes were not required. Some still watched, however, from the corners of their eyes.

"Protecting my honor, Dahken Cor?" Thyss asked with a disdainful laugh. "I shall return by morning."

She held her arms to the sky above, and a slight wind blew across the grassy hills. It was almost as if Thyss caught the wind with her body and then melted into it. Cor watched as her physical form simply disappeared, turning to a mist or wisp of cloud in the wind. In a few seconds, she was simply no longer there, and the wisp of cloud rose into the air on the breeze and joined itself with a particularly fluffy white cloud. He looked into the sky longingly in the direction she had blown away and got the distinct impression that she watched him and laughed. Cor sat back down to brood and shook his head; the woman was truly beloved of gods.

It was shortly before dawn when Thyss returned, and it had been a bad night for Cor. Despite her claims, Cor worried over the elementalist from Dulkur. He spent the night pacing around his refugees' encampment, impatiently staring up into the sky in hopes of seeing any wisp of cloud that seemed to move of its own accord. Eventually, he stopped his nervousness and sat. He even tried to sleep, but every slight breeze brought him to his feet, but he did not see her arrive. Thyss simply appeared, joining him from out of the gloom. He was exhausted from lack of sleep, she weak from exertion, and they slept until the sun was highest in the sky.

"Explain to me exactly what you did last night," Cor said as they ate a lunch of nuts and dried fruit.

"I changed my elemental form," Thyss explained. "Your body is made of three of the four elements. It is mostly earth and water, but there is a bit of air also. I simply changed myself to a form of air and water so that I would look like a cloud or fog."

"You can do that at any time?" he asked.

"Not exactly. It is very tiring, and while I gain my strength quickly, the body cannot take such stresses regularly. But it is not the change itself that is exhausting; it's the constant struggle to maintain my identity, my sense of self. Elemental forces are primal and chaotic, and when you release your body to become one with them, you must fight constantly to not lose your mind to them as well."

Cor nodded; the explanation seemed simple and clear enough, though he still did not understand the actual magic itself. He never would, but one thing did occur to him as he thought her words over.

"So, I was in no danger of losing you to a Loszian crossbow, but I could have lost you forever otherwise?" he asked.

"I was not aware, Dahken Cor, that you owned me," she replied. Her words carried a hard edge, but her eyes did not hold the danger that he had seen there on several occasions. He did not answer her immediately, but in fact waited a few moments before speaking again.

"I thought," he started slowly as he tried to piece it together, "you controlled fire?"

"Hykan is my patron," she answered, "but I can make use of all elemental magic. My abilities with fire are far more ... potent, but I would never transmute myself into fire."

"Why not?"

"Because I would never come back," Thyss said, and Cor could see by the look in her eyes that it was true.

After their brief lunch, Thyss mapped out what she found. She saw the entire Loszian fort from the sky and committed every detail to memory, and the first thing she noted was the complete lack of pickets or advance guards of any kind on the approach to the garrison. Apparently, Menak did not consider an attack from within Losz to be of any concern. At night, it appeared that only four crossbowmen stood watch on the wall overlooking the mountain pass, with another two soldiers down on the ground guarding the mechanism that opened the door. Six more guards, these armed with swords, patrolled the cluster of buildings, and two stayed outside of Menak's quarters at all times.

There were only six men separating them from the relative freedom of the mountain pass. The other eight were either on patrol, and therefore not immediately able to get in on a fight, or guarding Menak, and they would be loath to leave their posts for any reason. In fact, it seemed safe to assume that should a fight break out, one would rouse Lord Menak, and the other would wake the hundreds of other soldiers. But it would take them time to organize, and there were only six at the wall and gate. It was about a half mile from the furthest out building to the gate, which, on horseback, they could cover in a matter of minutes. Cor knew he could handle the two guards on the ground.

"Do not worry about the crossbowmen on the wall," Thyss had said, a familiar gleam in her eye.

The bigger problem that Cor saw was that their group was comprised mostly of children. Keeping them on horseback at a gallop would be difficult for some of the younger ones. Also, should any fall or become separated, he feared there would be no time to save them. They must reach the gate before the alarm went up, then eliminate the guards and open the gate within a minute at most. Hopefully then they could slip into the darkness of night in the pass and make their escape. Traversing that rocky terrain at night presented another problem altogether, but one he would worry about later.

Cor opted to tie all the horses together with Thyss' rope, with her assurance that it would withstand whatever stresses the horses put upon it. He left his own palomino and Thyss' horse off the train to give them the freedom that would be necessary. The four oldest would be responsible for keeping track of the others, for they would be riding fast to reach the wall.

The guards on patrol represented another problem, and both Cor and Thyss knew it. They could hope with such a large area that they would not be seen by one of these men, but there was little doubt that the guards would hear them ride in. Cor did not plan on trying to be silent; if he had, he would have discarded the horses altogether. No, speed was needed here. The guards would most definitely hear some commotion, but they would try to investigate the noise before raising any alarm. Hopefully by the time they knew what was going on, Cor and the Dahken would be at the gate.

They ate a cold meal shortly before the sun began to set, and Cor forced his group to remain as still as possible and rest. He knew they would need the rest, for the hardest part of the journey was yet ahead, but requiring children to reign in their boundless energy was not so simple. As the sun dipped below the horizon, the air's temperature dropped substantially, and this helped calm even the younger children. Eventually, they all began to huddle close to each other for warmth and drifted off to sleep, except for Cor. He could not calm his nerves, and he noted disdainfully that even Thyss had stretched out languidly and slept.

Cor woke them up before midnight, starting with Thyss and the older Dahken. He and Thyss tied the horses together and made other preparations while the teenagers aroused the younger children, and he noted with satisfaction that it took little effort to get the entire group up and moving quickly. The infant remained asleep, and Cor hoped he would stay that way for some time. He did not look forward to having a screaming infant adding to the din of battle and confusion that was sure to come, but Cor had little faith that the child would sleep through the mad dash for the Loszian wall.

The horses were tied into two rows; he and Thyss would each lead one. Once their few belongings were collected, Cor had the Dahken mount two to a horse. He had several dismount and move to different horses, trying to find the best mix of older children with younger and so forth. After a few minutes of this, Cor gave up with the realization that this was an at best imperfect solution. At worst, it was downright foolhardy, and they would all be killed. Finally, he declared that they were ready, and he mounted his palomino. He was glad that the moonlight was partially obscured by clouds so that he could not see the fear he knew would be on the children's faces.

Cor set a slow pace at first, just walking the group toward the Loszian fort. According to Thyss, they were only a few miles away, and even at a slow pace, they would arrive at the outskirts of the fort in about an hour. At times they would top a hill, and Cor could see glints of moonlight reflecting off objects in the distance. While he could not see any torches or distinct shapes from this far away, Cor was certain that the reflections came off the Loszians' ubiquitous black stone. The buildings emerged from the gloom as they approached, first as indistinct shapes, but then more clearly. A few flickering torches cast a constantly shifting orange light in the paths between the black buildings, and Cor halted the horses. He saw none of the patrolling guards, but there were several forms moving on top of the wall.

"This is it," Cor said to those behind him. He turned his horse about so they could all see him and spoke in a loud whisper. "We'll be riding as fast as we can. The horses are tied together so just hold on and don't fall off. Once we get the gate open, we'll ride through and into the mountains as fast as we can."

They started towards the fort at a walk, and Cor slowly urged the horses onward, faster. He had the group almost to a full gallop as they reached the first outbuildings. Cor risked one look over his shoulder to see how his charges were handling the rough gait and decided that he dare not push the horses any faster, as many of the smaller children held on only with the aid of the larger. The baby, strapped to the wet nurse's chest, had begun to cry, awakened by the terrific bouncing motion of her horse. Cor pushed it from his mind as he focused ahead.

They moved quickly through the clusters of buildings, and he saw the immense gate clearly ahead of them. It seemed that the huge stone doors were each opened and closed by large upright wheels interlocked with some sort of gear system below the ground, similar to the mooring mechanisms he'd seen at the docks in Tigol. Cor hoped they would not be difficult to operate, though he realized he only needed to open one door. One man guarded each wheel, and he counted four more upon the wall's walkway, just as Thyss had reported.

It was then that the alarm went up, not from in front, but from behind them. A black mailed guard, likely on his path patrolling through the buildings, shouted in Loszian that intruders rode through the compound, and Cor looked over his shoulder to see the man running for a large building he assumed to be one of the barracks. Cor pushed his horse faster, causing some of the children behind him to bounce dangerously close to losing their holds on their mounts, but he saw little option. At any moment, Loszian soldiers would come pouring out of their barracks.

The guards in front had turned their attention to the oncoming group, and the first volley of crossbow bolts fired their way. Cor could waste no look behind him to see if any of his charges had been hit by the attack, and he charged his horse in a full gallop towards the men guarding the gate mechanisms. To an observer, it would have looked as if the Dahken intended to ride by the first guard, but just as he was about to pass, Cor half leapt, half fell from his saddle into the unsuspecting soldier. The impact jarred both men as Cor landed on top of the guard in a heap of arms, legs, and steel.

The Loszian received the worst of it as Cor's helm slammed into his face, breaking his nose and splintering his teeth. Cor quickly scrambled to his feet, drew Soulmourn and ran the man through while he was still fighting for breath. A weak blow clanged off the back of Cor's hauberk as the other guard had attacked him poorly from behind. He quickly glanced to his left to see one crossbowman screaming, arms flailing as he fell off the wall fully engulfed in flames. Another lay burning, his body still and on the battlements, while the other two frantically reloaded their weapons. Thyss charged up the steep stone steps, curved sword in hand, and thinking Cor's attention diverted, the guard launched another attack with several high, broad, sword strokes. Cor easily ducked the first two, before parrying away the third. The poor man had no chance of regaining his balance before Soulmourn rent its way through his left arm near the shoulder and into his midsection.

Cor looked around and knew his situation was about to deteriorate quickly. Thyss had torn through the third crossbowman, and the fourth had closed in on her with twin daggers. He felt a twinge of fear and wanted nothing more than to run to her aid when he saw the fletched end of a crossbow bolt jutting from her left thigh. But he could not afford to help her, for only a few hundred feet away the first Loszian soldiers were charging toward the group.

Dropping Soulmourn, Cor gripped the spokes of the closest wheeled device. He heaved his weight into it one direction and found it completely unmoving. He shifted in the other direction, and the massive wheel began to turn, spokes interlocking with a large gear set into the ground. He could hear a great clicking as the gear teeth interacted with metal, no doubt other gears beneath the ground, and there was a mild vibration as one black stone door began to swing open. He pushed the wheel until the door had opened perhaps three feet.

"Keth, Geoff, get them through!" he yelled at the two older boys while sheathing Soulmourn, and nodding, they began to herd the horses out the great door. "Thyss, we leave now!"

The fourth crossbowman dispatched, Thyss lithely jumped from the top of the wall, landing in a roll. She screamed once in pain, clutching the crossbow bolt embedded in her leg, as she made impact with the ground, but she forced herself to her feet and limped to her horse. Cor looked back at the oncoming soldiers, counting that he had mere moments before they were upon him. As the crowd of horses quickly filtered through the open gate, Cor saw the shape of a small girl lying face down in the dirt two dozen paces away.

"Dahken Cor," Thyss shouted, now on her horse, "leave her!"

This girl was here now only because of him, and he ran to her unmoving shape without hesitation. Behind him, he could hear Thyss swearing eloquently in her native tongue. Scooping the girl up, he noticed a large knot forming on the side of her head. She must have fallen off her horse when they came to a stop. Something whizzed by Cor's left ear, and as he turned to run to his horse, white hot pain lanced through his left hand. His palomino anxiously awaited him, her eyes wide as her tail swished back and forth.

Just as he reached her, a wave of immense heat nearly knocked him off his feet. Thyss sat on her horse, arms raised to the heavens, and a wall of orange flame over twenty feet tall and twice as wide separated them from the oncoming horde of soldiers. Crossbow bolts were shot into the flame, only to be incinerated, and Cor slung the girl's limp body over his left shoulder as he stepped into the saddle's right stirrup. Soldiers with crossbows flanked the wall of flame by climbing the stone wall's steep steps, but just as the first men reached the top of the wall for a clear line of fire, they fell, suddenly punctured by long Western arrows that arced over the battlements.

Cor did not have time to wonder about this, and he kicked his horse into action and shot through the open gate. The heat subsided, and he saw Thyss charging after him, clearly having ended her spell. Cor expected it to be dark in the ravine outside of the fort, but there were a number of lit torches in front of him. He saw the Dahken still mounted but behind a dozen men who fired arrows towards the Loszian fort. One approached with a longbow in hand, and Cor recognized him as Thom, the commander of Fort Haldon.

"Dahken Cor. Queen Erella commanded me to provide you aid. We must make haste," he said.

The rangers continued to fire arrows at the Loszian wall, and the opposing soldiers could do nothing but stay under cover as they were out of range with their crossbows. Thom's expert marksmen neatly skewered the few who were brave enough to venture through the small opening, but the gates were beginning to open wider. Shouting for everyone to follow him, Cor spurred his horse deeper into the mountain pass. The archers remained behind for just a moment to loose a few more arrows before following.

They traveled the pass at a dangerous pace, considering they had nothing but intermittent moonlight and a few torches, but they had no choice. Cor could occasionally hear a large Loszian force on the move not far behind them. They were well beyond crossbow range, and the rangers from Fort Haldon did not stop to blindly fire their own longbows. More than once a horse stumbled, or someone fell due to the treacherous ground. While he could not afford to dwell on it, Cor was amazed at the dexterity of these men who had saved them, and when someone did fall, the rangers seamlessly picked the child up and kept them moving. The men ran alongside the horses, keeping pace almost effortlessly.

"We must keep this up for a bit longer," Thom would say to him over and over, raising his voice over the sound of the horses' hooves. "Just a bit longer."

Cor wanted to ask the man just how long a bit longer was.

He tensely rode through the pass, and he could feel his muscles begin to protest with exhaustion. He could only imagine how the other Dahken, the children, were handling the pace. The girl had not moved in his arms once, and he was afraid she was not breathing. Cor looked over his shoulder and saw most of the rangers ran with steadying hands on small forms. These men astounded him.

Cor shook his head to keep his wits about him, for they had been at it for hours, something he could judge by the moon's passage across the sky. The group tired, having already been through so much, and even the rangers seemed to be wearing down. The sound of the Loszians was not as far away now as the group's pace continued to slow, and someone in the rearguard announced that the Loszians were gaining. Thom implored Cor to keep the group moving, and he sprinted into the gloom ahead, saying he would be back soon. Cor watched the man disappear ahead, surprised at the commander's sudden departure and that he had such energy left in him.

Their pace had slowed to almost a walk as both horses and riders were exhausted from both the forced march and the uneven ground. There was little more Cor could do, and he readied himself to turn and fight. He would die, holding off the entire Loszian garrison, if necessary, if it bought enough time for the rest of the group to escape. He continuously looked over his shoulder and more than once caught Thyss' gaze. She looked ragged and exhausted, and her leg no longer bled though the crossbow bolt still jutted from her thigh. Watching him, the corners of her mouth turned up in a slight smile, and Cor could see the immutable fire burning in her irises. He knew she was with him, and he knew together no one would defeat them.

The Loszians would not expect him to turn and attack, and he was just formulating his plan when he heard an odd sound. Cor stopped his horse suddenly, straining to hear the sound of a hundred tiny whistles as they passed overhead and behind them into the distance. And then men screamed in the gloom from behind, closer than he realized, a hundred arrows found openings in armor. A shout came from the darkness ahead.

"Dahken Cor! Do not stop now! You are very nearly safe!" the voice implored as another volley of arrows was loosed at the Loszians behind them.

3.

"However, Dahken Cor, Her Majesty did not inform me that you would be bringing a nursery with you," Thom said. Cor sat with Thyss in Thom's private quarters, eating their first hot and hearty meal in days, and though he was loath to admit it, Taraq'nok did set a fine table. The rest of the Dahken ate in one of the mess halls, attended to by Thom's men.

Thom had explained to Cor the receipt of Queen Erella's message and orders, and that he and his best men had come across the mountains. As it turned out, Thom was a fair strategist, and he had surmised that, though the Loszians would have been confused by the sudden attack from beyond their wall, they would not stay that way. He assumed they would pursue in force, and before leaving Fort Haldon, Thom had given orders to his second in command to follow with nearly the entire garrison. He had hoped to rendezvous with his garrison before the Loszians could chase them down, but the children had caused him some grief, however.

"Believe me Thom that when I left Aquis, I had no idea that I would find them."

"They are all," Thom paused, not sure how to continue, "like you then?"

"They are Dahken, yes," Cor answered, bringing a laugh from Thom.

"My apologies then! I thought your name was Dahken Cor, but Dahken is your? People?"

"I suppose Dahken Cor is my name as much as anything else. We spring from Dahk, the Blood God," Cor explained. "We are a race, essentially, but we come from all over the world. As all people have blood, you have as much chance of having a Dahken son as I."

"Dahk the Blood God," said Thom, leaning back in his chair. "Sounds nefarious."

"I thought as much myself when I first found out," Cor replied. "How did the queen know I was coming back to Aquis?"

"Oh, Dahken Cor, don't ask me such questions. As someone who cannot exist without a god, you of all people know the gods have their own wills in our lives. I am not a particularly pious man, but I know Her Majesty occasionally has words with Garod," Thom explained with a shrug. He changed the subject without a second thought. "What are your plans now?"

"If its all the same to you, Commander Thom, we'll stay for a few days to let the children rest. Then I suppose we'll make for Byrverus. I believe the queen and I have some matters to discuss. Is that acceptable to you, and can you send a message to her?"

"Yes, to both questions," Thom answered, pausing before he continued. "What of the poor girl?"

Once the garrison had repelled the Loszians, the group had taken a few moments to regain their wits. Thyss allowed the Westerners to remove the bolt in her thigh and treat the wound, and amazingly, no one else was injured in the party with two exceptions. A crossbow bolt had shot through the soft flesh between Cor's thumb and index finger on his left hand. He remembered it happening but had paid it no mind at the time. The bolt had continued on and into the back of the little girl he had scooped up off of the ground, and she had died at some point in their flight from the Loszians. When they discovered the cause of her death, it had taken several moments for Cor to fully realize what had happened. His vision turned red as rage consumed him, and Thom had to very nearly throw a bucket of cold water on him before he calmed down, as he was ready to charge headlong back to Losz and fight the remains of the entire garrison himself. Her name was Liya.

"In their history, the Dahken always buried their dead warriors together in catacombs under their strongholds," Cor explained to himself as much as to Thom. "But we have no strongholds or catacombs anymore, and she wasn't a warrior, just a little girl. Perhaps you have a suitable place for her here?"

"We will find her a resting place, Dahken Cor."

On the southwestern coast of Aquis, a consciousness began to dream. In this dream, it had a body. It was male clearly, judging from its anatomy, and its arms were lean and strong. The body's hands were agile and calloused from the use of tools, weapons perhaps. It floated, completely suspended in liquid, but the mind realized it did not have to breathe. It should have to breathe; it knew it had to breathe at some point in the past. It willed the body's eyes to open, but it saw nothing but red. It was not sure it could see at all, so it closed its eyes again, and an odd, metallic taste filled its mouth.

The being sensed movement, like a push from below or perhaps a force lifting him from where he lay. He still floated in the red medium, but something caused his body to move in a direction that felt like up. He had no sense of time, and he could not judge how long this went on for before his body broke the surface. There was warmth on his face and body, and he opened his eyes to see a dark orange sun and a red sky overhead. He turned his head slightly and saw that he floated on the surface of a blood red ocean that extended as far as his eyes could see, and he realized quite suddenly that he needed to breathe.

"It was not yet your time," a voice said, booming in his mind. "You have much work yet to do."

He closed his eyes for a moment, and when he reopened them, the ocean of blood was gone. In fact, he could see nothing but darkness, and he could feel that he lay on a cold stone surface. He inhaled sharply, as if for the first time, and coughed horrendously as the air around him was thick and musty. The coughing went on for several minutes as his chest cleared of thick, sticky globs. As his vision adjusted to the dark, he could see that he was in a small room that was not completely absent of light; a thin ray streamed through the crack of a slightly ajar door. Finding his legs wobbly, but strong, he set himself to escape the musty prison.

Cor awoke early. Disentangling himself from Thyss' naked arms and legs, he stepped outside of the spare junior officer's tent Thom had found for him. It was early yet, and the sun had not broken the horizon. His breath came in white puffs in the chill air, and Cor thought of the journey that was to come. Thom had assured him that Queen Erella would have received the message by now, so today Cor would take his nursery, as Thom had called it, to Byrverus and the queen.

He stood facing the mountains to the east before cocking his head slightly as if he heard a subtle noise. Cor slowly turned, scanning the horizon as he went. He stopped facing just south of west, staring at the horizon over the great grassy hills and plains of Aquis. He had no idea what he looked for, but it was as if something hovered just beyond his sight or perhaps just below the horizon. Something waited for him out there, and he felt the stirring in his blood, a sensation he had not felt since he fought with the thing that once was Lord Dahken Noth.

Cor ducked back into the tent and, as silently as possible, began strapping on his black armor. Thyss stretched languidly and then transfixed him with one open eye. It made Cor think he had disturbed a comfortably sleeping cat rather than a deadly sorceress who was also in her own right a deadly warrior. She opened the other eye halfway, considered him for a moment and then rolled over on the cot to go back to sleep. The cat imagery not remotely dispelled, Cor fought back laughter as he turned to again leave the tent.

Thom had sectioned off part of the least full barracks to accommodate the rest of Cor's group. As it turned out, most of the soldiers at Fort Haldon were delighted to have children around. Many had their own families, and it served to remind them of what awaited them at home when their postings ended. The men very nearly lined up to be included in whatever game the youngsters played, while Keth and Geoff had taken some beginner's lessons on swordplay. Fully armored, Cor checked on the Dahken and found most of them still asleep.

Realizing he had little else to do, Cor proceeded to the stables to look in on his horse. Kelli, of course, always seemed glad to see him, and he thought in the silence as he fed her sugar cubes and brushed her coat. He had told the Dahken that they would be traveling with him to Byrverus and that they would meet the ruler of Aquis. As most of them were of Loszian slave stock and very young, Cor was not sure they had an inkling of what this meant. Regardless, afterwards they would be free to go where they chose, but without families, he had no idea where they would go except with him.

Cor hoped that he and Queen Erella could now put the past behind them; hopefully, she would be convinced that he harbored no ill will toward the Shining West. She would want to know his intentions, and he needed to build a new Dahken stronghold or castle where he could train those he had rescued from Losz. He would also need to go forth and find other Dahken, as there was little doubt that more were about in the world, but the trick was finding them before the world killed them. He would explain to the queen that his only aggressive intentions were toward the Loszian Empire, and he intended to bring it down completely.

"Why bother with the Loszians?" Thyss had asked him a few nights previously.

"The Loszian Empire is an abomination," he explained. "It operates under a strict caste system in which the bottom level, half or more of the population, is slaves. These people have no free will. They are completely unable to serve their own desires or needs but break their backs at the whims of a decadent and disgusting ruling class of necromancers. Put yourself in their position and tell me what you would do."

Thyss took a moment to answer, and when she did, her voice was merely a whisper, "I would burn it all down."

"Remember that the next time you think to ask me that question," he had said to her, perhaps more harshly than he intended.

Cor did not know what he was going to do with Thyss. He knew she would come with him to Byrverus, and no doubt find some way to challenge the queen. But he had no illusions, for Taraq'nok's description of her had been terribly accurate. She would not wait around for adventure while he spent the next five or ten years training and teaching the Dahken. No, she would grow bored, and she would leave him to go elsewhere, anywhere.

The thought turned Cor's stomach upside down, and he was not sure how to handle the feeling. He wondered if he may be in love with the elementalist from Dulkur, and it was a bizarre thought. In his time at Sanctum, he had read many scrolls, journals, and memoirs of Dahken, and he could not recall any of them discussing love. Even Lord Dahken Rena, the previous wielder of Soulmourn, had described her encounters with lovers in exacting, thorough detail, but she had never once discussed the emotion of love. Perhaps as the Dahken secluded themselves from the rest of society and continued to build their own strength, they lost sight of certain parts of their humanity.

He wondered if Thyss loved him. He wondered if that would be enough for her.

Lost in these thoughts, Cor failed to realize that the sun had broken the horizon, and the fort's activity level picked up. Patting Kelli one last time, he left the stables and returned to his tent to find Thyss awake and beginning to dress. He waited for her to finish, admiring her as she did so, and together they left for Thom's quarters.

There were no long goodbyes in this military camp. Thyss and Cor breakfasted with Thom while the other Dahken arose and ate their own meal. Thom had dispatched his quartermaster immediately upon waking to make sure the Dahken were properly provisioned for the trip to Byrverus, and the group left Fort Haldon well before noon. Thom wanted to send an escort with the band, but Cor declined. The two men clasped each other's arms, and Cor genuinely hoped that he would again see this ranger and captain of men.

A quiet ride through the country, which lasted Cor and two soldiers of Aquis a mere week not so long ago, now took him almost twice as long. Though well rested and incredibly resilient, the children logistically required more time to travel than three men. They needed more sleep and required more time to eat meals, but Cor pushed himself to be patient. The threat of armed pursuit had passed, and there was no need to rush onward.

Cor spent most of his time thinking, and due to the lack of conversation, Thyss had dropped into a sort of belligerent melancholy. He ignored her for the most part during the day but gave her whatever attention she craved once they had stopped riding to rest. He thought over the coming audience with Queen Erella, and how he would explain to her his plans for the future. He needed money to build a new Sanctum, a stronghold in which his Dahken would live and learn of their strength. He thought of the jeweler in Worh, and with any luck, the man would have a sizeable sum awaiting Cor from the sale of a gem that was fit for a king. Perhaps, he could convince the queen Herself to aid in the construction, considering his long term goal was to reclaim Losz for the Shining West. He would need to train the older Dahken first, and then he would send them forth into the West to find more of their kind. Cor continued to lay down plans in his mind, and he decided he would have to spend the next fifteen years at least training the Dahken he had with him now.

Thyss would not wait fifteen years.

Cor continued to feel an almost magnetic pull from the west, slightly south of the setting sun. It had been easy to ignore at first, but it grew stronger with each passing day, and he knew he would have to deal with it, perhaps right after meeting with the queen in Byrverus. They were just over halfway through their journey to the capital of Aquis when Cor felt a startling sensation, as if his blood may try to exit his body through his pores. Whatever or whomever it was, the thing that called to him was moving, and he was certain that it was coming toward him.

The rolling hills had long given way to rich plains as they traversed the road between Fort Haldon and Byrverus. Cor knew they were within a few days journey when the great plains began to change to occasional farms, followed by huge sprawling farms and small village centers. The huge farms then turned into smaller farms and large numbers of cottages with inns, mills, and smiths. They began to see many people about these places, and there was no shortage of long stares from the commoners. Though they were still several miles away, Byrverus was in sight now; so massive, the city gleamed in the sun like a beacon for all who would travel there. Within a mile of the city walls, a score of armored men stopped Cor and his group. Cor recognized the man at their head, the same captain who had brought him before Queen Erella months before.

"Dahken Cor, welcome back to Byrverus," he said. "Her Majesty sent me to meet you and escort you to Her palace."

"Thank you, Captain. Might I assume that Her Majesty's hall can accommodate my companions?"

"I am certain She would expect no less, sir."

With that, the mailed soldiers took up flanking positions on either side of the Dahken, and the captain led them into the city. Cor's Dahken gasped in awe and stared at the awesome city; apparently, they had never seen anything of the like. They traversed the heart of the city, heading directly for the palace and main temple of Garod, and this time, there were no stares or fingers pointed at the group. The city dwellers of Byrverus were too busy with their day to day tasks, and most of them had seen it all as far as they were concerned. However, the children openly gawked, and he was content to let them do so. Even Thyss failed to completely mask her interest with her practiced look of disinterest, and her eyes drank in every aspect of the largest city in the Shining West and possibly the world.

Beyond the weather having cooled, it appeared that nothing had changed at all in the great city. Everything was exactly as Cor remembered, including the beautiful plaza connecting the palace and temple. Despite the constant bustling activity, the city was peaceful in a way, as if the people were content and sure of their safety from the dangers of the outside world. Cor wondered what most of these Westerners would do if real war were to again come to Aquis.

They dismounted outside of the palace, and the guards escorted the group into the palace. The children continued to stare and point in awe, while the teenagers and Thyss had finally settled into calm interest. The wet nurse, Celia, paid little attention to any of it; she simply followed the group, her attention focused on the infant she carried. There was no wait for admittance into the palace's great hall, as no doubt the queen awaited him for days, and she was prepared to see him immediately upon his arrival.

Upon entrance into the hall, he saw her sitting upon her throne, examining his group with a practiced eye, but relinquishing no clue as to her thoughts. The old man who was her advisor stood to her right, and he coughed lightly into a small handkerchief. Cor approached her raised dais slowly while removing his helm, and then, somewhat uncertain as to why, went down onto one knee before her. Most of his group hesitantly followed suit, excluding Thyss, whom Cor noted held a disdainful grimace upon her face.

"Rise, Dahken Cor," she said. "It is interesting to me that you now show respect. I would ask what you found in Losz, but the answer seems obvious between your black armored countenance and those who follow you. I truly did not expect to see you again. Why have you returned to Aquis?"

"I have slain the Loszian lord responsible for my parents' murder," he answered. He then half turned and motioned as those behind him. "Majesty, I present to you the future of the Dahken and perhaps the future of the Shining West."

"Interesting, and who is this exotic foreigner?" she asked. Cor had not expected the queen's interest in Thyss, and the question gave him pause.

"I am Thyss of Dulkur, Elemental Priestess of Hykan," Thyss said in her thickly accented Western.

"You show this court no respect, Thyss of Dulkur, and you dare mention the name of a heathen god before my throne."

"A heathen god in your eyes, but King of the Gods in mine. A god of whom you dare not deny existence, Queen of Aquis," Thyss retorted, and her voice contained a dangerous note of challenge. The assembled crowd hissed and murmured to each other about the audacity of this woman, and the old man called gently for silence.

"As I must treat you as a dignitary from an empire we have little relations with, I will allow your tone to pass Thyss of Dulkur, but do not push too far lest you find yourself unable to return," the queen said softly. She then turned her eyes to Cor. "What do you here, Dahken Cor?"

"I have come to discuss with you my plans and hopes that the Shining West and the Dahken may find common ground, Majesty."

"And what ground would that be?" she asked in response.

"It is time to free the Westerners who remain enslaved to the Loszian Empire. It is time to end the reign of evil over half of this continent," Cor declared loudly. The onlookers had mixed responses, from mild cheers to guffaws.

"How, Dahken Cor, do you expect to accomplish that? With an army of children?" Queen Erella asked, and this evoked laughter from the assembly.

"Majesty, the Dahken are among you, regardless of what you know or believe of them. We are born to all classes, in any nation, and we are ostracized or even murdered at birth. Only the Dahken can help you defeat the Loszians. The children you see before you represent the first of the new generation of Dahken warriors and more will follow. I will build a castle in Aquis, a stronghold such as Sanctum once was, and as was once done, I will find more Dahken and bring them to our stronghold to learn of their power."

"And you would expect me to allow this?" the queen interrupted him. "To create a small army comprised of your kind? You would expect Aquis to allow you to erect a castle so that you may destroy us from within with the power of your evil god? You would expect me to allow you free reign over the lands of the Shining West to find more of your abominable race? You expect much, Dahken Cor."

Queen Erella stood from her throne as she spoke, and her voice had risen as if with a violent rage, though her face remained as impassive and calculating as always. The crowd had gone completely silent, some of their eyes locked on their queen, while the rest bored into Cor's back like daggers. He expected she would have this reaction, having played through this scene in his mind many times over the past days, but he hoped for otherwise. It showed just how entrenched her beliefs of the Dahken were, and as he replied, he kept his voice as calm and reasonable as possible.

"The Dahken are not evil. The god from whom we spring is Dahk, the God of Blood. All Rumedians have blood, and as such, a Dahken may be born to anyone. I neither worship him, nor any god, but they all exist in our world and must be recognized. The Dahken history, as translated by The Chronicler, shows that the Dahken didn't stand with the Loszians, but neither did they help the Westerners in their plight. That was a mistake, and they paid for it dearly when The Cleansing came to them.

"I am here to make amends for the mistakes of the past. I ask you to judge neither me nor the Dahken based on your view of history. Judge me for who I am, what I have done, and what I will do."

"You admit to having murdered a venerable priest of Garod and twelve of my soldiers, do you not?

That is a crime punishable by death," she said, her voice very quiet though it carried well through the hall.

"I admit to having defended myself against men who killed my mentor and tried to kill me also. One even dealt me what should have been a killing blow, had I not spilled his blood before I died. I have no guilt over it. And if you wanted me dead for that crime, you would have had me killed last time I came before you. Certainly, you would not have risked the lives of Thom and his garrison to save me from the Loszians," Cor reasoned. "Majesty, I know that you don't trust me, and you'll likely not be surprised to learn that I don't much trust you. Powers in this world, Her Majesty included, have worked to manipulate me from the day I was born, but trust starts with one person. I have never lied to you, and I ask you to trust me. In return, I will make myself your loyal servant, and together we will free the rest of Garod's people."

Queen Erella dropped back heavily in her throne in shock of this man who stood so confidently in front of her. He was barely out of boyhood, but he spoke with a well reasoned mind. This Dahken Cor was far wiser than his age, and he spoke in a way that made one listen. And here he was, standing in her hall, with over a score of his people and one exotic, arrogant foreign woman standing behind him. What was it about him that made people listen to him and follow him? Even now, she, Queen Erella of Aquis and High Priestess of Garod, wanted to stand and proclaim her agreement to his ridiculous claims. She needed to think over the entire situation.

"Captain, please find comfortable chambers for the Dahken and arrange for them to have meals as necessary. Dahken Cor, I will consider your words, and we shall speak more tomorrow."

She stood, and the entire assembly excluding Thyss knelt to the ruler of Aquis. The two women locked eyes for a moment, an imperious gaze fighting a defiant stare, and Queen Erella of Aquis exited the great hall with her aged advisor trailing behind her.

4.

"Surely, you don't expect me to stand around for twenty years while you train your children," Thyss stated derisively from her place on the plush bed.

The rooms they had been given in the palace were huge and airy, even compared to those in Taraq'nok's castle. Thick, plush carpets and rugs lined the floor, and silk tapestries and wall coverings abounded. Of course, there were no slaves in Aquis, but paid servants who steadfastly did their duties waited on them heavily. The other Dahken were given rooms all located down the same corridor, and Cor rested somewhat uneasily having solid walls and doors separating him from them.

"You will be her loyal servant?" Thyss asked with a sneer. "Perhaps I was wrong about you, Dahken Cor. I think perhaps I should take my leave of you."

She stood up from her place on the bed and stared at him intently, her legs set wide apart. Though they had only known each other for about a month, Cor had been with Thyss long enough to know when she issued a challenge. He also knew he had two choices – he could meet her challenge, or he could let her walk right out the door. Somehow, he knew it would be the last time he ever saw her. Cor lifted himself out of the chair he had sat in after removing his armor and walked to stand directly in front of her, mere inches away.

"I need the Westerners to understand that the Dahken are not evil, that we are no threat to them," he said to her. "To do that, I need Aquis to support me. It is the heart of the Shining West."

"I would have just demanded what I wanted. She would have given it to me, or I would have destroyed her precious kingdom and urinated on the visage of her god," Thyss replied imperiously.

"And you would have died in the doing of it, killing the rest of us with you. Thyss, I love you, but you need to learn that sometimes destruction is not the answer."

"What did you just say?" she asked, her eyes narrowed.

"Sometimes destruction is not the answer," Cor replied, "You can partner with people to create. Creation can be just as random and elemental as destruction."

"No, you said you love me."

"I," Cor was about to deny it until he thought carefully over the words that had come so easily. "Yes, I did. I do."

"Then I have finally broken you."

They made love then, and no fire of passion was contained. Lying there afterwards, Thyss asleep against him, Cor realized what she had always sought. Everyone wanted Thyss. How could they not? She was beautiful, powerful, and dangerous, but she didn't need to be wanted. She wanted to be needed.

"I find myself in a most interesting predicament, Dahken Cor," Queen Erella said. She had called him to her chambers just after he breakfasted. She expected him alone, and he very nearly refused, having expected Thyss to join him as always.

She left him to visit the queen alone, saying, "Creation, not destruction. Besides, I would like to look around this wondrous city a bit." So, he went alone as asked, and it did not escape his notice that half a dozen guards were in the room.

"What predicament, Majesty?"

"You were right, I don't trust you, but I find myself daring to believe in you. You have already accomplished something I deemed impossible – your entrance into and escape from Losz. You claim to have slain one of their necromancers, of which I have no actual proof, but I do not think you are a liar. What if I agree to your terms?"

"Well," he paused in thought, "First, there is something I must do in the west, but I don't believe it will take long. Then I would need to select a suitable site. My family owned land near Martherus. I assume it belongs to me now."

"One thing at a time Dahken Cor. Do not think I am going to let you plant a small castle just anywhere in the Aquis countryside. No, *we* will select a suitable place that will allow me to monitor you," she paused briefly, studying his face. "What task awaits you to the west?"

"I don't know, but I don't believe it will take long," he repeated. "I can't fully explain it, but whatever it is, I can feel it coming to me as we speak."

She continued to study his face, searching for any hint of deception before shrugging the matter away. "Very well. I will grant you land and title that you may hand down to successors as you will. However, I will garrison your holdings with a force of no less than fifty times the number of Dahken that stay there. If I agree to help you build a fortress or castle, how do you intend to finance it?"

"Hopefully, I have a great sum of gold awaiting me in Worh," he replied.

"It must be a great sum indeed. I will send someone from my exchequer to Worh to retrieve your wealth. You will fill him in on the details. Where Dahken Cor should I place your castle?"

"I see an easy solution, Majesty," Cor said, walking over to a map that hung on the wall of the queen's office.

"Here," he said, putting his finger on Fort Haldon. "You already have a large garrison there, and it is a strategic point for entry into Losz when the time comes."

"Or into Aquis," she replied, closing her eyes slightly. "Unfortunately, the location makes perfect sense. I will warn you Dahken Cor. Should you betray me and the Shining West to the Loszian Empire, I will destroy you and every Dahken ever born."

"Of course, Majesty."

Cor decided that he would travel west alone. There was no need to bring the other Dahken, for soon they would have to travel back to Fort Haldon. When he informed Thyss of his decision, she punched him hard in the jaw, asking how dare he make that decision for her. She certainly was not going to stay cooped up in this castle, as impressive as it was, while he went forth and faced Hykan knows what. He should have known better, and rubbing his face where she struck him, he agreed.

They left the next day, putting Keth and Geoff in charge, as they were the oldest. Before leaving, Cor explained to the Dahken that they would not be gone long, and when he returned, they would have one more journey to make. It seemed that his very presence near the younger children made them feel safer, and many of them asked him not to go. He supposed that this is what fatherhood felt like, and he assured them it would be only a matter of days.

This time, there were no visions or subtle hints to guide Cor on his way to whatever his blood sought. Somehow, he just knew that he'd know when he got there. Thyss accepted this explanation. The entropy of the world was something she simply accepted as the way of things, but even so, Cor felt anxious and uneasy. There was also the fact that not only did they ride toward this thing on the horizon, but it also moved toward them. Whether it was a person or not, it was being guided to him, and Cor hated feeling manipulated by anything, even the blood in his veins.

They traveled the western road out of Byrverus, a road that continued all the way to the Endless Sea over a thousand miles away, though they needed not go that far. They passed through settlements virtually identical to the ones they had passed through a few days ago on the other side of the city. As the villages thinned and turned to farms, the cobblestone road ended, and a dirt road began. The weather was favorable, cool, and crisp, and they covered the miles quickly. Cor felt as if he might jump out of his skin, and he did not want to stop even to sleep.

They had ridden the dirt road for three days, and Cor's blood felt as though it may boil at any moment. Every time they rounded a bend or crested a small hill, he was sure that he would see whatever pulled at him. They passed few people now, just farmers transporting late harvests or supplies on wagons one direction or the other. It was when they passed a solitary figure on foot that Cor pulled Kelli to a sudden halt. Thyss continued a good dozen paces before she realized he had stopped, and she turned her horse to face him.

"What is it?" she asked.

"I don't…"

Cor turned his horse to face the direction they had come, and he saw the lone figure, a man, standing in the road. He had also turned in his tracks and stood staring at the mounted pair. Cor could see little about him, as he wore a heavy wool cloak used by many travelers during colder weather, and the cloak had a hood that hid his features well. The man was not large, but Cor was sure he was built solidly. He stood like a fighting man, and Cor thought he saw a glint of bluish steel underneath the robe.

"I have come far, Dahken Cor, much further than you," came a distant but familiar voice from beneath the hood.

"Who are you stranger, that we seek each other?" Cor asked, slowly walking his horse toward the figure, as he drew Soulmourn. He was not sure why, but something about this man unnerved him.

"I am not sure of my name, but I am sure that we are no strangers, Dahken Cor. Certainly we are not enemies."

The man reached his hands to his hood and pushed it back over his head. He then pulled the robe's ties at the neck, allowing it to fall to the ground, revealing an armored countenance. He was middle aged with shoulder length hair that appeared to have recently gone gray. He was unshaven, but very little growth was on his face, and his eyes were gray, cold, and hard. He wore full plate armor that oddly reflected the sunlight blue, and strapped to his back were a large shield and a longsword. The man's face and hands were as gray as the dead, as gray as Cor's.

"This cannot be," Cor whispered. He dropped from his horse and sheathed Soulmourn. "You were killed. I saw it. I carried you back to Sanctum and entombed you below."

"Yes, I did die, and I became one with Dahk. Adrift in a sea of blood, I knew nothing, but He has caused me to return to this world," the man paused for a moment, studying Cor's open mouthed, bewildered look. He then asked in an almost childlike fashion, "Who am I?"

"You are the man who saved my life. You are Lord Dahken Rael, my teacher and my friend."

"Yes," the man whispered, memories flooding into his eyes. "That was once my name, but I think now I am only Dahken Rael. You... you are Lord Dahken Cor."

5.

The ride back to Byrverus was full of explanations and stories. Cor of course introduced Thyss and told Rael everything that had happened to him after the battle on the road that connected Sanctum and the port town of Hager. He included as much detail as he could remember, from the vision Soulmourn had shown him, to the dreams involving Lord Dahken Noth, to his journey into Losz and so on. Rael listened and responded rarely, his face stoic and impassive throughout the entire narrative, and he had little comment, even regarding Thyss. Cor explained that he had found his parents murderer, at least, the lord who was responsible, and that Taraq'nok collected Dahken for some master plan to take over the whole of the Loszian Empire and the Shining West. Cor took his revenge and somehow managed to get the Dahken back into Aquis, most of them at least. After several hours of storytelling, he finally explained his latest meeting with the queen and his ideas for the future.

"I do not understand your plans though," Rael said. "I understand building a new home for us and rebuilding the Dahken, but why the alliance with Aquis and The Shining West? Why are you so determined to destroy the Loszian Empire?"

"Their empire is an affront to freedom, to free will," Cor answered. "I will not allow it to exist any longer than it must."

"Is the West any different?" Rael asked. "They change history and control their populace through their religion."

"But at heart, they're good people, Rael."

"I still do not understand, but then it is not my place to understand," Rael conceded. "You are Lord Dahken now."

"How about this for a reason, then. Most of the Loszians kill Dahken on sight, even as soon as they're born."

"I suppose that is reason enough."

At Cor's prodding, Rael explained his reliving as well as he understood it. He remembered being one with Dahk, part of a great sea of blood that went as far as one could see. He was suddenly expelled from that sea and returned to life. He could barely recall, as if from a dream, a voice telling him he was not yet meant to die, that he still had purpose. He remembered nothing else clearly; memories of a life that once was flashed through his mind unbidden and in a confusing jumble. However, when Cor spoke his name, they returned all at once, clear and ordered.

Rael awoke in the crypt that Cor had made for him, and he remembered collecting a number of items that were entombed with him – a sword, shield and armor mostly. The door opened easily enough, but his exit was half blocked by rock and earth. It was the work of several hours for Rael to move enough detritus out of the way to climb out of the crypt and stand amongst the caved in remains of Sanctum. Through some amazing bit of luck, or perhaps some form of divine providence, several of the crypts including his had been spared by the destruction, but most had been flattened or buried, their history and treasures lost.

Climbing out of the huge crater had been work worthy of a titan. Nearly every bit of ground Rael climbed created a landslide, several of which threatened to take him. It took two slow and arduous days to reach the mouth of pit, and his muscles ached from the constant, painstaking exertion. Many of his fingernails were cracked, torn off, and bleeding from his efforts to hold onto the smallest amount of purchase. From there, he simply walked east, eventually picking up a road and following it until he found Cor. He had no recollection of where he had gotten the cloak or what he had eaten over the days or weeks since his reawakening.

"If not to lead the Dahken, why has Dahk restored you?" Cor asked him.

"I was never a leader, Cor. Of course, there's never been many Dahken to lead, and I claimed the title of Lord Dahken only to make certain the line went unbroken," Rael explained. "You, however. You led a group of children through a heavily fortified border and seem to have gained their trust and loyalty. I can see no better Lord Dahken."

"You still haven't answered my question," Cor insisted.

"I believe I am here to train the Dahken."

"Then tonight I will pray to Dahk and thank him," Thyss interjected, "I was not enjoying the prospect of standing around for twenty years while Cor raised his Dahken brood. I may just have thrown myself from the castle ramparts."

"Really? I'd have thought you would just run off with someone more interesting," Cor retorted. Thyss' eyes flashed angrily for a moment, but then cooled, leaving only an enigmatic smile on her face.

"I don't think you appreciate what had to occur for Dahken Rael to return to Rumedia," she said. "I have had some dealings with my own gods, and they do not interfere with the mortal world lightly or easily. To outright resurrect one who is dead would have required an extreme expenditure of power on Dahk's part."

"He's a god."

"Such a Western thought that the gods are all powerful. Dahken Cor, they are not, and it is likely that Dahk will not intrude into our world again for years for his trouble. Think on that," she replied.

"What happened Rael? How did Jonn kill you?" Cor asked. After a short silent moment in which it became clear that Rael was not going to answer, Cor continued. "When he knew I was going to kill him, he used the same magic, and I walked right through it. Everything I read about Dahken said we were immune to such power."

Rael sighed. "I am honestly unsure. To say Dahken are immune may be a slight exaggeration, but mostly accurate. I had only once before faced Garod's power, and in that instance I prevailed. I am afraid my death was necessary at the time for you to truly become Dahken Cor."

"Sounds like talk of destiny," Cor said, and he spat to one side. "I will no longer accept that the death of people I love is necessary or unavoidable. Not anymore."

"How grand," Thyss said, and her words were weighted with the greatest sarcasm. Cor ignored them.

When they returned to the palace in Byrverus, Cor and Thyss received a hearty welcome from the Dahken. One boy wrapped himself around Thyss' left leg, and she shot Cor a pleading, pained look at which Cor laughed quietly. Thyss did not seem to know what to do with children; clearly a mothering instinct was not innate to all women. The younger children received Rael warily, and the older boys clasped arms with him as men might. Rael was only the second adult Dahken any of them had ever seen, and Cor hoped that the knowledge that they were not aberrations would help bind them together.

Cor awaited Queen Erella's summons impatiently, pacing to the far corners of the chambers he shared with Thyss, and he walked the palace halls, no doubt under the watchful eye of the queen's guards, just to keep himself busy. He had no desire to wait around any longer. Thyss also seemed anxious and impatient like a caged tiger looking for any opportunity to escape, and she learned quickly to avoid Rael, as he seemed disinclined to engage her in conversation. It was a response she was not used to, and she did not like it.

Rael, for his part, began to train the Dahken within hours of arriving at Byrverus. He divided the children into two groups based on age. At times, he would bring the groups together and lecture them on the history of the world and the Dahken. When their attention wavered, he would separate them again. The older children, including the four teenagers, began combat training in one of the palace courtyards. The guards would not provide Rael with real weapons but instead made available padded wooden practice swords. Rael grimaced at these but accepted them as the best that could be done for now. During the training periods, he would allow the younger children to watch or simply play as children might. Cor observed and noticed that death and rebirth had not changed the man one bit; he was always precise and to the point.

It was nearly a month before the queen again summoned Cor to her chambers, and Cor sighed with relief when the summons came. This time, he did not go alone, choosing to bring Thyss and Rael with him. The two would play important parts in his future, and from here on he would include them both in all of his decisions. They entered her chambers, finding Queen Erella looking tired and seated at her desk, stacks of administrative work strewn about. Rael and Thyss stayed slightly behind Cor on either side of him, and behind the queen stood Thom. Cor smiled slightly, nodding his head to the older man who had very recently saved his life and those of the other Dahken.

It was then Cor realized that Queen Erella stared at Rael, her gaze like a surgeon's knife. She seemed to look deep inside the man, directly into every fiber of his being. Cor found it most unnerving, but Rael merely stood and allowed the queen her long examination. Eventually her gaze softened, though it lingered on the older Dahken's face for several long moments.

"Dahken Cor, I was told that you had brought another with you, a Dahken named Rael who now trains your people," she said.

"Majesty, this is my friend Dahken Rael," Cor said, turning his head to indicate the man. "He seems to have returned to help me."

"Indeed," the queen said quietly. "Dahken Cor, I'm not sure what your friend is, but I don't think he is a Dahken. I see him, but it is as if he is not there."

Cor turned and clasped his friend's shoulder. "I assure you, Majesty, that he is real enough."

"Very well," she very nearly whispered. She paused before speaking again, this time with more strength. "Everything is prepared Dahken Cor. Your jeweler in Worh was holding a note worth a mighty ransom. I have taken possession of the note to finance the building of a castle at Fort Haldon, and I have already dispatched architects to the site.

"Your land grant is marked accordingly," she said, pointing to the map, "It is approximately twenty five hundred acres the eastern border of which is the Spine. Lord Paton is your immediate neighbor, and he was not overly excited about giving up the land. I paid him with the knowledge that he would no longer be the first line of defense should war with Losz occur.

"Commander Thom has agreed to stay at Fort Haldon permanently as garrison commander. The two of you seem to be on fair terms, so the choice was simple for me. He will relocate his family, as will most of his men. The garrison and the castle will be maintained by Aquis as it always has been, but you will need some income to support your Dahken."

"Majesty, I still have a fair amount of gold and some gems," Cor said.

"That may do for the short term, but you must have citizens to tax," she replied. "I have offered land to commoners and farmers who desire opportunity within your grant. I will assign an administrator from my exchequer's office to you for the purpose of establishing an equitable tax system. I hope you are prepared for the mundane life of a lord, Dahken Cor."

"I hadn't considered it honestly," Cor said. Near as he could tell, the Dahken in the past survived on accumulated wealth of centuries, likely from their many adventures. But now that wealth was gone, and he would need a way to support his people, for several years at least. The fact did not dawn on him until just then.

"Before I allow you to leave, I must be clear about one thing. I have no reason to trust you, the Dahken, as your history by the way I remember it is an unsavory one. I am still not certain whether you are good or evil, or whether your desires are best for Aquis and Garod. However, I am certain that you are not a liar, and you have given an oath to serve me. Make no mistake, I am ruler of Aquis, and I answer to no one but Garod. You will obey my will as quickly as one of my palace guards. If that is clear, you may take your leave of me now.

"And one last thing Lord Dahken Cor," Queen Erella called after him as they turned to leave her chambers. "In the future, I expect that you and your subjects will show proper respect when entering my presence."

Cor simply nodded and continued his exit. It dawned on Cor later that night that Queen Erella had labeled Cor with the same title that Rael had been using. Yet somehow, he was sure the title did not carry the same meaning to each of them.

6.

Palius slumped in his chair behind his desk, eyes closed, and the bridge of his nose pinched in his left hand. He sat very still, deep in thought as to the state of things, though he was completely conscious and aware of his surroundings.

To look at him, one would think him asleep, even dead if not for the slight rise and fall of his ever thinning mass. Occasional coughing broke his peace, and he would sometimes fight for breath. Palius rarely ate these days, and he had originally assumed it was from the constant rigors and stress of his position. A priest had told him otherwise. He was dying, and he knew his time was limited. Queen Erella knew it too, but she had never spoken to him about it. Palius understood most of Garod's priests could see illnesses in people, especially those that would lead to one's death, and sometimes, even they were powerless to stop it.

For weeks Palius had discussed matters with Queen Erella, imploring her to see reason. Discussion reached the point of pleading argument, as he could not understand how her angry outburst at the Dahken had turned to understanding and acceptance. He had come at her from every angle he could conceive, and yet, she refused to agree with him.

"The Dahken are dangerous, My Queen. They cannot be trusted."

"We should have let the Loszians rid us of him."

"Kill them now, at least Cor and Rael. They've committed crimes against the crown and Garod."

"If not kill them, exile them from the West, taking Cor's wealth as reparation for the death of Jonn and your men."

"My Queen, we cannot trust a boy who slays at will, and now he is rejoined by one we thought dead. Their god, a blood god of evil, has resurrected the one just as a Loszian might."

"Even if we can trust Dahken Cor, that makes him an idealist, and his idealism will lead us to ruin! Open war has not existed between the West and the Loszians for centuries for good reason! We cannot win such an endeavor! It will mean the end for us as we know it!"

This last argument he made shortly after the Dahken had returned with his sorceress slut with yet another Dahken in tow, and at this Queen Erella grew angry. She became very quiet and fixed Palius with a cold, hard stare. In a way, it was better than the way she had been looking at him over the past few months, a soft gaze full of concern and sympathy as she watched him slowly waste. At that point, Palius excused himself from his queen's presence, and she had not called on him since.

Palius hated them all because he truly believed that Queen Erella's original interpretation of that first dream long ago was correct. The Dahken would, one way or the other, bring about the fall of both the Shining West and the Loszian Empire. He loved his queen, he loved his country, and he loved the world as it was.

The worst case scenario was unthinkable, disturbing, and frightening at the least. Dahken Cor would lead the West to war with the Loszians, and he would turn traitor at just the right moment to allow the Loszian necromancers free entrance into the West. Palius did not think this out of the question, as the blood god was no doubt evil, closely related to those of the Loszians.

Perhaps the Dahken was truly an honorable and honest man, boy really. Again, that made him an idealist, and there could be nothing more dangerous than an idealist. He would inspire thousands in the West, perhaps even the Queen Herself, to rally and form armies, and they would launch an attack upon the Loszian Empire, with the Dahken at the forefront. And it would not go well. Its armies broken, the Shining West would retreat to its side of the Spine, only to be crushed and again enslaved for millennia by the Loszians in an orgy of blood, rape, and death.

Or perhaps the Dahken would succeed in toppling the Loszian Empire with the help of the West. Then what? Too far from home, the soldiers of the West would be unable to maintain order, ignoring that they would no doubt long for home after such a long and certainly terrible campaign. The newly freed peoples of that land would have no idea what to do with their freedom, and total chaos would ensue, perhaps leading to the rise of new powers just as evil as the Loszians. The Dahken, servants of an evil heathen god, would come to be known as the saviors of the West, and the people would throw off the yoke of Garod, destabilizing the strength of Aquis and Queen Erella.

In any case, it meant the destruction of the Shining West, and Palius refused to allow that to happen. He simply would not allow his great queen, for whom he had sacrificed his entire life to secure her power, to let it all crumble because she was caught up in some idealistic fervor. He continued to think, barely moving for hours.

Palius finally opened his eyes and sat straight in his chair, sliding it closer to the oak desk with a spine shivering scrape on the floor. From a drawer he pulled a blank parchment scroll, and he wrote upon it with a quill pen in shorthand that he invented and that only a few people in Aquis could read. Palius was as loyal an advisor as any ruler could ask for, but sometimes he had to handle things in his own way and had done so for over fifty years. At times, things to which Queen Erella would never agree had to be done.

After he wrote his message, he sat and poured over it several times, silently except for the occasional dry cough. Satisfied, he sealed the scroll with plain wax using no insignia and slid it into a soft leather case. Palius could not entrust this message to a palace guard or runner of any sort, as he never did when he was forced to use his shorthand. He knew he would have to venture out and deliver this himself.

The old man dressed as warmly has he could with thick cotton undergarments below his white cotton robes that were emblazoned with his queen's insignias. Over the robes, he wore a heavy brown wool cloak that completely closed around his form and had a hood that he could pull up over his head to hide his face from the elements or other things, such as prying eyes. Palius removed his house slippers and pulled on a set of soft brown leather boots, swearing during the entire process as he pushed his feet into them.

Before leaving, he hid the scroll inside his cloak and unlocked one of his large iron banded chests, from which he produced a small sack that was heavy with coin. This also disappeared inside his cloak. He coughed loudly as he exited his rooms.

"Going out for a walk. The night air will do me some good I think," Palius said to the now ever present guard that stood outside his door. Truly, he needed no explanation, but it was better to have a reasonable answer to the question in the man's eyes. It did not escape Palius that Queen Erella had always respected his request for no guards, but that changed as his health worsened.

Palius made his way through the palace halls and then to the outside. It was dark, but this part of

Byrverus was always kept well lit with torchlight that danced off the white stone walls of the nearby buildings. There was nothing to be wary of in this part of the city. Guards were posted regularly, and no one would dare assault a known advisor to Queen Erella. However, that would not always be the case for Palius tonight, at least not where he would have to go.

As he left the palace and temple complex, he passed the estates of nobles and extremely rich merchants, most with their own tall white walls. Many of those villas had their own guards, and their masters knew Palius for who he was. The estates continued to shrink in size until they gave way to large homes, those that belonged to well to do inhabitants. These had no guards, no tall white walls, but they continued to be well lit as the city received the greatest portion of its tax wealth from this class of citizen.

Off a side street, he picked one of these homes and approached its massive oak front door, pounding the iron knocker loudly. He could barely make out his surroundings as he waited, as this house had no lantern or torch anywhere near it, and he could see only by the moon and the meager light cast by the light sources of other houses. A low voice, barely more than a hiss, whispered from the shrubs that lined the front of the house, and Palius felt as if he nearly jumped out of his skin.

"It is late to be out, milord," the voice said, "perhaps too late for an old man to be about."

"My affairs," Palius replied strongly, though his heart hurt his chest it pounded so hard, "sometimes keep me out late at night to deal with the likes of you."

"How true, milord," hissed the voice. "What needs have you of me?"

"I have a message that must reach Larnd."

"I shall take it straight away, milord, for the right price, of course."

"No," Palius said; he was calmer and surer now. "No, I must deliver it myself. You are to make sure I am unmolested as I deliver it. For the right price, of course." With that Palius produced his hand from his robe, two of the queen's mint gold coins in his palm.

"That, milord, is the right price," the voice hissed, and a man dressed completely in black stepped out of the bushes into the light.

Palius could barely see the outline of his form in the dim, flickering light cast from lamp across the street, but he wore black boiled leather from head to toe, excepting his soft black leather boots and matching cloth cowl. Palius couldn't even make out any portion of the man's face or hands, and it occurred to him that the cutthroat likely had some sort of ink or tar on his skin to hide the white flesh. Palius knew the man, and of what he was capable, well. His name was Marek.

"It is quite a walk to Larnd's place, milord," Marek said, "and I assume you wish to move as fast as possible. Don't fear if you cannot see me, I will not be far, milord. I will have to move ahead to make sure my brothers do not bother you."

Marek silently turned on his heel and made around the side of the house. Palius followed and caught up to the man around the back of the place as he opened a door set at an angle into the ground. Palius assumed it to be the entrance to a cellar, but upon following Marek down the steps found he was quite wrong. The small staircase opened into one of Byrverus' many underground sewer passages, and Palius wrinkled his nose in distaste, standing as if he had no intention of going any further.

"It is the fastest way to cross the city, milord," Marek said, and he immediately started down the tunnel to the right.

Palius sighed loudly and resigned himself to following the cutthroat. Palius had no idea that the sewer system under Byrverus was such a twisting maze, and without Marek, he would never have found his way out again. Marek moved through the tunnels assuredly, occasionally stopping to look at markings on the tunnel walls at intersections. After less than an hour, Marek declared them to have arrived at their destination. He climbed a small set of steps and pushed the pine door open from the inside, and though winded, Palius climbed the steps up two at a time to breathe deeply of the crisp night air.

They had crossed the entire city, and there was a hint of garbage and other refuse in the air, as was expected in the Commons. Commons was a bit unfair, as this part of the city was home to the most uncommon and unsavory inhabitants of Byrverus. Queen Erella abhorred criminals and what they wrought, but it was impractical to think the city could be rid of them. Besides, sometimes a little debauchery could be put to good use, as long as the miscreants kept to themselves most of the time. Buildings in the Commons consisted mostly of small granite structures with wood roofs. The granite used was cast off from the larger construction projects around the city as it was too low grade or too small for city walls or municipal structures, and the people in the Commons were able to buy it cheaply. There was little light here, except that of the moon, and what buildings had lanterns or torches had them to draw business. They were brothels and bars, mostly.

Marek wove his way through the streets, down alleys and between the buildings. Palius, on the other hand, stayed to the main roads with his hood pulled up and tight to hide his face from onlookers. More than one cutpurse, thief, or whore watched him longingly, but they already knew not to accost the man in the heavy brown cloak. True to his word, Marek had cleared the way for Palius, and fortunately, the old man knew where he was going.

When Palius reached Larnd's home, place of business, abode of dark dealings, whatever one would call it, Marek was already there and leaning against the wall next to the front door. It was a squat structure, perhaps only eight feet tall, made of poor grade granite and fairly long at almost fifty feet. The building had no lead paned windows or any portal at all except the heavy iron banded elm door. Palius thumped his fist on it three or four times with a flat quiet thud, and the door creaked open just a few inches, spilling warm orange light into the street.

"What?" came a rough voice from inside.

"I have a message for Larnd," Palius said, producing the scroll case and holding it out in front of the slight opening.

A man's hand, small and calloused, shot out and roughly grabbed the scroll, and the door immediately pulled shut behind it. Palius looked questioningly at Marek, who still stood leaning against the building, and the man simply shrugged and began picking his teeth with a shiny steel dagger. Though Palius' eyes had well adapted to the darkness, the man was still hard to see dressed as he was, but his teeth stood out brightly, a shock of white in the darkness. After several minutes, Palius thumped on the door again.

And again, the door opened, and the voice issued forth, "Larnd needs payment. A lot of payment."

Palius reached into his robe and held out the heavy sack that he knew contained exactly fifty gold coins, no paltry sum.

"Leave it," commanded the voice.

Palius did as he was told, dropping the coins heavily in the stripe of orange light on the ground. He and Marek turned as a hand retrieved the gold, and they returned to the tunnel and the sewers. Upon returning to the palace, Palius realized he stunk horrendously from the sewers, and as he passed them, several guards took obvious note of it.

"I slipped and fell into a ditch full of horse dung. Very upsetting," he lied to the man outside his door.

When Palius entered his rooms, he stripped off all his clothes, including his boots, and cast them all into the fire.

7.

It was early when Keth roused the Dahken for their morning exercises. Dahken Rael would always wake him first, because he knew he could rely on Keth to get the others moving while Rael set a small breakfast and made sure that a practice area was available. He was the eldest of those Lord Dahken Cor had saved from the Loszian Taraq'nok, and he had immediately taken on a sense of responsibility for the younger children, starting with the flight from Losz. It felt like so long ago, but it had only been a few months.

Keth was a Westerner whose parents were slaves in the Loszian Empire, slaves to Taraq'nok himself. The Loszian had of course found it advantageous to have the boy born right under his nose and allowed him to live and grow as a slave. Eventually Taraq'nok came to fear the boy would be discovered by other Loszians, and he put Keth's parents to death. He then forced Keth to drink a vile potion, and the young Dahken awoke mere hours before Lord Dahken Cor avenged himself upon the Loszian.

Keth was sixteen years old. At least that's how old he was when his parents were murdered, and he had no way to know how much time had passed. He was a few inches shorter than Cor and Rael, standing about five foot eight, and he had been that height since he was twelve, so he figured he was done with growing. Keth's body was made well enough; a slave and the son of slaves, he had toiled hard in the fields alongside his parents, and that built a degree of hardiness into one's body. He had a thick mane of light brown hair that curled after it had grown a few inches and large dark brown eyes framed by a wide, gentle face.

All the Dahken save Cor slept in rooms that branched off of one main corridor in the eastern wing of the palace. Queen Erella posted guards at the entrance to this corridor presumably to assure that no one could access them without first having to face Rael, though Keth was sure it was to keep an eye on the Dahken. Through these rooms Keth moved one by one, awakening the Dahken, excluding of course the infant. He always saved his hardest battle for last.

Geoff was a year younger than Keth, and though younger, he was actually a couple inches taller. He had an oddly narrow frame with long legs, arms, and fingers, to the extent that some wondered if Geoff had any Loszian blood in him. Keth didn't know Geoff's background, and to his knowledge, he hadn't ever discussed it with anyone. The younger boy had jet black hair and hard gray eyes just like Rael, and he had a face made of hard angles with a hawk nose, sharp cheekbones, and a pointed chin. He had constant dark rings under his eyes, giving them a sunken in look, and combined with the pallor and coughing fits that all Dahken shared, it made Geoff look even more like one of the walking dead. He spoke little, but Keth knew he saw all.

Geoff almost never wanted to rouse himself in the morning, at least ever since they reached Byrverus and Dahken Rael showed up. In the flight from Losz, he had been very helpful, even responsible, but now he undertook every task asked of him with lackadaisical effort, if not grumbling disdain. Keth was sure it had to do with the training; Geoff had shown no aptitude at swordsmanship at all and had no success with using his blood, as opposed to Keth, who advanced nicely to the point that he and Rael now fought with live steel, under the watchful eye of Western guards.

Keth knew Geoff resented him.

"It is time," Keth said, merely poking his head through the crack between the door and its frame. He knew Geoff was awake, though the boy lay on his side facing the wall. "You need to get up."

"Why?"

Keth sighed, "Because it is time. Dahken Rael wants a short training session, and have you forgotten? Today we leave for Fort Haldon."

"I'd rather just stay here, and I don't much see the point in having Rael bleed me some more," Geoff responded as he rolled onto his back and sat up. He lay naked in his bed, and Keth saw dozens of small scars on the boy's arms and chest, most of them fully healed. A few were fresh.

"Geoff, its there, its in you. You just have to find it."

"Maybe I couldn't care less. Did anyone consider that?" Geoff asked, swinging his legs over the edge of the bed.

"I don't have time for this today," Keth said. He pushed the door all the way open and turned to leave but thought better of it for one moment. "Remember, Cor freed us from Taraq'nok, and he gave us the *choice* to come with him and learn. I am sure the other choice is still open to you."

Geoff watched as Keth stalked off down the hall. He clenched his jaw as he sat staring at the cold stone floor of his room. He should just leave; no one would stop him, but then he would probably spend his entire life running from Loszians and Westerners for the power they thought he had but didn't. Geoff closed his eyes and sighed, slumping slightly. He then pushed himself up from his small bed and dressed himself.

Keth burst shouting into Cor and Thyss' room in the late morning. Cor almost never slept late, as Rael typically would not allow it, but today was their last day in Byrverus. Thyss had kept him up late, well past midnight, in a furious session of lovemaking, and while she chaffed at the inactivity over the last several months that had kept them well into the winter, Cor thought she would miss the plush pleasures of Queen Erella's palace soon enough. Not that she would ever admit it.

"Lord Dahken!" Keth shouted as he charged into the room, startling the couple awake in their bed.

Cor bolted upright, inadvertently yanking the warm down blankets off Thyss' naked body, who only growled and rolled over for the trouble. Keth stood doubled over with his hands on his knees, gasping and trying to catch his breath while his eyes fixed inadvertently on the bare skin of her back. It seemed he had sprinted a good distance.

"Keth, what's wrong?" Cor, also naked, slid out of the tall bed to plant his feet on the cold floor, and Keth yanked his eyes away from Thyss.

"You must... come see... Geoff in... in the practice yard," Keth wheezed out.

Cor yanked on a cotton tunic and breeches, the same he had discarded at the foot of the bed the previous night. He ran from the room, leaving Keth gasping and coughing as Thyss slowly crawled from the bed without any sense of modesty before the young Dahken.

Rarely would Thyss move hurriedly in the morning hours, and Cor knew she would move especially slow with the knowledge that she would soon be in Rael's presence. The two had no use for each other ever since a recent incident, and it put Cor in an aggravating position of balancing the two and their idiosyncratic personalities. Generally, he thought it would be best if they stayed away from each other.

In very little time Rael made it clear that he disapproved of Thyss' very presence. He considered her a distraction and said that she would only disrupt Cor's attempts to rebuild the Dahken. The older Dahken said that like all women, she was too prone to emotional outbursts, especially since she mirrored the mannerisms of irrational and unpredictable gods. Thyss took exception to his comments to say the least.

"Once you have gotten everything you want from him, you will leave. And what will you leave him with?" Rael had said. "You are just another whore."

Thyss had drawn steel in a practiced move meant to take Rael's head clean off. A seasoned warrior, the Dahken avoided the maneuver, and the two set to fighting in earnest. They would not listen to Cor's shouts for peace, and he had to insert himself between his companion's blades to make them stop. Rael was stoic and seemingly emotionless, but his jaw was set and his eyes hard as steel. Thyss seethed, and Cor knew she restrained herself with only the greatest effort.

"Rael will watch the wagging of his tongue, or I will burn it to a crisp within his mouth," Thyss growled. She sheathed her sword and stalked away angrily. Rael merely nodded quietly under Cor's angry glare and went his own way.

As he ran through the halls, Cor's mind raced as to what could cause Keth to behave so; the boy was only a few years younger than he and always very respectful. It simply must be bad. Rael gathered all the Dahken, even the small children, early in the morning to practice fighting and help them learn to feel their blood. It had been slow going;, as none of them seemed to be able to tap into it as easily as Cor had, but Rael had said that was normal. Rael seemed generally unconcerned.

Except with Geoff. Keth and Geoff were the two eldest, and Keth seemed to be learning at a pace that satisfied Rael. Geoff on the other hand had been completely unable to accomplish anything, and he was a poor fighter. As he ran through the palace toward the practice grounds, Cor genuinely feared the boy had been seriously hurt or worse.

The practice grounds consisted of a large flat area, open to the sky, but wholly contained within the palace. Only the Queen's Guard, the elite of Aquis' warriors, practiced here typically, but Queen Erella had made an exception for Cor's Dahken. It suited their needs, but no doubt helped her to keep an eye on them. The grounds were roughly fifty yards across and over two hundred long with archery targets at one end. There were also several rows of practice dummies, really just tunics stuffed with straw and stuck on a stake in the ground, and they reminded Cor of limbless scarecrows. Racks of weapons were scattered about the grounds, many containing real, battle-ready items, while others held wooden practice swords, blunted arrows, and the like.

At the far side he saw the Dahken gathered in an area bounded on either side by two racks of weapons, both live and practice. All the children save one hid from the disturbing scene, watching from behind the weapon racks. Cor could see Geoff on the ground unmoving, and Rael stood perhaps twenty feet away with his sword and shield readied. Between the still Geoff and battle-ready Rael stood a thing the likes of which Cor had neither seen, nor even imagined.

The thing was easily seven feet tall, towering over any of the Dahken including Rael and Cor. It was relatively lanky in appearance, but nothing like a Loszian; it was thin of limb and body, but not stretched and narrow. The monster, for Cor could think of no other word for it, had no muscles of any kind that he could discern, nor joints, nor even a face. Cor could make out no fingers or toes, and it had no ears on the sides of its head. With no details at all, its shape was completely smooth and fluid, and as far as he could tell, it was made purely of blood. It held a huge, six foot long two handed sword, also red as blood though it glinted in the late morning light like steel.

Realizing he had stopped in his tracks upon entering the practice grounds, Cor started to sprint the hundred or so feet that separated him from Rael, garnering a sidelong glance from the older Dahken. As he ran, Cor reflexively reached for Soulmourn and Ebonwing, only to find he left them above in his room. He was close, less than twenty feet from the scene, when the thing suddenly jumped several feet to its right and stood with its legs slightly bent to lower its stance. The quick move made Cor stop his run, coming to a skidding halt next to Rael, and he swore he could see the creature's chest rise and fall as if it breathed heavily.

Cor momentarily diverted his attention to the unmoving form of Geoff on the ground some feet away. A small wooden buckler shield was strapped to his left arm, and a shortsword lay on the ground near his right hand. The boy had three shallow wounds on his legs that were no longer bleeding. In fact, only a small amount of blood showed around the boys wounds at all, already growing sticky and dry. Why Geoff was unconscious, perhaps near death, and what this thing was, Cor had no idea.

Rael sheathed his longsword and held his hand out to Cor to indicate silence. Cor didn't speak, as he worked to control and slow his breathing.

"This is a blood ghast," Rael said softly. "I have never seen one before, but I have read of them. It is a rare gift, and the first Dahken to manifest one was Lord Dahken Drath."

"The one Tannes sent into the north," Cor said, remembering the Dahken history he had read what seemed like a lifetime ago.

"Indeed. For all purposes, Geoff's body is dead as we speak. His essence is in the ghast. I can only explain it by saying that it is the manifestation of Geoff's true Dahken self," Rael continued. The blood ghast stood on the balls of its feet as if ready to strike, still appearing to breathe heavily, but it did not move otherwise. "That thing is as deadly a warrior as exists. If you strike it, you will wound Geoff, and its attacks will become more deadly. If it wounds you, it will feed your strength back to him, making it stronger and healing his wounds. Do you see that Geoff's wounds do not bleed?"

Cor could only nod.

"There is no blood in him now, but if the ghast returns to him before the wounds are healed, they will begin to bleed again."

"What if I deal the ghast a mortal wound and it returns to Geoff?" Cor asked.

"Then he would likely bleed to death," Rael answered.

"What is the point?" came a female voice from behind them; it seemed Thyss decided to dress and follow Cor down. "Couldn't I easily slay the boy now? He is vulnerable."

The wraith's head snapped to the side when Thyss posed her question.

"I do not know for certain," replied Rael, "but I imagine the blood ghast will immediately attack anyone who attempts to harm Geoff or the wraith itself. What matters is this – Geoff must learn to control the ghast. He must learn to transfer his consciousness to it and return when he wills it. As it is, the thing manifested without warning."

"How long do you think it will last?" Cor asked. As he did so, he slowly approached the ghast with his hands open, palms up in front of him. The blood ghast allowed Cor to approach within a few feet of it so that he could look more closely. Cor had the odd sensation that it was doing the same thing, even though it had no eyes of which to speak.

"I cannot say, but I do not think long."

Fortunately, Rael thought correctly. He collected the others and left the practice grounds for the purpose of finding a snack, leaving Cor and Thyss in quiet regard of the blood ghast. Somehow knowing that neither was apparently armed, the ghost wandered back to Geoff and stood over him silently, but it seemed no less ready for battle. After close to an hour, the thing dissipated. Its skin, for lack of another word, started to bubble and then boil, turning into a translucent pink vapor that swirled in the air around it, not unlike the dust devils Cor had occasionally seen on the farm as a child. Eventually the ghost's entire body had boiled away into this vapor, a seven foot tall swirling mass that could not be seen through and was more red than pink. A tendril broke away from the blood tornado and snaked its way to Geoff's nose, followed by another to his ears and yet a third to his open mouth. Several others made their way to his open wounds. The tendrils of blood thickened as the swirl became shorter and narrower and began to lighten. After a few seconds, there was nothing left of the swirling vapor, and even the tendrils disappeared, leaving nothing but a light trickle of blood out of Geoff's left nostril.

The boy, only three or four years Cor's junior, opened his eyes as the wounds Rael gave him began to bleed.

"What happened?" he asked when his eyes cleared.

"By Hykan, that was fucking incredible," Cor heard Thyss say behind him.

"Lord Dahken Drath was the obvious choice to head into the unforgiving Northern Kingdoms," Rael later explained. "Tannes selected him purely for his ability to spawn the blood ghast. It allowed Drath to search those frozen lands when he felt a Dahken born, as it was common practice among the Northmen to leave them out to die in the elements. The Northmen viewed our pallor and coughs as weakness, an affront to their sensibilities. Drath could sustain his blood ghast for days at a time, even a week, and no one ever defeated him in battle. It was said that he knew how to use his mind to communicate with others through the blood ghast."

For his part, Geoff felt extreme relief; just this morning he wanted to quit Dahken Rael's teachings, to run away. All he knew was that before this morning, he had failed at all of Rael's attempts to teach him anything. He failed at wielding any weapon put in his hand, and he had failed at "feeling his blood" as Rael so often called it. He had the scars to prove it. Now he knew he wasn't a failure, and he knew that he was more powerful than Keth, who had shown great promise. Over time he would become more powerful than Dahken Rael; for the way Rael spoke about it, the blood ghast was nearly indomitable, and Geoff took quiet pride that one day he may even be more powerful than Lord Dahken Cor.

8.

Larnd managed to get his man into a minor foreman's position so that he could plan the assassination. The plan was simple. They would strike the night the targets arrived shortly after they fell asleep, as they would be exhausted from their travels. By all accounts, their targets were extremely dangerous, deadly warriors that also wield magic, and it would make sense to minimize their readiness as much as possible.

Lord Dahken Cor and his people would reach Fort Haldon very soon, and they would need housing, as the construction of the planned keep would take at least three years. Most of them could be pushed into temporary tents with cots, the type an army on the move would use. However, the Lord Dahken slept with the bitch from Dulkur; they and also his second, the middle aged man, would need something a little more substantial.

The new foreman asked to be assigned the task of building two small shacks, one for the man called Rael and the other for the Lord Dahken and his wench, the second obviously larger. It was a simple squat design, nothing special or particularly inventive, but each building had a false ceiling about two feet tall inside with a nearly undetectable access point near where the bed would be placed. One man could hide in Rael's quarters and two in the other. All he had to do was make sure his murderers slinked their way into the ceilings after Cor's group arrived, but before they retired.

If they waited until their prey slept soundly, it would be a quick and easy job. Larnd was always good to him. The jobs were dangerous and required more discretion, but they paid well. It was a simple plan.

It was a long, cold ride back to Fort Haldon, taking nearly two weeks longer than the reverse trip had taken months earlier. Queen Erella, though she hadn't seen them off, over tripled Cor's retinue with everything from accountants to cooks, and while Fort Haldon already had such support staff, more layers would need to be added to support a legitimate castle and its lands. A small number of citizens also came along and more would follow as the families of Fort Haldon's men came to join their husbands and fathers that were now part of a permanent garrison. The short days combined with the simple amount of time it required to get four score persons, half of whom were women and children, up and moving slowed them substantially. The winter storm that hit them halfway there made the going even slower.

Having grown up in either southern Aquis or a sailing vessel, Cor had experienced few snowstorms in his life. Truly, the only one he remembered was the blizzard that struck his home on that one frightful night many years ago. This was nothing of the sort – a ceiling of hard gray clouds dropped wet fluffy flakes steadily for hours. It was quite beautiful, and even the warm blooded Thyss found it wonderful to watch. However, after almost a full day of it, the snow came nearly up to a man's knees. The footing underneath grew treacherous, and general feelings of those who traveled in the storm grew gloomy as the clouds overhead.

Nothing could be done about it however, and Rael did not let up on his training regimen for the young Dahken. During the months in Byrverus, Rael had rewritten as much of the Chronicler's histories as he could remember, as closely as he could remember it, and he lectured on it during the cold, snowy nights.

Commander Thom would listen in on the history lectures, often quietly smoking a pipe, and occasionally remarking that he had never heard of something that Rael related.

Rael continued teaching the Dahken to fight, something which Thom joined. Cor watched as the venerable ranger and garrison commander showed great interest in the gray skinned children, helping Rael teach basic swordsmanship, and Thom in fact spent many hours with Keth during the evenings. There was nothing more Rael could teach the young Dahken about his blood, and the boy now only needed to become a more skilled fighter.

Having never before seen a blood ghast, nor ever known a Dahken who had, Rael had no direction to offer Geoff. At Rael's behest, Cor agreed to allow Geoff to spend time by himself away from the main camp to work on manifesting the creature and controlling it. Rael wanted no accidents. On several occasions, Cor would stand on one of the crests of the rolling hilltops near the Spine and watch Geoff in the small valleys below him. More than once he saw the reflection of Geoff's meager fire playing off the "skin" of his blood ghast, and sometimes the thing even moved despite there being no foe to combat.

There was something else that concerned Cor about the boy; he would occasionally find Geoff staring off to the east, into the mountains that were now not far away. Cor knew what the boy felt, and Rael had of course explained to all the Dahken about the pulls they would feel as they grew powerful. Even still Cor felt a need to discuss it with the young Dahken, and he did so on an early morning when the sun's light was just beginning to outline the mountains in purple and blue.

"Something calls you, doesn't it?" Cor asked, coming to stand to Geoff's left on a hillcrest.

"I think so. I'm not sure, Lord Dahken," Geoff answered, his stare unmoving. He did not act as if Cor startled him, but also showed no sign that he had heard Cor's approach.

"Have I told you how I was led to Soulmourn, and how I recovered Ebonwing? As time passes, that pull you feel will become stronger, and sooner or later you'll have no choice but to go to it."

"Do you think it's in that strange place where you found your fetish?" Geoff asked, motioning at Ebonwing.

"No, that would be more south of us than anything. No, you're looking into the heart of the Loszian Empire past Fort Haldon. If I had to guess, I'd say you are feeling something in the catacombs below Noth's obliterated tower. We Dahken have a long history of robbing the dead. Perhaps that's why we've always placed our fallen in tombs instead of the ground."

A shiver ran through Geoff; for the winter morning air, the talk of Losz, or other ghoulish things, Cor could not be sure.

"How will I find it?"

"When it's time, you'll be led to it easily enough," Cor said. He turned and placed his left hand on Geoff's shoulder before walking back to oversee the packing of camp.

It was late in the day when they finally arrived, the winter sun already low in the western sky, and Fort Haldon had changed substantially since Cor had seen it just a few months ago. Activity bustled everywhere as stonemasons, carpenters, laborers, and foremen crawled across the area like ants as they performed various tasks. Several new but small buildings had popped up, and there were a large number of workers in an area against a cliff face. He noted also that the wooden palisade protecting the pass was being reinforced on the outside by huge granite blocks. Cor knew it would eventually turn into a true wall with battlements and a massive gate.

On the way, Thom went over the entirety of the construction plans with Cor, Rael and Thyss, though Thyss' interest was nearly nonexistent. The cliff face was a convenient location for the keep, and a curtain wall would be placed in a semicircle around it. Cor wanted an additional wall that would surround the entire complex on the Aquis side, just in case an attack came from that direction. At first Thom argued the point that such a thing was highly unlikely, but he eventually conceded, though they agreed that it would be the last thing to be built. Queen Erella's architects estimated that the entire project, excluding the additional wall, would take close to seven years, and by then Cor hoped to have over a dozen full fledged Dahken warriors.

Cor took a brief tour of the site with Rael, Thom, and a continuously listless Thyss, but they did not spend too much time pouring over details. They had tomorrow and many months to come to review the details. Famished, their stomachs ached for a real meal instead of travel rations, and they quickly ended their tour and moved on to dinner. The Dahken shortly settled in to bed early, including Keth and Geoff, sleeping two to a tent much like the last time they had been here.

It was a simple plan. The "foreman" waited outside the buildings in the darkness dressed in black, tar coating his face and hands. He presumed they would all come together and then separate, but the plan could not be left to such chance. He would wait and watch for the marks to come to their quarters. Once they arrived, the two lovers in one building and the older man in his own, he would pelt each roof with a small stone. The men inside would then start counting down. Each had a half hourglass, and after four full turns, they would kill their marks.

He didn't have to wait long before the marks approached with the garrison commander. They were exactly as described by Larnd, lean and dangerous, but that didn't matter. The most deadly warrior would fall beneath the blades of his assassins if that warrior was asleep, and he left nothing to chance. A killing stroke would not be necessary as the blades were coated with a relatively quick and deadly poison. Arms were clasped, and the garrison commander soundlessly took his leave back to his own quarters. The trio separated exactly as expected. After he heard both doors open and shut, he signaled his men inside and sat down against one of the buildings to wait with his own half hourglass.

The two men in the false ceiling turned their glasses and waited, listening intently for the lack of moving sand that they should turn them again. Their targets were a young warrior and a beautiful witch from the east, potentially two dangerous foes, but the plan neutralized that. They heard the expected fumbling around – thuds from footsteps between the rooms, the clinking of armor as it was removed and the sound of bodies flopping into a soft bed with contented sighs.

They turned the glasses over, starting the flow of sand through the next half hour. As the minutes passed, other sounds came from the bedroom below, and the muffled grunts and moans made it obvious what transpired below them. Perhaps it wasn't a terrible surprise now that they had private quarters and a soft bed after a long ride. It was all the better for the two would exhaust themselves even more, and that would make the job that much easier. The assassins turned their glasses a third time.

The sands ran out again, and they turned the glasses the fourth and final time. In a half hour, the sands would run out, and it would be their time to strike.

But the couple was still at it, showing no signs of slowing. They could wait, but the third assassin would have no idea that the plan had changed. If the other murder didn't go well, the two below would be warned, and the whole affair would come apart. Larnd would not be happy, a bad thing to be sure.

The sands ran out.

The assassins silently and without delay removed the panels that would allow them into the bedroom below, weak flickering candlelight barely penetrating the darkness. They could make out the form of the woman with her flawless bronze skin and golden hair astride the young man with the gray skin. On his back, he momentarily opened his eyes to look right at the pair of assassins as they prepared to drop. As they came down, landing on the packed dirt floor soundlessly, the warrior threw the witch off of him.

The assassin meant to kill the witch sprung, dagger in hand, and it was then that his world exploded into light, colors of yellow, orange, and red. A heat unlike anything he'd ever felt infused every fiber of his being, like the warmth of the sun on your face on a winter day, but it instead was ten thousand suns. He tried to open his eyes but found he couldn't, and something boiling hot stung the cheeks of his face. Someone screamed incessantly, pausing only long enough to take another breath and scream again. His dagger gone, he could think only of escaping the heat into the cold winter's night air. He found a door pull, the cold metal very soothing against the skin of his hand, and yanked the door open. The assassin then ran screaming into the night.

Cor paced Thom's quarters, his temper raging as he clenched and unclenched his fists. He felt a tingle in the back of his skull, Soulmourn and Ebonwing pushing him to action, begging him to slay. He ignored it, though he allowed the sensation to fuel his anger. Thom for his part sat quietly, coolly with his feet up on a small table while they waited. Rael stood solidly and placed a hand on Cor's shoulder in a suggestion of calm as the Lord Dahken paced by.

Rael had easily dispatched his would be assassin with a sword thrust through the heart from behind. The Dahken said he had always had trouble sleeping in unknown places, and he'd been sitting in a corner of the room quietly, just listening to the night. The assassin came down facing the bed where his target should have been fast asleep, and he hadn't stood a chance.

As it was, things could have gone badly for Cor and Thyss. Hee had wanted to go straight to sleep, but the always hot blooded elementalist had other plans. It was pure luck he'd been looking up at that exact moment, and Thyss reacted instantaneously with anger and power, lighting a blue ball of flame in her palm. She blew into it as if blowing a kiss, and the flame changed colors and streaked in a sheet toward the two men, instantly setting their hair and clothes ablaze. One man fell dead almost immediately, while the other ran screaming into the night. He didn't get far.

Thyss' magic managed to set half of the room on fire as well, and it was all they could do to retrieve their clothes, armor, and weapons before the ceiling came crashing down around them. In their exit, they nearly ran headlong into Rael, and the older Dahken watched the building's roof burn and fall in while Cor and Thyss dressed themselves.

They immediately ran to Thom's newly expanded quarters, waking him and his family as Cor barged right through the door. He did not suspect the veteran of duplicity, but anything untoward that happened at Fort Haldon was Thom's responsibility. Thom, a true professional, shook off sleep quickly and laid out the plans for the current stage of construction. He called for two of his men to retrieve the foreman responsible for the buildings, thinking that perhaps there they could find some answers. After a wait during which Cor seethed and Thyss dozed, the men returned with no sign of the man.

"Find him!" Cor yelled at them, causing Thyss to open both eyes and glare at him. "Wake the entire fort, search, and find him. No one rests until we do! Go!"

The men paused uncertainly, edging toward motion, but looking at Thom.

"Lord Dahken Cor is your lord and mine. Obey his orders without hesitation," Thom said and paused; after the men left, he said to Cor, "The men are not used to taking orders from anyone but myself. I apologize Lord, I will correct it immediately."

Cor waived it away saying, "I don't care about that right now, Thom. I want to know who just tried to kill me, us."

"Hykan damn it, Cor!" Thyss swore loudly. "Don't you understand? He's gone, and if he's any good at his job, we'll never know who he was. Now I am going to sleep in Thom's bed! Is *anybody* joining me?"

Cor watched open mouthed as she stormed through a doorway into an adjacent room. Thom chuckled softly to himself, leaning his face heavily on his palm. "Lord Dahken," he said, "please go with her. My wife sleeps with the children for the rest of the night, and I will be fine here."

Cor turned and followed her, ignoring Rael's sigh.

They met the next morning with clearer minds and calmer tempers. It was clear that the last assassin, the foreman that arranged the entire affair, was gone. The only trace left behind was a set of tracks in the snow leaving Fort Haldon, but these disappeared quickly as the sun shone and warmed the air. Thom showed great concern over his lord's safety, but Cor convinced him that they needed to protect the younger Dahken as well. Whoever wanted Cor dead may very well strike at those who had not yet learned of their powers.

They would build a small barracks, a dormitory for the Dahken, and it would have one large room in which most of them would sleep and about a dozen small rooms for the older Dahken. These would have little space for more than a bed on which to sleep. Four sets of larger quarters would be adjoined to the barracks, one for Thyss and Cor and one for Rael, with two to remain empty should they be needed later. They designed the building with large double doors at either end of the building's length, to be always guarded, as a handful of other men walked a perimeter. Thom hand picked the men for these positions; no new faces from Byrverus would safeguard the Dahken.

An architect drew up the plans quickly, as they were rather simple, and ground broke on the project before the day ended. Cor wanted the building complex finished immediately, and no small part of their resources were diverted to the project. There was little doubt in Cor's mind that the attempt on their lives had its roots in either Losz or, more likely, Byrverus. He doubted that the Loszians, as lazy and self absorbed as they seemed, would have gone to the trouble. As such, it would be about two weeks before the person behind the attack knew of its failure. And then, what would happen next?

9.

Palius sat in his chair before a raging fire, wrapped in a heavy brown robe over top of the normal white robes he wore daily. He had found this winter to be increasingly cold even though most considered it relatively mild other than one recent snowstorm. He knew he was dying, as did Queen Erella and most of the palace, but he refused to make a bother over it. The old man coughed occasionally, something he tried to remedy by adding more layers or stoking his fire, all the while saying that he merely had a cold. In his chair before his fireplace is where Palius could be found more often than not, for he could not stand the deep cold of the rest of the palace. All his meals came to him here, as did Queen Erella when she needed him for counsel or aid, and she came to him with decreasing frequency as the days advanced. Those who entered Palius' chambers typically found themselves sweating in a matter of minutes or even seconds.

This day, like most days, Palius sat in his chair and stared at the fire, waiting. He waited for his queen to need him, he waited for news that he may think over, and he waited for the icy hand of death to close its grip about him. He coughed loudly twice, a deep rumbling cough from down in his chest, accompanied by wheezing and the momentary sensation that he was drowning. Palius inched his chair closer to the blazing hot fire, unaware that his underclothes were soaked against his body.

He thought of the Dahken and Fort Haldon every day. He wondered how they fared making the journey from Byrverus back to the outpost, especially having to trudge through a good bit of cold, wet snow. And the snow would have been worse closer to the Spine. It would make life easier if a few of them had died from exposure on the way, and it certainly would help his conscience if he didn't have to arrange the slaughter of children. On the other hand, he did it all for the Shining West and Queen Erella, and Palius knew that Garod and his queen would forgive him in the end. The death of every Dahken at Fort Haldon was absolutely necessary to the security of Aquis and its queen. He must force the Dahken back into obscure history as they were before the birth of Cor Pelson, and in a generation or two, no one would even remember the gray skinned abomination. Any Dahken babes born in the future would be thought of only as sickly children and oddities, and their existence as a race would be finally and completely purged.

A knock at his oak doors broke him from these thoughts. Slightly irritated, he turned his head to consider the sound as the knock came again somehow more insistent. If it were the queen, she would have simply entered, but no one else had such privileges. He considered ignoring the knock in the hopes that the offender would just go away when it sounded a third time, this time the dull thud of a palm being slammed against the heavy door.

"Enter," Palius called resignedly.

"Sir," a guard captain in mixed plate and chain armor with the seals of Aquis emblazoned upon it entered Palius' chambers. "A man, an undesirable I might say, is at the palace entrance demanding to see you. He says he has an urgent message for you. We pushed him off, but he wouldn't leave. I suggested that he use proper channels tomorrow, but he says the message cannot wait, nor does he trust it in anyone's hands. One of my men got a little rough with him, and well, it didn't turn out well. Sir, I know you don't feel well, but perhaps you could come look into this?"

Palius sighed as he turned his face back to his fire. He really had no desire whatsoever to leave his chair and the warmth of his chambers, but it seemed that his duty intruded. It was not uncommon for someone to have a message for him and him alone, but an undesirable as the guard captain put it was something new. Palius sighed again and pushed himself up from his chair. The brown robe was somewhat undignified for a man of his position, so he chose to discard it slovenly over the back of the chair. Palius looked down in surprise at his official white robes, soaked and clinging to his aged and unhealthy body. He pinched at the cloth idly with a thumb and forefinger, pulling it away from his skin before releasing it to hang limply.

"I will need a moment," Palius said, and the captain excused himself.

After changing, Palius strode quickly through the palace corridors toward the main hall. He thought it was unforgivably cold, even with clean dry clothes, but he ignored it and in fact allowed the air to invigorate him. It felt good to be out of his chambers and moving around, and he almost didn't notice the rumble in his chest and the regular, low cough. The old man had spent so much time in his chambers lately that he had really lost all sense of it, and the hour was obviously late as few people were about, excluding the occasional servant and the usual guards. Upon reaching the main hall, Palius turned left to cross plush carpets toward the antechamber that lead outside. He briefly glanced at Queen Erella's throne upon its raised dais, finding it empty. No doubt she had simply retired to her own chambers for the night to handle certain mundane matters of state, but the sight of the vacant throne disturbed him for some reason. Palius wondered, then wishing he were more involved with the priesthood, who would be selected to rule when Queen Erella's reign came to an end. As he left the throne behind him, his footsteps again echoing through the hall as the carpet ended, Palius realized grimly that it likely wouldn't matter as far as he was concerned.

Pushing open one of the heavy doors leading into the antechamber, he found several palace guards, one of whom had blood running down his face from a nose that was mashed to one side. The man's armor lay on the floor next to him, and his right arm was twisted unnaturally. Palius did not even break stride as he crossed the room and pushed open the set of doors leading into the cold night. A half dozen guards stood here in a semicircle, blocking any access to the doors leading inside, their breath coming in large white puffs in the frigid air, and at the bottom of the steps stood a man that made Palius' brow furrow. He was a Westerner with black hair and large brown eyes, and he wore plain brown trousers and a white cotton shirt. It was the man's stance, his lean form that seemed as if it could disappear while standing right in front of a crowd, that caused Palius' eyes to widen in surprise. Palius hoped his reaction would go unnoticed by those present.

"I am told you have an urgent message for me?" Palius asked.

"I do, milord," Marek answered. "It is most important. I couldn't entrust it to anyone."

"Most wise of you, good sir. Please if I may?" Palius held out his hand. Marek approached, a sealed scroll in hand, and the guards parted to allow him to place it in Palius' outstretched palm. Palius replaced it with a gold coin.

"Thank you, milord," Marek said with a quick slight bow of his head.

Palius watched as the rogue that he had found so useful stepped easily down the well lit broadway. Within moments, the man had completely vanished into the night, despite the light thrown by torches and lanterns in close proximity to one another. Palius returned directly to his chambers.

The old man sat in his chair, much in the same position he was in before the guard captain informed him of the man with the message, though this time without a heavy cloak about him. He sat in quiet consideration of the scroll in his right hand; it was made of new parchment and not discolored from age. There could be little doubt of the source of the message based on who delivered it, and Palius' hands shook slightly as he considered the implications. He rarely used Larnd, for rarely did he have need of Larnd's special skills and network of cutthroats. The master rouge had never failed him before, and Palius thought it possible the man had never failed at all. He was a consummate professional, and certainly Larnd had never felt a need to contact a customer to convey success.

Palius carefully and deliberately broke the black wax seal on the scroll and unrolled the cylinder of parchment. He found nothing, no words, no marks, and no message. He sighed deeply as he slumped further in his chair, the blank scroll in his hand slipping to the edge of his fingertips, threatening to slide into his lap and fall to the floor. The messenger was the message; Larnd sent his own brother, the man Palius used as his contact with the lord of Byrverus' underbelly, to convey failure. The scroll was incidental, a decoy. With a flick of his wrist, Palius discarded the piece of parchment into the fire and watched it disappear as if it had never been.

If only he had murdered Dahken Cor as a child. So many accidents could have befallen someone so young.

Palius knew that the power of the Shining West depended on him, that he stamped out this fire before it raged too hotly. It was time to try a different approach – what Palius now needed was an ally not a hireling, someone who would help him destroy Lord Dahken Cor and his people for the good of the empire. If he could only distract the Dahken with something substantial, a large force perhaps, he could strike at them from within. Some good men at Fort Haldon may die, one way or the other, but their sacrifice would secure Aquis' future.

Palius stood and half carried, half dragged his chair over to his heavy desk. He then walked to one side of his office to stand before several of his large chests as he considered what he sought. Producing a key that he had taken from his desk, he knelt and unlocked the chest furthest to the left, throwing back its heavy lid. Palius stared at its innards, many diverse and odd items that he had collected from various persons over the years for various purposes. He knew that many of them had their places in dark rituals for evil gods and some had powers he dared not consider. Queen Erella and the priesthood would not approve of him holding these objects, but he had always thought they one day may come in handy.

Palius found the particular thing for which he looked and disengaged it from the rest, taking care to touch as few of the myriad items as possible. After closing and locking the chest, he carried the item by one end by pinching it between his thumb and middle finger as if loath to touch it and gently placed it face down upon his desk. The thing was a mirror, round and about eight inches across with a curved handle that extended roughly six inches. The mirror glass itself was set into a very slightly translucent stone that reminded him of the jade from Dulkur, though it had hues of purple instead of green.

Over twenty years ago, Palius had taken this mirror from a spy, a shit of the lowest order who used it to contact his master, conveying all he saw or heard. Palius watched this man for a long time before he was sure of the treachery, and he finally caught the man in the act of using the vile mirror in a broom closet. The spy's remains still lie on an iron table far below the palace in a dungeon the existence of which Palius was not sure even the queen was aware, his joints stretched and pulled out of place. As the spy was castrated and his guts ripped asunder, he screamed that he only did it for his family – some nonsense of how the emperor himself would mate with his wife and daughter if he were successful. The men Palius used for the deed were promoted, made wealthy, and moved to separate boring garrisons throughout Aquis, excluding one whom Palius kept close to him for other needs.

    Palius wasn't sure how to use the thing. He only hoped that if he held the mirror with its glass facing him, eventually someone would take notice.

10.

Sovereign Nadav was bored, and now he realized just how monotonous life had been before the death of Taraq'nok at the hands of a Dahken. With a little investigation, everything became clear to the Loszian. Apparently, Taraq'nok had been collecting Dahken when he came across them, rather than eliminating them outright as had been the edict in Losz for hundreds of years, and for some reason, he had a particular interest in a young Dahken named Cor Pelson, a Westerner by birth. Perhaps it was because the boy already knew how to use his powers, or he had hopes that the boy would lead him to other more powerful Dahken. It seemed Taraq'nok intended to use the Dahken to overthrow Nadav, take control of all Losz and invade the Shining West. Taraq'nok may have been disloyal and arrogant to the point of blindness, but the half breed (not truly accurate, but seven eighths breed didn't roll of the tongue as well) was nothing if not superfluously ambitious.

Eventually Dahken Cor sought Taraq'nok out and killed him, with little resistance on the Loszian's part, and with the sorcerer's magic broken, Sovereign Nadav could not simply transport himself into the dead Loszian's castle. It upset him to no end that he had to physically travel by horseback from Ghal, perhaps one of the most disgusting and uncomfortable experiences of his life. By the time he arrived to find Taraq'nok dead, the Dahken, his nursery, and a fire breathing bitch from Dulkur had already fought their way through Lord Menak's outpost near the Spine, the very place the boy had originally come through to find Taraq'nok.

Menak's men nearly stopped their escape if not for sudden help from Westerners with longbows, and Nadav still scratched his head over how the men from Aquis' Fort Haldon knew to be there at that precise moment. They could not have been there waiting, watching; Lord Menak was adamant that his spies and scouts checked the pass daily.

All this Sovereign Nadav gleaned from long, frank discussions with both Taraq'nok's steward and Lord Menak, and he had no reason to doubt either's veracity, as they both bore the scars of Nadav's rather insistent questioning. The steward convinced Nadav of his truthfulness after the glowing hot poker pierced and melted his right eye and threatened to enter a particular orifice. Menak on the other hand had never been a liar, but Nadav kept that other hand as a souvenir just to be sure. He suggested that perhaps a gleaming steel hook or even a serrated knife blade would make Menak substantially more dashing than he was with two rather boring hands.

Nadav never understood why none of his subjects seemed to have a sense of humor. He thought he was rather clever, even if his statements were full of puns, irony, or crude humor.

After months of riding smelly beasts, Sovereign Nadav returned to Ghal with relish. He had found no other place in Rumedia as beautiful with its massive black and purple walls and spires, his of course being the tallest of them all. A handful of lords also made their home in Ghal, and these were careful to never outshine their Sovereign who was certainly the most powerful sorcerer in Losz. He loved the smells of the city as well as the sights - the blood and sweat of slaves and the risen doing their master's bidding, excrement and detritus rotting in the streets and alleys. It was home, the center of Sovereign Nadav's power.

Only days after returning to his palace and sinking with a sigh into the plushness of his bed and slaves did he realize just how uninteresting was his life. Nadav spent the last thirty or forty years never leaving the comforts of Ghal and his palace, indulging in all his desires and trying to become one with the universe through various intoxicants. He spent more time drunk or drugged than he did lucid and sober, and most of his lords had become just as lazy and decadent as he. Despite the hardships of riding, the smell of the animals, the dust in his nose and throat, and exposure to the outdoors, the adventure of it all awakened something inside Nadav. He was home only briefly before he longed for activity, intrigue, violence, and death. The entire affair was, for lack of a better word, fun.

On the southern wall of Nadav's bedroom, twelve foot tall curtains of blood red silk waved slightly in a breeze. Nadav wandered over to these, pushing one aside to step out onto a balcony. The balcony was over eight feet long and only about three feet from the entrance to the edge with no rail of any kind to prevent one from plummeting to a sure death far below. Nadav's chambers were of course at the top of the tallest tower in Ghal, at least several hundred feet in the air, though he did not know the exact height.

The night air was warm, and the black city seemed rather peaceful from this far above it. Facing the southern side of the city, Nadav could see three other towers, all of which belonged to lords and sorcerers of course, and even hundreds of feet away from the closest, he could see light spilling from their windows and balconies. The temples were far below, the tallest no more than a quarter the height of Nadav's tower. The Loszian necromancers worshipped their gods privately, and the temples were mainly for their lessers. The dark purple towers and temples reflected moonlight in a variety of dark hues to be oddly absorbed by the black basalt used in the common buildings. Large fires spotted the city here and there, and Nadav was certain debauchery most foul was afoot in many places hidden from even his view.

A slight sense of vertigo, coupled with a cold but powerful gust of wind convinced Nadav to leave the balcony. Letting the curtain close behind him, he leisurely crossed the room to stand at a full length mirror, admiring his naked body, well built and strong. He was tall, even for a Loszian, standing over seven feet tall with shoulders only about two feet across, narrow even for a lowly Westerner of average height. The joints of Nadav's arms, hands, and fingers were more elongated than many Loszians, accentuating his pure blood and making it so that the tips of his fingers dangled at his kneecaps even when he stood fully erect. His forehead, the widest part of Nadav's skull, was not quite six inches across, and his face narrowed consistently down angular features to the wicked point of his chin, a mere inch across. Despite his age of over a century, Nadav's skin stayed completely flawless over the years, retaining its pale white color that showed the networks of blue veins across his body underneath, and like most trueblood Loszians, he was completely and totally devoid of hair. Staring at his reflection with violet eyes, Nadav knew he was the picture of pure Loszian beauty and power.

Standing there admiring himself, Nadav decided it was time to end the Loszian decadence. For too long his lords plotted against each other or even him to expand their power, and for too long, the Loszians sat in studies or trances to heighten the strength of their magic. A true leader, Nadav recognized that he too was as much to blame as any of them for allowing it.

All of the strength, power, and wealth the Loszians could want was right in front of them, ready for the taking if they were but bold enough to claim it.

The Shining West was no better than them. A decrepit old hag ruled their most powerful kingdom, and surely her power paled when compared to his. They arrogantly guarded their borders with nothing but men and longbows, and few of their garrisons even had sorcerers, Priests of Garod by their label, to help combat any invasion. Regardless, Nadav refused to believe the complacent Westerners stood a chance against a well planned, overwhelming invasion.

Nadav needed to think it out a bit, but he couldn't concentrate as the feeling of vertigo returned, this time with a tingle in the back of his brain. It grew insistent, infuriating the emperor until he realized the source of the sensation. It was something he hadn't felt in years, and Nadav was knew this particular slave died at the hands of Westerners long ago. He turned from the mirror, crossed his chamber, and passed through a portal that led to his laboratory.

Nadav fumbled through a variety of alchemical devices before selecting a plain bowl carved of pure ebony, which he filled with water. With a muttered word, he watched his reflection in the water change to one that was wholly unsettling. An old man, a Westerner stared back at him, and surprise momentarily registered in his aged eyes before turning back to a cold stare. He was ancient by Nadav's reckoning with thinning white hair that he kept closely cropped and a heavily lined face with sagging white bearded jowls. The man looked exhausted, swollen purple pouches lining his lower eyelids, and Nadav's stomach turned as he took in the Westerner's visage.

"Who are you, old man?" Sovereign Nadav asked venomously.

"I am Palius, counselor to Queen Erella of Aquis," said the face, rippling in the water as it spoke. "I presume you are a Loszian of import to have had a spy in my queen's palace."

Nadav screamed in fury, "Some import? I am Sovereign Nadav, Emperor of all Losz, you steaming pile of horseshit! How dare you address me as such!"

"Please accept my sincere apologies, Sovereign Nadav," Palius replied with a long nod of his head, his voice completely calm and even. "I humbly request to speak to you about a danger to both of our empires, a Dahken by the name of Cor Pelson. I believe we can help each other, eliminate him, and secure our empires' mutual future."

Nadav's eyes narrowed as the man spoke, and he took a long moment to respond. "Very well. Let us speak."

When Sovereign Nadav made the call to council, he had given his lords two weeks to make whatever preparations they felt necessary before coming. Over three hundred were called, many of them lesser lords owing fealty to others of greater power, but all of them answering to him in the end. Knowing that many would transport to Ghal almost immediately, some out of a sense of duty or others out of a need to ingratiate themselves to the emperor, Nadav had prepared the city for their arrival. The first lord to transport himself did so in only a few hours, and over half of them arrived over the first week. Some without the ability to use magic rode horses and chariots into Ghal, and most of these pushed to the time limit. The last few days of his wait chaffed Nadav as impatience worked its fingers into his brain, heart, and joints.

To say he called forth a council was not entirely accurate. The simple fact was that Nadav was Emperor of Losz and answered to no one, be it one of the lords or all of them together. Not to say he could ignore the combined strength of all the lords, but fortunately Nadav directly controlled over half of them. And the rest of them were too fragmented, too divided to mount any form of resistance against him. The council would force the lords to unite as one.

The conquest of the Shining West was the topic at hand. The excitement of the last few months made Nadav's blood boil, and he hungered for action, for blood, and for the horrors of war. He would order his lords to form armies, the size of which would be determined by the size of their holdings, and the necromancers themselves would lead them into battle. The Loszian Empire could crush the Shining West, of that Nadav was sure, and now the old man called Palius had opened the door for the terror that the Loszians could bring down upon their world.

The old man was very concerned about the safety of the west and, oddly, of Losz as well. He spent some time elaborating on Dahken Cor, now Lord Dahken Cor thanks to the queen of Aquis, and frankly, Nadav found the entire story somewhat boring. He couldn't have cared less about where the boy came from. However, his interest piqued when Palius discussed the Dahken's plans to invade and free Losz, and Nadav puzzled over this idea, for he had no idea from what Dahken Cor expected to free the Loszians. They were already free, and the Westerners who lived underneath them certainly enjoyed a better life than they would otherwise. At least in Losz they could hope to mate with their Loszian masters and advance themselves, whereas in Aquis, they would always be under Garod's yoke. Regardless, the old Westerner seemed to think that a Dahken led Western invasion of Losz would, one way or the other, lead to the fall of both.

It nearly stunned Nadav into silence when Palius suggested an alliance. Perhaps alliance was too strong of a word; collaboration or collusion would be more appropriate. The old man put forth that they could rid both empires of the Dahken with some coordination, starting with an attack on Fort Haldon by the Loszians with a sizeable force. While the garrison fought to repel the onslaught, a group of Westerners chosen by the old man would eliminate the Dahken from the inside – not just Lord Dahken Cor, but all of them, children included. Palius assured the emperor that his time as Queen Erella's prime advisor had made him many loyal subordinates in her army's ranks.

"Why do I even need you old man? Why do I not simply crush Fort Haldon and then the rest of Aquis?" Nadav had asked.

"Because you cannot win, Sovereign," he replied. "Garod's people pushed you from the Shining West ages ago, and you cannot break His power. The men of Fort Haldon have held that pass for centuries with their longbows and will continue to do so, especially with the strength of the Dahken and that damnable woman from Dulkur. A force large enough to break it would be spotted well in advance, allowing them to send for help, and Her Majesty's armies stand ready. Besides Sovereign, let's be honest. Both our empires thrive in their own way as things stand. Let us not destroy the peace that has made us both powerful."

"Very well," Nadav whispered, conceding Palius his point. "I will consider your words Westerner, but I make no promises for now. We will discuss this again in one month. Do not disturb me before then."

Nadav broke the spell by contemptuously flinging the bowl aside.

The sack of sagging flesh had no inkling of the insult he had thrown the way of Sovereign Nadav to even suggest that the Shining West could defeat the hordes of Losz or that Garod was greater than Nadav's own gods. Nadav would visit the meteor, the great vessel that brought the Loszians to Rumedia, and he would prostrate himself before it. The gods would bestow upon him their favor, enhancing his power, and Nadav would raise vast armies long dead. An army never before seen in Rumedia, a hundred thousand strong, would obliterate Fort Haldon and the Dahken. He would crush Aquis with a wave of death, shattering all in his path, and Nadav would sodomize Aquis' ancient bag of bones queen even as his magic turned her flesh to maggots.

Nadav leered viciously at the thought.

The lords gathered in Nadav's great purple hall. The necromancers, none of them as tall or beautiful as Nadav himself, dressed in their robes ranging in color from blood red to purple to black, carrying markings of their power. There were a number of crossbreeds as well; many of these were not sorcerers, at least not to the extent of a full blooded Loszian and wore various types of well wrought and beautifully adorned armor. Only a few stragglers arrived as late as the appointed day, a number of malcontents and those who had to ride to Ghal, and Sovereign Nadav was well aware of who the former were.

He mused that if each Loszian here could raise a small army of one thousand, regardless of whether it consisted of crossbowmen, soldiers, slaves, or the dead, the empire would be unstoppable.

Nadav sat upon his throne, perfectly still and straight, barely moving even to breathe as he glared out at the crowd. He had forced them to assemble here with no slaves or servants, and no personal guards. The general paranoia of his race made them mill about uncomfortably, as if each one of them expected at any moment to be slaughtered mercilessly. Keeping one eye on Nadav, the Loszians began to coalesce into pockets of strength, groups that were like minded or even allied with one another. They watched Nadav, but they watched their enemies more closely as they waited for their emperor to explain why he brought them here. He waited until the tension seemed to crescendo before he stood from his throne, a towering giant standing on his dais that brought the whispering crowd to a hush.

"We are weak," Nadav began slowly, and the hushed whispers began again in earnest. "We have lost sight of who we are, of what we are capable. We have allowed the Westerners to keep us trapped on our side of the Spine, content to scheme against each other from our towers. We are decadent, happy to eat, drink, and fuck our way into oblivion as we attempt to strengthen our powers.

"My subjects, today is a great day," he announced, changing his tone as he threw his hands toward the ceiling high overhead, "for today we begin to forge our future, a future where once again the Loszian Empire extends from coast to coast over the west. We shall raise armies such as Rumedia has never seen and retake what belongs to us, the lands of the Shining West. We shall crush their feeble resistance, casting their armies aside as a storm capsizes a fishing boat, and then we shall cast them upon the rocks, shattering their civilization. We shall claim their lands, their riches, their women, and children, and we shall defecate on the images of Garod."

The mass of Loszians stood quietly, without even hushed whispers breaking the silence. Most of them simply stared back at Sovereign Nadav, their thoughts hidden behind practiced inscrutable masks, while others furrowed their brows in thought as they stared at their feet or the domed ceiling above. None spoke, and it certainly was not the uproarious applause Nadav had expected. He stood sweeping his gaze over them expectantly, and after a moment, some mumbled conversations sprang up within the group, though the lords immediately at the forefront were careful to neither move nor speak.

"Damn you all," Nadav swore, "why do you have nothing to say?"

"Why should we risk our lands, our wealth for your fools errand?" asked a loud voice. Nadav could not see the voice's owner, though he recognized it well. It emanated from one of the groups to the left of the carpeted main walkway and close to the rear of the hall. Nadav heard some grumbled agreement throughout the hall, and a few of the lords nodded their heads, though perhaps they should have remained still. His temper flashed at this, but Nadav instead focused on the verbal challenge.

"As if my command is not enough? It is the right and destiny of the Loszian race to rule all the west, if not the world. Fool's errand? Words spoken by a coward no doubt!"

The last brought a great amount of rumbling from the assembled Loszians who could no longer contain themselves. Some shouts went up from the rear of the mass, and a group of about a dozen necromancers came forward on the left side. Those between Nadav and the approaching lords hastened to part and allow them through. At their head was the one who dared to argue with Nadav – Venid'kos, a pureblood Loszian only a few inches shorter than the emperor himself. He stood arms crossed defiantly in all black robes emblazoned with platinum lettering, his stance more reminiscent of a Westerner than a Loszian, and his yellow eyes blazed as he returned Nadav's long, hard look.

Venid'kos was older than Nadav and had long viewed himself as the rightful heir to the throne. But the lords selected the emperor, and it was a game more of wealth and politics than true power as a sorcerer. Venid'kos often stood against Nadav, and it was widely rumored that he intended to challenge the emperor for his throne. The only thing that had stopped him was lack of support from the other lords, and should he defeat Nadav, it would likely bring outright rebellion. This was Venid'kos' opportunity to dethrone Sovereign Nadav, for he knew the emperor asked more from the lords than they were willing to give freely, and Nadav had expected the challenge.

"Reconsider the path you would take us on Sovereign," Venid'kos said, the threat plain in his voice. "We are strong and secure in the empire. We have no need for anything beyond our borders. You demand that we risk much for naught."

"You are wrong, Venid'kos," Nadav countered. "The murder of Taraq'nok at the hands of a Dahken proves it. We are weak and decadent. We drink, we sleep, we fuck, and we hide in our towers to prove to ourselves that we are strong. The Loszian Empire has too long stayed in its strongholds behind the protection of the Spine. We will enslave the Shining West and rape it as we desire."

"We will not follow you to ruin!" Venid'kos nearly screamed as he pointed a long, spindly finger at Nadav. To this, there were many calls of agreement, but also Nadav's more staunch supporters edged forward in anticipation. Their eagerness polarized the Loszians, rallying the quieter lords to one side or the other, and with a quick mental count, Nadav knew he had more supporters than Venid'kos. Many seemed to be unsure, but that would change.

"You will follow me wherever I should lead! To say otherwise is to incite revolution, treachery, and you shall pay dearly."

"I would not call for a revolt," Venid'kos said. "I would not dare so weaken the empire by causing a civil war. Nor would I risk the empire by waging war on the Shining West. I do say you are unfit to be emperor, Nadav, and I would see you destroyed. Allow council to select a new emperor, me if they desire or not, but you will fall."

"Does that mean," asked Nadav softly, deadly, "that you dare challenge me?"

"For the throne, yes," Venid'kos replied as he stepped forward.

The other Loszians cleared away from Venid'kos to avoid being struck by errant magic, but the battle lasted scant moments. Venid'kos found his magic virtually ineffective, unable to penetrate the wall of wards that surrounded Sovereign Nadav. The emperor enveloped his opponent with a great black cloud of pestilence, transparent enough for those in the hall to watch Venid'kos' fate. He screamed horribly as his skin changed from merely pale to gray, and his fingernails grew immensely, inches and then feet in just a few seconds. The skin of his face and his scalp pulled tightly around the Loszian's skull, drawing blackening lips back to reveal white teeth that began to change colors and decay. The screaming ended, leaving its echo as Venid'kos' skin, hair, ears, and eyes turned to dust, and the bones encapsulated by his robes fell to a pile on the floor.

The other Loszians stared unspeaking, some aghast and others merely contemplative, for no Loszian had killed another in open combat for decades. However, the humiliation of Venid'kos was not yet done as his bones began to rustle and move under the empty robes. Within seconds, they had reformed themselves fully, a skeletal reflection of the necromancer they once were, and the skeleton jerkily climbed the steps of the dais to stand behind Sovereign Nadav, its robes just barely hanging loosely upon its form.

"And so it will be with all of my enemies," proclaimed the emperor.

11.

While construction on the hall hadn't even begun, Cor felt it appropriate to hold the ceremony where all future ceremonies would take place. Eventually the hall would be the official meeting place for the Dahken, that is all the Dahken that chose to reside at Fort Haldon. When Cor discussed it with him, Rael had been against any such ceremony, as they never before existed in Dahken history, but Cor insisted. He wanted to make sure recognition was given properly for those who deserved it. Rael conceded the point of course, but with one parting comment.

"How very Western," he said.

Cor had carpenters build a table of walnut and mahogany, long enough to seat a dozen persons on each side and one on either end. The finished product was a gorgeous piece of polished furniture that gleamed powerfully in the light. It had several pedestals supporting it down the middle, each about a foot thick that splayed out into three stylized griffin talons. Armchairs of the same design lined the table on each side, with a larger chair at each end. These were finished with rich burgundy velvet cushions on the seat and back.

It would be an evening affair, as deep into spring, the nights were staying warm until well late, even at the edge of the Spine, and as the sun set to the west, Cor would speak to those he found in Losz and recognize one for what he was – a Dahken not only in race, but in his strength. As the gloaming thickened from the sun disappearing below the horizon, servers would light torches on stanchions and bring out food.

The Dahken would feast in celebration, and Cor hoped it would serve as inspiration to others to become powerful as well. In the end, everything was left to them, their choice if they stayed or left. Even if they used him only to learn to feel their blood and then went down a separate path, Cor would accept it. Certainly, he hoped they would choose to stay and strengthen his ranks, but he would not force them to nor attempt to control their fate as the world had tried to do to him.

Cor sat in his chair at the northern end of the table and waited. He tried to be patient but found restlessness getting the better of him; even still, he forced himself to sit and wait. As the sun neared the horizon, the Dahken climbed the hill where the hall would eventually be built. Directed by Rael, Keth, and Geoff, they took positions at the table, the youngest toward the middle. It was then that Cor realized just how much work lay ahead of them, for he was surrounded by children, over half of whom were less than ten years old. In fact, it amazed Cor how any of them were left alive; somehow, only one had been lost and that one to a Loszian crossbow bolt.

Thom stood to Cor's left some two dozen feet from the table. The stolid, reserved commander had become one of Cor's most trusted advisors, and as such he was invited to the proceedings. He would be invited to all the Dahken meetings, but he chose to merely observe rather than be directly involved. It was his choice, and Cor respected the man's sense of propriety.

Cor felt a presence next to him, and he turned his head to his right to behold something that made his heart leap into his throat. A long, fit feminine leg the color of bronze stood out from a red silk dress that nearly touched the ground. The sides of the dress were slit to well up the thigh, and following the dress up, Cor found it to be sleeveless and held up barely by two thin silk straps. The straps crossed and trailed down a bare back to again meet the dress just above Thyss' buttocks. The front of the dress was no less revealing, the thin red silk accentuating her breasts and nipples. She was beautiful, supple, but at the same time well built for battle. To drive this point home, she carried her alien scimitar by its leather scabbard in her right hand. Cor felt as if his heart were being crushed and simultaneously set on fire, the latter of which was not impossible considering the subject of his gaze.

"Thom's wife said I should dress differently for this occasion," she said. "It seems you approve."

"I didn't expect you to come. I thought you'd be bored. Where did you find *that*?"

"I bought it before we left Byrverus," she replied, and she laughed at his surprise. "Believe it or not, Dahken Cor, I do occasionally enjoy wearing pretty things."

Cor opened his mouth to speak, but sudden silence snapped his attention away from the enflaming sorceress to the assembled Dahken. All of them sat watching the pair, not a word passing amongst them. Keth sat immediately to his right and Rael at the other end of the table with Geoff to his right. Cor cleared his throat before standing before them in full battle regalia with Soulmourn and Ebonwing at his sides, his black armor clean and polished. He left his insectoid helm off, instead allowing it to sit on the tabletop facing the onlookers.

"Just a year ago, I was alone in this world. A Loszian killed my parents, and a priest of Garod killed my friend Lord Dahken Rael, leaving me with no one. I took my vengeance on the priest, and I later avenged my parents death by killing Taraq'nok, the Loszian from whom I freed you," Cor paused for a moment. He had planned an entire speech, but now he could not remember a word of it, so he just said what felt right.

"The Loszians would have us killed for fear of us, and the Shining West would just as soon see us disappear back into history, their version of history. But we have escaped the clutches of those who will destroy and control us, and now we stand poised to build a new world for our kind. The faces you see across the table will be the first, and I believe that Dahken Rael has been returned to us for this very reason.

"The history of the Dahken is gone, wiped out by a world who hates us, the last known written accounts erased by Taraq'nok at Sanctum. I have told you the story. The history is gone, and with it goes whatever traditions existed. Now, we start our own traditions.

"When a Dahken has reached the point where we can teach him no further, we will summon all of our race who reside at Fort Haldon, *our sanctum*, to this very table, in a hall that has yet to be built. There is one such Dahken among us now. He has learned everything there is to learn from Dahken Rael, the most knowledgeable among us, and now, this Dahken must only work to strengthen himself. He will feel and need to answer the calls in his blood, and they may lead him to anything – artifacts, other Dahken, or even the Chronicler Himself. But for now, he is here with us, and we are content to honor him.

"Please stand, Dahken Keth!" Cor announced.

As Keth arose, the other Dahken, especially the children applauded in a growing storm by pounding their feet on the ground and their palms on the table. Keth had always been popular among them for his caring, helpfulness, and kind words. Rael and Cor joined in the applause as Keth's smile turned into an embarrassed, almost stupid, ear to ear grin. Cor grasped his arm warmly.

"Let us eat!" shouted the Lord Dahken, loud enough for the nearby servants to hear.

There was much rejoicing amongst good food, good company, and lots of wine. Of course, the servants understood the proper place of things, and the children were limited or even disallowed from the wine depending on their age. Cor noted with satisfaction that Rael drank little compared to what he remembered; perhaps the man's death and rebirth had cleansed him of some of his demons. Cor for his part, partook a little too much, encouraging Keth to do the same.

One other Dahken ate little and enjoyed the wine too heavily. After less than an hour, Geoff told Dahken Rael that he felt ill and would retire. He concentrated immensely on his balance so as not to stumble and fall as he walked away from the table. He barely made it back to the Dahken barracks and his rooms, stopping once to vomit a little more than halfway there. When he reached his door, he could barely keep his eyes open while he unlocked it and pushed it open. Once inside, he passed out on his bed without even closing the door. He wasn't out long, maybe a few hours, when he woke up to the sound of someone pulling his door shut from the outside. He stood up to lock the door and found that his legs betrayed him, and the world spun. He felt terrible, and it only added to his chagrin and anger.

It should have been him.

Keth was nothing compared to him, a stray dog eating from rotten garbage. Geoff's blood ghast contained strength and power of which Keth couldn't even dream. Older by a year he may be, but Keth couldn't hope to defeat him in battle. Geoff knew what he could do with the thing, and even Dahken Rael didn't have such power. And Lord Dahken Cor had never done anything to prove his strength. What had he done in his life? Killed some decrepit priest and a Loszian necromancer whose sorcery couldn't even affect a Dahken? He avoided someone's attempt on his life only because of that slut he was always fucking. Geoff knew

Lord Dahken Cor would have no chance against his blood ghast. They said that they could teach Keth nothing further, but what could they possibly teach him?

It should have been him. He should have been at Cor's right, now called Dahken Geoff. They would soon find out how much they had to learn.

12.

Keth noted that Rael hadn't shaved in a few days, and thick stubble in a mix of black and white covered his face, an interesting effect against the older Dahken's gray skin and the bluish steel of his armor. There was a slight chill in the air this spring morning, one's breath coming in white puffs, but the sun already worked hard to warm the day. Today Rael began the task of training two more of the Dahken children to learn to fight as Dahken, Marya and Celdon, a girl and a boy who were perhaps a few years younger than Keth.

Marya was thirteen, still just a young girl, but Keth knew that she budded into womanhood, a fact that her loose fitting clothes hid well. Shortly after they arrived in Fort Haldon, Keth had accidentally walked in on her naked in a bath. He blushed; at least, he felt the heat on his face, though no color showed in his gray cheeks, and she laughed out loud at his embarrassed reaction. Marya was barely five feet in height and extremely thin, a mere slip of a girl. Once the grime of slavery had been washed from her, Keth found her rather pretty with her long, auburn hair that curled slightly at the very end. She walked more like a boy than a girl, and the hazel eyes that both matched and contrasted her hair seemed to be at once playful and angry.

Standing by her side, Celdon seemed to be Marya's physical opposite. He was tall for his age, almost as tall as Keth, and at least two stone heavier. When Cor had first liberated them and fled to Aquis, Celdon had been downright fat, but he had lost a fair amount of weight in the past few months. Even still, he had a decidedly pudgy countenance, made more apparent by the short bowl shaped way he kept his hair. Keth really didn't know much about Celdon or where he was from, but it seemed the boy was a born fighter, having taken quickly to training with Fort Haldon's men.

This would be the first time either of them had held live steel. Since coming to Fort Haldon, the Dahken's access to resources expanded immensely. Thom had assigned several veteran soldiers to the task of teaching the Dahken swordsmanship with wooden practice swords, which got larger and heavier as the user advanced in skill. Cor hoped that all of them could learn to fight before Rael began the harsh task of wounding them over and over. Rael saw the value of the lessons, though he showed disdain for Cor's concern, saying the children would learn the way all Dahken had learned.

Rael started with the boy, Celdon, at first simply parrying the boy's attacks, allowing him to learn the weight and balance of a real weapon before Rael inserted his own strikes, attacks that were easy to parry or avoid altogether. They became more dangerous, more precise, and Celdon had an increasingly more difficult time deflecting them. Then the first wound came, a shallow cut to the boy's upper right arm, above the small, round buckler shield he carried. Having never been wounded before, Celdon lost focus on what he was supposed to be doing as he cradled the wound. Rael ceased his attacks and sheathed his sword. He spoke to Celdon in the usual way, coldly talking about his blood and how the boy must learn to feel it. He must find the heart of the pain and use it to fuel his own attacks. They would give him strength, and his own blows would heal him. The mock battle continued with Rael landing two more blows, to give Celdon shallow wounds. The boy was unable to return the attacks with any force, and eventually fell to his knees crying.

Rael sheathed his sword and motioned to one of Thom's soldiers, as several were on hand for these training sessions for multiple reasons. The man, whose name Keth could not recall, gently helped Celdon to his feet and half carried him away to see the garrison's surgeon. Rael sighed and turned from the group to be alone with his thoughts for a moment. Keth knew that one day this task would be his, and he didn't think it would be easy to bleed children while telling them to fight back.

Geoff sauntered up to lean on a post next to Keth.

"What are we doing now?" Geoff asked, yawning.

"You know what. Where have you been?"

"I overslept," Geoff responded indifferently with a slight shrug of his shoulders.

As far as Keth could tell, it was true. The rings around Geoff's eyes looked darker than usual, and he still smelled of wine and maybe something a little less savory. Rael called for Marya and began the same way he had with Celdon.

"Turning into a bad habit of yours," Keth said. "Maybe I should talk to Lord Dahken Cor about disallowing us access to the fort's wine."

"It's my choice, Dahken Keth. Isn't that what Cor is all about? Choice?" This last word he spat with venom.

"Lord Dahken Cor, Geoff. You would do well to remember that."

"As you say, *Dahken* Keth," Geoff said, making no attempt to hide his distaste.

Marya fought Rael with less coordination than Celdon had, but she made up for it with energy and a desire to prove that she was as good as a boy. It was interesting to watch as she was only half Rael's size, but Keth pulled himself away as he saw the soldier returning with news of Celdon. He watched out of the corner of one eye as he was told that the boy would be fine, news no different than what he expected. Rael in the meantime had wounded the girl once, and as he ceased fighting to talk to her in the same way he had to them all, the girl suddenly and angrily swung her shortsword at his head. Keth smiled and turned his full attention to the soldier in front of him.

Rael had wounded the girl a second time, and no doubt prepared to wound her a third, when the soldier stopped talking, his mouth just handing open in mid sentence. It took Keth a moment to realize the man stared at something behind him, and he turned quickly, though in his mind it seemed to take hours. Rael for his part caught just a glimpse of something, perhaps reflecting light, at the edge of his field of vision. It likely saved his life as he reflexively blocked the first blow with a crash on his shield, knocking him back several feet.

His foe stood before him, a full foot taller than he and gleaming red in the morning light. Keth stood, struck dumb in shock as Rael faced a being apparently made of blood. The thing leapt forward to the attack, swinging its six foot blade, each attack at Rael a killing stroke. Rael evaded as best as he could, parrying strikes when necessary, and occasionally taking a blow to his shield that would stagger him. He'd never felt such strength, but he dared not strike the ghast for fear of harming Geoff. Keth tore his eyes from the scene that he feared could not end well and found Geoff, his body on the ground and unmoving. He couldn't even see if Geoff's chest rose and fell, and he appeared dead, as he always did when the blood ghast appeared. His shock broken, Keth made to run to Geoff's body, perhaps somehow wake him.

"No!" he heard Rael shout as steel rang. "The ghast will come for you! Get Cor!"

Keth hesitated for a moment, his first instinct to disobey and wade into the fight against the ghast, against Geoff. Rael's shield, a large kite shield made of steel that gleamed blue in the light with a large gem set in the middle, was battered and bent. The gem, a blue stone the size of his fist, was cracked and crushed, half of it missing. Keth turned and sprinted to Thom's quarters, leaving the sounds of the battle and crying children behind him. He was unsure where to find Cor, but Thom would know. If only he could run fast enough.

Rael continued to fight the onslaught, but he had no idea how long he could keep it up. The thing hit with the strength of a giant, so Rael assumed as he had never fought a giant, and while he grew tired and worn, the ghast did not slow at all. In fact, the more fatigued Rael became, the harder the thing's blows seemed to land. He hoped the more it attacked, the more exhausted Geoff would become, and eventually it would return to his body. His only other hope was that he could reach Geoff through whatever senses the thing had.

"Geoff, you must listen," he shouted as he fought. The blood sword rang against his no different than the hardest steel. "You must come back. You must hear me!"

The blood ghast quickened its attacks, swinging its sword and recovering for the next blow almost faster than Rael could follow. One came that he could not parry, and he took it against his now battered shield. The sword bit into it and ripped away most of the top of the shield, and Rael let go of it, allowing the shield to slip off his arm as he dodged the next strike.

"The blood ghast is your essence. You can control it! You can stop it! You must bring it back to you!" Rael pleaded.

And to his amazement, the manifestation of Geoff's blood essence stopped its onslaught. It stood in place on the balls of its feet, sword still at the ready, and it appeared to breathe heavily in and out as if from exertion. It reminded Rael of the first time he had seen it back in the palace in Byrverus, but he was wholly unprepared what happened next. He heard one simple word in his mind, as if a hint of a whisper in Geoff's voice.

"No."

Stunned with horrible realization, Rael barely brought his sword up in time to fend off the next attack. The strike was so powerful, it shattered his longsword and drove him back a few steps as steel splinters glistened in the sunlight. Off balance, Rael could not avoid the sword as it tore into the steel plate on his right shoulder from a massive two handed overhead strike. The cruel weapon drove deeper into his body downward and at an angle, rending steel flesh and bone. It stopped just at his breastbone, having ripped through over eight inches of steel plate across his chest, and rivers of blood ran down the blade, Rael's chest, stomach, and back. Idly, he realized he had lived over a hundred years to die twice since he had first met the boy Cor just a few years ago.

Cor sped, with Keth on his heels to the grounds Rael used for training the Dahken. He had been sitting with the chief architect to determine which and how many rooms in the keep would be allocated to the Dahken when Keth burst into the room. Cor couldn't comprehend what Keth meant by Geoff's blood ghast attacked Dahken Rael, but he knew he needed to get to them quickly. As they approached, he could see great throngs of garrison soldiers and laborers surrounding something or some scene. Those in the outer rings parted readily for the Lord Dahken, but he had to push his way through those close to the middle who fought for a better view.

As he finally reached the center, he stopped dead in his tracks, a cold sick feeling running through his gut. Most of the Dahken were gathered here, most of them crying, and on the ground were Geoff and Dahken Rael. Rael's armor showed a huge gash, starting over the right shoulder and down through the breastplate. The man's steel reflected red in the sun, and blood covered the ground underneath him, growing sticky. Geoff sat on the ground to Rael's right, on his knees with his legs tucked underneath him, and he fiercely gripped Dahken Rael's right hand. As Cor approached dumbly, he cast his shadow over the pair, and Geoff looked up squinting into the sunlight. The young man, boy, was also covered in blood, though none was his, and streaks of tears stained his face.

"I'm sorry. I don't know how..." Geoff said weakly, his voice trailing off.

Cor knelt to Rael's left and quietly placed his hand on the man's forehead and closed the dead man's eyes for the second time. He then closed his own eyes and bowed his head silently for several long moments, whether in prayer or thought one could not be certain. Cor then sighed softly and stood, his hands on Ebonwing and Soulmourn who sang softly to him. It was odd as they only did this in times of danger, but that thought would not occur to him until later.

"Take Dahken Rael to his quarters for now," he said to some of the nearby soldiers. "Bring Geoff and Dahken Keth to mine. I wish to speak with them, Geoff first."

And he stalked off, leaving the crowd to murmur as his commands were carried out. As the men collected Dahken Rael and gently carried him away, Keth stared down at Geoff and the blood soaked dirt. Geoff coolly returned the gaze, tears still running down his face, but

Keth saw no sorrow in his eyes. He saw nothing there at all, except a small glint of satisfaction.

Cor paced his rooms tensely, annoying Thyss to no end. The sorceress had slept late, as usual, and was only just rising when Cor stormed in and told her Rael was dead. She showed surprise, but that was all; Cor knew the two hadn't ever come together in any way. The polite knock came at his door while she still dressed, and he ignored it. Moments later a second, more forceful at the door drew his ire.

"Wait outside gods damn you!" he shouted.

When he was ready, or rather when Thyss was ready, Cor opened the door and admitted the blood and tear stained Geoff, closing the door on Dahken Keth and several soldiers. Still fuming, he pointed to a chair in the corner of the room while he collected his thoughts and calmed himself.

"What happened?" Cor eventually asked, once he was certain that he would neither shout nor cry.

"I'm not sure," Geoff answered sullenly.

"Start from the beginning and leave nothing out."

"I... I overslept and missed the beginning of training," Geoff started haltingly. The Lord Dahken had a dark look on his face, but Geoff continued. "I had too much to drink last night. Keth says I probably drink too much. I was talking to him while Dahken Rael started with Marya. It was fine at first; you know, the usual, the same wounding that we all went through from Dahken Rael. The second time he struck her, I wanted to stop him. She's just a little girl! But then I felt faint and blacked out.

"I started to realize I was attacking Dahken Rael with a huge sword, and I thought I was dreaming. It was strange. I saw everything, but it was strange and dizzy. I could feel the vibration of my sword in my hands as I fought him."

"When did you realize it wasn't a dream?" Cor asked, his tone calmer, softer.

"When I heard Dahken Rael's voice calling to me, telling me to stop. He said the blood ghast was me; that I could stop it, control it. But I couldn't! I couldn't..." Geoff cried, covering his face as tears again welled up in his eyes.

Cor's anger dissolved completely, and he looked at Thyss, as she looked on in concern, even sympathy to the young man.

"I don't see that you can be blamed for this. I wasn't your fault," Cor said as he dropped to one knee. He placed both of his hands on the young man's shoulders. "I will not lie to you. I am furious at Rael's death, but I think the blood ghast appeared because you felt the need to protect Marya. And protecting your weaker sister is nothing to be ashamed of.

"We will honor Dahken Rael. We will entomb him as was the Dahken way before and as will be again. You can most honor him by learning to control the ghast. Geoff, go now to your room and rest. We'll talk more later."

Cor regained his feet and opened the door. Geoff slowly stood and walked outside into the sunlight, and he appeared exhausted, slumped and sullen. He absently gazed east as he walked away. Cor motioned for Keth to enter and related to the young Dahken everything Geoff told him. Keth could add nothing to the story but suspicions that he kept to himself.

"I should have helped Dahken Rael. Together we could have beaten the blood ghast," Keth said after several minutes of silence between them.

"How can you be sure? Rael was fully armored and ready for battle, and you had nothing but your sword," Cor argued. "Geoff could have just as easily killed you both. Even if you are right, you would have killed Geoff. Is that a better outcome?"

"As opposed to Dahken Rael dead?" Keth questioned incredulously. "Yes, I would rather that. Geoff has never proved himself in our eyes."

The statement brought about more fury from Cor than he had ever known. How could Keth, who was essentially a brother to Geoff, say such things? Cor howled his anger, or perhaps it was his grief. He reached down, and in one fluid motion, gripped the underside of the solid oak desk he had learned to keep for administrative issues and upended it, flung against a stone wall. The action and the power of it, shocked Keth into silence, and even the unflappable Thyss leapt to her feet in alarm.

"You will not say such things!" Cor shouted at the younger Dahken, and he brought his face within inches of Keth's. "Geoff's ghost attacked Rael because he felt he was protecting Marya! I will not condemn him for such a thing!"

Seeing Keth and Thyss' reactions, Cor quieted himself, turned his back and forced himself to calm. After several deep breaths, he slumped into the heavy oak chair that matched his now damaged, perhaps useless desk. He sat quietly for several minutes, staring ahead at nothing.

"I have told Geoff that he must learn to control himself, but I don't know how to help him with that. We must learn together, I think. In the meantime, we must build a tomb for Dahken Rael. I will discuss it with Thom. Dahken Keth, you must now teach the Dahken."

Keth again sat stunned into silence, for one by the sudden change in Cor's demeanor, but also for this development. "Lord Dahken, I believe that should be your place. I am so new to it."

"No, it must be you Keth. The power of my blood came to me with no teachings from anyone, Dahken Rael only helped me to better recognize it.

However, you had to work at it, and you are still growing in strength. The Dahken can learn with you. Besides, by now they know you better than me. I intimidate them, but you are their brother. I see no better choice."

Keth stood and said, "Then I can only hope to honor both you and Dahken Rael."

The two men took each other's arms, and Dahken Keth left to contemplate what to do next.

The stonemasons built Dahken Rael's tomb in just over a day, Cor having made it very clear that this project was of the utmost importance. Dahken Rael would be interred as he had before, as all Dahken had before, in a granite tomb roughly ten feet in every dimension. The door was made of solid oak, almost a foot thick and banded with iron multiple times. To Cor's knowledge, the Dahken tombs had always been in catacombs beneath their castles or towers, but it would be different now. Construction on the keep had barely begun, and there were no catacombs of which to speak. Instead, a suitable site had been chosen just a half mile south of the fort, and it was situated on a tall, hilly rise, well away from the mountain river that fed Fort Haldon its fresh water. Dahken Rael's tomb would be the first so placed, and as such was at the apex of the hill. Other tombs would eventually be built around it descending downward, hopefully later than sooner.

Rael had been placed in repose upon his bed, the room sealed and guarded that none would enter with less than Lord Dahken Cor's presence. The battered remnants of his shield and the shattered pieces of his sword were laid out beside him with care. His body still wore his damaged armor, and that was how he would be entombed. His only other belonging, a journal that he began upon his rebirth, resurrection, lay at his feet, and all of these effects would go with him.

The weather on the day of his funeral was in stark contrast to the day's grim deeds. Sunny with only a few fluffy white clouds, a warm wind blew from the west over the hills and mountains, but the warmth of the sun and wind brought no cheer to the hearts of those involved. Four bore Dahken Rael upon their shoulders, Lord Dahken Cor and Commander Thom under the dead man's armored torso and arms, Dahken Keth and Geoff under Rael's legs and lower back. The stiffness of death still held Rael somewhat, making the going easier. Behind them came Thyss who carried Rael's useless shield and Marya who carried a silver tray. A burgundy satin sheet lay on top of the tray, weighed down against the playful wind by the pieces of Rael's shattered longsword. The rest of the Dahken trailed behind Marya, as well as a good many of the soldiers who had come to know the fallen warrior.

They carried him from the Dahken barracks up and down the rolling hills to the south of Fort Haldon until they reached the tomb that would hold his body. To Cor, the climb up the hill approaching Rael's final resting place seemed far more arduous than the previous half mile, and as he looked up the sloping hill at the gray, granite tomb, it struck him how little it matched the warm spring day and cloudless sky behind it. On the farm, a day like this reminded one of life, new and vigorous, but this felt like the harsh, somber reality of death.

The heavy door had been left open, and an amount of dust and loose dirt lay on the stone floor within a few feet of the doorway, blown into the tomb by the near constant breeze. A blank stone slab of granite, almost three feet tall, made up the eastern wall, and this is where they laid Dahken Rael. As Geoff and Dahken Keth filed out of the tomb, Cor separated Racl's legs slightly, and here Thyss placed the pieces of his shield. Last, Marya laid the silver tray with his broken sword and its shards on the floor directly next to the slab.

Lord Dahken Cor shot a last hard look at his dead friend, mentor, and the huge gash in his solid, steel plated torso. More than once, Cor had torn Soulmourn through solid steel, but the force necessary to rip through ten inches of steel, flesh, and bone still awed him. He doubted that Dahk would bring His son Rael back to Rumedia again. Cor silently ushered Thom and Marya from the tomb and pulled at the door behind him. Though immensely heavy, it closed easily and silently on well oiled hinges to boom loudly when it shut, and two Rumedian glyphs forged of steel were mounted on the door.

Cor locked the door with a heavy iron key. The lock was simple and would not keep out determined intruders, but it needed only to keep out curious onlookers, the weather. and wild animals. He turned to see the gathering, those that had followed. Some cried, mostly the children, while others stared at the ground quietly, and yet others watched Cor as if expecting something from him. In his life, Cor had rarely been at a loss for words, but this was one exception. With nothing to say, no comforting sentiments to offer, he simply and silently walked down the slope back toward Fort Haldon. Thyss and Thom fell in behind him, as did some others.

Dahken Keth chose to stay for a while in consideration of the tomb, as if the granite itself might provide him with some insight. He thought of Geoff, but Keth did not see him amongst those who remained, nor had he gone back with Cor. Widening his search, Keth found him sitting halfway down the eastern side of the hill, staring toward the Spine. Keth had seen Geoff looking to the east for months, and for just a moment he felt envious, for he had never felt his blood call to him as Cor and Rael had talked about. He knew Geoff would be leaving soon, going to the gods knew what.

13.

Aidan, Lord of Byrverus, sat his ponderous bulk at a ponderous table in one of the temple's large dining rooms, gorging himself on all manners of food available to one of his position. No one had the privilege, or misfortune, of supping at the same table as the fat lipped priest, and nor would they after seeing the grotesque manner in which he sated himself. Pork, chicken, beef, and duck – no kind of meat was ever absent at his table, and he ate better at each meal than most of his subjects did in a week.

Such was the advantage of power. As Lord of Byrverus, Aidan lived in the temple next to the palace, and he was at the top of the ecclesiastical food chain, only behind the queen. All the priests and priestesses of the city deferred to him in the end, and his was the largest share of all the tithes that found their ways into the temples' coffers. After all, the temple required great amounts of coin to maintain such an edifice. While he technically wielded no more power than the Lord of Martherus, or other of Aquis' great cities, he controlled the capital, which in his mind was the key to one day controlling Aquis.

Aidan answered directly to Queen Erella, and she generally allowed him the freedom to run the city and its surrounding lands appropriately. He answered to her accountants and advisors far more often than the queen Herself, especially Palius. In deference to Garod, Aidan would never wish any harm on the old man, but he was most definitely an aggravation. Of course, Palius' death was now a forgone conclusion, and Aidan, always one to take pity on others, hoped he passed smoothly and without incident.

Aidan approached forty, and he worked very hard not to think about the inconvenience of aging. In fact, he spent no small amount of silver and gold on various treatments to help him ignore it, such as brown dyes for his graying hair and creams from Tigol to smooth his skin, especially around his deep, brown eyes. He'd risen to his great position with extraordinary quickness, partially thanks to the wealth he had inherited upon the death of his father, a somewhat wealthy merchant, but also due to his sharp intellect. Aidan knew how people worked, how they thought, and how they felt. He assumed it was a gift he'd inherited from his father, who used it to great effect in business dealings. Aidan used it to become Lord of Byrverus.

Queen Erella had already been on the throne for decades when Aidan was born, of course, so it was through no fault of his own that he had plateaued ten years ago. It was acceptable; after all, the view from on high was spectacular, and it wouldn't be humble in the eyes of Garod to complain about such things. Like all children of the Shining West, Aidan had been taught that one must always accept one's position with contentment, but that didn't mean he should not plan for the future. He was destined to be King of Aquis, and for ten years he had never denied a favor to a lesser priest. Aidan would one day need their support, for even Queen Erella's grace would eventually end.

The fat priest sat debating silently on whether to eat more duck or begin his dessert course, finally deciding to start dessert because after all, to eat more duck and then start dessert would be gluttonous and certainly not pious. Aidan had just begun some sort of cheesy cream pie when the royal messenger arrived carrying a dispatch with the queen's seal in purple wax. He barely acknowledged the man's presence, motioning to an empty place to his right while he ate; the man left the rolled parchment, bowed, and left. Aidan politely ignored it while eating, as one ignores his own stench, with the assumption that Queen Erella did not have immediate need of him.

Even after he finished, he refused to touch the scroll as he leaned back in a great oak chair, throne like in its size and the intricacy of its woodwork. Aidan had learned long ago that reading such things was bad for the digestion, and he instead folded his hands over the brown robes covering his great girth. He allowed his eyes to close and even snored lightly, as he always did, while the lowly acolytes cleared the table. He started awake when the lack of sound indicated that they were finished.

Still refusing to break the seal, Aidan took the parchment in a sweaty hand, crushing and staining the roll as he did so, and slowly orbited the table to head for his cell. All the priests and acolytes residing in the main temple complex had identical cells, fifteen feet square, which they were allowed to modestly make their own. Of course, Aidan was Lord of Byrverus, and a big lord at that, so he'd had three walls removed to allow himself a bit more room to breathe. And as the Lord of Byrverus must not smell unclean, he had installed a comfortably sized marble bath, which he now had filled with steaming water and rose and lilac petals. The queen's message sat forgotten as he relaxed and again dozed off.

The cooling bathwater roused Aidan, and he finally lifted his massive bulk from the water, careful so as not to lose his footing on the slick marble. The drying of his body required a fair amount of time and many soft towels, after which he powdered the nooks and folds of his body extensively. He dabbed a sickly sweet smelling perfume from a beveled glass vial onto his skin and pulled a loose fitting brown robe over his head. Sighing heavily, he finally picked up the parchment roll and broke the queen's seal.

The message was but two simple lines requiring him to be present in the royal hall exactly two hours after sunrise. Aidan looked at it dumbly and then read it again, certain that there was much more to be read and that he'd merely missed it all. However, the scrolling script did not change, and Aidan dropped it on a table in quiet disgust. Queen Erella had a task for him or perhaps a favor to ask, and she chose not to ask it privately. That meant one simple thing – he would not like it, and she made sure that he could not refuse, for he could not refuse his Queen, his High Priestess in public. He knew he was in a trap from which there was no escape.

Aidan slept fitfully, plagued by nightmares that forced him to wake up often and yet returned immediately when he closed his eyes. He dreamed of Erella, giant and standing dozens of feet above him while she beat him repeatedly with the Scepter of Garod, and the old man Palius laughed grandly all the while. He dreamed of Byrverus, beautiful and magnificent, its limestone and marble spires crumbling before a great black storm, and Aidan was powerless to stop it. He awoke freezing and soaked with sweat as the sun's first light shone into his grand cell, as one final nightmare of a burning lake of blood faded out of his consciousness.

"My queen, how may I serve you?" Aidan asked, kneeling in reverence.

He was tired and haggard, the fat pouches below his eyes seemed to hang dangerously, but he had come as commanded. The hall was not as crowded as usual, and even Palius was absent. Apparently, Queen Erella needed only a handful of witnesses to be sure he did not refuse her in whatever hardship she had planned. She wore her ornate white robes with both secular and religious badges of office embroidered in gold thread. Her most official crown, heavy gold and reserved for the most important state affairs, sat upon her head, and the scepter rested across her straight legs.

"Good Aidan, you show your loyalty to Garod and Aquis as always," she said, though the praise even more committed him to whatever task she asked of him. "Garod has great need of you, or more specifically, your unique skills in protecting and spreading the faith."

"I live only to serve, Majesty," he replied, and he saw the very slightest hint of a smile upturn her lips.

"I need you to journey to Fort Haldon and oversee the foundation of a proper temple. Garod must be present there and faith in Him protected amongst the masses. I see no better choice than you."

"My queen," Aidan said slowly as he chose his words carefully, "what of Byrverus? Surely there are other priests who are just as pious with less responsibility."

Queen Erella's eyes turned hard as granite, and Aidan knew the discussion was over. "None so much as you, good Aidan. You need not worry for Byrverus, for I shall care for the great city. I care for all of Aquis already, what is the addition of Byrverus to the weight already on my shoulders. You must leave immediately. Go forth and make certain Lord Dahken Cor shows Garod the proper reverence."

Aidan couldn't believe what she'd done to him, what she asked of him! He, Lord of Byrverus and the next ruler of Aquis, was being sent to the edge of the realm and the edge of the world as far as he was concerned, to brave the cold of the mountains, Loszian invasion, and worst of all, a gray skinned demon and his heathen witch seductress. He mumbled his gratitude and returned to the temple to prepare for his journey. It was in a sudden fit of panic that Aidan realized he'd never once left Byrverus and had no idea how he would survive outside of civilization.

14.

Cor sent for the architect nearly an hour ago, and he paced around the table with great impatience. Ever since he almost destroyed the desk in his quarters, he'd taken to overseeing most matters from the long heavy table that would soon be surrounded by the Dahken's hall. It was covered or even moved indoors during poor weather. Though that was not an issue today as the weather was beautiful, and Cor had been looking over the new plans for Fort Haldon. Outside the keep and in the main cluster of buildings that would support the fort was a large building labeled as "temple".

The plans had been revised slightly several times over as more people came or intended to come to Fort Haldon to make their homes. About a hundred new soldiers had arrived from Byrverus, but more importantly, hundreds of commoners had come from various parts of Aquis, brought by opportunity. Land was offered readily in great amounts for very little to entice them to come, despite the proximity to Losz that always seemed like a looming black cloud to the Westerners. Even still, they came with their families to establish new homes. As the population grew, as homes and farmsteads were established, Fort Haldon itself would need to grow more into a small city than just a defensive fort.

None of the previous plans had included a temple, at least nothing labeled as such, and Cor wanted an explanation. After all, this was his land as given by the queen Herself, and all changes to the plans had been discussed with him directly, except this one. Cor wanted to know who had added it to the layout of Fort

Haldon and its intended use, though the general intention was clear enough. Every city or town in Aquis, and most of the smaller villages as well, had temples to Garod for the local populations to attend, worship, and tithe.

At this moment he wished Thyss were near him so that he could discuss the matter with her, express his annoyance. She had taken to exploring the mountains, journeying into the Spine in search of anything that wouldn't bore her. "Perhaps I will find my own giant spider to slay," she had said. At first, Thyss would only disappear for a few hours at a time, but lately she had made her expeditions longer, as much as several days. He worried for her safety for no rational reason. Thyss could more than handle herself against virtually any foe, but even still, her trips or rather the lack of her presence twisted Cor's stomach into knots. He couldn't much complain about it, since it kept her busy and took her mind off how mundane their existence had become since returning to Fort Haldon.

Excluding Rael's death of course.

Cor looked down the grassy slope that led to the center of Fort Haldon and saw the architect, a short man of only five feet or so in height named Karl, as he climbed his way upward. Cor had been informed that architect wasn't entirely accurate, as the man had several architects underneath him who handled most of the drawings of the individual buildings. Karl called himself more of a civil planner, whatever that meant exactly, and he was an odd man who spoke very quickly in short, clipped phrases when he felt the need to speak, moving quickly from one topic to the next. Though not very long, Karl's light brown hair always stood on end in a most unruly fashion and often fell into his eyes as he spoke. Cor found him oddly comical.

It was the man that followed a few steps behind Karl that drew a long, hard look from Cor. He was a

Westerner to be certain, roughly halfway between the height of Cor and Karl and very wide of frame. His straight, dark brown hair was combed and kept very flat and still against his scalp in a stark contrast to the shorter man he followed. The stranger wore a full brown robe complete with hood, though this was down behind his shoulders as it was a warm day, ornamented with markings indicating him to be a priest of some import. As the two men drew closer, he could clearly see the priest's round, jovial face with fat lips that looked as if they slightly smiled even while he slept, and the man's robe did little to hide an equally round figure. The priest had dark brown eyes in perfect concert with his hair, and Cor watched as they took in every detail.

"Lord Dahken, I apologize for the wait," Karl said as he reached the top of the long slope, huffing slightly.

"I understand you have many duties Karl," Cor replied. He looked to the priest who distinctly smelled of flowered perfumes, likely to cover the unpleasant scents that usually accompany one of such bulk. "Who are you?"

"Aidan, Lord of Byrverus, servant to Garod and Queen Erella. I arrived yesterday to oversee the proper establishment of Garod's order in Fort Haldon."

"I would expect someone such as yourself to announce his arrival to me immediately, not whenever he felt like it."

"You have no authority over me Cor Pelson. I come with the authority of Queen Erella Herself. Fort Haldon is set to grow, and it will soon be a center of order for the people who live within your grant. It is necessary that all proper services are available to the people, including the proper religious guidance," Aidan said, unmasked superiority in his tone. "Immediately upon arriving, I instructed Karl to include a temple befitting of the King of Gods."

"You will not call me by name, priest," Cor growled angrily. "You may call me Lord Dahken only. This is Fort Haldon, not Byrverus, and I am law here. Fort Haldon is mine, land and title bestowed by the queen, and I do not bow to you, priest. The Dahken do not worship your god."

"This is not open to discussion," Aidan replied, crossing his arms. "The queen commands the temple because the people of Aquis need Garod and the guidance of His priests. We protect them and teach them how to live in freedom."

"You put the yoke of your god upon them," Cor said, his temper flaring. Anger boiled inside him, and he strode purposefully to stand a mere foot from the priest. His palm longed to feel Soulmourn within it, but he repressed the feeling. "Garod's priests have enslaved the minds of Westerners as much as the Loszians once enslaved their bodies. You force them to live as you would have them live, at any time imposing your will as the will of Garod's. I will have no part of it at Fort Haldon."

"You tread dangerously Dahken. I know of your blasphemy before Queen Erella, but She will have none of it in this matter."

Aidan's voice turned hard as cold steel, and the portly priest's jovial face had become stone. They, Cor and Aidan, stood staring each other in the eyes for a long moment, each challenging the other, and Cor's brain hurt with the screaming call to action from Soulmourn and Ebonwing. Finally and abruptly, he turned from the priest and slowly wandered back to the north end of the table where Fort Haldon's plans were laid out and weighted at its corners from the wind. Aidan's face softened a bit, and the satisfaction of a victory shone in his eyes.

"Karl, am I correct in assuming Garod's Temple is nearly as large as the keep itself?" Cor asked, his head bent over as he leaned his hands on the tabletop.

"In ground area, yes Lord Dahken."

"Very well." Cor stood upright and turned quickly to again lock eyes with the priest. He approached Aidan as he spoke, "We shall build Garod His temple, but we shall decrease the size to a quarter. I recognize the need of some to worship Garod, but there are other gods we must pay homage to as well. We shall build a temple to Dahk, the blood god and the god of my people, and it will be of equal size to Garod's, no smaller, no larger."

Cor relished Aidan's reaction as his face turned from arrogant satisfaction to anger, but he was not yet done outraging the priest. "Also, in deference to my Thyss, there will be a temple to the elemental gods, of which Hykan is King, again no smaller or larger than Garod's. I command you to erect one last temple, a temple to the dark gods of Losz. I'm not sure what such an edifice would entail, but perhaps you can research it a bit."

Aidan had surpassed anger and moved on to pure, unbridled hatred and disgust. His face turned red and very much resembled a tomato to Cor, and his fleshy lips trembled with seething. The priest's hands had dropped limply to his sides with the shock of Cor's audacity, and it was a long moment of silence before he realized that Cor merely stood before him, awaiting an answer.

"You go too far, *Lord Dahken Cor!*" he sneered, these last words riddled with disgust. "Your blasphemy knows no bounds! You think yourself as powerful as Queen Erella, perhaps even Garod Himself, but you are no errant flame. No. You are a vile insect, vermin, and I will see you stamped out of existence for your blasphemy! I shall make sure the queen knows of this!"

"Please, tell her yourself, and tell her now," Cor said smugly, and with that, he struck Aidan near the shoulders with both open palms, all his weight behind the blow.

The ponderous man could do nothing but fall over backwards and roll down the slope away from Cor and Karl. At first, he fell head over feet, but after a few such somersaults, began to simply roll sideways through the grass, his large waist acting as a wheel of sorts. He ended his roll with a great splash into a puddle of mud at the bottom of the long slope, and the laborers moving from here to there on various tasks stopped to stare. As Aidan lifted himself, his great brown robe soiled and dripping with mud, the men around him began to laugh heartily at his expense. The priest bit his tongue to subdue a curse as he looked uphill at Cor who laughed for all to hear, and he turned his great bulk from the scene to collect his belongings.

Cor ceased laughing and turned to Karl who stood staring after Aidan, a look of the utmost shock on his face. "Karl, would you please strike the temple."

"Lord Dahken, that may not have been wise."

"The queen and I have crossed words before, and we may again. But Karl, there are other gods in this world who are no less real than Garod. I have no qualms with Garod, but I will not force the worship of Him because a priest says I must. No, it is time for the Shining West to change."

In the weeks since Rael's death, Keth had taken to training the Dahken, as Rael would have, and he worked with Marya and Celdon daily. In Rael's quarters, he found volumes of history covering a wide range of topics, all of them written in Rumedian and in Rael's hand, and Keth assumed that Rael had scribed them from memory. Cor had told him the story of

Sanctum, its destruction, and the vast wealth of knowledge that Taraq'nok had burnt with it. With these Keth enlisted Marya's help, as she had picked up the Rumedian language far more readily than he had. In fact, most of the younger Dahken, the children, seemed to adapt their mind more easily to the ancient tongue. And that was exactly it – Keth simply could not learn to think in any other language. When he read a text in Rumedian, he found himself translating each glyph one at a time, whereas Marya could simply read it unhaltingly as easily as he could read Western.

Today Dahken Keth fumed, and the momentary diversion of the fat priest rolling down a hill into the mud below did little to raise his mood. His session with Marya and Celdon had gone well, and he thought the two advanced as well as he could expect. It was Geoff that made him so furious. He arrived at the training grounds in his usual disheveled and hungover form, but this time he still drank from a wineskin. Keth endeavored to keep him from distracting the others, and after a few minutes Geoff wandered off, likely back to his quarters. Keth disbanded the group for lunch, in fact deciding that they were done for the day.

He had not yet gotten used to wearing his armor, but Cor made it clear that he must do so every day, especially now that he was so involved in training the younger Dahken. Shortly after they arrived at Fort Haldon, Cor had the blacksmith begin to fashion armor for both Keth and Geoff, though the latter never wore his. The smith had given them some options, and Keth chose a relatively plain chain shirt with cowl and a steel breastplate with a high shine that strapped on around his sides and over his shoulders. He also wore steel plate legguards and sabatons over leggings of chain. The plate pieces shined silver in the sunlight, a bright contrast to the hard gray of the chainmail. Keth postponed any combat for the first few days after he began wearing the armor while his muscles learned to work while encased in steel. It was a strange sensation, and he found it tiring.

Dahken Keth very nearly climbed the hill to speak with his lord, but when he reached the bottom of the slope, he instead turned about to confront Geoff himself. If Geoff didn't want to be a part of the Dahken and Fort Haldon, it was time that he left, that he went east to answer whatever called to his blood. These thoughts carried him to the Dahken barracks and Geoff's quarters, one of the large rooms immediately adjacent and attached to the barracks, but not directly connected. Keth beat on the heavy door, his blood growing to a boil the more the considered the coming conversation. The door's hinges whined slightly as it opened just a few inches, revealing Geoff's haggard face. Keth thought his eyes looked even more sunken in than usual, the dark rings under his eyes swollen and more pronounced.

"What do you want, Keth?" he asked.

"Let me in. I need to speak with you."

"Go away," Geoff retorted, and the door began to close.

Keth's temper flared, and he leapt to throw his entire weight against the door, impacting its center with his right side. Not expecting the sudden force, Geoff went sprawling to the floor of his room as the door was flung inward, and the room was flooded with the bright light of the noon sun. Keth's momentum carried him inward, and as the door swung wide, he landed heavily on top of Geoff, making the smaller, younger man groan. The only light in the room came from outside, and Keth decided he need not look around too much. The room stank horribly of piss, shit, wine, and vomit. Keth shifted to keep Geoff somewhat held down, but so that he could breathe.

"Get off of me, gods damn you!" Geoff huffed at him.

"Not until you listen to me, Geoff. I am done with you; do you understand me?" Keth shouted in Geoff's face. "I am a Dahken by the word of Lord Dahken Cor. You will show me respect. You will respect him. Either come to training with the others or don't. I care not which, but you will no longer make this example for the others!"

"Get off me Keth or I -"

"You'll what? You'll kill me, just like you killed Dahken Rael? Yes, I know what you've done; I saw it in your eyes, and I will make you pay for it," Keth threatened, and in his anger, Keth's spittle struck Geoff in the face. He drew his sword to hold the point mere inches from Geoff's throat.

"Think this through, Keth," Geoff said slowly after he thought for a moment. "Whether you kill me or not, you will never be able to prove that I meant to kill Rael. But if you're right and I did use the blood ghast to murder him, what chance do you have? Rael used his powers for over a hundred years. You? A few months maybe? Put your sword away and get off me, Dahken Keth."

Keth very nearly rammed the point of his blade into Geoff's throat to sever veins, arteries, and spine, but he felt his anger slowly diffuse and leave him as the full meaning of Geoff's words became clear. He knew Geoff was right. Keth sheathed his sword and stood, removing his weight from the prone Geoff, and with a fistful of cotton tunic, he yanked Geoff to his feet and pushed him against one of the room's stone walls.

"I will leave you be Geoff, but -"

"But what?" Geoff asked deliberately, confidently.

"Gather your things and go east. Go into Losz, go find whatever is calling you," Keth said. "I've watched you, so don't deny it. I know Lord Dahken Cor has talked to you about it. Go tell him its time for you to leave, or I will tell him that you murdered Dahken Rael. And he *will* believe me."

15.

The Loszian had followed the woman with the golden hair for three days, ever since she left Fort Haldon by simply walking out its new huge double doors. He had briefly glimpsed her a few weeks previously as she left the Spine and entered the Fort, and as he waited and watched Fort Haldon for any signs, any changes that would require report to Lord Menak, he never dreamed to see her again. When she entered the pass, he stealthily shadowed her movements, but the woman didn't stay in the pass more than a few hours, climbing up one side and striking out south through the mountains.

He had never seen anyone like her; she was tall, nearly six feet, lithe and graceful, but clearly with muscles as strong as iron. Her bronze skin and golden hair made it obvious she was neither Westerner, nor Loszian. She didn't just move about the land, but instead attacked the mountains, crevasses, and cracks ferociously with zeal. She was dressed in a solid black tunic and pants that seemed to be made of silk, though they occasionally glimmered in the sun like steel. She carried a long rope apparently made of the same material, and it was immensely strong as she often used it to support her own weight. She brought no other climbing equipment of any kind, using her hands and sandaled feet with great skill.

He followed her for three days as she camped when the sun passed below the horizon, and she awoke when the morning sun's first rays touched her face. He was Lord Menak's best pathfinder and spy. The men of Fort Haldon had never detected his presence, even when he was mere feet from their new granite wall and neither did the woman with the golden hair. As was normal for him, he made not one misstep, did not knock loose one pebble, or rustle one bush. He followed, watched, and waited for any indication of what purpose upon which she was set.

On the fourth morning, the Loszian decided to act. The woman sat on the ground with her legs crossed breakfasting on dried meat as she stared into the direction she had been traveling over the last few days. Her long curved sword lay on the blanket to one side, easily accessible to be sure, but he knew he would be upon her before she could react. The Loszian had no intention of ravishing her, as enjoyable as the prospect seemed, for he knew that he would have mere moments before her corded sinews would threaten to push him off of her. He wanted to know what she did out in the Spine, in the case that the intelligence would be of some use to Lord Menak.

He stole one final silent, furtive glance from around the rocks behind which he had hidden through the previous night. His prey had not moved, and with no trace of sound from beneath his soft leather boots, the Loszian slowly crossed the short fifteen feet or so that separated him from the woman with the golden hair. He crouched slightly as he walked, his straight bladed knife held low and pointed toward her back. He would take her by that golden ponytail, wrenching her head back as hard as he could, and force her down upon her stomach. With his knife's edge at her throat, he would glean what he wanted to know.

"It took you long enough," she said, still looking ahead. "So perhaps now that you've decided to stop hiding, you will tell me exactly what you're doing."

Her speech shocked the Loszian into indecision, and his every muscle froze in place. He was Lord Menak's best, the most stealthy and subtle, and he knew this section of the Spine like no other. It was simply impossible that the woman with the golden hair knew he had been following her. Nevertheless, in his moment of unsure immobility, she stood, turned, and faced him with her vicious curved sword in hand. The blade reflected the sun with an eerie green light, and the Loszian knew he had likely forfeited his life in following her through the Spine.

"So, you are only part Loszian then," Thyss said in accented Loszian, sweeping her eyes across his form. "I know something of the Loszian race and how it breeds with Westerners, and I'd say you are less than a quarter, spawn of some necromancer and slaves several generations back, I am sure. Whom do you serve?"

While speaking, she had closed the distance between them to a mere four or five feet, all the while watching him with a predatory gaze. Even though her swordarm hung loosely at her side, he knew his life was in clear and sudden danger as she looked upon him as a cat looks upon a trapped mouse. A coward at heart, the Loszian sought to escape, pivoting quickly to run back behind the rocks and hastily make away from this woman. He made but one step in that direction when roaring yellow orange flames burst from the rocky ground to bar his way. The wall of fire burned well over his head, and he instinctively turned to dart to his left. He halted immediately as another flame barrier appeared before him.

Thyss laughed haughtily behind him.

"You're going nowhere spawn of some Loszian rapist, so let's have a talk about why you followed me and what you were doing so near Fort Haldon. Speak plainly, and you may yet live."

"If I speak, my lord will surely have me slain anyway," he replied, "so kill me now."

"Oh, you will speak worm. Is there something wrong with your foot?" Thyss asked, pointing at his left boot, made of soft brown leather and perfectly pliable for both climbing and moving silently.

The would be assassin thought to retort her foolish statement, but in hesitation he noticed a slight warmth on the toes of his left foot. The warmth grew suddenly, changing first to uncomfortable heat and then an excruciating burning as his boot smoked at the toe, and he screamed as the searing pain took him. He raised his burning foot off the ground, frantically clutching at the boot with both hands to remove it, and the Loszian fell onto his backside, his great dexterity forgotten in the mad rush to remove the offending thing. When he finally pulled it off, he found no relief from the pain. He watched in horror as the toes themselves burned, as the skin blackened, pulled tight and split from the flames. The sickly smell of burnt human flesh wafted slightly into the air, and he batted roughly at his disfigured toes, grunting in pain each time he struck them. The fire resisted all his attempts to extinguish it and finally went out on its own, leaving him with charred bone nubs where the toes of his left foot once were. He sat on the rocky ground, cradling his ruined foot with streaks from several tears making clean tracks down his dirt encrusted face.

"Now," Thyss said, kneeling to his level, "shall I continue with the right foot for symmetry? Or would you prefer the left hand?"

Cor sat in shocked silence. "You want to do what?"

Cor had been in the place he usually handled his day to day tasks, upon the hill at the Dahken's table, when Geoff climbed the grassy slope. He had greeted the boy warmly, as any interruption was a respite from signing property documents and taxation agreements, and to be honest, Cor had no idea what he actually signed. The appointee from Queen Erella's exchequer handled it all, simply pointing at each sheet of paper in turn, saying "Sign here. And here." Geoff's dark face and quiet somber tone told Cor something was amiss, and they retreated back to his rooms to discuss it.

"Lord Dahken Cor, I need to go east of the Spine, into Losz," Geoff repeated. "I cannot fight it much longer. With each passing day, the urge becomes greater and greater."

Cor searched the boy's face long and hard for a hint of anything, duplicity, fear, anger, but could read nothing. The boy's face was haggard, tired. The whites of his eyes were bloodshot, and his eyelids themselves looked swollen and painful. Geoff perpetually had rings under his eyes, giving him an exhausted appearance, but now they were darker, deeper. Cor had watched Geoff for months, ever since they left Byrverus, as he gazed to the east, and he remembered every time he felt the pull on his own blood, the last of which only a few short months ago when he discovered Rael resurrected. It was a need the likes of which he couldn't clearly explain to anyone even himself, a hunger that could not be sated. Geoff was like a lodestone, inexorably attracted to some piece of iron that he could not see, only feel.

Cor sighed and then said quietly, "Geoff, I understand, and I know you can't tell me what it is you seek. But if I let you go into Losz, I let you go to your death."

"My ghost will protect me from harm," Geoff answered. "It will stand against an army of Loszians."

"A very sure, even arrogant statement when you don't know how to control it," Cor retorted, and he thought for just an instant, anger flared in Geoff's eyes. "I don't know how your power works, Geoff, but I do know what happened last time the ghost appeared. What if you can't make it appear? What if it doesn't manifest on its own when you need it? Would you take that risk with your own life?"

Cor took a deep breath. Geoff opened his mouth to answer, but Cor silenced him with an upraised hand.

"It doesn't matter, does it?" Cor asked resignedly. "If I deny you, you will simply leave anyway and find another way through the Spine, won't you? Don't bother answering me one way or the other; I can see it in your eyes. If you're sure you need to do this now, then you may leave as soon as you are ready. I can spare no one to go with you, but I will see to it that you have a horse, silver, and supplies for two weeks or so. I hope you know how to live off the land; you'll need to do it as much as possible.

"Geoff, I don't know what you go to or how you will get past Lord Menak and his garrison, but when you return, if you return, we will welcome you back as Dahken Geoff."

Cor stood from his chair and clasped arms with the young man who was only three years his junior. He motioned toward the door, and as Geoff left, Cor returned to his chair, sat heavily, and rubbed his eyes. Now more than ever, Lord Dahken Cor wished to return home, to the simple life of a farmer or even a sailor on the Narrow Sea. He wondered what became of his parent's home, the farm he had known as a boy, and of his friend Captain Naran, the huge Shet from central Tigol. But the world would not allow Cor Pelson such a simple life, for even he had made enormous claims and plans, and all of this was just one more step along the way. As Cor left his quarters to return to his normal vantage point, he asked himself why he simply didn't disappear. He looked to the south in the vain hope that he may just see Captain Naran's sail on the horizon despite the thousand miles of land that separated Fort Haldon from the Narrow Sea.

16.

Thyss silently cursed the dead Loszian almost constantly as she trudged across the rocky terrain dragging his scorched corpse behind her. Once content that he had no more information to offer, she decided to end his life mercifully and return to Fort Haldon. She thought it best to bring his body along, just in case anyone doubted her story, and started by carrying him across her shoulders. However, this did not work out as she had hoped; even with her well developed sinews, his weight wore her down quickly, and the ground was treacherous.

She instead used her rope, the black cord woven from the silk of a great creature in her homeland, to tie the Loszian's feet together, and she dragged him across the rough terrain. More than once she turned to see the grisly trail his corpse left behind as the rocky ground tore through clothes and charred flesh, and more than once she yanked his body over a hill or off a small ridge to watch it fall to the ground with a sickening thud, bones cracking. Over the trek, the Loszian's skull cracked upon the rocks, and gray matter slowly oozed its way out onto the ground. The entire scene made Thyss at once grimace in civilized revulsion and smile in wicked satisfaction.

Something else had bothered her on this outing into the Spine, something she could not understand. The entire affair seemed slightly more arduous than usual, and she found herself feeling somewhat queasy on more than one occasion. She ate irregularly and even vomited once right after, an action and accompanying sensation in which she was wholly inexperienced. She vomited again on her trek back to Fort Haldon, hauling the twisted carcass, and she cursed her body's betrayal.

The longer she dragged the dead Loszian, the more she realized the irrationality of saving his body, since she knew that Cor would never doubt her word. Regardless, she felt a need to show him the dead Loszian, and the further she pulled his corpse, the closer she was to Fort Haldon. After a few days, Thyss finally dropped into the pass connecting Aquis and Losz across the Spine, the early afternoon sun overhead warming the day substantially. She rested briefly, feeling the sun on her face, before starting the last few miles back to the fort.

As Thyss approached Fort Haldon, a horn sounded from the granite battlements that were steadily replacing the old wooden palisade. The new wall was a massive feat of modern engineering, towering dozens of feet over the original palisade, and it seemingly interlocked perfectly with the cliff faces that created the mouth of the pass. The horn sounded again, and Thyss knew it was to inform Lord Dahken Cor of her return. One of the massive doors opened inward to admit her and her prize.

Cor sprinted toward the gate, toward her from across Fort Haldon's compound, weaving between workers and soldiers as his black hauberk reflected the afternoon sun. When he came to a stop before her, he lifted her in pure adoration as far into the air as his arms would stretch and turned so that the radiant sunlight shined through her golden hair. Thyss laughed, and as he lowered her, she locked her strong legs around his waist and kissed him fiercely, the Loszian's corpse forgotten. They cared not for the scene they made. After a long moment, she released her leg's hold upon him, dropping her feet lightly to the dusty ground, but they held the kiss until a voice broke the spell.

"I am ready to leave, Lord Dahken Cor."

Thyss turned from her lover to see Geoff standing only a few feet away, looking exhausted and worn with a drawn face and swollen eyelids. The ever present dark rings under his eyes had deepened to shades of black and purple like she had never seen among the living. All this, combined with the gray pallor of his race, reminded Thyss of the walking corpses raised by the Loszian necromancers. Geoff was dressed for traveling and held the reigns of a horse that stood patiently behind him.

"Then go safely, Geoff, and I hope that you find your way home soon," Cor said, and Geoff merely nodded and led his horse through the still open gate.

"Where is he going?" Thyss asked, jerking her chin toward Geoff as men quickly closed the door behind him with an echoing boom.

"I don't know. His destiny, I'm afraid."

"I don't believe in destiny, Dahken Cor," she replied, and Cor could hear the curse in her voice.

"Perhaps not, but there's no point in discussing it now. There is one thing I want to ask you," Cor said, and he pointed to the charred, broken corpse Thyss had dragged with her from the Spine, likely only devoid of flies and maggots due to its burnt status. "What in the gods is that?"

"A present, my love," Thyss answered with a wicked smile.

It was late in the afternoon when Thyss related her tale, starting when she knew the Loszian followed her, less than an hour after leaving Fort Haldon. At her suggestion, Cor called Thom and Keth to the future site of the Dahken hall, the latter of which brought the young Marya with him. Seeing the state of the corpse she brought with her, Cor very nearly sent the girl away.

Thyss stopped him saying, "No, allow her to stay. Make her grow strong."

163

The Loszian's name was Jor'lek. He was a servant to Lord Menak on the other side of the pass, a grandson of the lord in fact, though the Loszians never claimed their Western descendants as blood. He had ranged the Spine for years, reporting to Menak anything out of the ordinary, simply keeping an eye on the border with Aquis, but his task had changed recently. Lord Menak had sent Jor'lek to specifically spy upon Fort Haldon and report any activity, no matter how small. He took great pride in his duties, some nights getting so close to the palisade as to hear the archers above talking or snoring. When he reported that ground had broken on a keep and that the wood wall was being replaced with a true granite curtain wall with battlements, Lord Menak showed no surprise. Jor'lek thought his master expected war, and soon.

All this he told Thyss in earnest in between his screaming fits as she slowly burned away his digits, hair, and flesh. As Jor'lek screamed, she promised a reprieve if he told her everything she wanted to know, everything he knew, which was surprisingly little. By the time she was done, he was barely alive with every inch of his flesh charred black, and his voice gurgled out from its disfigured face begging for mercy. Certain that no man could endure such pain without speaking honestly, she finally ended it with a sword thrust that cleanly removed his head. His hands twitched frenetically in a most disturbing fashion until she pulled the blade free.

Cor sighed deeply and slowly tilted his head to one side while turning his face the other way as if to crack his neck. He looked in turn at the face of each person seated, all of whom had become trusted lieutenants, with the exception of Marya. He was convinced the girl should not have heard the story Thyss related with such relish and gruesome detail. Thom grimaced slightly as his hard stare pointed at the table's mahogany top, while Keth remained almost perfectly impassive.

How like Rael, Cor thought. *I don't know what he's thinking, but he will tell me if I ask.*

He looked at Marya last, having almost forgotten the girl, and found himself surprised. How old was she? Twelve? Thirteen? The girl looked in awe upon the beautiful Thyss, and on her face was a vicious smile, not too dissimilar from the elementalist's own. Keth spent much of his time working with Marya, and he had told Cor of her rather tenacious personality. She was bright, he knew, but she was constantly asking Keth to spar with her using live steel. She was a little girl who'd discovered strength, and it seemed she longed for an opportunity to use it. Cor decided he needed to spend more time with Marya and the other young Dahken.

Thom was the first to speak, "I don't see that this changes anything, Lord Dahken. Long before your arrival, we lived here under the assumption of imminent attack. So, the Loszians watch us. We watch them as well. I have men in the mountains, overlooking the Loszian side of the Spine, and should an army capable of invasion begin to form, we would be the first to know. We also have more men than before, trained soldiers, but commoners as well. With the advance warning, I know we can hold for reinforcements."

"You're very certain, Thom," Cor stated. "I wish I could be. Keth?"

"Lord Dahken, I barely know battle, and I don't know anything about war. You gave me back life and the lives of Marya and the others, and I'll follow you to my end."

"I've never asked for that, Dahken Keth, and I never will," Cor sighed, looking up into a sky that glowed orange in the afternoon light.

"Lord Dahken Cor, there is one other thing to consider," Thom said. "I have never met anyone as extraordinary as yourself and Lady Thyss. Together, the two of you led a band of children past a trained garrison of Loszians with swords, pikes, and crossbows, not to speak of black sorcery. Your people have a power beyond my ken, and while I've always been too pragmatic for faith, I know you must be gifted by the gods. My Lady, I know not of your land, but I know that you summon fire and command it to work your will. In a short time, I have already seen you do the impossible. Surely, no Loszian host can defeat Fort Haldon so long as you both are here."

Cor, Lord of the Dahken and Fort Haldon, breathed deeply as he mulled over Thom's words, and he closed his eyes as he considered them. He knew he needed to tell Thom he was wrong, to tell Keth to take Marya and any of the other young Dahken away to live a quiet life somewhere. He questioned himself and his decisions that led him and a group of children to the least safe place in Aquis. Cor had always told them to go where they will and live as they choose, but they always followed him. They followed him from Losz, straight away into danger and death, and he realized then that they had no choice to make. They were children looking for a parent to protect them, and he offered the only security they would find. Cor opened his eyes and looked at Thyss, his beautiful, deadly, and even malicious Thyss.

"And you?"

"Let them come Lord Dahken Cor," she said, her dulcet voice a barely audible whisper. "Let the Loszians come, and we will burn and hew our way through their legions. When faced with our fury, they will run, and they will hide in the shadows within their purple towers."

"And what if they don't run?" Cor asked. He could see the flames burning deep in her eyes, and he knew the answer that was forthcoming. Just as her mouth opened, she was interrupted by a younger voice from further down the table. It was a bit higher pitched and less melodious.

"Then we'll kill them all," Marya said.

17.

It did not take Geoff long, only into his second day crossing the Spine, to curse himself, Keth, and the gods themselves. The more he tried to remember about his days before being frozen by the Loszian necromancer Taraq'nok, the less he could recall. All he knew was that traveling alone with limited supplies was miserable work, and he almost wished he had let Keth kill him. Actually, he wished he had called forth the blood ghast and slain Keth. It would have been easy to explain; drunk, Keth attacked him out of jealousy, and Geoff purely defended himself. He sighed with the knowledge that it was too late for what could have been.

The weather was the only thing that made the trip remotely bearable. The days had been warm as of late, even in the mountains, and it cooled substantially as he made camp the second night with threatening clouds overhead. He awoke the next morning to find the clouds had passed by harmlessly, loosing only a few drops of rain to help keep the dust down, and the air retained its cooler temperature. As such, he didn't feel the need to draw on his water supplies as often, but he felt he really could use a large quantity of wine. It had been a long time since he had been this sober, and he did not like the feeling.

Geoff tried to remember back to the last time he traveled this pass in the hopes of recognizing any landmark, any sign to indicate how close he was to the Loszian side. Unfortunately, it was to no avail; he could remember nothing of that harrowing night except exhaustion and the sense of danger as the sounds of Loszian soldiers closed the distance behind them. The more he thought about it, the more he couldn't understand how they had all survived that night. Well, almost all – one little girl had died, but who was she?

It was late into the third day that he reached the end of the pass. The sun had begun to set, having already disappeared behind the mountain peaks and casting shadows across his path. A great wall wrought of black stone with battlements and four square towers blocked the way ahead, and Geoff knew the last time he had come through its iron portcullis was in the middle of the night some months ago. As he approached slowly, still out of crossbow range, a cry went up from the wall to announce his presence to all on the other side. Uncertain as to how he should proceed, he halted his horse. At the least, Geoff knew he did not want to be filled with crossbow bolts like a pincushion.

With a familiar sound of steel chains quickly scraping stone and metal, the black portcullis began to lift and out came over a dozen men, most of whom were armed with crossbows and clad in black chainmail. Geoff considered that he may have made a mistake by coming here, and he turned his horse with thoughts of escape. As he did so, two men dressed in supple leather appeared from behind fallen rocks and brush, and they too were armed with crossbows, a smaller sort that was held easily in one hand. Geoff could not ride his way out of the trap, lest he make himself an easy target for the scouts who had snuck up behind him, and he dismounted under the assumption that he had no choice but to fight. One of the approaching soldiers held up a black gauntleted hand, and they all stopped, their crossbows still trained on Geoff. He prepared to defend himself, but the apparent leader spoke.

"Dahken, my lord has commanded that I immediately escort you through the gate to his presence," he said from behind a black basinet helm.

"If he plans to kill me, I'd rather fight and die here," Geoff responded.

"I do not know of his intentions, nor is it my place to question. I know only that I am not to kill you, so let us keep this peaceful."

Geoff prepared to retort, but then nodded with the logic of it. Whoever the Loszian's lord was, his intent was likely not violent, for if he wanted Geoff dead, he would have had the crossbowmen finish it here and now. Geoff took his horse's reins in hand and walked slowly toward the line of armored crossbowmen, and the two behind him followed. As he approached, the line opened to allow him passage through its middle and then folded to envelop him.

The group passed through the open portal into the Loszian fort; it was large enough to allow three men at a time. Seeing the place in the late afternoon sunlight, Geoff noted how little different it was from Fort Haldon in size and layout, and the Loszians too seemed to be building large numbers of outbuildings, many of which were made of darkly colored basalt. Most of the men dispersed as they passed through to the other side of the wall, but their leader and one other escorted him to a large square building of purple Loszian stone. Two more guards stood outside the entry to this building, a heavy oak door that was banded with black iron. They stood at attention and did not move as Geoff's captor opened the door himself and ushered Geoff into the room beyond.

As if hit by a falling rock, Geoff suddenly realized he was about to meet a Loszian named Menak, the lord of this particular part of Losz. Menak's abode was one giant square room, just as Cor described, with a ceiling that must have been ten feet tall, no doubt to offer ample comfort for the tall Loszians. The walls and ceiling were all made of purple and black Loszian stone, and Geoff thought sorcery must be at work to hold up the ceiling with no interior supports whatsoever. Torches burned smokily, creating a gray haze near the ceiling and casting flickering shadows throughout the gloom. In the far corner, a true Loszian in dark burgundy robes sat at a bench with a host of alchemical materials in front of him.

Geoff and his captor walked to the large table in the room's center and waited quietly. Geoff looked around the room interestedly, but after an interminable amount of time he began to grow bored. It wasn't long after he began to fidget that the Loszian spoke in a startlingly loud and deep voice.

"You have brought me the Dahken?" he asked, though it seemed more of a statement expecting a reply than a question.

"I have, Lord Menak," the soldier answered as he removed his basinet helm. "He came without unpleasantness."

"Excellent," Menak said, still focused on his beakers and vials.

He cursed and sneered as he stood, knocking over several of them with the back of his spindly hand. He turned and made his way to the center of the room. He seemed to be in no apparent hurry, but his long stride made short work of the twenty or so feet between them. Now closer, Geoff could see that Menak's robes were not actually burgundy, but of a blood red silk. Only one hand hung from the sleeves of his robes, the other apparently tucked into the folds. The pale Loszian studied Geoff intently.

"What are you doing here, Dahken?" Menak asked as he sat at the table, but his voice sounded almost disinterested.

"Standing, talking to you, Loszian," Geoff replied, and he paid for it as a chain gauntleted hand smacked the back of his head. It hurt sharply at first as lightning bolts and stars exploded into his vision, but quickly faded to a dull ache. He looked at the soldier, clearly a Westerner and not a Loszian, and said darkly, "Don't do that again."

"Dahken, let us keep this simple," Menak said, pulling back Geoff's attention. "The last time a Dahken came through this pass, I did not obey laws that had been set since before Nadav became emperor. It cost Taraq'nok his life, and I, my hand. I do not intend to make the same mistake twice. So very simply, who are you, and why have you come to Losz?"

"My name is Geoff, and I don't know. Something pulls at me, pulls me east."

Menak merely nodded and said, "I have heard something of how the Dahken blood works. I assume you are one of the Dahken who escaped from Losz. We know you returned to Fort Haldon some months ago, and the Westerners began fortifying the place. Perhaps you can provide an explanation?"

"An explanation of what?"

"Why, he is dense isn't he?" Menak asked of no one in particular. "Why have the Dahken returned from Byrverus to Fort Haldon? Why does Aquis reinforce the garrison and build additional defenses?"

"I assume for the same reason the Loszians build on their side," Geoff answered.

"Not as dense as I first thought, then. Geoff, I don't particularly care why you have come to the Loszian Empire, but I do care that my Sovereign knows that I am as loyal a subject as possible," Menak said, and he stood from his chair. "Therefore, the only solution is that we travel to Ghal immediately. Nadav despises unannounced visitors, but I think his ire will turn to great pleasure in this instance."

"I don't think I want to go to Ghal to see your emperor," Geoff said, and even to his own ear, he sounded like a petulant child.

"I don't think you have much choice, Dahken. Refusal will only lead to your death. Yes, you may very well kill me, but you will not escape the thousand under my command. One way or the other, you will die if you choose the path of resistance," Menak explained. He paused, perhaps for dramatic effect, before saying, "Come with me to Ghal, and maybe you will live just a bit longer."

An unexpected sensation jolted Sovereign Nadav and brought him to his moment of ecstasy before he expected it. Normally, such an occurrence would infuriate him, sending him into a rage that would end the existence of any number of breakable objects. However, in this particular instance, Nadav was mating, a peculiar activity that was wholly necessary for the survival of his race, but one he did not enjoy in the least. Lady Veltrina, from the northern part of Losz, was the first to fulfill his expectations for raising an army, and in fact, she had exceeded them considerably. Nadav was not above rewarding excellent work, but he cringed when she decided upon the boon that would be granted. She too was pure Loszian, and no doubt she expected his seed would help her produce an exceptionally powerful sorcerer. He removed himself from her, rearranging his robes and turned as she looked over her shoulder at him expectantly. Realizing that he had no intention of continuing, Veltrina picked her own robes up off the floor and headed for the long stairs that spiraled downward.

Nadav lightly pulled a gold chain that he knew would bring slaves running from the chamber immediately below his while he considered what brought the vile engagement to an end. Someone had transported into the palace, and as Nadav focused, he knew that the person or persons had come from Menak's holdfast. Two young boys with gold collars around their necks entered from where Veltrina had just passed.

"Find out who has come into the palace by way of Lord Menak's beacon," he commanded. As they began to leave, Nadav looked down at his stained robes and wrinkled his nose at the smell of woman. "Bring me new robes as well."

They left to carry out his commands, and he pulled the robes over his head to throw them to the far side of the room. Nadav knew that mating with the women of his kind was a necessary evil, but he hated the stench of the less fair sex. He drew a scalding hot bath and stepped into it as if the heat would burn away the shame he felt. He was just beginning to feel clean when an entourage of his slaves arrived bearing clothing, various powders, and news. A teenaged boy, a Dahken, crossed the Spine into Menak's hands, just the same as it had happened months ago. Menak captured the boy and brought him directly to Ghal. Nadav was pleased; he may just give the lord back his hand, which now sat preserved in a jar of clear liquid.

Once he felt clean and dry, Nadav started on the long spiral down. As he descended, he chose to meet Menak and the Dahken while standing on the dais before his throne. It would be a fully formal affair with a full complement of slaves, beautiful in their chained nudity, and soldiers, resplendent in their black armor. He would make a spectacle of destroying this Dahken, as he would destroy all the rest of their kind at Fort Haldon.

Nadav fussed over the condition of the hall containing his platinum throne. He made the slaves and servants reposition the gold carpet that marked a path from the floor up the steps to his throne at least a dozen times. He inspected the condition of his soldiers' armor, sending several of them back to make certain it shined as was proper. Exactly twenty four slaves were placed precisely upon the twelve steps leading to the dais, one boy and one girl on each side of the golden carpet. It took the better part of two hours for him to be satisfied.

Finally, he called for Menak and the Dahken boy, who waited in a nearby antechamber, and the two armored soldiers nearest to it left the hall. They returned quickly to retake their honor guard positions at the columns that lined the hall, and Menak's familiar form, less a hand of course, entered the hall. Behind him came a figure at which Sovereign Nadav stared long and hard. He seemed to be a boy somewhere in his middle teens, but he was tall for his age and race as judged by his black hair. Dahken aside, the emperor suspected this boy was not a pureblood Westerner; the joints of his limbs and fingers were longer than normal, and his frame was thin and narrow. The boy's facial features were angled and sharp, and it was his pointed chin, as opposed to the solid round chin of a Westerner, that confirmed Nadav's suspicions. The two came to stand in the middle of the golden carpet, only a few feet from the bottom of the steps, and Menak immediately prostrated himself before his emperor.

"You stand before Sovereign Nadav, Emperor of Losz!" Nadav thundered, standing quickly from his throne.

Startled, the Dahken dropped to a knee and lowered his face, though he did not demean himself as obviously as Menak. Nevertheless, Nadav was satisfied after a moment, and he settled back into his position upon the throne. Sensing this, Menak hazarded a glance up and stood, pulling the Dahken up with him.

"Welcome back to Ghal, Lord Menak," Nadav said formally.

"Thank you, Sovereign," Menak said with no hint of sincerity. "I have taken this Dahken crossing the narrow pass that separated our lands from Fort Haldon. I believe him to be one that Taraq'nok had collected, and I thought it wise to bring him directly to your presence."

"Wise indeed," Nadav answered pensively, as if he did not already have this information. "What is its name?"

"My name is Geoff."

With the boy's answer, Menak decided to remain quiet until the emperor put a question directly to him. *I will not speak. Allow the Dahken to dig his own grave*, he thought.

"Geoff, it seems you have returned to Losz. Perhaps you longed to see your homeland or maybe your family?" Nadav asked. "You have Loszian blood in your veins, do you not? Tell me where you are from, that is, before you ended up in Taraq'nok's cellar."

Geoff did not answer, but his eyes visibly darkened. He set his jaw in such a way that the hard angles and points of his teeth ground upon each other, and he lowered his eyes to stare at the carpeted steps instead of the tall Loszian made giant by the dais and throne upon which he sat. Menak sighed and slowly, cautiously backed a few steps away from the boy.

"Tell me!" screamed Nadav, and it jolted everyone in the hall except for Menak, who had expected the reaction.

"Both of my father's parents are part Loszian. They live in the eastern part of the empire," Geoff explained. "They expelled my father from their household when he married a Westerner."

"As well they should have," Nadav interrupted. "Where are your parents now?"

"Dead at the hands of Taraq'nok. They lived quietly near the Northern Kingdoms and raised me and my sisters. Taraq'Nok came and killed them all and took me prisoner."

"They were weak, barely Loszian then, to allow one such as Taraq'nok to eliminate them," Nadav spat as he said the name. "The loss of so many of impure blood is a boon for the empire!"

Geoff's gray face screwed up in anger, and his darkly ringed eyes closed a bit as his forehead furrowed. It gave them an even more sunken appearance, making him look like some Western ideal of a Loszian demon. He clenched his teeth so hard that they felt as if they may crack, and he resisted every urge in his body to charge up the dais and beat the Loszian emperor to death with his bare fists. The effect made Nadav leer, and Menak was now fully off the gold carpet to one side to make Geoff stand alone.

"I've made it angry!" Nadav said gleefully as he rose from his throne. He came to stand at the top of the stairs, and he knew it made him appear twenty feet tall to those below. "You are an abomination, Geoff! An abomination of both men and the gods! That one gifted by his parents with Loszian blood would choose to mate with a Westerner for any other purpose than creating slaves or servant is disgusting, an affront to all Loszians! The Dahken race itself should be extinct, and I will take a step toward that end right now!"

Nadav threw his arms and open hands out before him as if to push an enemy who stood just in front of him. A great black, semi-transparent cloud extended from his open hands and billowed toward Geoff, who stood fearfully of the approaching magic. Even Menak shuddered as it enveloped the boy, well aware of the fate about to befall him. Geoff stood in the center of the cloud, at first frightened almost completely out of his senses, but his fear began to abate after a moment, as it was clear that the magic had no effect on him, at least no more effect than a slight tickling sensation.

Geoff began to laugh mirthlessly at the seething emperor and his obvious frustration as Nadav dropped his hands to his sides and the pestilent cloud dissipated. It seemed that Rael's stories of Dahken resistance to

Loszian necromancy were true, and now Geoff would have his turn at dealing death. He quieted his laughs and sat peacefully on the carpeted floor, lowering his head, and closing his eyes in concentration. He focused his mind into the sound of his heartbeat and felt his essence pour from his body into the open air. Within seconds, his blood ghast, seven feet of animate blood and death, stood at the bottom of Nadav's steps.

"Protect your sovereign!" Nadav screamed as he backed away.

Geoff's essence bounded up the steps three at a time, but it only managed to reach halfway before bodies closed in about it. Armored soldiers rushed from all parts of the hall, but they were still precious seconds from intercepting the threat. Also, several dozen shambling forms, corpses and skeletons animated by magic moved in from the dark places of the room, but they were even slower. Unexpectedly to Geoff, it was the slaves that slowed him from reaching his target. While they were all children, none of them even half the ghast's size, the sheer mass of their combined bodies prevented him from closing any further. They grabbed a hold of his arms and hung limply and wrapped themselves around his torso and legs. He reaved relentlessly, ignoring the fact that they were only slightly younger than he. Geoff backhanded one hard and heard its body thud sickeningly at the bottom of the steps, and another he kicked in the face – a small boy whose neck snapped instantly. A third was shorn clear in half by the ghast's great sword, her blood and innards spilling everywhere to stain the steps and make them slippery. A fourth was decapitated by the return stroke.

Nadav's guards, armored in black plates over chainmail, rushed in to the attack, and the child slaves released the ghast in attempts to slink away from the battle. Geoff's essence hewed through the first soldier with one blow and immediately turned to find itself facing several others. It fought with blazing speed and cold detachment as it spilled blood, heedless of the blows that landed upon its body.

Menak watched from the side of the hall with great interest, but it was Geoff's prone form, not the battle that held his gaze. He watched, and as the ghast was struck, a wound appeared on the boy's body. The wound did not bleed, as if all the blood was gone from him to form the creature, and it healed just as quickly as it appeared when the ghast bled its foes. Menak drew a dagger from beneath his blood red robes. It was a ceremonial weapon with a wickedly curved blade and a gold hilt inlaid with precious gems, deadly sharp, but clearly not meant for combat. He rushed over to the boy's still body and knelt beside him with the thought that he could end the battle now before it got out of hand, as it threatened to do.

For a moment, the ghast's instincts overrode Geoff's conscious thought, its most basic of which was to protect Geoff's physical form. The thing ceased its fighting and leapt from its place halfway up the dangerously slick, blood soaked steps. The distance to where Menak knelt over Geoff, dagger in hand, was easily twenty feet away with a drop of a good ten feet, and the ghast landed lightly and easily to stand over them both. Menak froze for just a moment, looking up at the menacing ghast above him. He regained his senses just in time as he fell to his left, narrowly avoiding the massive red blade as it struck the stone floor where he just had been kneeling. Menak turned and scrambled to his feet. As he retreated, hot ripping pain tore through his left leg, and he collapsed forward onto his belly, suddenly no longer able to run or even stand. Nadav's guards and undead servants now surrounded Geoff's ghast as Menak's life poured from the stump just below his left hip.

"Enough!" thundered Nadav's voice, and he again stood at the top of the black steps. "Dahken Geoff, I demand that you end this. You may destroy many more of my servants, but you will die in the end. I know you can hear me, and I promise peace between us."

The ghost stood on the balls of its feet unmoving for several seconds, and both of its hands stayed on its great red blade, ready to strike. It even seemed to breathe heavily as if from exertion, its great torso rising and falling. Finally, it began to dissolve, streaming back to Geoff's body from whence it had come. As the threat dissipated, Nadav became distinctly aware of the cries of the dying around him, including Lord Menak.

"Do shut up, Menak," Nadav said disdainfully as Geoff's eyes fluttered open. "We'll be sure to get you a peg or some other contrivance to help you walk again. You men, make sure our Lord Menak does not bleed to death on my floor. Though, I am afraid it is too late to save my carpet.

"Dahken Geoff, I welcome you to Losz," he said, turning to the quietly brooding boy. "I am curious, however. What has brought you here?"

"I…" Geoff started, but he could not find any words to continue. For months he had felt a call in his blood pulling him east past the Spine, and for the first time in months, he felt nothing. It was as if he had found it. "I don't know."

Nadav's laughter filled the hall amidst the spilled blood, innards, and body parts of the dead and dying.

18.

He had no idea how long he slept, but he was sure that it was late into the day. His rooms had several windows that faced east, and the sun was not to be seen through them. Geoff had been given a suite several floors above Nadav's hall in the palace's great tower, and he knew the emperor occupied an entire floor well above his. Despite the unpleasantness that ensued on his arrival, he had to give his host credit for hospitality. The bed was clean, with sheets of fine silk and was perhaps the most comfortable thing on which he'd ever lain. There were also several soft divans, and a thick layer of plush carpet covered the cold stone floor. Nadav explained to Geoff how he could merely touch certain stones, and they would provide differing levels of light, depending on what his wishes were. The Loszian also assigned him a trio of slaves to meet his every need for as long as he stayed, and it was not long into the night that Geoff realized they were also there to indulge any desire he may have. Just the previous day, he had been ready to kill the Loszian emperor, but he was starting to think that he instead preferred the lifestyle that friendship with Nadav would afford.

As he lay on the soft bed in consideration of the unadorned ceiling, Geoff felt an urge as he often did when he first awoke, and he climbed atop the girl that slept next to him. As he took her, he gave no thought to her cries, whines, or the fact that she was about two years younger than he. She was about the same age his oldest sister would have been. He finished, climbed from the bed, and found his discarded clothes on the floor near a divan. As he dressed, he demanded food of the other two slaves, who hastened from the suite. Geoff waited, looking out a window over the black city below, which looked oddly serene during the day in stark contrast to its devilish appearance at night. Indeed, he could truly enjoy this life.

The slaves returned after a short time with two trays of food, including a suckling pig, some slices of rare beef and a host of different fruits and cooked vegetables. As Geoff ate, he thought long about the events of the last day or so, and he wondered what the new day would bring. After the bloodshed, Sovereign Nadav seemed friendly, even cordial in the way he spoke to the young Dahken. He said the future would hold great opportunity for them both, and they would come together tomorrow after Geoff had plenty of time to rest from his travels. Geoff briefly had the feeling that things were about to spin out of his control, but the tenderness of the meat and a look at the naked girl in his bed replaced it with other thoughts and feelings.

A servant, a man clearly of mixed Western and Loszian blood entered the suite unannounced. He was unremarkable, and he had a bundle of silver silk draped over his arm. He strode across the room to kneel directly in front of the divan on which Geoff sat as he ate. After a brief pause, he raised his head and stood politely.

"My lord, Sovereign Nadav commanded that I make certain all of your needs have been met thus far," he said. Receiving a nod and mumbled response from Geoff, he continued, "Sovereign Nadav asks that you join him when you are ready."

"Where?" Geoff asked around a mouthful of pork.

"In his sanctum at the top of the tower," the servant answered, and he placed the silks on the divan next to Geoff. "Merely exit your suite and climb the stairs until there are no more to climb. I shall inform the

Sovereign that you will join him shortly. He has provided this elegant set of robes for you, something more appropriate for a man of your stature."

Geoff watched as the man silently left, and he stared at the silver robes left on the next divan as he chewed absently. They were in fact of fine silk and excellent workmanship, and he had already accepted Nadav's hospitality in multiple ways. Even still, something about adopting the style of dress common to a Loszian sorcerer gave him pause. The Loszian hierarchy had brought his parents pain and sadness, and even Nadav himself made clear his disgust for those who rejected their Loszian blood. A realization suddenly broke in on Geoff's thoughts – the servant meant that Nadav expected him immediately, not whenever he was ready.

He jumped from the divan, pushing the food aside, and caught a glimpse of his reflection in one of the several floor to ceiling mirrors in the room. The Loszians were clearly a narcissistic lot, or maybe it was just Nadav, but the mirror served its purpose. Geoff was quite disheveled, and his clothes caked with dust and dirt from his short travels through the Spine. He looked disdainfully at the silver robes and decided that they would do; he would wear them only until he received a new tunic and breeches or had these washed.

He needed little time to don the robes, as they were in fact the simplest form of clothing he'd ever worn. As he looked over his new appearance in the mirror, Geoff thought the robes had the opposite effect of what he expected. They were not made for him, but it seemed for a pure Loszian of similar height. The sleeves swallowed his arms whole, and his fingertips did not even peek out from them. His legs were not disproportionate to his torso like a pure Loszian, so several inches of the silk dragged upon the ground. The gleaming silver threads did not provide the contrast against his gray face that he expected, not to mention that he had never seen a Loszian in anything other than rich, dark colors. Instead of bringing out his Loszian blood as he expected, the silks made it even more clear that he was not pure.

Satisfied that Sovereign Nadav would not like the effect of his choice of robes, Geoff began the long climb up through the cylindrical tower. He counted steps as he went, discarding the thought as he reached fifty, and instead counted floors. Just as he passed the eleventh, he caught sight of the servant again – the man had been coming down the steps from a floor above, and upon seeing Geoff, hurriedly turned and ran up the steps two and three at a time. Geoff shrugged, mentally at least, at the realization that he obviously hadn't come as quickly as expected.

He was exhausted, and his heart thudded heavily in his chest when he finally reached the last of the spiraling steps. They ended at a small landing with a set of opened double doors that led to an open suite of rooms that obviously occupied the entire floor. He could see windows and balconies on the far side, and it suddenly struck him that he had to have passed through at least two dozen levels in the tower. The very thought of the dizzying height at which Nadav's tower must overlook the city of Ghal gave Geoff a sudden sense of vertigo, and he had to put his hand against the cold black wall to steady himself. That was interesting also – the Loszian stone was cool despite the warming sun.

The manservant appeared once more from inside the suite and said, "The Sovereign Emperor of Losz expects you, my lord." As Geoff passed, the man whispered, "Be sure to show proper respect."

As he entered the first room, which was clearly Nadav's sleeping chamber, he looked for the Loszian, but carefully kept his eyes from the open windows and balcony to avoid a return of the dizzying vertigo. Nadav kept his abode plush and neat. Silk tapestries and wall hangings covered the walls, and superfluous carpets covered the floors, though furniture was spartan. A few slaves in various states of undress moved about on one task or another – one straightened Nadav's bedclothes, while another crossed the room carrying a glass apparatus Geoff couldn't identify.

He found the emperor in the next room, and though the rooms were immediately adjacent and not separated by something as vulgar as walls, there was a notable difference between the two spaces. The carpets ended, leaving uncovered, cool stone floor, and there were no rich silks hanging from the walls. A large, intricately carved table stood to one side, and it was covered with tools and devices that Geoff only assumed came with the necromancer's trade. He suddenly realized that Nadav's rooms were substantially larger than any of the tower's other floors, which seemed simply impossible based on Geoff's limited architectural understanding. Nadav later explained that he used sorcery to make his sanctum transdimensionally incongruous, as if that explained everything.

Nadav sat in a huge throne-like chair made of a rich dark wood that had been polished to a high shine, and he stared contemplatively at a large map on the floor. It pulled at Geoff's attention immediately, and it was unlike any map he had ever seen. It rose from the floor in three dimensions, and it was partially transparent, as he could see the floor beneath it. It displayed the western continent in its entirety, both the Shining West and Losz. Cities were marked with small castles, and topographical features such as the Spine were plainly obvious. Also, Geoff noticed figurines spread across the Loszian countryside, and there were a few in Aquis also, including a tiny one at Fort Haldon.

The map quite suddenly vanished, leaving nothing but a black floor, and Geoff looked up at Nadav.

The emperor now stared at Geoff expectantly, and his right index finger was raised in the air, presumably to dismiss whatever magic had created the now gone display. The Loszian was stark naked. Geoff knelt, as he knew he should, though he did not prostrate himself entirely as he had seen Menak do the previous day. His kneeling position brought him to perfect eye level with Nadav's uncovered manhood, and the fact unsettled Geoff greatly. The Loszian dropped his finger back to the chair's arm, and Geoff took that to mean he should stand, careful to keep his eyes centered on the emperor's face.

"Thank you for joining me, Dahken Geoff," Nadav said. "I can only assume by the late hour that you found your accommodations satisfactory. I must say the silks of a Loszian lord most definitely suit you, and I hope to see you in them more often."

Geoff was at a loss for words. After a flustered moment, he could only manage to say, "Thank you, Sovereign."

Nadav hadn't thought twice about trying to kill him just yesterday by his own hand. When the magic failed, the Loszian set his more concrete forces against him, but now Nadav was cordial as if they had been friends for years. Nadav called him Dahken Geoff, the title he had rightly deserved at Fort Haldon. What was happening?

"Great power and wealth, every luxury you could desire awaits you, Dahken Geoff," Nadav continued, and his voice grew darker. "Yes, I could have had you slain, but it would have been a waste of so much strength, so much potential. I have heard how the blood of the Dahken sometimes demands your race to travel or seek out objects, persons. Is that what brought you through the Spine to Losz?"

"It is, Sovereign," Geoff replied, now finding his voice.

"Before you came to Ghal, do you know to where your blood pulled you?"

"Not exactly," Geoff said, unsure as to where the discussion would end. "I felt like I needed to ride directly for the rising sun. Due east."

"Interesting, but Ghal is southeast of Menak's holdfast. So, to where do you feel pulled now?" Nadav asked as he leaned forward, seemingly very interested.

"I..." Geoff's voice trailed off as he focused. "I don't."

"Then I would say you've found what you were looking for."

"Why would I want to find you?" Geoff asked the Loszian, barely containing a sneer.

"Isn't it obvious?" Nadav asked. He seemed nonplussed by the question, but Geoff thought it was an act. "There's a darkness in you, a darkness that any Loszian would be proud to have. I saw it when you jumped to attack, when you murdered unarmed children in your attempt to strike me down. I doubt you have wept one tear for them or anyone else you've slain, and I know there have been others because you killed those who meant nothing to you so very easily. You've taken full advantage of my hospitality, and I know what you have done to one of the girls I left with you below. You may be a Dahken, but you are a Loszian in your soul.

"Geoff, you are like me – we are both gods among insects in this land, unmatched by any of those around us. We must only be careful not to offend those gods from which we receive our power, and fortunately, they rarely care for the designs of mortals. Together, we are indomitable."

"I don't need you," Geoff said boldly. "You can't hurt me, and I can kill you with one arc of my ghast's blade."

"I would have you know that I have many magicks at my disposal, and what you saw was only one of my most mundane. If you believe what you say, then try," Nadav challenged quietly.

Their eyes were locked in a silent combat. Geoff didn't know if it was the Loszian's words or his relishing leer, but he no longer felt sure of himself. He broke the contest by dropping his eyes to Nadav's feet, and the Loszian sat back in his ebony chair in victory.

"Very well," Nadav continued. "Now, tell me about Fort Haldon and the goings on there."

"Why should I?" Geoff asked, but it sounded childish even to his ear.

"Because if you don't, I'll have you skinned alive until you do of course," Nadav said with a sigh. "But I'd rather not. Besides, what loyalty do you owe those people?"

"Lord Dahken Cor freed me from Taraq'nok," Geoff said hollowly.

"Yes, he did, but you and I both know Taraq'nok would have freed you eventually anyway," Nadav said with a shrug. "What does the lordling Dahken plan?"

"He trains the other Dahken, teaches them to be like him," Geoff said, not knowing why he spoke of it. "He intends to invade Losz and free the Westerners here."

"Free them?" Nadav asked, genuinely perplexed. "Free them from what? Why? So that they may starve? Without their masters, they wouldn't know how to survive. We care for them as children, but it is of no matter. He would invade my empire with a handful of children?"

"Soldiers arrive from Byrverus weekly, and the fort is reinforced. He believes he can lead an army to destroy the Loszian Empire and unite all of the West."

"And what do you believe?" Nadav asked quietly. "Where do you fit in his army, his new order?"

"I... I don't. Lord Dahken Cor refuses to recognize my power."

"Of course not," Nadav said with a dismissive wave. "He fears you. You are more powerful than him, and he knows it. With the proper allies, the proper master, you will lay waste to armies and cities. I offer you the chance to fully realize your strength, to use it for your own will. All Dahken born in the West will be brought to you to teach, train, and command. You will be honored as a king, even worshipped as a god, and you will live in luxury where none of your desires are denied. Would Lord Dahken Cor ever offer you such?"

"No."

"Then he is a fool," Nadav spat. He leaned forward, and his fingers clawed into the throne's arms as he spoke. "All this I can give you, and I offer it to you for the taking. Only one thing do I require in return - your unfailing loyalty. Serve me as I require, and you will be more powerful than Cor could ever be. He will kneel before you in fealty as you fuck his woman, or he will die.

"Of course, Dahken Geoff, I could not expect you to answer now," Nadav said leaning back in the chair with a sudden calm. "It would be unwise, rash to make such a decision after only a moment's consideration. Please, continue to enjoy my hospitality. I will see you no more until you have made your decision, as I would not want to unduly influence you with my ambitions. Take up to a week and simply climb the tower once you've made your decision. If you choose against what I see as your rightful destiny, I will gladly send you on your way with no wronged feelings."

Realizing he had been dismissed, Geoff bowed as he felt was appropriate, quietly turned and left the emperor's presence. Thoughts and feelings swirled about within him like a maelstrom of the sea, a great thunderstorm in the sky. Everything Nadav and Losz stood for was evil and wrong, and the way he had indulged himself was also. But Nadav was right! He was more powerful than Cor, more powerful than Cor and Keth combined, and the powerful should have what they are able to take. Geoff worked to clear his mind on the long spiral down to the rooms he'd been provided, and his heart and breathing eventually began to slow. He must avoid thinking about it for at least a few days just to approach the whole idea with a level head.

It was only two mornings later that Dahken Geoff made his decision. He'd had too much wine the previous night and had fallen asleep on one of the plush rugs on the floor. As usual when he drank too much, he slept fitfully, tossing and turning throughout most of the night with dreams that he could not remember.

However, there is one that he recalled quite clearly. He was here, in Nadav's black tower, but he occupied a set of rooms to rival Nadav's. Fully naked, Thyss was bent over and screamed in agonized pleasure as Geoff took her from behind. Shoulders slumped in defeat, Cor knelt on the thick, plush carpet and watched dejectedly as Hykan's priestess called for more, and the once Lord Dahken's armor and weapons were hung on Geoff's walls like trophies. Geoff thought he heard laughing from somewhere in the tower's recesses, but he paid it no mind. Eventually, the dream faded, and he slept soundly well into the daytime hours.

When he awoke, Geoff felt like his blood boiled. His body was sore from sleeping on the floor, but other parts of him were enflamed for other reasons, especially as he looked at several of the slave girls in the room. He picked one and took her over and over, heedless of her cries, and the entire time he envisioned Thyss begging him to continue. Once sated, he bathed and then dressed in a set of silver robes that were identical to those he had worn before Nadav two days previously.

Sovereign Nadav smiled wickedly, as he knew the Dahken boy was on his way up the tower. Brazenly, he would leave the apparatus he'd used to manipulate Geoff's dreams right on his worktable, but the boy would have no idea for what purpose they had been used. The Dahken was easier to sway than he'd expected, no doubt due to the sliver of Loszian blood that ran through his veins. Of course, if he had not been convinced, he would have had to die. This time clothed in his robes, Nadav again waited for the boy in his ebony chair. It was not long before Geoff knelt before him in a show of loyalty, the rings under his eyes even more black and prominent than usual.

"Stand, Dahken Geoff," Nadav said. "I assume you have reached a decision."

"I have, Sovereign," Geoff replied. "I accept your offer."

"Most excellent," Nadav said impassively, and after a brief pause, he added, "Lord Dahken Geoff."

19.

Keth's sword whistled through the air. It was a high strike, intent on severing the head from the neck of his target, but as usual, Marya used her smaller size and agility to easily duck underneath it. They sparred daily as she constantly worked to improve her skills, and she had become extremely adept at simply evading most blows. In fact, Marya almost never parried Keth's blade, and she never used the small buckler shield that was strapped to her left arm, a fact that caused Keth no small concern. He virtually had to aim a blow at the shield, and even then, she often just moved away from it.

Adding to his frustration, Marya almost never landed a blow of any sort on Keth. Only at first, when Keth worked with her until she understood how to feel the strength in her blood, did she wound him, and that was of course necessary. In the last month or so, the matches became fights in earnest, and she seemed to genuinely want to hurt him. Though, it was her shortsword that was the prime problem because Keth's longsword had a good two feet of reach over Marya's shorter weapon. He'd tried to get her to discard the blade and use something longer, but she found everything else ponderous and difficult to maneuver. She discarded the idea within minutes, returning to her three foot long blade.

Keth advanced at her with blow after blow, the majority of which missed completely as she danced away. Some she parried, always returning with her own attack, but he never had trouble parrying her counters or simply blocking them on his large, round shield. He brought his sword down from above and across his body, and she ducked while lurching back and to her right, causing the sword to miss altogether. Keth quickly recovered, whipping his sword back at her shield arm. Off balance, she couldn't leap away from his blade in time, and it caught her left arm well above the shield. She yelped loudly, and her arm dropped to her side completely limp.

Keth knew not to lower his defenses, and he was rewarded with a jarring impact to his shield, as splinters flew and the metal bands stretched and bent. He was loath to strike at her again, and sensing this, Marya doubled her efforts, allowing her wound to fuel her attacks with great strength. Sparks flew as their blades notched each other. Keth overextended a thrust, and Marya saw her opportunity; she brought her own sword down upon his, forcing it down to impale the ground. She smiled at him wickedly, gloating as blood ran freely down her useless left arm. It would be a simple matter now to bring her sword up and open his abdomen for all the other Dahken to see, until her vision clouded black, purple, and red as something huge and round crashed into her right shoulder and head. Marya landed on her back several feet away from where she just stood claiming her victory, groaning from the bashing force of Keth's shield.

"Damn it Marya," Keth said, kneeling next to her as she regained her senses. He had left his sword and shield behind, right next to her shortsword where it had fallen. "Are you all right?"

"I can't move my arm," she said, her right hand rubbing at her forehead.

"Of course, you can't. Had I actually been trying to hurt you, I would have taken it off! Why don't you ever use your shield? You should have easily deflected my attack."

193

He inspected the wound in her upper arm and found that his longsword had cut through the meat clear to the bone, severing many muscles. It had rendered her arm useless, and her elbow, forearm and hand were coated in slick blood. Keth always kept a dagger at his side, just in case, and he drew it now. Closing his left hand tightly around the cold steel blade, he grunted in pain when he jerked it free, cutting his palm and fingers to the bone. He placed his blood covered hand over Marya's wound, and she grimaced and groaned.

"Do it," Keth commanded.

Marya nodded and focused on her arm. Interestingly, the pain had disappeared moments before, and the wound didn't start to hurt again until Keth put his own deeply cut hand over it. She could feel Keth's blood mixing with hers. She sensed his Dahken strength, and she could feel the pain of his deeply sliced hand. She brought the pain of the two wounds together until they became one, and then just as quickly, they disappeared altogether.

Marya tiredly opened her eyes to see Keth standing over her with his left hand extended out to her. She reached up with her own now healed arm, and he helped her up to stand on unsteady feet. Keth released her hand and wiped each side of his dagger's blade on his tunic.

"Gods damn this thing!" she screamed as she stripped the shield from her arm. She then flung the metal disk across the practice yard.

"I think," Keth said slowly as he sheathed the dagger, "you should go rest. We've been at it for a while, and the others are restless. Let me work with Celdon while you get some sleep."

"I don't need sleep!" she shouted at him angrily. She stole his dagger from its sheath and ran past him to her sword. She picked it up and backed away from his sword and shield. "I'm not done with you yet, Dahken Keth!"

He sighed deeply and looked at the other Dahken, including Celdon, whose faces had turned from abject boredom to a renewed sense of interest. He turned and walked to his sword and shield, and as he bent to pick them up, Marya jumped backward a few feet. He stood facing her – shortsword in her right hand and his dagger in her left.

So focused on her sword, Keth ignored the dagger that she held low near her waist, and she stuck him with it in only their second series of moves. The watching Dahken gasped in surprise, and Celdon even cheered with a pumped fist. It was a light wound that glanced off his ribs, but it hurt and drew his blood none the less. He learned quickly to be wary of the small blade as she flicked it in and out of their exchanges as quickly as a viper may strike. It was completely impossible to parry the dagger's thrust, and he began to use his shield as a barrier from its bite. They danced this way for the better part of an hour, and while Keth still got the better of her, Marya had still managed to wound him several times.

"Enough Marya," Keth said in a commanding tone, and he lowered his sword. He disentangled the dagger's sheath from his belt and held it out to her. "Take it, keep the dagger. I can't teach you how to fight this way, but maybe Thom has someone who can. If your wounds are healed, why don't you go rest. We'll talk later."

He watched her as she walked away, headed toward the Dahken barracks. She walked with pride, her face up towards the sun and a haughty spring in her step. She carried both her sword and new dagger in hand, not bothering to clean the blood from the blades or sheath them. He could have stayed locked in battle with her forever with no sense of victory for either, and she knew it.

"Celdon, stay here with me for a bit," he said, drawing his attention back to the other Dahken. "The rest of you, go find something to eat and have some fun."

They trained well past midday, until Keth's own stomach began to growl with ferocity, and they adjourned to find a pair of roasted chickens. Keth liked Celdon; the lad was quiet but affable. While he had dropped some weight, mostly from training with Fort Haldon's men at arms, he still had an impressive appetite. Keth looked at him as a younger boy but had to remind himself that only three years or so separated the two of them. Soon, those few years would mean little to nothing.

After they ate together, Keth released Celdon to do as he might. Keth needed to find Cor and Thom, and as he climbed the grassy slope, he knew where he would find the former. Temporary steps of timber had been set into the hillside to make the walk up and down easier to manage, but even still, Keth felt exhausted after the long session with Marya. His effort was rewarded as he found both men seated at the mahogany table pouring over an extremely detailed map of the pass connecting Aquis to Losz.

"I assure you of its accuracy Lord Dahken," Thom was saying. "The topography has been charted by my best rangers time and time again. We spent two years alone working on this project."

"I'm not a cartographer, but it looks like the narrowest part of the pass is blocked by our wall?"

"It is," Thom agreed.

"What about these cliffs?" Cor asked. He touched the map on either side of the wall.

"Its true that the wall can be flanked by climbing those cliffs and coming down on our side, but not by any sizeable force. Anyone coming down would be easy targets for our longbows," Thom explained. He then said with a smile, "Also, I always keep a small group of men on each cliff to deter such an action. Trust me Lord Dahken, we are well protected here. Fort Haldon has stood for hundreds of years."

"Very well," Cor conceded, and he looked up to see Keth standing at the far end of the table. The Lord Dahken rose from his chair to take the younger Dahken's arm. "Keth! I feel like I haven't seen you in days."

"You haven't, Lord Dahken," Keth responded quietly.

"I hadn't realized. You need me then?"

"Actually, I need both of you," Keth replied, momentarily glancing at Thom.

"How advantageous for you then. What matters bring you here?"

"Its actually the same matter; it's about Marya," Keth said, and he shifted his gaze to Thom. "Commander, I hope you have someone here, a soldier or man at arms, a fighter who fights with two blades? In training today, Marya came at me with a shortsword and dagger at once, and I found it most difficult to ward off. It seemed to be very effective for her and the way she tends to weave about in combat."

A flash of memory, an image of his very first battle came to Cor's mind, and he immediately understood what Keth meant. He remembered the short and stocky Tigolean that came at him with two daggers, and how the man bobbed and danced around. He hadn't even been trying to harm Cor, and Cor now knew that if the pirate had wanted to kill him, he wouldn't have stood a chance. Not back then.

"I have just the man, Dahken Keth," Thom said, nodding. "His name is Jory, and he claims that some Tigolean hermit taught him some ancient art to wield steel with both his hands and feet. Its all bluster and rubbish, I'm sure, but there's no better man to fight with two blades. He mans the wall from sunup to midday, but I could reassign him."

"No please, Commander," Keth said, extending his fingers and slightly shaking his head. "If he would give Marya an hour every afternoon, I'd be most appreciative."

"Settled," Cor said, "but I'm still trying to figure out why you needed me."

"Lord Dahken, it is time to hold the ceremony for Marya as you did for me," Keth said, and as he watched Cor's eyes widen, he knew he must explain further. "She controls her blood well enough and will only get better at it. I can't teach her anything else. She needs to work with Commander Thom's man to develop her on fighting style, but as far as being a Dahken is concerned, she is ready."

"I think we're getting ahead of ourselves. You've been training her for what, a few months? I don't think she's ready, Keth."

"You said when we can teach someone nothing else," Keth argued. "Marya channels her strength at will. She fully understands herself and her abilities. There's nothing else she can learn from me."

"There's more to it than that," Cor said, shaking his head. "Rael was impressed with you and said you'd only become stronger with or without his instruction. Marya is so young, she's… just a child."

"As am I, Lord Dahken. As were you when you first began to discover your powers. We are rebuilding our race, as if I even know what that means, and I need to focus my energy on those who need more help. Like Celdon."

"Is she ready to teach someone else?" Cor asked, and as Keth hesitated to answer, Cor continued. "You say she won't learn anything else from you, but she must be ready to teach another. If she isn't, then she isn't prepared to be a Dahken in name as well as race. Can you tell me she's ready for that?"

Keth considered the question for a few seconds before conceding the point, "No, Lord Dahken, I can't."

"Then this discussion is over, Dahken Keth."

"Very well, Lord Dahken," Keth said, and he turned to leave. Before he began the descent, he turned to see Cor retaking his seat to pour over the map of the pass. "I might say, I think one day soon she'll prove herself to you."

Cor glanced up for just a second and said, "I'm sure you're right."

Keth strode down the timber steps slower than he would have liked. The further he went, the faster he went. He wanted to break into a run, but he knew that would only end with him falling and landing in a heap at the bottom like the fat priest. He was aggravated at Cor's refusal, but the Lord Dahken was right. As he crossed the common areas of Fort Haldon en route to his quarters, Keth noticed a sticking pain in his side. It occurred to him that the feeling had been there for an hour or more, and he was somewhat winded by the time he reached his destination.

He shut the door behind him and looked at the chair and table he had scrounged from Rael's belongings after his death, the latter of which was covered with the various texts Rael had written out. Only the window on the east wall lit the room. Actually, it was nothing but an open hole that shuttered from the inside, and only ambient light came through at this time of day. Keth sat down heavily in the chair with a sigh, gingerly inserting his fingers under the left side of his chain shirt. There it was – a small wound where his dagger, Marya's dagger, had nicked him. It was not deep, but it bled and hurt as his fingers traced it. He began to tiredly pull off his armor.

"Why didn't you tell me you were hurt?"

Keth looked up to see a girl leaning in the doorway that led to the room in which he slept. Between the dim light and that she had recently bathed, her combed backward hair that was usually auburn appeared black. Marya wore an off white shift that hung loosely from her shoulders down to her ankles. It clung to her in places where her body was still wet from bathing, and Keth found it difficult taking his eyes from her form.

"I didn't realize it," he said, looking at his blood covered fingertips.

She crossed the small room in just a handful of steps with a gait that didn't match the shift she wore. The more she learned about her race and the strength she could tap, the more arrogance Marya adopted in her walk, in her very being. He had never seen it more than right now, and the effect was oddly feminine, though he had never seen another girl walk in such a way. Except for maybe Thyss.

She stood over him and took his hand to look at the blood from his wound, then reached down with her other hand to grasp the hilt of his sword. She drew it from its sheath as she released his hand, and it was awkward for her, as it was substantially longer than her own. Carefully, she ran her own fingertips against its edge and allowed the blade to cut into them. She bit her lower lip as she did so, the cold steel bringing both a searing pain and a fiery pleasure. As the blood welled up from the blade's cut, she pressed her fingers against Keth's wound and bent down to kiss him.

20.

This morning, like most as of late, Cor ate alone at the Dahken table and watched over the progression of Fort Haldon. He knew little of engineering, carpentry, or masonry, but it was explained that the foundations had to be dug and placed before anything else could occur. That task had started right where he now sat, where the Dahken Hall would be and extended outward from there. Progress seemed so slow that Cor was certain the stronghold would never actually be built.

Marya arrived at the table, looking stronger and more like a woman every day. While the other children ate together below, Marya had taken to joining Keth at the site of the hall. Cor had little to say of it, as she had shown herself more than willing to stay at Keth's side through all things. Cor wondered if her loyalties lay with him, with the Dahken, or with Keth, and he decided to discuss with Dahken Keth the nature of his relationship with the young woman.

In truth as Cor understood such things, Marya had only just begun her journey into womanhood, and Cor endeavored not to notice the fact. She was a full foot shorter than he, and he wondered what bloodlines had mixed to create the color of her hair. Her matching eyes showed defiance, but Cor thought it a ruse meant to guard some truth. She was a slender girl and her features were sharp, the bones of her face clearly defined beneath her gray skin. There was something else about Marya – arrogance, a swagger in her walk that wasn't there when he first saved her from Taraq'nok. Cor had seen the same in Thyss and in the vision of Rena so long ago. Cor realized that he was staring at the girl, and he averted his eyes.

Thyss trudged her way up the slope, and Cor looked at her in concern. Things hadn't been quite right since her trip into the Spine two or three weeks ago, when she had brought back the dead Loszian. She always seemed tired, fatigued, and she rarely left their bed in the morning hours. He was convinced she was angry with him. Everything he said seemed to anger her, and they hadn't made love since the night of her return. As she approached, she looked exhausted and disheveled, having not tied her hair into a ponytail as he'd seen her every day since they first met. Thyss' usual formfitting tunic and pants, made of the foreign black silk that shimmered in the light and was as strong as steel, were nowhere to be seen in favor of loose wool. Her sword, however, never left her.

"Don't feel well?" Cor asked, feeling stupid for even asking the question as she sat immediately to his right.

"No," she said.

The cooking fires at Fort Haldon raged from sunup to sundown to feed over a thousand people two if not three meals each day, and as such, it was only a matter of minutes before a porter placed a large plate of food in front of Thyss. She stared at it for a moment and then proceeded to poke a piece of roasted pork with a small knife. Discarding the idea, she instead bisected a tuber that looked as if it had been fried in oil and picked up one half with a thumb and forefinger. As quickly as she placed it in her mouth, Thyss violently pushed away from the table. Rushing from the table, she fell to her knees after about ten feet and vomited onto the bare foundation. Cor moved to her side, but she pushed him away angrily and wiped her mouth with her wool sleeve.

"Damn you, Hykan!" she screamed to the heavens. Standing, she strode to the table while drawing her wicked blade. In a great two handed strike, full of rage and fury, she brought the scimitar's edge down onto the middle of the plate, shattering it into a half dozen shards. The gleaming green steel pierced the thick mahogany of the tabletop, penetrating deeply. Thyss stormed away, her sword imbedded in the wood, leaving Cor and Marya to stare after her. Cor looked back at Marya, who merely shrugged and returned her attention to her own breakfast.

Cor later found Thyss in their bed, still clothed as she was and curled into a fetal ball. Her scabbard with its leather strap lay discarded on the floor, and Cor gently slid her sword back into it and leaned it against the wall near the bed. When he sat next to her on the straw mattress, he realized that she cried silently. Never once had he ever seen Thyss cry, and Cor felt surprised that she was even capable of such.

"What do you want?" she asked in a mumble full of venom.

"I'm just worried about you, worried if you are well."

"Of course not, you gray skinned bastard!" she lashed out, sitting upright. Cor was used to Thyss' harsh emotions and reactions; it was her way, but this was different. Her flawless bronze face was a visage of fury and disgust, and at this moment, he could feel it all directed at him.

"What did I do?" he asked as he reached up to caress her face.

She slapped his hand away. "You have to ask that? How stupid are you, Dahken Cor? Do you understand nothing of women? For fifty years Hykan has given me power over fire and dominion over my own body, but now he has forsaken me! He has allowed your demon seed to quicken inside me!"

Cor stared at her blankly, dumbly, for a moment before his eyes cleared in understanding of what she said. The thought had never occurred to him. On the farm, most children learned of such things naturally, as farmers tended to have many children. His parents had never had another child, perhaps for fear of another sickly babe, and certainly the priests would just as soon explain conception as Garod's will and nothing more. What Cor knew of it all, he had learned on the open sea, listening to bawdy sailors talk of their wives and children at home and their whores and sweethearts abroad. The sudden thought of being a father made him want to piss his armor, and he didn't know why.

Thyss belched, an odor of vomit suddenly in the air, and she laid back into the position in which he had found her. "My body betrays me. Hykan has forsaken me," she repeated.

Cor dropped off the bed and onto the floor, kneeling so that his face was level with hers. "I love you," he said. "What can I do?"

"Leave me to my misery."

Thyss stayed in bed and slept nearly the entire day, only once coming out into the afternoon sun to eat a very small meal of bread and cheese. She considered eating again in the evening, but the smell of cooking meat again evoked nausea. It was at night, as they both lay in bed awake in frightened consideration of parenthood, that something Thyss said came to Cor's mind.

"Can I ask you something?"

"What," she said in sullen expectation, and he breathed a little easier as it seemed her fiery anger had abated for the time.

"You're fifty years old?" he asked.

"You have no manners, Dahken Cor," she stated. "Were you never told not to ask a lady her age?"

"Manners have never seemed to be a concern of yours," he answered dryly, lightly poking her side below the ribcage with a forefinger. She elbowed him forcefully in response.

"I stopped counting," Thyss said with a sigh, "but I'm at least sixty years old."

"Really!" he exclaimed, and he received another elbow for it, this one much harder. "I'm sorry. It just surprised me."

"Gods, you can be stupid sometimes," she said as she leaned up on one elbow to face him. Thyss could barely make out the hurt on his face. "How old was Rael? How old is Queen Erella? If you don't get yourself killed first, you will live well over a hundred years yourself, perhaps even two hundred. Dahken Cor, you of all people should know that those of us gifted by the gods outlive the others. Sometimes, it amazes me how much you still think like a Westerner. You must learn to think like a Dahken, like a giant among ants."

She kissed him hard on the mouth and then flipped over onto her side, her back to him. As Cor listened to her breathing slow, he wondered what it would be like for two giants to raise a normal child of mixed race, half Western and half Dulkurian. Somehow, it didn't seem right for them to stay young as their child grew up, aged, became frail and died, and as Cor drifted off to sleep, a feeling of deep sadness washed over him.

21.

The ride from Byrverus to Fort Haldon, and then back again after only one day's reprieve, had not been kind to Aidan's substantial backside. He had never been one for horses, but he didn't have to be, considering that he never left his beloved white city. However, it was his pride that was truly offended, making his face as red and angry as his rear. Pride or otherwise, this Cor person was a danger to Aquis and Garod, and Aidan would make certain that Queen Erella understood just how perilous the matter was.

As he rode back to Byrverus, the entire affair became more distorted in his mind, and his memory of the happenings mutated into something vaguely recognizable as what occurred. He remembered a fully armored and battle ready antagonist, who swore and shouted blood oaths to Dahk and other foul gods. This figure threatened to stick him with a longsword while waiving a skull headed fetish in the air, saying that he would make a blood sacrifice of the poor innocent priest. Aidan looked to the queen's architect (Karl was his name?) for help, but he could see that the poor man was as powerless and frightened as he. In the end, Aidan was saved only by a misstep, having tripped over a large rock that lay on the ground just behind him as he backed away from the murderous Dahken. That led him to roll in a most undignified way down the hill, but at least it saved his life. He ran for his belongings and horse while Cor laughed maliciously from on high, and he rode hard away from Fort Haldon. He dared not look back for fear that the Dahken may chase him down with his sword in hand.

All this, Aidan told Queen Erella, relating the entire story moment by moment with as much detail as he could muster in her main hall, in front of a crowd. Occasionally, he would return to an earlier detail to elaborate more fully, and he watched as Erella's face remained passive, all except for her eyes. Her eyes betrayed her true thoughts, as they widened momentarily when Aidan explained Cor's plan to erect a temple to both Dahk and the Loszian gods. As he depicted the culmination of their brief meeting, the queen's face turned hard, her eyes smoldering, and Aidan knew she finally understood. The assembled guards, commoners, lords, and priests spoke in frenetic hushed tones to one another, having turned fully against Lord Dahken Cor on just Aidan's word, until Erella called them to silence.

"What would you have me do now, Majesty?" Aidan asked after finishing his tale.

"Return to your duties attending Byrverus with my thanks," she said. "Your faith and loyalty in this matter and all others is widely noted by all and Garod."

"May I offer further assistance in this matter?" he asked, bowing his head in a practiced move of fealty.

"No, good Aidan. I will summon Lord Dahken Cor to court and consult with Palius while I await his arrival," she replied.

"He will always be your loyal servant, Majesty. I prayed for Palius' health over the weeks I was away."

"No doubt you did," she said softly, and Erella stood from her throne. As everyone, Aidan included, bowed in her presence, she purposefully crossed the hall and exited toward her chambers. Within minutes she had signed and sealed an order for Lord Dahken Cor to return to Byrverus in haste, as there was an important matter to be discussed that could not wait. She dispatched a rider with the authority to use the queen's horses as necessary and stalked the halls to find Palius.

Of course, Erella knew precisely where he would be, as the poor man never left his own chambers anymore. Everyone in the palace knew that his time grew short, and Palius rarely even left his bed except to use a pot. As she entered, she found him sitting upright in bed reading a large leather bound tome, and the room was sweltering with its ever present roaring fire, despite the fact that it was a warm spring day.

"Majesty!" Palius exclaimed at her entry, and he was positively beaming, though he wheezed heavily as he spoke. "For what affair do you require counsel that you would visit a dying man?"

"I wish I could say that I was here for pleasure only, that I did not need your counsel on any matter," she replied as she pushed a chair to his bedside and sat upon its velvet cushion. "You are rather cheerful for a man who says he is dying."

"My queen, I know I am dying and so do you, so let's not insult each other with such words," he replied, placing a slightly shaking hand on hers. "But to answer you, I find that since you no longer need me for daily duties, I have much time on my hands. I've never taken the time to read for pleasure before."

"What is that?' she asked, pointing to the tome he had set to the side.

"Oh, theological essays by Kris... Kris... Kris-something."

"Kristonn," Erella said. "He was one of the first priests of Garod, a child found and taught by Werth, and he helped Werth liberate the West during The Cleansing."

"Majesty, what is the matter at hand?" Palius asked. "I'm sorry, but you are not here to discuss my leisure reading or the history of the Shining West."

Erella sighed. "I sent Aidan to Fort Haldon. I wanted him to have a temple built there and make certain that our Lord Dahken paid proper reverence to Garod."

"A prudent idea, Majesty, if for no other reason than to extricate Lord Aidan from the all consuming politics in which he tends to involve himself."

"That was not my intent," she shot back.

"Of course not, Majesty. I assume things did not go well?" he asked.

"You well know that if it had, I wouldn't be here now," the queen replied, and she related everything Aidan had said to the best of her memory. Palius pinched his nose and closed his eyes as she spoke, his chest rumbling as he breathed deeply through his nose. When she finished, he did not move for at least a minute, momentarily causing the queen to wonder if he had fallen asleep. Finally, he opened one bloodshot eye and looked at her worried face.

"No, Majesty, I am not asleep, nor dead quite yet," Palius said. "It would seem that our good Lord Aidan has yet again made a spectacle as he is often wont. I have no doubt he has embellished the story, and he chose to relate it publicly to cause the people to stand against Lord Dahken Cor."

"I am afraid that is my fault. I called him to court to give him his task publicly."

"Ah," Palius said with a nod. "But my queen, if even a quarter of what he says is true, then the Dahken has ignored a direct command from Your Majesty. And if half of what Aidan says is true, then we have been betrayed, and Cor assaulted one of Garod's preeminent priests."

"I know, Palius," Erella said with a sigh as she slumped back in the chair. "You tried to warn me months ago, and I am afraid I was blinded by what might have been. I have dispatched orders to Fort Haldon, demanding Cor's presence in Byrverus immediately. I do not think we're compatible, the

Dahken and the Shining West, and I am afraid that at the least I will have to exile he and his ilk from Aquis."

"Majesty, that day may come, but for now let me read to you from Kristoff," Palius said, lifting the heavy tome back into his lap.

"Kristonn."

His queen had sat with him for a good while longer than he had expected, listening as Palius read ecclesiastical essay after essay. She was rather silent with only an occasional comment, though she was attentive, and Palius had no doubt that Erella had been an excellent student, likely the pride of her tutors and priests when she was a child at least fifty years before his birth. He had never loved her more than he did while she sat with him, making time for her dying advisor and friend, despite their recent disagreements. Eventually, he feigned massive fatigue and exhaustion, and she left him to rest.

Loyal to Erella and Aquis to the end, Palius would protect them as he had always protected them, even if it were the last action he took in this life. She had little notion of the things he had done over the decades, or if she did, she did not voice it. Sometimes things had to be done, and it was better if his beautiful queen did not have to bloody her hands with such actions. Palius thought of Aidan, and he wondered if the corpulent priest would be up to the task at hand, if his conscience would allow it. No, Aidan's way was the way of politicians and their entangled webs of deceit, favors, and beholden tasks. Palius was far more direct; pay the right person to do a job, and it gets done.

It wasn't that Palius actually believed Aidan's narrative as related by Queen Erella. He had no doubt that the priest had embellished it, but to what extent he was not sure. However, Aidan failed at his task, and he had failed quite thoroughly, which only meant that something close to what he described had happened. In the end, it only reinforced one simple fact, a fact that Palius had known for quite some time – this Dahken Cor and his kind were dangerous and untrustworthy, and it was time to solve the Dahken problem.

Larnd had sent assassins the first time, professionals at striking down persons unaware in the dark, and they had failed miserably. All they had managed to do was put Cor on the defensive, and he immediately made plans to segregate his people into their own enclosure. Additionally, he had halted or at least slowed severely the flow of new troops to Fort Haldon. It was time for something more direct, overpowering, and the timing was perfect. Cor would be away from his protection at Fort Haldon as he crossed miles of open country on his way to Byrverus.

Palius pushed himself from his bed and sat on its edge, and his bare feet hovered several inches over the rug. He pushed himself off slowly until his feet touched the floor gingerly. It was something he did every time he arose from bed, and when he was sure that his legs would still support his weight, Palius slowly walked to the corner of the room that held his chamber pot.

Once relieved, he tottered to the adjacent chamber that still held his desk, where he handled state business. He stopped briefly as he passed a mirror, suddenly aware that he hadn't shaved in months, and his beard was several inches long at his chin, scraggly and inconsistent. The top of his head was completely bald now, and the white hair around the sides and back of his head hung long and unkempt almost to his shoulders. The combination of his beard and hair lent him a particularly insane appearance, like that of some poor, homeless old man.

Palius sat at his desk, which had gone unused for months ever since Queen Erella had pointedly stopped asking for his help in state affairs. He arranged its surface with blank parchment, ink and pen, and wax to seal the message he began to compose mentally. Palius started to write a message to Larnd but found it a difficult task as he halted every several words. He folded the parchment in half and started again, this time intent on sending the message to Marek. He found this no easier however and again folded the parchment, placing it to the side after only two words.

Palius leaned back in his chair, closed his eyes, and pinched his nose as he tried to gather his thoughts. He couldn't possibly make the journey through the city to Marek or Larnd. Beyond the fact of his failing health, it would raise many eyebrows to see him about the palace and even leaving it, and he dared not write a letter directly to Larnd because he couldn't trust anyone to deliver it safely to one of the kings of Byrverus' underworld. In fact, a message of any kind just seemed unsafe at this point, which meant Palius needed to send for one of the men to come to the palace. Marek was the obvious choice as the cutthroat was a master of disguise, and no one would guess him to be Larnd's brother, a former soldier, and murderer of notably ill repute.

Opening his eyes, Palius pushed away from his desk and picked up the two failed letters. He shambled his way to his fireplace, the blaze now reduced to hot coals and cinders. He still had a small amount of fuel available, and he dropped a piece of tinder onto the iron rack, lighting it painstakingly with flint. As the fire caught and grew steady, he caught the corners of the parchment sheets in the open flame. The dry parchment lit easily, and he held it in front of his face, watching the fire grow and move across its surface. When it was half consumed, Palius dropped the burning parchment onto the flaming tinder, and he reached to the side for a small piece of split wood, which he added to the small blaze.

He stood and went back to his bed, wheezing somewhat with the exertion of it all. Most certainly, he would not make it to the palace's doors, much less into the city somewhere, without collapsing. Lying down, he reached for a small bronze bell that he kept on the table at his bedside for use when his breath would not allow him to call for the guards. Mere seconds after he rang the bell, one of the soldiers who stood outside his chambers entered. "Get me Sergeant Holt," Palius said to the man.

Palius liked Sergeant Holt, and he had used the grizzled veteran for a large variety of tasks over the years. He was a pragmatic old soldier, well past the age that most fighting men hung their sword upon the mantle and told their grandchildren great tales of their exploits. Long ago, he had realized that Palius' only concern was for the safety and security of Aquis and its queen, and as such, the then young soldier had made himself available to Palius' every need.

Holt had done it all in the service of Her Majesty and more in the service of Palius, from guarding the queen Herself to hunting down bandits in the Aquis countryside. He had sailed the Narrow Sea for six months as Aquis helped Roka defeat a pirate flotilla that pillaged the trading lanes. He had even helped put down a rebellion on the western side of the nation, summarily executing over fifty men who had murdered a local priest and burned his temple to the ground. Palius assigned that particular task to him, and the entire affair had never reached the ears of Queen Erella. It was Holt who most brutally and efficiently tortured the user of the Loszian mirror that Palius now possessed.

It easily took Holt an hour to arrive at Palius' chambers, and the dying old man was most aware of the passage of time. A year ago, he would not have noticed due to that peculiar perception that time seems to pass more quickly as one ages. However, now he was dying, and every minute, every second seemed more important than a great sack full of gold coins. He would have given anything to go back and tell himself how important time was, to make every moment count as if it were his last. His life could have been something else entirely, could have been so different.

The old soldier trudged into Palius' rooms, having pushed the door open and entered with no announcement. He clinked as he walked a steady pace, no doubt set by years as a soldier marching from place to place. Holt's face had been tanned like leather from years of the sun and elements with eyes that had been closed from exposure and were yet sharp as a hawk. He shaved occasionally enough to avoid growing a full beard, giving him a constantly stubbled appearance. As opposed to the plate armor worn by the younger soldiers, Holt always wore a full suit of gray chain mail and hard brown leather boots. Attached to the back of the shirt, a chain cowl covered his once black hair now grayed to match his armor. Everything about Holt shouted practical and uncompromising efficiency, including the unadorned sheath that carried his double edged longsword with its plain steel guard.

"My Lord," Holt said in his distinct gravelly voice, "I came as soon as I was able."

"I understand you have duties beyond my needs," Palius replied, wheezing from his bed.

"My duty is whatever Aquis demands, sir. What does my home require of me?"

"Ever loyal Holt, Aquis faces a grave danger from within, and I must take action beyond the usual channels," Palius said. "Unfortunately, my failing health prevents me from contacting those I need to handle the problem. I'm afraid I may not be able to breathe much longer, and a walk across the city would speed my breathe away from me."

"I understand. It would be my honor to serve you as always. Where do you need me to go, lord?" Holt asked.

"There is a man who lives in the city, not far from here. His name is Marek, and he lives in the part of Byrverus past the rich estates and private villas."

Holt nodded several times as Palius spoke. "I've been around, lord. I know who he is and where to find him, but I believe it's his brother that you truly need."

"Indeed, but Marek's brother could never come here or anywhere even near the palace. On this matter, I will deal with Marek, and he will have to deal with Larnd. And I'll need your help, Holt."

"Of course, lord," Holt said, and then he simply listened.

22.

Sergeant Holt dreamt, and he knew it, for these events had happened over twenty years ago. He was still an old man, a worn old soldier over sixty years of age, but when this actually happened, he had been middle aged. It always disturbed him that of all the things he had done in life it was this dream, this memory, that stayed with him and haunted him every time for the last ten years that Lord Palius needed something from him. He always saw himself as an old man, as he currently was, instead of the younger, vigorous version of himself that perpetrated the events.

Palius called for Holt, and they had discussed what happened in hushed tones behind closed doors. A village near the far western edge of Aquis had fallen into revolt against the crown and therefore the priesthood. Palius had heard of it weeks ago, rumblings of discontent among the commoners there, and that they had ceased tithing. When the local priest warned them of their actions and even went so far as to impose an additional tax on those who would not tithe, things turned ugly. The small handful of soldiers the priest had at his disposal was overrun by an organized mob mostly wielding farm tools as weapons. The farmers burst into the temple and brutally beat the priest to death to the point that he was wholly unrecognizable. Five soldiers were killed and the sixth sent to Byrverus with a message, a message that Palius intercepted so that Queen Erella would never hear of it. Palius loved his queen more than anyone, but he knew she was too benevolent a person and incapable of the unpleasantness that must be done.

Palius' image never changed in Holt's dream memory, always appearing as he did those years ago. He was thin and fit with a straight, tall back that had not yet hunched over from age and weight. Palius had a full head of hair that had only just begun to turn from near black to white, and his full white beard was gone in place of a trimmed goatee that matched his hair. One thing always remained the same however – Palius' face was always drawn and exhausted, with dark rings under his eyes on a face that was not yet lined from age.

The queen's advisor explained to Holt that the situation must be handled and handled properly, that no hint of rebellion or challenge to the order of things could survive. Those responsible must disappear entirely, so their dangerous actions and thoughts do not spread elsewhere in Aquis. It would weaken the Shining West for decades, and Aquis would no longer be able to protect its people from the horrors of the Loszian Empire.

"Yes, lord," Holt had said. "I'll take a group of men I trust. We'll handle this."

"No," Palius said a little more forcefully than he had planned. He again hushed his voice to a whisper. "It must be you alone, Holt. If you take more soldiers, even a small force, it will be apparent to all that a battle occurred. There will be too much evidence, too much proof that the queen put them down forcibly."

"Lord, how might I defeat at least two score men, farmers perhaps, but men none the less."

"Holt," Palius said, placing a less than reassuring hand on the soldier's shoulder, "I have faith in you."

"Garod help me," Holt mumbled as his eyes sank to Palius' white slippered feet.

"He will, Holt. For everything you do, you do for Him and Aquis."

Holt left Byrverus immediately and traveled west by horse to the city of Harus. The journey required a solid ten days of him, even at the steady pace he kept, and he had worked out his plan in the meantime. Palius had given him ample gold as well as blanket authorization to commandeer whatever resources he needed. Once in Harus, Holt acquired a small wagon, which he loaded with two barrels of whale oil, two steel chains, two heavy locks, and a small barrel of white glue made from some kind of fish organ. The vendor claimed it to be the best – sticky and very fast to dry. He also bought a couple large brushes meant for staining furniture, a torch, and some flint before setting off again.

He'd detached the wagon in a small grove not far from the village, a few miles at most, and rode the horse the rest of the way. Holt wore his armor as proof of his position in the queen's palace, but he left his weapons behind in the wagon. He wanted no cause for the villagers to attack. As he entered the village from the east, he found it oddly deserted. He rode in slowly, cautiously, with his sharp eyes and ears open for any movement or sign of danger. Doors to small houses were left open in the breeze, and there were none of the sounds of a village about him. No farm animals snorted, clucked, or bayed, nor did he hear children's laughter or shouting parents. He rode for the temple, easily distinguished as the largest edifice among the quaint collection of buildings and painted white to match the great temples of the cities.

Holt approached the white building from the side, as its main doors faced south through the village center. He slowly rode around to the front and the main street, such as it was, a growing sense of uneasiness growing in his gut. Someone watched him, he was sure, and his suspicions were confirmed as he saw three men slinking between the small houses and shops to come up behind his horse. He watched them carefully with one eye, very aware that they were about to cut him off from the way back to his wagon. The men wore clothes of peasants and farmers, and they each carried a tool turned weapon – pick, pitchfork, and hoe.

"What do you here?" shouted a voice.

Holt stopped his horse and turned his attention forward. Standing in an open doorway to one of the apparently deserted homes stood a large man, easily over six feet and muscled to be as strong as iron. He had extraordinarily fair skin and strawberry hair not seen among Westerners, which was parted down the middle and combed to each side, to fall almost to his shoulders. He had a broad, clean shaven face with a jutting forehead and wide features, giving the illusion of stupidity and barbarism, and Holt suspected that at least the latter was accurate. Holt eyed the proper sword that hung across the man's back. It was a large weapon held in a sling of sorts with no sheathe or scabbard, the blade of which was longer than Holt's own, and the hilt looked as if it could be used either one or two handed. It was a bastard sword, the weapon of a Northman.

"I said what do you here!" shouted the red haired man, and this time, it was a statement and not a question. His voice was deep and strong.

"I'm here to talk," Holt said evenly, careful to make his voice heard but still sound passive. He was distinctly aware that the farmers had finally blocked the way back.

"Talk! Talk is for lovers!" the Northman retorted with a laugh. "Leave now and tell your queen we are free!"

"I am here only to discuss your grievances and end the bloodshed. You see that I'm alone and unarmed," Holt reasoned, and he held his open palms into the air for all those watching to see. More men began to slowly filter from the surrounding buildings, and he knew he had their attention. "You wish to be free of the queen's rule and the laws of Aquis. Very well, I am here to offer you that freedom in peace."

"And how would you do that, dog?" boomed the Northman.

"Let's meet in peace here in the temple at noon tomorrow, and I will present the queen's offer. You need only listen to me, and then you may kill me if you wish. I'll die having done my duty, but I don't think that'll happen," Holt replied.

"I lead here," the Northman said with arrogance. "I will meet with you now."

"No. I will meet with all of your people tomorrow. At noon."

"Why?" asked the red haired man, his head tilting slightly in suspicion.

"Because it's about freedom. Your people joined you for freedom from Queen Erella, did they not? Then they all deserve the freedom of hearing what She offers."

The Northman looked about the gathered people and knew he had lost. Several dozen had come out of hiding to listen to the soldier's words, and many whispered enthusiastically amongst themselves, while others nodded. He had raised this rabble with talks of freedom and had now lost control of them due to the same words coming from the mouth of a soldier of Aquis. He sighed deeply.

"Very well. We will meet you at noon tomorrow," he said, turning back into his home and slamming the door.

Holt turned his horse and rode back the way he had come, the three armed farmers parting to allow him passage. Once out of the village, he rode swiftly a rather circuitous path back to the grove hiding his wagon. Once there, he removed his armor and waited patiently. When the Northman crept, sword ready, into the grove just after nightfall, Holt neatly skewered the man with two arrows to the chest, and as he lay dying, gasping for breath as blood filled his lungs when Holt severed his head from his body.

Holt managed only a few hours of sleep, and he felt exhausted and ragged when the morning sun lit up his world. He wasted little time in breakfasting and donning his chainmail. He rode into the village well before midday, having left his wagon behind holding the body of a red haired man that now collected flies. He was the first to the temple, and he tied his horse to a fence nearby and went in to wait.

The people began to arrive just before noon, slowly filtering in and then arriving in groups. Holt counted nearly forty, and more still straggled in one or two at a time. The absence of their leader did not go unnoticed, and some left to search for him. Many implored Holt to talk, to present the queen's offer, but Holt curtly refused, saying, "I will when everyone is present. I'll not have Her words repeated second hand." The search for the Northman turned up nothing, and the people began to whisper that perhaps he had deserted them. Finally, Holt stood up before the assembly.

"Outside of the Northman, is everyone here?" he asked, and the searching glances, nods and whispered comments answered his question. "Very well, one moment as I must retrieve something from my saddle bag. I believe you will all be most relieved."

Holt strode up the center aisle and pushed his way out of the temple's front doors. Once outside, he sprinted to his horse and removed the items he needed to finish his mission. He returned to the doors just as a farmer who had just yesterday menacingly brandished a pitchfork opened them. The man looked over the chain, flint, and torch in Holt's arms, and his eyes widened in understanding just as Holt planted a swift and heavy kick into his groin. The farmer doubled over and fell to the ground moaning as the assembled people stood at once in surprise, and Holt quickly dropped his load and roughly threw him back inside. He slammed the doors shut and wrapped the chain around the pulls as tightly as he could. Just as the people inside began to pull and push at the doors, he slid the lock home through several of the chain's links.

He walked around the perimeter of Garod's temple, torch in hand and set small, loose brush aflame. He had spent the previous night placing random and inconspicuous enough debris right up against the temple's exterior walls and then dousing it and the walls in the whale oil, which was expensive but highly effective. Holt had also crept inside and painted whale oil on the inside walls, rafters and in rows across the floor. The loose brush caught immediately, and flames climbed the walls almost before he could blink. It was mere minutes before the flames spread inside, and he heard the cries and screams of those trapped inside, mostly men but not all. They realized too late that the rear doors were already chained shut, and all of the lower windows were shuttered and sealed tightly with Holt's glue.

A few found a way to reach one of the upper windows, easily twenty feet above the ground. They thought they could escape by bursting through and falling to the ground. They discovered they were wrong as the first man received an arrow to the chest and fell back into the temple; a lifelong soldier, Holt was a skilled marksman. He had brought two full quivers and consistently hit his marks. One peasant was lucky enough to drop to the ground, having stayed low to avoid Holt's arrows, but there was an awful wet snapping sound when he landed next to the blazing temple. This one Holt approached and ran through with his longsword.

Holt silently begged Garod for forgiveness as he retreated from the heat. He no longer heard a clamor from inside, and as he watched thick black smoke pour from the broken windows, he knew no more would attempt escape. He heard a soft tread of running feet and turned to see a small girl, no more than seven or eight, running south through the village away from the burning temple. Swearing softly, Holt notched an arrow and drew back his bowstring.

23.

"Will you need an honor guard?" Thom asked.

Cor sat with Thyss and Fort Haldon's commander as they ate a midday meal in Dahken Hall, or at least what was very quickly becoming Dahken Hall. The room was still open to the outdoors, and a hot sun shone down on them. The workers had finished the foundation and floor and had begun building a skeletal structure around and above with heavy timbers. Just a few weeks ago, Cor felt as if the construction made no noticeable progress, but now he knew that the hall would be done in a matter of weeks.

"No," Cor answered. "I can take care of myself."

"Lord Dahken, in light of what happened when you first arrived here, I have an issue with you going alone."

"He won't be alone," Thyss said with a note of finality. As the spring season turned to an early summer, the sickness of her pregnancy disappeared, and it was replaced by a small but noticeable roundness about the lower part of her belly. Even still, she gingerly picked at her food for fear that she may suddenly become ill.

"I didn't think…" Cor began to say, but he stopped himself when he saw Thyss' blazing glare. "Can you ride?"

"I've been riding my entire life," she said hotly. "Don't think I'm going to let this stop me."

"I suppose I'm just wondering if it's safe."

"Lord Dahken," Thom intervened, "my wife has ridden her entire life including the several times she was with child. A midwife explained to me that if her body is used to such exercise, then there should be no concern." He looked at Thyss as he spoke, and her gaze softened toward him, perhaps in a show of gratitude.

"Very well," Cor said, sheepishly returning his attention to his food. He had known that Thyss wouldn't stay at Fort Haldon no matter what his reason, but he hadn't expected Thom to so soundly reason for her. It was just a trip to Byrverus for the gods' sakes.

"You still need a retinue, Lord Dahken, someone to watch your back."

Cor looked back up to meet Thom's insistent stare. "I will bring Dahken Keth along, and no doubt Marya will come with him. Between the four of us, we will be safe enough. We'll leave first thing in the morning."

"What would you have me do with the Dahken, the children?"

"Protect them," Cor answered. "I doubt we will be gone for much more than a month. Its been a long time since they've been able to be just children."

After eating, Cor went off in search of Keth, as he had not yet informed the younger Dahken of the summons back to Byrverus. Of course, everyone knew what it was about, but Cor didn't let it concern him too much. Keth was not at the training yards, likely having already dismissed the children as the day grew hotter. He made his way to the Dahken barracks, a building that would become obsolete as the hall and its surrounding rooms were completed. Passing the guardsmen outside, he found the interior full of his Dahken children, some slept, some ate, and others played various games. Many of them looked up as he entered, and in seeing him, approached him for an embrace or a kind word.

"Do you know where Dahken Keth is?" he asked them.

"In his room, I think," one boy said.

Cor made to leave but thought better of it. The children had very little exposure to him since they came to Fort Haldon months ago, spending almost all their time with Rael and then Keth. Cor knew that Marya had taken on the role of teacher to some extent as well, leaving him wholly to deal with the grander matters of Fort Haldon. Looking around at over a dozen gray skinned children, Cor reminded himself he must be Lord of the Dahken as much as Lord of Fort Haldon. As such, he spent well over an hour just talking and spending time with them.

After the assassination attempt, the barracks had been designed with four separate suites adjoined to the main room. Suite was perhaps too grand a description, as they were little more than a small cell of a bedroom with a slightly larger general purpose room attached. Originally, Cor and Thyss, Keth, Rael, and Geoff had occupied them, but with the latter two now gone Marya and Celdon had moved into the two vacant sets of rooms.

As Cor knocked on Keth's door, he suspected that if he found the younger Dahken inside, he would not find him alone. After a moment, the door opened revealing Keth's form. He wore a simple tunic and trousers, having clearly changed clothes after the training session, and Cor could see his discarded armor and undergarments on the floor behind him. Keth stood in the doorway as if to bar entrance into the room beyond, and his questioning face changed to a look of surprise when he saw Cor before him.

"Lord Dahken," he said, "I didn't expect you."

"There's something we need to talk about," Cor said as he entered, Keth reluctantly moving aside. He stood over Keth's discarded armor and sweat soaked garments, and he hazarded a quick glance toward the bedroom. Seeing nothing, he turned and said, "You really should take more care with your armor."

"I know, Lord Dahken. Today was hot; I was rushing to get out of it," Keth hurriedly explained, and Cor could see a worried look on his face, perhaps guilt as well.

Cor waived it away. "It doesn't matter. Keth, I've been called to Byrverus."

Keth released a breath he didn't know he had been holding. "This is about that priest, isn't it?"

"I'm sure. I leave tomorrow with Thyss," he said. "You're my right hand, I need you to come with me."

"Of course, I am yours, but wouldn't it be better if I stay here with the Dahken?"

"No," Cor disagreed, very subtly shaking his head. "Thom will watch over them for us, and I trust him completely. But I need someone to watch over me and Thyss, and for that, I trust you completely. We'll breakfast at sunup and leave for Byrverus within the hour," Cor concluded, heading toward the door.

"Very well, Lord Dahken," Keth said as he moved from Cor's path.

"Keth, there's one other thing," Cor said in a hushed tone just as he passed back into the hot afternoon sun. "As a friend, not as Lord Dahken – please be careful with Marya. I know the two of you have grown far closer than an ordinary teacher and student, but she's little more than a child."

"Nor am I," Keth replied.

"Perhaps, but just make sure whatever happens is what she wants as well as you. See you both in the morning."

As Cor turned and stalked back the way he had come, Keth stood in the doorway and stared after the Lord Dahken. He closed the door behind him and leaned hard against it, once banging his head on the hardwood while staring at the ceiling. He heard a rustling from his sleeping area, and looking up, he saw

Marya's slender form standing in its doorway with a thin wool blanket wrapped tightly about her body and tucked under her arms.

"I guess I'm glad I disposed of my armor in here," she said.

Keth sighed. "He knew you were here."

"Does it matter?" she asked, approaching him.

"Probably not," he muttered, shifting his gaze to his feet.

"Then why do you sulk like your father just caught you with your hand in a honey pot?" She was close to him now. As she leaned up against him, he scented the sweat she'd worked up during their exercises. He looked down into her face, kissed her, and forgot about Lord Dahken Cor.

After, Marya lay on her side with Keth wrapped around her as he snored softly in her ear. She wondered if it were normal for a man to simply drift off to sleep, as Keth had done all three times, whereas she simply wanted to bathe. She was no longer scared of the act, as she terribly was the first time, and in fact was starting to find it pleasurable. Most certainly, it was painful as well, but Keth had taught her how to turn her pain into strength while using a sword. Apparently, it worked the same way during the act of love, and the result nearly shattered both of their senses.

Marya elbowed Keth in the stomach, and his snoring came to an end with a sputtering snort.

"What was that for?" he asked as he flipped onto his back.

"I'm going with you tomorrow," she said.

"I know that and so does Cor."

"Good."

Marya sat up and swung her legs over the side of the mattress that sat on a solid wood platform, allowing the blanket to fall off her. Keth's eyes traced her spine from the base of her neck and down her back to her buttocks. As she stood, Marya was aware of a somewhat uncomfortable wetness between her upper thighs – third time and the aftermath still disgusted her. She began to dress, first by pulling on her underclothes that had mostly dried but now held a somewhat salty stench. She then clasped and buckled on her armor. It was a mix of gray steel plates and gleaming rings, specifically modified to fit her petite, five foot form. The armorer grumbled as he worked it, complaining that she would only grow out of it, not to mention that armor was not meant for a woman. Honestly, as he watched her encase herself in steel, Keth was certain it only made her more beautiful.

"Get up you lump," Marya spat, vehemently striking the mattress' platform with her boot. "We got things to do if we're leaving these kids behind."

Keth stretched, sighed, and climbed from the bed.

Once out of the foothills near the Spine, the Aquis countryside in the early summer was exactly as Cor remembered it as a boy. The roads led through lush, green grasslands and prairies, around bountiful farms, and through quaint villages filled with the sounds of every day life. Cor sighed as he watched people go about their duties, and more than once he wished for the simplicity of a farmer's life, even though he knew Thyss would have none of that. The weather was warm and generally clear, but several times they were caught in a sudden storm, full of thunder and huge, pelting raindrops the likes of which were common to Aquis this time of year.

Often, they slept under the stars, favoring the outdoors any time the weather was fair, as opposed to the occasional small inn or the queen's wayside outposts. It was better that way, Thom had reasoned, as

Cor had clearly made some enemies in Losz, Aquis, or both, and it would help minimize the risk of the small party being trapped indoors for would be assassins. Thom asked one more time to send an honor guard for added protection, and Cor again refused.

Before they left, Keth had all the Dahken assemble to breakfast together; it surprised Cor at first, but when it was all over, he had been happy Keth had done so. It allowed them all to enjoy a few minutes together before the four departed Fort Haldon and assure the others that they would be back soon. After the meal, Keth pulled the pudgy Celdon aside and explained to him that as the oldest, he was to oversee keeping the Dahken on schedule. However, Cor waived it away and told the boy to simply help Thom keep track of everyone; there would be plenty of time for training and learning when they came back.

As the four checked their horses for adequate supplies, Cor couldn't help but notice that Keth and Marya brought only one bedroll between them. He sighed deeply, setting his jaw with clenched teeth; it did not anger him as much as it just created another complication. Before leaving, he quietly attempted to broach the subject with Thyss.

"So, what," she had said. It was a statement, not a question, making her thoughts clear.

"Its just that, well," Cor stammered, suddenly wondering why it bothered him so. "They're very young."

To this she laughed heartily, making no attempt to quiet herself and said, "Surely when you were their age you had some village strumpet you were ravishing nightly!"

"When I was their age, I was either sailing the Narrow Sea with a huge Shet captain or learning about myself from an old, bitter man in a broken, old castle."

"Dahken Cor, the fable your life has become from the meager beginnings of a peasant farm boy, and you're worried about two people who've learned what it is to fuck?" she said, and her candor surprised him as it often did. "It is what it is. It's been happening for thousands of years, and it'll keep happening."

"I think it is a little more complex than that," he said.

"Oh," she said in a most drawn out fashion, "I think you're afraid she is more loyal to Keth than you. Think on this Dahken Cor – leaders inspire loyalty. When you led the Dahken from Losz, they followed you without question. Since we've come to Fort Haldon, you've been too busy managing all this to lead them." The last she said with a grand circular motion of her left hand at all of the activity around them.

Cor wished he had never brought it up to her. He should have known how she would respond, and her blunt way of putting things always left him feeling somewhat sheepish. She was right of course; there was nothing he could do about it, nor should it bother him. He was sure that eventually one of two things would happen – either Marya would be forced to choose between her Lord Dahken and her young lover, or as they grew older, the love would grow stale and sour to push the two of them apart irrevocably. Eventually either way, Cor would lose control of the situation.

Why did he need to control them? The question bothered him, weighed on him heavily, and Cor spent the first several days of their ride in near total silence.

They were over halfway to their destination when Cor decided they had little choice but to find a place to stay indoors. They had endured two days of soaking rain in warm, muggy air. On the first day, the water worked its way through the cracks of overlapping steel armor and into the wool underneath, causing their skin to pale and chaff. The constant and steady rain turned the road to mud, and the horses slogged through it in a most despairing manner. Eventually even Thyss grew soaked and miserable, unable to continue warming her body to ward off the wetness, and they camped the night in a nearby orchard Cor had seen from the road. It seemed too well kept to be wild, but no one disturbed or threatened their attempt at repose. The trees provided a degree of shelter from the incessant rain, and they laid their blankets and bedrolls underneath them on the ground. It was a miserable, sleepless night for the four of them, and they were ready to keep moving when the sky lit up just enough to see that they would have no respite from the dark gray clouds.

It was a village that offered them protection from the weather, and they came upon it shortly after midday, at least so it seemed as the only way to tell time was by the grumbling of their stomachs. It was little different from any other village in Aquis, except to say it was larger than most as per its proximity to Byrverus, and as such it had a seemingly sizeable inn close to its center. Cor pulled Kelli to a halt as he stared at the building – a gray stone edifice with an oak door, shingled roof and a few lead paned windows. He then looked northwest for several slow heartbeats, as though he could see Byrverus at this distance, and then dismounted.

"Stay here," he said as he removed his helm, "while I make sure they have enough room for us and the horses."

Inside was little different than he expected with a large common room that was stiflingly hot due to its two roaring fires. There were an even dozen tables in the middle of the room, all of them vacant, with a bar opposite the fires. Here was the only sign of occupancy with a man behind the bar, refilling drinks with a bored expression for the few patrons that sat there, all of whom appeared to be local farmers and such.

"Wut ya' need, lord?" the bartender asked, eyeing Cor's black armor and sword.

"My companions and I seek hospitality. We require two rooms, stabling for four horses and plenty of room to dry ourselves out."

"I 'xpect ya' got coin then," the bartender said warily.

An apparently heavy purse allaying his concerns of Cor's monetary situation, the proprietor busied himself with making sure appropriate rooms were ready and dispatching a hand to take care of the mounts. Cor retrieved the others from the soggy weather, and they immediately moved their important belongings into the awaiting rooms. The Dahken stripped themselves of their armor, and they returned to the common room to stretch out before the substantial fires to dry their soaked clothes and blankets. It was too warm in the year for fires of such size for anything other than cooking, but Cor was glad for them now.

They sat and lay about the common room languidly, slowly drying out and dozing in and out of sleep, and no one bothered them, as it seemed this inn was not particularly busy. None of them noticed one of the men at the bar as he watched them closely, and nor would they for he was excellent at his job. After a few more hours of practiced drinking of spirits that looked more potent than they actually were, the apparent farmer paid and seemed to stagger from the inn. Neither Thyss nor the Dahken saw as he retrieved a horse from the stables and galloped northwest out of town.

Holt awoke from his dream calmly, almost begrudging that he lived another day to serve Aquis. For years, he had woken up in a fright, sweating profusely and sometimes even shouting as he did so, but now he had become so used to his nightmare, his memory, that it was just a matter of course. As he sat up and considered the rising sun with squinting red eyes, Holt knew that he hated Palius. In fact, he hated himself and everything he had done over the years. His one comfort was that he had done it all for Queen Erella, and Garod would forgive him the multitude of sins when it was his time to be judged.

He couldn't even remember the village's name.

Holt pushed himself out of the bed in which he'd slept and stretched, feeling several twinges and cramps begin to work themselves out. Whether they were from his steadily advancing age or from having slept in a strange bed he neither knew nor cared. He dressed himself in a simple, light wool tunic and breeches and belted his sword about his waist while staring at the new armor he'd bought in Byrverus. It was plain and unadorned steel plate – a hauberk and legguards. Holt had left his real armor behind in the barracks so as to avoid anyone connecting this operation with the queen or Aquis. He went down into the noisy lower level of the inn to eat and see if Marek had yet arisen.

He found the lean, wiry man in the common room with his back in a corner eating as he watched the door to the inn. Also on the table was a second plate, this one still stocked with fried pork sausage, eggs, and a hunk of bread. Holt sat across from his murdering companion and systematically began clearing his plate. He wasn't really hungry, but he had learned long ago to eat when food was available.

"I went ahead and ordered you breakfast, Sergeant."

"How many times I have to tell you?" Holt asked in his gravelly voice without looking up from his food. "I'm just Holt for now. How close are we to being ready?"

"As soon as you're done eating, milord. They're all here now."

"What?" Holt asked, his mouth full of grease soaked bread. He looked around the common room and saw men of all sorts across the room breakfasting, many of them armed. In fact, he counted about a score in all. "Do we have enough? These people are hard to kill, I hear."

"There are only four," Marek said, answering his own question.

"You are sure? And you are sure that we're on the right road?"

Marek sighed and leaned back in his chair, staring at the ceiling for several breaths while Holt merely gazed at him and chewed. Marek dropped his chair to the floor and leaned forward. "Look, I'm a professional. I placed several good men on the three most likely routes from Fort Haldon. They come this way, and there are four of them – three with gray skin and the woman.

"I'm surprised that a lord and lady would travel with so little protection, even if they're as deadly as these two are claimed to be," Holt grumbled, unconvinced. "What if others join them along the way?"

"We'll have advance warning of any changes. Besides, I'm not worried about a few peasants turned soldier. These men here are the best professional soldiers money can buy."

"Mercenaries. Larnd -"

Marek cut him off with a loud coughing fit, spraying Holt's plate with crumbs. He made quite a show of regaining his breath, followed by a long, deep drink of not the clearest water. After being sure that no one paid them any mind, or at least no one other than the men they had hired, the black haired Marek said, "Don't talk anymore. Yes, they're all here. Yes, that's how fast we move. Yes, they're ready to fight, and they know some will die. But none of them think they'll be the ones. Frankly, I think the whole damn business is stupid and foolhardy, 'cause we don't really know how many we'll have to fight, and we know one of 'em breathes fire or something. I think my brother is blinded by that whole chest of gold we carted away from the old man for the job. I'd just as soon say forget it, but I'm contracted now. So shut up, eat your breakfast, and let's go."

The old soldier stared at the murderer, locking eyes for a long moment, partially in disbelief at the man's candor. For a moment, anger that a lowly criminal would dare speak to him in such a way roared in Holt's mind, and he weighed the consequences of breaking the man's jaw. Finally, Holt's eyes cleared, and he went back to his food with nothing else to say on the matter. The mission was the most important thing. As he finished his meal and pushed the plate away with a belch, Marek stood from the table and leisurely made his way for the inn's exit. Holt quickly followed, and as they passed, armed men followed suit one after the other. After a few minutes, only a few Westerners and one Northman remained to look about in surprise at the now empty common room.

24.

Holt, Marek, and their mercenaries had holed up in a barn just off the main road that eventually connected Fort Haldon to Byrverus. They paid the farmer well for his hospitality and discretion, with a sum easily worth a year's harvest. Of course, he politely refused at first, a refusal that changed abruptly when coin was produced in great quantity, and Holt promised that they would not impose upon his family for long. It was there they waited on the evening of a second full day of rain when one of their watchers returned with news.

"Perfect," Marek said to his scout. "The weather should break by tomorrow, and they'll ride straight to us. Did you see a suitable place?"

"Suitable place for what?" Holt asked, his voice the dulcet tone of two rocks being ground together.

Marek turned to look at Holt for a moment, exasperation plain on his face. "What don't you get? A place to ambush them."

"No," Holt said, shaking his head. He ran his hand up his jaw and found it covered with rough white stubble, as he hadn't shaved in days.

"What?" Marek asked incredulously.

"We come at them directly."

"What?" Marek again asked. He looked around to see the men staring, waiting. He tapped the old soldier on his shoulder and said, "Step outside with me a minute."

The day grew dark as the sun neared the horizon, though it could not be seen for the great dark clouds that hung overhead spilling their contents. It was definitely warm, and the constant rain added a horribly humid element to the air and a general feeling of misery to those who stood in it. As they exited the barn, their feet squished and sank into the waterlogged mud, which sought to work its way into their boots.

"We ambush them. They won't stand a chance. I have heard stories of these grave colored people, and there is three of them plus the fire witch."

"It is time for you to listen to me," Holt said, and his face was as hard and constant as chiseled stone. "I have done terrible things in service to my country, my god, and my lord, Palius. He dies now, and this will likely be the last thing he ever asks of me. Upon his passing, I will retire from the queen's ranks to some quiet countryside in the West, hopefully to pass soon myself. I will not have my last act under his command be carried out with shame or dishonor. We fight them face to face, with live steel only - no bows, no poison, just the metal of our trade. We fight for Garod and Aquis, and we will be victorious."

"You are set on this, are you old man?" Marek asked rhetorically as he rubbed his eyes. "More men will die than is necessary."

"I am set upon this course," Holt said. He then added, "What do you care? The more who die increases the size of your share."

At this, Marek dropped his hands limply. He looked into Holt's eyes for a moment and then looked through the rain across the farmer's field. With nothing else to say, the two men returned to the dry of the barn.

Upon close inspection, the inn was not the cleanest of establishments, having been overrun by all sorts of pests due to general ill use. Rats moved around the walls and in the corners of the main room, even brazenly crossing it in plain view after a fallen morsel of food. The buckets used for chamber pots had been dumped though not cleaned regularly and had a foul odor from the buildup of human waste. The straw mattresses were full of fleas and lice, and the stables were even worse. Even still, the three Dahken and the woman from Dulkur slept deeply, almost as if dead, and they somehow ignored the filth when faced with the prospect of another night in the rain.

Cor rose slowly, deliberately savoring the pure sunlight that showed through the windows as the storms had finally passed in the middle of the night. Realizing how fair was the weather, he felt a sudden need to leave the inn behind, and he woke the others. He pushed them into motion, and they gathered their now dry belongings. He breakfasted faster than the others, eating quickly to move on to the task of making sure the horses were well kept and ready, and within the hour they rode away from the village and its inn.

They were not far down the road when they spotted a group of men approaching on foot. At a distance, Cor could see little except the glint of steel, but as they grew closer, it was plainly obvious they were fighting men. Under cloaks and concealing robes, he caught glimpses of sword hilts and armor, and while they did not seem to form a cohesive unit, they still marched as fighters. Perhaps a hundred feet away, Cor counted about a score of them, seemingly led by a picturesque, grizzled veteran. He pulled Kelli to a halt.

"Dismount. Now," he ordered as he swung out of his saddle. "We approach them on foot. Leave the horses to graze."

"Lord Dahken?" Keth questioned.

"I've never learned to fight on horseback. Have you?" He watched as Keth surveyed the approaching men and grimaced, meanwhile a slight and mischievous smile crossed Marya's face. Both she and Thyss quickly dismounted with nothing to say.

"You expect a fight then," Keth said as he followed suit.

"I'd rather expect a fight and not have one then have one and not expect it."

They approached slowly together, in no hurry to cross the distance. The approaching men did not slow or falter when their prey dismounted, and they halved the distance. The men had no heraldic symbols on their armor or shields, for those who carried them, and Cor somehow doubted this was an escort to Byrverus. He suddenly realized he had left his helm attached to Kelli's saddle, and he had to fight every instinct to run back to her for it. No doubt such an action would only spur on whatever was about to happen.

"You two stay together," he said calmly and in a hushed tone. "Protect each other."

"Who's going to protect you?" asked Keth.

"I'll protect all three of you," Thyss whispered from behind them, and Cor smiled despite what approached them.

They came to a stop perhaps fifteen feet from the oncoming men, who also stopped and formed a line that measured eight men across. More filed out from behind this line and formed two more lines on either side of the wide road, essentially boxing in Cor's party, though the rear was still open to them. Cor noted that, but he was sure they would be unable to make a run for it before the sides of the box closed in upon them.

"Lord Dahken Cor?" asked the old warrior directly in front of him. The man's voice was rough, grating, and he carried himself like a professional soldier.

"I am," Cor answered strongly, working hard to control both his voice and his muscles as they tensed for battle. There was something else – a low sound in his ears that added to his anxiety, and he noted absently that his right hand was clenched so solidly that it hurt. He forced himself to release the fist. "Who are you, and why have you stopped us?"

"Who I am, we are, doesn't matter, my lord. All that matters is that we've come before you to draw steel, to fight honorably. Your death, and the death of your companions, is our task. Now, join us in battle."

The leader, the white haired and bearded soldier, drew his sword, and all his compatriots also readied their various weapons. However, none of them approached, but simply watched and waited for Cor to also move. Perhaps they were under orders as such. Cor placed his hands on Soulmourn's hilt and Ebonwing's handle, feeling great comfort in their presence against his palms, but he hesitated. There were so many to fight, and he had no doubt they were all true warriors, professional fighters, and killers.

Learn to be of action, he heard Naran say.

Cor pulled his weapons and charged headlong to his left. It only made sense – Keth and Marya stood to his right, and Thyss would no doubt buy him a few precious seconds. As he crashed into his first opponents, the roar of flames and a sense of heat to his right rewarded his judgment. He dared not pull his eyes from those in front of him, but Cor knew that Thyss was in action. He could hear the clang of steel and shouts of battle behind him. He fought seven men with the foolhardiness of a crazed man, ignoring blows and dealing his own to those before him, to his left, and right. His blood flowed; he knew it, but he also knew that he let their blood in greater amounts than his own. As he felt his wounds give him strength, Soulmourn sang through the air, rending armor and cleaving limbs. Cor lost his senses in the chaos, allowing Soulmourn and Ebonwing to guide him as much as he controlled them. Men screamed in agony and frustration at this black armored demon that simply would not die, no matter how hard or often they struck him.

Having never been in battle before, the two younger Dahken hesitated as Cor attacked, fraught with indecision. Keth recovered just in time to parry an incoming attack and dodge another from a great, two handed mace. Marya was slower to react, and she was saved only by intervention by Thyss and a flash of her green saber. Thyss cut the legs out from under a man who laughed as he approached Marya, but in so doing, she nearly lost control of the blazing inferno she had invoked to shield them from six of their attackers. It didn't seem that Keth and Marya could hold their own against veteran warriors, barely able to defend themselves from blow after blow, but the hired killers did not understand the nature of their prey. Rather than go for the kill, they toyed with the young Dahken as a cat may toy with a mouse. As they wounded the Dahken, their blows were returned with doubled strength that rent through their armor and blades.

The others had split up and were now coming around the fiery barrier, just as Cor moved in on the last warrior on his side of the road. Thyss looked upon him in astonishment, just long enough to lose concentration, and the wall of flame dissipated as quickly as it had appeared. The young Dahken, bloodied and fighting more by instinct than skill, still faced three armored men, and three more rushed to join the battle.

The final three moved in to attack Cor from behind, who was drenched in both his own blood and that of his enemies, but he seemed unwounded by the time he thrust his sword cleanly through the steel breastplate of his last foe. Unable to aid Keth and Marya with fire lest she harm them as well, Thyss bowed forward and blew into her open hand as if blowing a kiss, and blue flames roared from her to engulf those who would attack her lover. Two died quickly and horribly, completely drenched in flame, and the third, a man protected by all black boiled leather as opposed to steel, turned away just in time to have only his left side ablaze. He dropped off the side of the road, screaming as he rolled across the still wet ground.

Cor turned just in time to see this happen, and he instantly reassessed the situation. With over a dozen men dead or dismembered, only six of their attackers remained, and Cor had little doubt that he and Thyss alone could dispatch the rest. Thyss already engaged with her sword, fighting alongside Marya, but she was too evenly matched with her opponent. This left Keth facing down four battle hardened fighters, including the old soldier who was their leader.

Cor sprinted across the road, and intent on causing as much confusion as possible, he collided with a crash of steel into the nearest of Keth's attackers. The two men went down together, taking out the legs of another, and the three ended up in a pile of arms, legs, and steel. Cor found himself dazed by his brash maneuver, having hit his unprotected head on one of the warriors sabatons. He rose shakily, trying to lift the fog from his mind, and found that only one of the men was moving, the other seemingly unconscious. His chainmail clad combatant was on his hands and knees, about to stand, and Cor brought Soulmourn down neatly upon the back of his neck. The chainmail may as well have been wool for all the protection it provided its wearer from Cor's blade.

Cor whipped himself around at the sound of a woman's scream full of anger and horror, and he saw Keth impaled through and through upon the old man's longsword. He'd aimed his weapon perfectly below Keth's chestpiece, and thick crimson blood and bits of innards dripped off the point that protruded from Keth's back. The scream had come from Marya, who stood still in shock. His head now clear, Cor moved toward the soldier, who yanked his sword free of Keth's abdomen and turned to face the new threat. Green steel flashed in the sunlight, and the older man's swordarm fell to the ground, blood spurting from the stump of his arm that was severed just above the elbow. Full of vengeance and hatred, Cor rammed Soulmourn through Holt's steel plate hauberk, instantly cleaving the man's heart in two. As they stood with their faces mere inches apart, Cor watched as a sense of peace, even gratitude, came over the old soldier's face before he faded into death.

As the body fell to its knees, Cor kicked it off his sword in disgust.

Keth lay in the road, his blood mixing with the brown mud, and Marya pressed her bare hands upon his stomach as if she could staunch the bleeding with them only. He breathed with great difficulty, and it seemed that he could not speak. His face was a visage of suffering as his body trembled, and Cor knew it was a mortal wound. If only Keth had been able to repay the blow, his body would have likely healed enough of the wound for him to survive. Cor kneeled next to his dying Dahken.

"We can do nothing for him," Thyss said, standing over them. Her body was covered with the sweat and gore of battle, but Cor could see tears forming in the corners of her eyes.

"I can save him," Marya whispered as she cried, tears streaming down her face and dropping to mix with Keth's blood.

"I'm sorry Marya, but no you can't," Cor said gently, and he placed his left hand over hers.

"Shut up!" she screamed at him. She choked back sobs and shook off Cor's hand, and she looked back to Keth and said softly, "I *can* save you. Let me do this."

Keth shook his head weakly but insistently, mouthing a word over and over. He looked at Cor, pleading for help, but Cor had no idea what he was supposed to do or not do. Marya pulled one hand away from his wound and placed it softly on his cheek to still his head, leaving a smeared bloody handprint across it. She kissed him gently on the lips, and then without warning slit her palm open widely upon her dagger; blood flowed freely from the flesh that was opened all the way to the bones of her hand. She then pushed her hand heavily against Keth's ruined belly, and he screamed in bloodcurdling agony. Cor thought to pull her away from Keth, but something held him back. She laid her forehead on his chest as he continued to scream, a scream that grew stronger as he started to breathe easier.

After a few seconds, he quieted and his eyes closed, and Marya slumped against him, as the wind carried Keth's scream across the plains. They lay unmoving, apparently asleep. Cor reached for Marya's hand and, in lifting it, found both of their wounds completely gone without a trace.

"What in Hykan's name just happened?" Thyss asked, still standing over them.

"I have no idea."

25.

"Dahken Cor, I must say that you never cease to amaze me," Thyss said as they sat around a fireless camp. This far from the mountains, the warmth of the oncoming summer was plainly apparent, and with Thyss' abilities, there was no need for a fire with which to cook. Besides, one attacker, the man armored in black leather had escaped, and Cor felt no need to draw attention to themselves in case another attempt was imminent.

After the battle, they searched the dead and found no sign as to who they were or who had sent them. They were professionals to be sure, as not one of them had lost their composure in battle or indicated a fear of defeat even as their brethren were cut down around them, but their origins were completely unknown. All except for one – the old man, everything about him and his sense of honor, screamed professional soldier or even lord. It was his grizzled face Cor inspected when he heard the slight moan of the one he'd knocked unconscious. Before he could stop her, Thyss neatly skewered the man's skull on her sword.

With no clues, they collected the horses and carried their unconscious companions across an empty, overgrown field to the tree line in the distance. It was hard work on a hot afternoon, and many times they twisted ankles or nearly fell on the uneven ground. It took far longer than Cor had anticipated, and it seemed as they walked, they got no closer to the shelter of oaks and elms. The trees only grew taller. As they finally dragged their feet into the trees' shadows in exhaustion, it was clear that this was an ancient, primeval forest with members that were hundreds of years old. Like many such forests, there was a noted absence of underbrush, as the large trees choked out most of the smaller plants in competition for nutrients from the soil. The place was full of the sounds of wildlife, as well as other sounds that Cor wished not to contemplate, and following the faint hint of flowing water, they found a small freshwater stream by which they made camp.

"I'm not sure what you mean," Cor responded.

"You are a juggernaut among men, wholly unstoppable in battle, and for some reason I do not yet comprehend, people listen to you. They do as you will and command." She paused as she lifted her eyes to his face. "And yet you know almost nothing of your race, what the Dahken are capable of or how the gods rule this world."

"I was raised a Westerner under the watchful eye of the priests," he explained with a defensive tone in his voice. "When I ran from home, I fell in with a big Shet from Tigol - a sea captain that worshipped no gods and relied on no one but himself and his crew. I only first learned of the Dahken four years ago, I think? Thousands of years of Dahken history were lost when Taraq'nok destroyed Sanctum. The only tie to it, the only source of knowledge I had was Rael, and he's dead."

"And that is also something I wonder about," she said reflectively shifting her gaze into the canopy overhead.

"You wonder if he's dead?" Cor asked. "You said yourself that the gods could rarely interact with Rumedia to that degree. I think its safe to assume Rael is not coming back this time."

"I'm not sure he ever came back," Thyss said quietly, and Cor stared at her in confusion. She cut him off just as he opened his mouth to speak. "I never knew him before, but I'm not sure that was the man you knew."

"I don't understand, Thyss. That was Rael. Everything about him was the same - the same personality, the way he talked, the way he taught the Dahken. He seemed to hold against you the same things he held against all women," Cor said.

This brought a glance as sharp as daggers from Thyss, and she sat up to face him. "You told me a bit of Lord Dahken Rael. You told me of a man who ate well and drank red wine often. How often do you remember him doing those things when he came back? Should I mention that when we first found him, he didn't even know his own name? And what did Queen Erella say of him?"

Cor thought back to that day several months before. He remembered his confusion at the queen's words and responded, "She said that she didn't think he was a Dahken. She could see him, but it was as if he wasn't there."

"And the priests and priestesses of Garod can see into people, can see their lifeforces, for lack of a better word. It is one of the gifts from Garod that aids them to heal the sick. I assume she meant that she could see no such thing from Rael."

"So, what are you saying?" Cor asked with a deep sigh.

"I don't know what I'm saying for certain," she answered, causing Cor even more annoyance. "I wonder if perhaps Dahken Rael was not actually resurrected, but maybe a simulacrum, some sort of duplicate."

"Why would Dahk simply not resurrect Rael?"

"Because as I've told you before," Thyss said, Cor's annoyance now shifting to her, "the gods are not all powerful. It would be far less consuming for Dahk to do something like that than truly bring Rael back to life, especially, if Dahk only needed him to train the Dahken for you."

"If that's so," Cor reasoned, "then its very possible that Dahk may do it again."

"Unless He has other plans."

"Not that it matters, but how would we ever know for sure about Rael?" Cor asked.

"There's only one way that I can see," she answered. "We would need to find his tomb in the caved in ruin of Sanctum and see if his body is still within."

"Oh, that explains it then!" Cor nearly shouted, as though he had an epiphany. "Rael told us how he pushed his way out of the tomb and climbed his way out of the ruins."

"Leave the understanding of magic to me, Dahken," Thyss responded harshly. "It settles nothing. If Dahk were to copy Rael, in both form and mind, I assume the copy would have to come from Rael's actual body. The copy would likely have completely ignored the image of itself laying in repose as if in a dream. I imagine that the doppelganger would be similar to the real person, but somehow a shadow, incomplete."

"It really doesn't matter, does it?" Cor asked.

"No," she agreed. "A magical curiosity and that is all. How long do we wait here?"

"Until they awaken," he answered, motioning at the two unconscious Dahken. They breathed softly and did not move, though their hearts sounded strong within their breasts, and Cor hoped it would not be long.

A short Westerner with jet black hair and blue eyes strode through the plaza bordered by Garod's largest temple complex and the palace of Queen Erella. No one had ever seen him in this part of Byrverus, for he never left his den of thieves and murderers, but many of the persons whose eyes followed him knew his identity. He nimbly avoided all those who got in his way as if they were only inadvertent obstacles, and in his passing, they were only vaguely aware that someone had even been near them. He noticed everything and everyone about him, a valuable skill for staying alive when one was involved in his trade, including the priest Aidan, who stood on the steps of the temple complex watching. The short man, his agile form dressed head to toe in fine black and blue silks that hid wiry muscles strong as steel chains, walked purposefully into the palace's main hall, right past guards who stared dumbly after the person that they swore they just saw. He stood in the grand hall, contemplating which direction to go, before striding up to a pair of guards.

"Palius. Take me to him now," Larnd said.

"Umm, sir?" the guard stammered. "What business -"

"Shut up. For the sake of your family, take me to him now. No questions."

The guard winced, knowing that should his identity become known to the man, who was a king in his own right, the lives of those he loved most would in fact be forfeit. Without further statement or question, the guard turned on his heel and walked briskly down a series of corridors. As always two more men stood outside Palius' rooms, the advantage and curse of being someone of import, and as someone used to going where and when he willed, Larnd allowed himself entrance unannounced. Guards attempted to follow him, and he shot them a hard glance full of cold fire and death.

Once certain the doors were closed, Larnd sprinted silently to Palius' bed and launched himself to land astride the man's chest, waking him frightfully. Palius immediately launched into a coughing fit, phlegm and blood bespeckling his lips. Larnd had produced a razor sharp dagger, the blade of which left a thin red line on Palius' neck as he coughed, and he waited for Palius' paroxysm to abate before speaking.

"They are all dead, you stupid old shit," Larnd whispered dangerously. "Only one escaped, my brother, and he is maimed and scarred. He will never again be able to serve me. His livelihood is gone because of your intrigues."

"For what I paid you," Palius said through halting wheezes, "I think he should be comfortable for the rest of his life, considering you don't have to pay any of the others."

"You idiot!" Larnd rewarded Palius' statement with a hard slap to the face, and the old man's pale skin gained a healthy pink color for a moment in the shape of Larnd's palm and fingers. "This isn't just about him. Do you have any idea what damage you've done to me, to my reputation? Now, every little gang leader will challenge my authority. In their eyes, I've failed twice to eliminate a minor lord. This man, this Dahken Cor, is a demon incarnate. A thousand men could not kill him and the witch that is always with him.

"I refuse to have any more to do with it. I would kill you now in your bed for my trouble, except that I see you already die slowly and painfully. I will take satisfaction in that." Larnd's dagger disappeared into his silks, and he climbed off the old man to stand at his bedside. He leaned over to whisper in Palius ear, "I expect you will not live long enough to call on me again, but should the idea occur to you, I will end your life before this consumption claims you. My organization is done serving your crown."

Only a few people in the Shining West could make such a statement without reprisal or sanction, and Palius watched as one of them stormed through his door forever. Truth be told, no one really knew who Larnd was or where he was from, only that he controlled much of the criminal world of Byrverus. Palius wasn't even sure that Marek was truly his brother or if it was some sort of cutthroat euphemism. He sighed as he touched the thin line of blood that ran across the left side of his neck. Inspecting his fingers, he decided it was little worse than a cut from shaving.

"Sir, is everything -?" came a voice from his door, and Palius looked up to see one of the guards sticking his head through the door in concern.

"Yes," Palius said with a wave of his hand, the one without his blood on it, "I'm fine, thank you."

The guard closed the door, again leaving Palius with his thoughts. He pinched the bridge of his nose in quiet contemplation, and he found it difficult to think. The rumbling in his chest distracted him from focusing his mind, and it happened often lately. *A thousand men could not kill him and the witch*, Larnd had said. He'd exaggerated of course, but Palius understood the sentiment. Therefore, the solution was not just a mere thousand but in fact thousands. It was time for the Loszians to bring their horde through the Spine and crush Fort Haldon and the Dahken. It would appear as if Aquis' armies arrived just in time to stem the invasion and send it back into Losz. He thought over his next steps very carefully, waking himself as he began to snore.

He hadn't meant to doze off, and Palius was aggravated with himself for the weakness. He climbed from his bed and wobbled away across his bedroom to his disused desk, using the furniture to hold himself upright much as a baby first learning to walk. He crossed the final, perilous ten feet with nothing to hold onto and half sat, half fell into his hardwood chair, wheezing and coughing heavily. Palius bent over and yanked open the bottom drawer of the desk, sifting through stacks of mostly blank parchment scrolls until his hand closed on the cold, purple stone mirror.

He held it with the glass facing him and began to speak, "Sovereign Nadav, can you hear me?"

Palius paused for several minutes before asking again. He repeated the process several times and was about to quit when the disturbingly narrow face of the Loszian appeared in the mirror glass.

"What is it, old man?" the visage asked.

"While you have gathered your forces, I made another attempt to kill Lord Dahken Cor. The man has proved very resilient."

"Not as resilient as you, I see," Sovereign Nadav quipped with a sarcastic laugh. "I suspect you have mere weeks left in that sagging skin of yours. Do you think your blessed god will accept you at his side?"

Nadav's voice matched the sneer on his face, and Palius ignored it. "It doesn't matter, Sovereign. All that matters is that I serve my queen. I hope your army is nearly ready to attack Fort Haldon. Even if I die beforehand, I can make certain that our army arrives just in time to appear to prevent full scale invasion. In fact, we will crush the Dahken between our forces and annihilate them from the face of our world."

"Oh, fear not, my armies are very nearly ready. Over five thousand have already arrived at the rally point, and another twenty thousand should arrive within the next few weeks. All total, close to fifty thousand stand ready to invade before the summers end, assuming I wait long enough for them all to assemble," Nadav explained, and he wore a predatory smile.

"Sovereign, I believe that the five thousand should be more than adequate," Palius said confusedly. He sat staring at the emperor's wicked face before his eyes cleared, and Palius fully understood what the Loszian planned. "For the stability of our empires, I implore you not to do this. This is only about eliminating the Dahken threat. Sovereign -"

"Shut up!" Nadav snapped. "I will eliminate the Dahken threat, right before I retake all of the Shining West and rightfully enslave its people to Losz. This whole mess with the Dahken made me realize just how lazy my people have become, and we're now coming for what is ours."

"You would start a war that may destroy us both!" Palius nearly cried. "I will warn Her Majesty, and she shall rally all of the Shining West's peoples against you."

"And brand yourself a traitor?"

"If I must. My salvation shall be that one last act of loyalty. Perhaps I was wrong about Lord Dahken Cor," Palius mused. "No doubt he would lead our armies in battle."

"Let him come! I have my own Lord Dahken, and he wields power the likes of which your pitiful Cor has never seen," Nadav shouted arrogantly. He turned to look to his left as he said his next words. "Come boy, meet the architect responsible for the fall of the Shining West."

Nadav's image moved slightly to one side of the mirror as if to share it, and another form entered the glass from the right. He was indeed a boy, scarcely older than sixteen and relatively small of frame, dressed in silver silk finery like that of Nadav's. The boy had sharp features, rigid cheekbones, and a pointed chin with a hawk nose. His eyes carried large dark rings underneath them as if the boy hadn't slept in days, but his gray skin, the pallor of the grave, told Palius everything he needed to know about him.

Palius gasped and said quietly, "I recognize you. You were with Lord Dahken Cor here in Byrverus. He saved you from Losz."

"And now I have returned to Losz," the boy responded. "I am Lord Dahken Geoff, and the Dahken will follow me or die at my hands."

"And who do you serve?" Nadav asked, never taking his eyes from Palius' face.

"I serve Sovereign Nadav, Emperor of Losz and soon all of the west."

Palius knew his mouth hung open in shock, and shocked he was. For perhaps the first time in his life, he had no idea what to say, and he had neither a well thought out plan to place into action, nor a sudden reaction from his quick mind. He was utterly speechless, and Nadav chuckled softly while his Dahken smirked wickedly. Palius regained his senses and grunted as he flung the mirror across the room, watching it shatter satisfyingly against a stone wall. This possibility had never occurred to him, but why had it not? He should have known better. He should have known that a Loszian could never be trusted, much less the Loszian emperor. Blinded by his loyalty to Aquis and Queen Erella – nay, blinded by loyalty to their power – Palius may have just handed all the Shining West to the Loszian Empire.

He could not allow it to happen; if he confessed it all to Queen Erella now, she could mobilize in time to stop it. Also, any grievances she had with Lord Dahken Cor must be set aside immediately. Cor would be eager to fight the Loszians, even take the fight to them, and Queen Erella would need his strength. *By Garod,* Palius thought, *Dahken Cor was never the enemy*. Assuming his queen did not execute him for treason, Palius would also confess his deeds to Cor himself. Perhaps Garod would still accept him in death.

He stood from his desk and wheezed and coughed his way across his chambers to his main doors, his disused muscles screaming in agony with every step. Once there, he pushed one open to face the two men who constantly stood guard outside. "I need to see the queen. I implore you to find her and tell her Palius needs her. It is a matter of the utmost importance," he said. They searched his face for a moment, and one of the men turned and marched down the corridor.

Palius barely made it back to his bed without collapsing, and it was several minutes before his coughing subsided enough that he could breathe again. His mouth was dry and tasted of blood and mucous, and Palius prayed that he lived long enough to tell the Dahken of the boy called Geoff. As his breath returned, he searched his memory, for he knew he had seen the boy here in the palace. Nadav said that Geoff was powerful, and there was something Palius thought he heard through the whisperings in the halls. The boy had turned into a ghost, or perhaps that he had summoned a ghost? Regardless, he knew it had something to do with a ghost seemingly made of blood, and he cursed himself for not listening more closely to what he thought were palace rumors and tall tales. Palius knew he must speak with Cor. Cor would know.

Mere minutes later, his queen glided in silently with a grace that still amazed him considering her advanced age, but her face was flushed as if she had run the halls to reach him. Great concern showed across her features, almost to the extent that she looked as if she may cry at any moment. No doubt, Erella thought Palius called for her because he was at his end, and in a way, Palius wished that was the case if only to avoid telling her what he must now confess. She approached his bedside quietly and sat down next to him, placing her hand over his.

"No, my queen," Palius said, unmoving, "I am not dying just yet, but I fear that time is close."

"Then what do you need, my old friend?" she asked softly. No relief came to her face despite his statement.

"My queen, I have never been a religious man," Palius confessed, "but in the end, I fear and trust Garod. My loyalty lies with my country, not just Aquis but the

Shining West. Though more than anything else, I love you Queen Erella of Aquis, and I've loved you since the first time I saw you. I've sacrificed every life I might have had to serve you, and everything I have ever done, I've done for you."

"I know," she said as she moved from a chair to sit on his bed with him. "Do not be afraid. In death Garod will grant you everything you may have once wanted – wife and home, children and grandchildren. His loyal servant deserves nothing less."

"Majesty, I've not always done the righteous thing, the moral thing in Garod's eyes. I have sins on my conscience and blood on my hands. I have made decisions and ordered horrible acts so that they would not stain your purity, and I am afraid that I must confess one of them now."

"Palius, you mustn't speak of it," she said, briefly placing a finger over his chapped lips. "Garod knows all, and he will forgive your sins for the light in which you committed them. I have often wondered how I reigned free from strife and unpleasantness, and it is because you protected me from such hardships. You have aided me to rule justly, and the people of the West have benefited greatly from your sacrifices. Garod will not condemn you for this."

"Erella, you must listen," Palius said. Never once over the decades had he ever called her by name, and it caused her to become silent. "I attempted to murder Dahken Cor, not once in fact, but twice. You know of the attempt on his life when he reached Fort Haldon. When you told me weeks ago of his disrespect of Aidan and that you had sent for him, I paid Larnd no small sum for a heavily armed force to intercept his party. I don't know specifics, except that Dahken Cor brought only a few with him, and Larnd's people were defeated soundly. He has become powerful, and you will need his strength for what is to come."

"What is to come..." she repeated. It was not a question, but he understood it as such. In fact, Erella still tried to comprehend the extent of Palius' connections and his attempted murder of a state official, a lord.

"I thought Dahken Cor to be the greatest danger to the Shining West in centuries. I thought he would bring down Aquis and everything it stood for in his challenge to Garod and the accepted order. I feared for your power and the power of the priests over the people of our nations. I know now I was wrong; your reign is not about power.

"I found Cor too resilient, too difficult to kill. After the failure to assassinate him at Fort Haldon, I sought an ally. Years ago, I uncovered a spy here in the palace who used a device, a mirror to contact his master on Losz."

"Who?" she asked with trepidation. Erella was shocked, and she found herself growing numb with each confession Palius made.

Palius paused long, his eyes searching her face, and he sighed and said, "Sovereign Nadav."

"The Loszian Emperor!" Erella gasped.

"Yes, my queen. Cor had already gallivanted through his lands and killed one of his lords, so I thought he would be a willing ally. I explained the Dahken's plans to train his people and invade Losz. I besought him to raise a small army, cross the Spine and attack Fort Haldon to rid us of a common enemy. While Lord Dahken Cor fended off the invaders, a small force of our loyal soldiers would end all of the Dahken once and for all."

"Palius, I –"

"Please, my queen," he interrupted. "Let me finish."

"I can hear no more!" she screamed at him. She stood from his bed and turned away from him, and Palius could hear the soft sound of her crying.

"You must listen!" he said, raising his voice as loud as he could with the rumbling of the phlegm and blood in his throat. "Nadav plans invasion of the Shining West, and he has his own Dahken to lead his armies."

"Palius," she said, and her voice was hard as granite. She turned, and he could see the tears that streamed freely down her lined face. "I will pray for your soul. Rest now and may Garod accept you."

Queen Erella of Aquis left him then, and as he watched her glide from the room as gracefully as she had come, Palius knew it was the last time he would see her in his life.

26.

"Marya can heal," Keth explained. "I'm not completely sure how it works, but by pressing her own wound to another's she can heal both. We've tried it a few times after she discovered the power, and we've figured out a few things. She must be wounded for it to work, her blood must mix with the other person's, and it weakens her.

"I didn't want her to heal me," he said as he looked over her still form. "I was afraid it would kill her."

"It didn't, but she still sleeps," Cor said. "She saved your life. If she hadn't done it, you would have died."

"She may yet die, and I'm not sure I can live with that," Keth said, lightly touching her cheek.

"I'm sure she'll be fine," Cor said. The statement didn't sound overly confident, but he was fairly certain that if Marya were going to die, she would have already. An idea struck him, but it sounded hollow even to his ears as he voiced it. "If Marya does die, she died to save you. Make her sacrifice worthwhile."

They had been in the forest for several days before Keth showed signs of improvement. He began to stir and eventually lifted his head and opened his eyes just slightly to try to make out his surroundings. The effort drained him, and his head fell back unmoving for close to another hour before he began asking for water with a parched croak of a voice. Within a few hours, he was sitting upright and eating, though he looked exhausted and felt worse.

Later, after Keth seemed more recovered and had taken full stock of their situation, Cor asked, "Why didn't you tell me?"

Keth looked at him uncomprehendingly. "About me and Marya? Or?"

"That she can heal others with her blood," Cor clarified.

"Oh. Honestly," Keth said while scratching the back of his head, "it never occurred to me. Perhaps Lord Dahken, if I may be so bold as to say so, you should spend more time with your people instead of looking over drawings and plans."

Cor's eyes flashed angrily, and he set his jaw to bite back angry words. He briefly felt the urge to draw steel, an impulse he fought and beat down with consideration of the speaker of the words that had angered him. He saw the look of concern on Keth's face that perhaps he had gone too far, and Cor used it to soften his own reaction. He held Keth's gaze for a moment and then dropped his eyes to the ground beneath his feet.

"You are right, Dahken Keth," he said softly with a sigh. "We will wait here through tomorrow. If Marya is not up and about by the next day, we will have to find a way to hold her on horseback. It may be slow going, but we must start moving again soon. I feel an itch to get back to Fort Haldon as soon as possible."

"If she still sleeps, she will ride with me," Keth said. "I'll hold onto her. We'll switch out our horse every couple of hours to not be too hard on the beasts."

It was the last night they slept in the ancient forest. Keth stayed near Marya into the evening hours, eventually arranging his bedroll and moving Marya into it before sliding in next to her. When Cor awoke, he saw their two forms intertwined and snoring loudly. Keth was slow to rise, waking only when the sun was well into the morning sky, and Marya crawled from the bedroll shortly after he. She felt exhausted and weak, hungry and thirsty, but she was overall well and able to travel. It was midday before they emerged from the trees and crossed the disused and overgrown field to again travel the road to Byrverus.

"Lord Dahken Cor, Her Majesty was most concerned for your well being," the armored man said. He wore gleaming steel plate armor from head to toe, shining mirror like in the sunlight and marked with the seals of the queen. "She expected you some days ago. Upon hearing of your arrival, Her Majesty cleared the court to receive you immediately. I've been instructed to bring you to the palace directly."

"We need no escort to the palace. I know precisely where it is," Cor responded. It was unfortunate that this man would feel his ire, followed by that of the queen, but Cor was done with having demands placed upon him. "Inform Queen Erella that tonight I will sleep in a bed of my own choosing, and that tomorrow I will come to meet with her."

"Sir, Her Majesty is unaccustomed to being disobeyed by anyone, especially one of her loyal subjects, peasant or lord."

"Then inform her that I am unfortunately becoming accustomed to attempts on my life and those I love. Even still, I will not simply walk right into another such trap. I will come at my convenience tomorrow."

The visor on the man's plate helm was up, and his face showed a range of emotions that turned from shock to outrage to anger. The four stood before him with wide stances and arms crossed in defiance, and not one of them budged or said another word as they stood and stared him down. Finally, he sighed heavily, and his face took on a look of sullen disbelief. He turned and marched back the way he had come.

"Was that wise, Lord Dahken?" Keth asked.

"I don't really care. If the queen or someone in her court is behind the attempts to kill us, marching right into her hands at a time she expects us is the worst thing we can do," Cor reasoned.

"Wouldn't they simply hold springing the trap until we arrive tomorrow?"

"Probably," Cor said, and he turned to show his companions a mischievous smile, "but at least this way we spring the trap when we choose."

Queen Erella hurled a vase across her office in unrestrained fury. A host of vile oaths came to her mind, and she desired to say at least one if not all of them. Unused to such language, she hesitated, unsure as to which curse would be the most appropriate under the circumstances, and she had to take what satisfaction she could from the frightful crash as the crystal shattered against a granite wall, spilling water, and flowers across her plush carpet. This man, this Dahken was the source of so much chaos. She had ruled for a hundred years without so much as a hint of disruption in Aquis and the Shining West, and yet Cor had caused a near total loss of control since the day he was born. He defied her at every turn, yet he had such lofty morals and goals for his people. His very existence and the lack of order it implied had led her greatest and oldest advisor and friend to betray her. It was too much; the Dahken must fall in line with her rule at any cost.

She closed her eyes and lowered her head, breathing deeply over and over in the hopes that Garod may help her find peace. When her heart no longer thudded, and she no longer felt the need to throw breakable objects, Queen Erella of Aquis opened her eyes to behold the two men in front of her. Lord Aidan sat red faced in his chair, outraged, and he looked as if he may burst at any moment. The captain she had dispatched to bring Lord Dahken Cor to the palace stood at attention, though he looked like a puppy that was afraid of being kicked by its master.

"You have no fault in this, Captain," she said to him, and while he still stood straight, relief was apparent in his being. "I will not see Lord Dahken Cor tomorrow as he intends. When he arrives *at his convenience*, you will show him to the suite we have prepared for him. Make sure another suite is available for the other two. They will sleep there tomorrow night, and I will meet him at a time of *my* choosing the following morning. You are dismissed.

"Lord Aidan," she said as the armored man clinked away, "you will now be of the greatest service to Aquis."

"How may I serve, Majesty?" he asked as he lifted his ponderous bulk. The redness of his face had begun to fade, leaving red splotches.

"You will now be in control of Fort Haldon. Lord Dahken Cor is nominally its lord; however, he will answer to you. I will dispatch you to Fort Haldon with the Lord Dahken and several hundred loyal soldiers, and you will carry with you a royal edict that will fully explain the situation to Commander Thom once you arrive. Lord Dahken Cor and his people will learn fealty to the crown and Garod, even if it takes years."

"Yes Majesty," Aidan said quietly, with a mix of satisfaction and resignation. He stood quietly as she wrote out her commands, and when she was finished, he took them and left her with a bow. Once outside of her chambers, Lord Aidan of Byrverus groaned forlornly.

27.

It was all Palius could do to lie in his plush bed, propped up by many soft pillows, awaiting death. He knew his time was short now; the rumbling wheeze in his chest grew louder and deeper with each breath, and he could scarcely move. He owed one more apology, one more recantation of his sins before his death so that he may meet Garod with a clear conscience. Rasping for breath with every few words, he could not call forth one of the guards outside his chambers and instead rang the small bronze bell. Palius besought the guard to find Lord Dahken Cor with all haste, for he did not know if he could wait any longer.

The dying old man waited, and every minute felt like hours as he watched the sands slip from the top half of his glass to the bottom. The glass held sand enough for twelve hours, and after having watched it spill time for so many years, Palius knew it would again need to be turned in about two hours. He doubted he would have the strength to do so when the time came. Palius felt as if he watched his own life slip through the tiny eye in the middle of the glass, and his time would be done once the last grain of sand finally fell.

His outer door opened, pushed in from the outside, and Palius looked that direction, moving only his eyes and not his head, as that would require what felt like massive effort. He expected the gleaming, black armored countenance of Cor, Lord of the Dahken, but instead found the golden haired Thyss of Dulkur entering his chambers. Palius watched her cross the room, sauntering with her arrogant gait toward him to stand several feet from the left side of his bed, arms crossed before her and feet set wide apart defiantly. She was as beautifully dangerous as ever, and he found himself staring at the slight bulge in her abdomen.

"Yes, I am with Cor's child," she said, her voice breaking him from his reverie. "What do you want?"

"I called for the Lord Dahken," Palius rasped, and he had to pause every few words for breath. "Why did he send you?"

"Cor meets with your beloved Queen, and the guard you sent said it was most urgent. I thought it better to come myself," she replied.

"Very well. Then I must ask you to pass this on to him, for I am afraid I am at my end."

And as such, Palius told her everything. He explained how he had arranged their attempted murder when they first reached Fort Haldon, as well as the attack upon them as they came back to Byrverus. He told her of his duplicity in colluding with the Loszian Emperor and that several hundred of the men at Fort Haldon were prepared to turn on them when battle was joined against the Loszians. As he spoke, Palius watched her beautiful, bronzed face change from surprise to anger and then seething hatred. He didn't care if she hated him, or if they all did, so long as she listened.

"But there is one more thing you must know, one more thing you must tell Lord Dahken Cor."

"I need not hear any more, old man!" Thyss screamed at him. "I will sacrifice you with fire to Hykan, and you may repent to Him in eternal flame!"

"Please, Cor must know!" he pleaded. But she had stepped back to the middle of the room, and Palius didn't think she could even hear his weak voice. Using the last of his strength, he pushed himself to sit upright and reached his open hand to her in supplication.

Thyss spat in his direction and raised her arms exultantly, palms open and up toward the ceiling. As she closed her eyes and turned her face upward, she thought she could hear the old man begging for something, his life she assumed. The temperature in the room grew quickly and raw untamed fires burst forth from the bed, igniting Palius' bed sheets and robe. The entire bed was engulfed in a column of flame, and immensely hot, it burned blue in the center. Despite being near death, Palius experienced pain and suffering unlike anything he'd ever imagined, and it lent him strength to flail his limbs and scream in a most horrific, heart wrenching way.

Mere seconds had passed when the guards threw the doors open to behold Palius barely writhing within the raging inferno. Cries went up of fire within the castle and the need for water, and Thyss merely stood in the center of Palius' bedroom as he moved no more, feeling the horrible warmth on her body and reveling in the ecstasy of it. She was vaguely aware of people with buckets of water, soldiers and servants alike, attempting futilely to extinguish the flames that now spread to carpets, tapestries, and drapes.

A set of cold, gauntleted hands grasped Thyss by her upper arms, and the sensation brought her back to consciousness of the here and now. A soldier held her, trying to force her arms down, trying to force her out of the room as it was full of heat, smoke, and fire. She jerked away, and the sudden motion broke her free from the metal grip. The guard thought twice about trying to catch her again, and instead he turned and fled toward the open doors.

Thyss held her open palm before her face and blew across it just as she had on the road only a few days ago, but this time a cold wind instead of more fire gusted across the room to extinguish the blaze as easily as if it were a lone candle. The gale left as quickly as it came and with it out the rooms' open windows went the heat and smoke, leaving a smoking charred ruin where

Palius' massive bed had once been. One could barely make out a blackened fetal form in its center. His hourglass lay shattered on the floor.

With the roar of untamed fire now gone, servants and palace guards slowly filtered into Palius' chambers to behold the gruesome sight. Over a dozen stared in disgusted awe, silent except for the sounds of their heavy breathing, and many still held buckets of cold water, which they set upon the floor. One, the armored guard who attempted to subdue Thyss and pull her from the room, looked in mixed fear and anger at the golden elementalist. He roughly turned another to face him.

"She did it!" he declared, pointing at Thyss. "Find the queen. Tell her the foreign woman has slain Palius. Go now!"

Aggravated, Cor sat in a plush chair off to the side in the chamber that served as Queen Erella's official office. He'd been sitting in the uncomfortably soft seat for over an hour, ever since he arrived for their meeting. When her guards announced him, she made a point of asking him to have a seat while she dealt with any number of seemingly pointless tasks of state, and after a short time, Cor began to fume as he shifted endlessly to find a comfortable way to sit and pass the time. Queen Erella was trying to break him down, weaken him so that she may establish dominance in the fight that was to come. It only angered him.

It seemed that Queen Erella had only one type of clothing in her wardrobe - white robes of the purest and highest silk. Her robes had varying degrees of heraldry, badges of office, and symbolism of Garod, Cor supposed depending on the tasks of the day. They always maintained a high degree of dignity and elegance for Aquis' ruler, but today she wore the simplest, plain white robes that covered her from foot to neck and a simple single starred tiara as opposed to the unwieldy, golden jeweled crown she wore officially.

Erella had only just called across the room for Cor to come stand before her when a palace guard suddenly burst through her doors with much surprise and shouting from those stationed outside. The man skidded to a halt on her plush carpeting and panted heavily as if he had just run a great distance in his plate and chain armor. Erella's aged face changed to that of great anger, and Cor could see it flash like lightning in her eyes as she stood from her desk with great strength and presence.

"How dare you invade my privacy? What is the meaning of this? Speak, damn you!" she all but screamed at the man as two of her personal guard raced into the room, taking their fellow by each arm.

"Majesty, I beg forgiveness!" he spoke with haste. "You must come to Palius! The woman – *his woman* – has killed Palius in his bed!"

For months, Erella had awaited news of Palius' final passing into the arms of Garod, and she would have sped it along herself had she discovered his treachery earlier. His penitence saved him that fate, reaffirmed her trust in him, and likely committed his soul to the right hand of Garod. Every time an unexpected knock came at her door, or a servant came to her with urgent news, she thought it would be of his death, but never had she expected this. She glanced at Cor, finding as much surprise on his face as she no doubt showed on hers.

"What?" she asked, her voice a mere whisper, barely audible over the summer breeze outside her windows.

"The woman with the bronze skin has murdered him. She burned him alive in his bed," the man said, his breathe coming easier now. "We tried to put the fire out, but it spread so quickly. We could not help him, and when it was done, she breathed the fire away."

Queen Erella shot from her chambers like a gossamer crossbow bolt, with a speed and agility completely unforeseen considering her apparently ancient and frail frame. Cor jumped into a run right behind her, and the guards, slightly slower to react, followed suit. The queen and her entourage charged through halls at a run, armor clanging in contrast to Erella's softly slippered feet, as servants, soldiers, and other onlookers endeavored to stay clear of their path. Cor had never been to Palius' chambers as he had never formally spoken with the man, but he knew as the queen's most trusted advisor Palius would not be far away from her. As such, Cor doubted it took even a minute for them to reach the destination.

When they turned a corner in the main hall, Cor knew they had arrived, for about another thirty feet down the hall stood a throng of perhaps twenty persons, mostly servants, trying to work their way through a set of double doors. As they approached, some looked up and saw their queen, immediately parting and calling for others to make way. Queen Erella, with Cor doing a fair amount of pushing others out of the way, made her way through the crowd through the double doorway. The smell of burnt wood and fabric assailed their senses, but there was also another smell, like charred meat but far more terrible.

Inside was another group of people, gawking and speaking in hushed whispers. Most of these were armored men who, upon seeing their queen, helped to clear the way for her to the center of the room. As they pushed closer, the air became replete with the terrible smell, and Cor steeled himself for what he knew was to come. As the final two bodies in their way parted, Queen Erella suddenly halted as she beheld the grim scene - the scorched and blackened remains of her friend. She stood wordlessly as tears began to silently fall down her cheeks.

Cor's eyes did not linger long on the remains of Palius and his bed, but instead found their way to one side, to Thyss. She stood rebelliously, haughtily, as she watched with open satisfaction at her handiwork. Even though armored men held each of her arms firmly, her gaze and stance held an open challenge for any who would dare oppose her. Feeling Cor's eyes upon her, Thyss turned her own to return his look, and he knew in that moment she had not simply murdered the old man.

"Take the witch away and secure her in a cell," Erella ordered. "Her fate is sealed, and justice will be done on the morrow at sunrise."

"Wait! You can't –," Cor started as the men restraining Thyss began to move, but he was cut off by the queen's authoritative voice.

"I can't what, Lord Dahken Cor? I am Queen of Aquis and High Priestess to Garod, and *I* rule here! She has murdered my oldest advisor and friend in cold blood, and you can see in her face she does not deny it!"

Then Thyss laughed, strong and melodious, interrupting the queen. "Of course, I don't deny it, you old hag! What you call murder, I call vengeance, justice! Let you have your justice tomorrow, and we shall see whose dominion reigns supreme over my fate, Garod's or Hykan's!"

"You blaspheme, witch! Be gone from my sight!" Erella shouted.

The remaining servants quickly cleared the room as the guards moved Thyss roughly toward the door. A fire grew in the pit of Cor's belly, and he clenched and unclenched his fists anxiously. There was a sound in his ears, a low buzzing as if a small bee hovered inside them, that tensed his muscles for action and made him breathe heavily through his nose as his teeth were clamped. He hadn't armed himself before going to

Erella's quarters, as it seemed improper, and he now regretted the choice. Cor longed for the warm feel of Soulmourn and Ebonwing in his palms, and he would slay everyone in the room to free his Thyss.

"I will go with you on my own, peons," Thyss growled as she yanked her arms free.

The queen raised her hand for calm, and the guards relaxed and led Thyss from the room. As she passed, she pressed one palm to the side of Cor's face. Her soft touch was as pleasurable as ever against his smooth shaven cheek, like the shock one felt after rubbing leather soled boots on thick carpeting and then touching steel, but it lasted forever instead of being gone in an instant. It calmed his sinews, and the buzzing abated a bit. Then she was gone, out of the room, as she was led away.

"Lord Dahken Cor," the queen said, pulling his attention from the doorway back to her, "you will return with me back to my chambers. We have much to discuss, I think."

"Yes Majesty. I would first speak with her if you would allow it."

"As you will, but watch yourself Dahken," Erella replied softly, and she stalked from the room with her guard in tow.

Cor pushed his way past the servants who still stood in the room, and as he exited into the hall outside, a fat priest nearly ran headlong into him. Cor recognized Aidan, the priest he'd pushed down the hill at Fort Haldon, and the good, pious servant of Garod, sneered at Cor as he passed around into Palius' chambers. Cor resisted every urge to kill the man, though images of bashing the man's brains against a stone wall or crushing his throat barehanded flashed through his mind.

"Lord Dahken!" Keth shouted as Cor entered the hall. The younger Dahken sprinted toward him with

Marya in tow, and Cor noted they were both armed. "We saw Thyss under guard and heard -"

"It's true," Cor interrupted. "I need you both to follow her, I suppose to the dungeons. Stay there and watch them. I will be there in a few minutes."

"I'll not allow them to jail her," Marya said with her hand on her sword.

"You'll do nothing, Marya," Cor said as he laid a hand on her shoulder. "I know you love her. So do we all, but Thyss will not allow any man to harm her. I just need you both there to keep an eye on things. I'll be right there. Go now."

The two turned and ran back the way they came, following the direction the guards had taken Thyss. Cor closed his eyes for a moment and breathed deeply. When he opened them again, he hazarded one glance back into Palius' room to see the priest Aidan kneeling over the scorched remains and mumbling some sort of prayers. Cor snorted and walked purposefully after his Dahken, but their paths parted when he stopped at the rooms they had been allotted on arriving at the palace.

He pushed open the door to the suite he and Thyss shared and strode to the bureau beside the large bed, upon which was his armor and both of their weapons. Cor quickly strapped on the black metal, though he felt he could not move quickly enough. Despite the urge to move faster, faster, his fingers did not falter, and he kept his nerves about him. Once finished, he fastened his swordbelt, Soulmourn and Ebonwing familiarly at his side, and last, he lowered his bulbous black helm over his head, yet again marveling at how he saw clear through the thing. Cor picked up Thyss' curved longsword by its sheath, the black leather strap by which it was secured to her back pinched between his palm and the gold leaf ornamented wood scabbard.

As the Lord Dahken left the plush suite, he was vaguely aware of the return of the low buzz in his ears and the accompanying warmth in his being that Soulmourn and Ebonwing always brought him.

28.

Locating the holding cells beneath the palace required little effort from Cor, just one question of a passing servant as he moved through the halls. He felt upon him the eyes of everyone he passed on his armored countenance, and he watched as the palace guards laid hands on their weapons as he approached, to relax as he passed. He found a dark stone stair that only led downward and emptied into a massive, dank hall with iron barred cells that extended as far as he could see in the flickering gloom. The entire level was illuminated by only a handful of smoky torches. Cor wondered at the need for the followers of such a supposedly beneficent god to need such a vast dungeon, and he somehow thought it likely extended to lower levels.

Four men sat upon crude wooden benches at a crude wooden table. Two were armored guards with longswords at their sides, their pikes leaning against the far end of the table. The other two were gaolers he assumed, one fat and bald in an open leather jerkin and the other young, thin, and scraggly wearing a brown wool tunic. The four men were intent upon a game of bones, each of them with a small pile of copper coins in front of them. The men looked up as he entered the room, but quickly returned their attention to the game, though one guard allowed his gaze to linger a bit longer as if in warning. They played with shouts of glee and forlorn moans as if the meager copper coins they wagered were of the most precious gold.

Cor saw Thyss in the first cell, a small enclosure that was only six feet in each dimension with old, filthy straw covering its stone floor, and a wooden bucket that sat in the far corner. Thyss, her ire plain, stalked the side closest to the dungeon's exit, walking its length, turning, and walking it again with an occasional glance up at those outside. When she saw him, she stopped, and Cor wondered if the gaolers knew just how dangerous a tiger they kept caged here.

Keth and Marya stood side by side near Thyss' cell. Keth had clearly waited patiently, impassive and stolid as ever, but Marya looked like a viper ready to strike. Cor could see the livid anger in her eyes, in every part of her being. How could a child, a mere girl of only thirteen be so prepared to kill for someone else? But the explanation was clear – she was no child; Marya was a Dahken. Cor wordlessly handed the pair Thyss' weapon and approached the bars.

"I'll get you out of here," he said.

"Don't be ridiculous Dahken Cor. I have spoken my piece to that bag of bones queen above, and she'll not release me," Thyss retorted.

"Tell me why, Thyss. I know your fury is as untamed as fire, but I also know you don't unleash it without cause. What happened?"

"It doesn't matter. Tomorrow my fate will be decided by the gods, by Hykan or Garod," she answered.

"It does matter," Cor said softly, reaching his hand through the bars to lay it gently on Thyss' abdomen.

"Hey, get yer 'and off 'er, you!" shouted the fat, bald gaoler, preparing to stand from his game.

Cor did as he was told, clenching an iron bar in each hand as if he could pull them apart for Thyss to exit. "I thought you didn't believe in fate or destiny. I thought you said the gods rarely interfered directly in our lives. What makes you think they will now?"

"Because my Lord Dahken, I can feel the fire of Hykan burning within my belly, and I know My Lord will not allow both of us to perish for the crime of justice," she explained. "I must believe he will save me."

"Don't wait for Hykan. Save yourself," Cor said imploringly. "Make yourself one with the air and blow way as you did in Losz. I will meet you back at Fort Haldon."

"Again, you are ridiculous Dahken Cor. Queen Erella would make war upon you, and even if the men of Fort Haldon followed you instead of Aquis, you could not hope to defeat her. Besides, I could not do that," she replied, and Cor could sense deep resignation in her voice.

"Why not?" he asked.

"Because it would mean the end of this," she said, now placing both of her own hands upon her belly.

Cor could only stare at Thyss' face with her ever present smile and the fire that burned within her eyes, but this time it was different. The fire, normally flames of defiance, arrogance, and independence now contained a different light, something he could only define as joy. He looked at her hands, still on her belly, and the full realization of her words sunk into his brain. He closed his eyes and dropped his head to the iron bars, causing a long ringing clang when his helm, invisible to his eye, hit them. *Because it would mean the end of this.* No, there would be no end to either.

"You never told me why you did it," he said as he raised his head.

"The old man betrayed us. It was he who tried to kill us, both when we reached Fort Haldon and on our way here. He even betrayed his queen; he said something about using magic to speak with the emperor of Losz. He earned my vengeance and Hykan's justice," she said, her voice rising in the strength he knew so well, the strength with which he'd fallen in love.

"He deserved it, then," Cor said, more to himself than anyone else. He paused and sighed deeply as he considered his next words.

"I'll have you free soon enough. You two," he said with a voice that brooked no argument as he released the bars and turned to his younger Dahken, "follow me."

Thyss resumed her pacing of the cell as the three Dahken left the room and climbed the stairs. They moved through the halls of Erella's palace at a quick pace, though they did not run, and he led them straight to Erella's chambers, outside of which now stood four armored guards. They eyed him with close suspicion now that he was armed and with two cohorts, both apparently ready for battle.

"You stay outside," Cor said to Keth and Marya, and to the guards, "The queen is expecting me. Allow me entrance."

Cautiously, one of the soldiers slowly opened the doors, and Cor entered and crossed the first room with long strides, making his way to the side doorway that led to Queen Erella's office. The guard closed the door behind them and moved hastily to keep up. Cor found the queen precisely where he expected, sitting behind her large desk, and the guard hurriedly announced the Dahken's entrance, almost as an afterthought as Cor stormed right up to the queen.

"Majesty, release Thyss to me," he said, and his voice had a hollow dimension from inside his insectoid helm.

"You dare come before me fully armed and making demands," she said without looking up. "I am not intimidated, Lord Dahken Cor, and be careful that you do not incur my wrath. As we speak, I sign the order for the headman to end her life at sunrise for murdering an official of the state. The matter is not open to discussion."

"I'm not here to discuss it," he replied. The tension returned to Cor's muscles, and his hands felt naked as they longed to feel his sword and fetish. The buzzing returned, and Cor wasn't sure that it wasn't in his brain rather than his ears. "Thyss murdered no one. She enacted justice on a man who admitted his own crimes to her. Your advisor hired men to kill us more than once. He's the one who was responsible for the attack on us as we traveled to Byrverus. No doubt, attempted murder of one of your lords and his subjects is as much a crime."

"It is not for you to decide what is justice in my own palace, Lord Dahken Cor. Understand now that your authority at Fort Haldon is reliant upon my support, my rule, and we have other matters to discuss in those regards," Erella said, clearly changing the topic of conversation.

"You must release Thyss to me. She committed no crime!" Cor shouted, and the queen's eyes hardened as her brow furrowed slightly.

"The matter is settled, and you will hold your tone, Lord Dahken Cor."

"It is *not* settled! Palius betrayed you as much as anyone, and you would murder Thyss for taking her vengeance? Wouldn't you have ordered death for him if he had told you?" Cor asked hotly, as he leaned forward placing his clenched fists on her tabletop.

"I am well aware of Palius' treachery," she responded quietly. "Palius repented his sins to me several days ago, and he has been forgiven in both my eyes and those of Garod."

Cor was speechless as he looked at the aged queen, and he closed his eyes, breathing out silently. He removed his fists from the oaken desk and stepped back to gather his thoughts, allowing her words to sink into his mind. She knew already, and she had known for days and took no action against the old man. Palius had been her friend, and her murder of Thyss was as much vengeance as anything Thyss had done. No. New anger began to build in his gut, and all his muscles tensed as his very skin tingled like thousands of ants crawled across him. Soulmourn and Ebonwing began to sing to him, as they always did when they urged him to action.

"You will not murder Thyss," Cor said opening his eyes. "That's what it would be – murder, not justice. It would have been justice if you had put Palius to death for his 'sins', but you wouldn't kill your old friend, would you?"

Now, Queen Erella stood from behind her desk, her voice growing in volume as she spoke, "Palius was forgiven his crimes. Justice only comes from the word of law, and *I* am the ruler of Aquis! The bitch from Dulkur acted of her own, outside of my laws, and that is murder! She will pay for *her* crime!"

"No!" Cor shouted again, and his face screwed into an image of hatred, though she could not see it for the helm. "I won't allow you to kill her, her *and* my child. What does your law say of that? What of Garod?"

"That is unfortunate," the queen said, lowering her tone as she was slightly taken aback. "I hadn't realized…"

"Then you will release her to me? I will take her back to Fort Haldon."

"No," Queen Erella said more strongly, setting her eyes back to his, "I'm sorry, but the course is set. She dies in the morning."

"I won't let you," he said again.

"Perhaps Palius was right after all! *You* won't let *me*?" Erella all but screamed at him. "Leave now, Lord Dahken Cor, and take your Dahken with you. Leave Byrverus and prepare for Aidan's arrival so that he may oversee the building of a proper temple for Our Lord. Leave now or meet Thyss' fate with her."

Cor opened his mouth to answer and shut it again, looking silently at the ancient woman who stood solidly before him. Her face, infused with anger, had taken on an aspect akin to granite, and her eyes were cold and uncaring. She would not compromise, and she would not discuss the matter further, having placed an ultimatum before him. Queen Erella had made her decision, and his muscles knew it was time to act. It all happened so fast, though in his mind's eye it seemed to take hours, and as slow as he moved, some part of him wondered why no one was able to stop him.

As Cor bounded over the great oak desk, a feat that required more strength than he knew he had, he could hear the battle song of Soulmourn and Ebonwing fill his being, drowning out all other sounds as he became one with them. His gauntleted left hand grasped the old woman by the throat, and his forward momentum sent her falling backward into her chair, crashing it to the stone floor and breaking its back with the force of the impact, along with some of her bones as his armored weight fell upon her. The thin, delicate skin of her neck ripped on the rough chain of the gauntlets, and her hands immediately flew to her throat in unsuccessful attempts to pry his fingers loose.

Queen Erella tried to scream, tried to gasp for breath, but nothing could pass. For a brief moment, Cor was distracted as something impacted his hauberk with the clanging ring of steel, and he let up just long enough for the queen to take in a sliver of precious air. It wasn't enough as her face turned blue, and her eyes began to bulge outward, partially in realized terror that she was powerless to stop him. The white hot pain of cold steel ripped into Cor's back under his hauberk, piercing deep into his abdomen, all the way through until it impacted the inside of the front of his hauberk, and Cor felt his life blood pour from him. It fueled his fury like throwing oil on an open flame, and incredible strength poured into his sinews. Erella's eyes went dark as he crushed her windpipe, and bright red blood sprayed across the invisible surface of his helm as his mailed fingers sank into her neck, rending arteries and veins.

Using his foot against Cor's back for leverage, the guard yanked his sword free, and Cor felt even more of his blood run from what should be a killing blow. But as Queen Erella's blood continued to spill onto her carpeting, Cor could feel his own ruptured organs and torn flesh seal themselves whole again. He gained his feet slowly and turned to face the man who dared strike him, having drawn Soulmourn in the process. The guard, one of Queen Erella's elite palace guards, dropped his sword and turned in horror, hoping to flee, but Lord Dahken Cor cut him down mercilessly from behind.

Cor ran for the doors and yanked them open to find Keth and Marya fighting back to back against several more of the Westerners. Three lay dead or dying, but four more bore down upon them. Keth and Marya were splattered with both the blood of their foes and their own as well, but no mark showed upon their bodies. Cor waded into the fray, striking down men who never saw him coming, and the fight was over in moments. As the three calmed for just a moment, Cor realized the buzzing in his ears had cleared, and Soulmourn's song quieted to low hum.

"Are you injured, Lord Dahken?" Keth asked, motioning his longsword to the massive amount of blood on Cor's hauberk and legguards, blood that already grew sticky.

"I'm well. Quickly we must pull them into the queen's chambers and shut the doors before we're found by more," Cor said.

"A few guards mean nothing to us, my lord. We are Dahken," Marya said disdainfully.

Cor sighed. "I know, but we can't fight the armies of Aquis or even the entire palace guard just the three of us. We must free Thyss and get out of Byrverus."

They set to the task of pulling the slain Westerners into Queen Erella's chambers, though they could do nothing about the massive pools of spilled blood that had formed. Marya found she was unequal to the task of dragging a fully armored man and instead sauntered inside to investigate Cor's handiwork. It was fascinating to Cor actually; she could drive a sword through steel plates, but only when her blood was up. Without it, she was still a thirteen year old girl. It was the work of only a few minutes for them to hide the dead guards.

"You killed her, Lord Dahken," Marya's voice said softly from behind them, "the queen of all Aquis, High Priestess of Garod."

"Yes," Cor answered, turning to face her.

"Good," Marya said, and Cor saw no mercy in her eyes. "She was an old hag, a weakling compared to us, to Thyss. We owed her nothing."

"She was also the closest thing we had to an ally," Keth said, stoically staring through the entrance to the room in which Queen Erella's body lay. He could just barely see her slippered feet and the white of her lower legs.

"We don't have time for this now," Cor said shortly. "We have to get to Thyss and find a way out of here without killing everyone in our path."

They left the corpses of the queen and her soldiers behind as they exited into the hallway, walking calmly across the palace's lower level to the stair that led to the holding cells. Cor wanted to charge across, to sprint his way to Thyss, partly to reach her as quickly as possible and partly to make their escape briskly. He forced himself, and Marya, to slow down, to walk the halls naturally, as the three Dahken rushing their way through would likely draw attention, especially as the entire palace was buzzing with word of Palius' death. On the other hand, Cor knew it was only a matter of time before some passing servant noted that Erella's sanctum was unguarded with blood spilled without and investigated within or a passerby noted the state of their armor, covered as they were by sanguine stickiness. The trio arrived at the dungeon, finding everything unchanged. Cor drew Soulmourn and strode directly to the end of the table at which the men played.

"Westerners, I have no quarrel with you," he said, hoping he sounded reasonable. "Unlock that cell and let her out. I don't want to hurt you, but to keep you quiet I'll brain you senseless and lock you inside. Someone will find you and let you out."

The men, two guards and two gaolers, made their decision. A rain of copper coins of little value clinked on the dirty stone floor as battle was joined. The fight did not last long, as the Westerner's had little chance against three armed and deadly Dahken, to say nothing of Thyss who merely watched with arms crossed from the shadows of her cell. When it was over, Keth handed Thyss' sword to her through the bars while Cor tried key after key from the gaoler's belt before finally unlocking the iron door made of bars. As the door opened outward to admit Thyss with a squeal from its hinges, a great cry could be heard from the upper level. Keth quickly turned and climbed the stairs two at a time to disappear into the hall at the top.

"What have you done?" Thyss asked as she fitted the leather strap about her torso.

"I'll tell you later," Cor answered. "Right now, I think we have a bigger problem."

After a moment, Keth returned and said, "They are coming. What now, Lord Dahken?"

"We fight," Marya answered quickly and a little too eagerly for Cor's liking, and he saw the thrill of battle flash through Thyss' eyes.

"Then we die," Cor said, somewhat softening the bloodlust on Marya's face. "We'll have to fight through an army of trained soldiers, and there'll be priests as well. Eventually, we'll falter, and this will all be for nothing. We need another way out."

Marya seemed unconvinced, but it was Thyss who provided the alternative.

"There is a way out of the palace down here somewhere," she said. "While you three were gone, apparently securing my freedom, two servants came down here to dump a collection of chamber pots." Receiving only a blank, uncomprehending stare from the three Dahken, she nearly shouted, "The palace has access to Byrverus' sewers! It must be down here somewhere!"

The echoing clamor of heavily booted feet and clanging steel made the decision easy for Cor, and he said, "Thyss, we follow you."

Thyss quickly darted down the cellblock, an open hall created by the iron bars of cells on either side. Taking torches, the Dahken followed, leaving the sounds of approaching soldiers behind them. Cor was right in his original assessment of the place – this floor was at least as wide as the main floor of the palace, though it didn't appear that any of the cages had been used in years. They were all empty and clean of refuse, but not of thick layers of dust that the four of them kicked up as they passed. As they moved further into the disused portion of the dungeon, they knew they followed a well worn trail, a particular path only a few feet wide that was free of dust, despite much of it on either side. The trail ended or rather continued downward at a set of stone steps almost identical to those on the far side from which they had just come, the side from which the sounds of steel clad men now came.

For a brief moment, a black maw that he remembered as the entrance to Sanctum's catacombs superimposed itself over the sight before him. He shook his head and closed his eyes, and when he reopened them, the image was gone.

"Down?" Thyss asked.

"We have no choice. Go!"

The staircase was not long, and Cor counted only ten steps before it turned and continued down for another ten. The ceiling was low, and all but Marya had to crouch as they carefully tread the narrow steps down into darkness. They held their torches low, and more than once the flames scraped on the walls in the confined space. Over halfway down, the gray stone blocks the walls consisted of gave way to natural rock.

The steps opened into a large cavern, the sides, low ceiling, and floor of which had been smoothed away by the hands of stonemasons. There was no light here, except that cast by their torches, and that flickering illumination could not penetrate too far into the depths. Just to the right of the stairway they exited was another continuing down, but the choking cobwebs and inches of dust on the floor denied that any living soul had passed that way in years. The path through the dust continued ahead between rows of iron bars set into the floor and ceiling. There was a rancid smell here, hanging old and stale in the air.

As they moved between these cells, Cor noted that these also hadn't been used in years, decades or even longer, but they weren't clean and empty like those above. Many of them held remains of long dead souls, nothing but piles of bones now, long picked clean by rodents and the remains of any clothing disintegrated by the ages. This was not only an old dungeon; it was a tomb, a tomb of the unnamed. The smell became thicker and clearer – a stench of urine and feces filled the air, and coupled with the faint sound of trickling water, Cor knew they were close.

Cor sensed a mild stirring in his blood, a magnetism that he knew all too well, but he ignored it as they quickly but carefully crossed the cavern turned dungeon. However, Marya broke into a run, stunning Thyss to a stop as she charged ahead of the group. Following the feeling led Cor to follow Marya, and he to began to run with Keth just on his heels. He had no idea what lay ahead, what called to them, but he knew it was no living thing.

The Dahken stopped at one of the iron barred cells, ancient and coated in thick layers of dust. Within lay skeletal remains, nothing but bones wrapped in a few layers of moth and worm eaten cloth that would no doubt crumble on first touch. The remains of the cloth wrapped around the skeleton's torso was rent open by something other than the ages, a blade perhaps, and it was stained with the color of rust. As they looked, Cor absently noted the air was hard to breathe, full of the putrid stench of piss and shit, and the sound of flowing water was near.

Thyss sauntered quietly to stand behind them. "What is it?"

"I don't know," Marya answered. "Its something about this man."

"He was a Dahken," Cor said.

"How do you know?" asked Thyss.

"I can feel it in his blood," said Keth as he pointed to the remains' ancient tunic, seemingly stained with rust. "I can't explain it."

"He's right," said Cor.

"How long do you think he's been down here?" Marya asked.

Cor sighed heavily, lowering his eyes to his feet. "A long time, but not long enough."

"What do you mean?"

"This is all very interesting," Thyss interrupted loudly, "but I do not think we have the time. How long do you think before they start exploring down here?"

"You're right," Cor said, turning. "Let's keep going."

"My poor, dim Lord Dahken Cor," Thyss said softly as she turned to point, "I'm afraid we are here."

Following her finger, Cor found a large trench that he guessed to be about four feet deep and wide, through which flowed a disgusting mass of human waste. The flow came out of a tunnel to the north, passed through the trench and then continued through another tunnel to the south. One way or the other, it was a clear escape route from the palace, for no doubt there would be other access points in the city. Between the group and their excremental escape stood floor to ceiling iron bars, spaced about eight inches apart, with no door of any kind through which to pass.

29.

"We have no choice now," Marya said with finality. "We turn and fight our way out."

Cor sat on the smooth cavern floor, leaning against the bars with his back to the sewer. He watched as Keth paced the row of bars, occasionally tapping or flicking one to create a dull ring. The younger Dahken paced the entire length twice, and Cor closed his eyes to calm the roaring song that threatened to fill his being. It tried to convince him that Marya was right; they had no choice but to fight and slay their way to freedom, but Cor knew it was suicidal. The battle song had led him to this, and it would not lead him to his end.

"They just toss everything through the bars, I guess. There is no way past," Keth said, sitting down next to Cor, and his Lord Dahken threw his head back against the bars, causing his helm to clang loudly. Thyss transfixed him with an exasperated glare.

Cor jumped to his feet and gripped a bar in each hand. Setting his feet widely, he pulled them in opposite directions, intent on making them bend. His muscles strained and began to burn. Cor focused on Soulmourn and Ebonwing, beseeching them to lend him strength for this challenge rather than fighting an army of Westerners, but the more he called on them, the more their song faded from his mind. He pushed all his weight against one, followed by the other, and finally exhausted, he opened his eyes and found that the bars had not budged. Cor released his grip on the bars and slumped to the floor, his head resting on the iron.

"They are wrought iron," Thyss chided, laughing softly. "What did you expect to happen? Marya's right, Dahken Cor. If we are to die, let us die in battle."

He had done all this to prevent Thyss' death, and now she resigned herself to it. He'd argued with the queen until he was out of breath, until his rage drove him to her murder. He and his Dahken had killed her guards, innocent Westerners who did nothing but serve their queen, to say nothing of the gaolers. They made their way through an ancient dungeon in the hopes that the servants dumped the palace waste in something more than a drain. They had found a huge tunnel through which to escape, but were prevented by solid, iron bars. Hard, wrought iron bars.

Cor snapped his head up.

"No one's dying today," he said, standing with new energy. "I can't bend the bars. They're too strong, too solid. But if they were *softer*, I could throw myself against them and make them bend." Cor pulled his helm off and dropped it to the floor as he approached Thyss, and he could see the understanding crossing her face as he gently touched her cheek with a gauntleted hand.

"Heating this much metal sustainably is difficult, my love," she said.

"I know you can do it, Thyss. I've seen you do incredible things. This is nothing to you."

"I know I can do it, you gray skinned bastard," she growled hotly. "Even if I do, how will you bend the bars? You dare not touch them."

"I'll throw my entire body against them. My armor will protect me well enough," Cor said.

"I hope so," she replied. "Very well, everyone stand back."

Cor replaced his helm over his head as Thyss took a wide stance a few yards from the wall of bars. She closed her eyes, and pure serenity crossed her face for just a moment before she reopened them with a look of sheer determination. She concentrated on the center point of the iron barricade, and for a minute nothing happened. The Dahken watched as slight red glow blinked into being on one bar and slowly spread in size up and down its length. The redness began to show on the adjacent bars as it expanded from the focal point, which now started to turn orange. Cor launched himself against the bars, jarring himself as his black hauberk and helm contacted the glowing metal, but he found them still quite solid. Even still, they were extremely hot, and he jerked away from them reflexively.

A clamor arose from the entrance to the dungeon as the sound of steel clad soldiers entered the far side with a cry of surprise and success. Men wearing the plate of the palace guard poured from the stairs, many carrying torches in lieu of their swords. Even in the gloom several hundred feet away, Cor counted half a score, and they approached cautiously. Facing the threat, Keth and Marya drew steel and shot impatient looks at their Lord Dahken.

"We can slow them down," Keth called out, and Marya anxiously shifted her weight between her feet.

"No, wait," Cor shouted.

He again charged the barricade, which now glowed in various shades across a circle roughly four feet across. This time the collision thudded dully instead of the ring of steel on steel, and the bars stretched and bent outward several inches as he rebounded off them. The advancing guards stopped for just a moment, but then broke into a run as realization struck them. Cor pushed his shoulder into the softening iron, heedless of the scorching heat that was dangerously close to his exposed skin, and the iron continued to bulge toward the sewer's entrance. But not quickly enough.

"Lord Dahken!" Marya called to hurry him. She then placed a hand on Keth's sword arm and said,

"Come. The two of them must escape. We'll follow after -"

"No!" Thyss screamed in interruption, and she whipped around to face the oncoming Westerners. She drew her open hand, fingers extended, across their path, and a wall of white hot flame exploded from the floor in front of them. The guards skidded to a halt, but one was not so lucky, charging headlong into the flames. He burst through, his plate armor glowing as brightly as the softening iron bars, and the linens underneath ignited spontaneously. Arms wheeling, he fell to the ground, screaming hideously.

Unable to withstand it anymore as his black armor also began to grow hot, Cor pushed himself away from his task just as Thyss returned attention to hers. She had lost valuable seconds in saving Keth and Marya, but no longer would she allow these inconvenient iron bars to prevent their escape. Silently, she prayed to Hykan for strength as she closed her eyes and raised her face upward. Thyss' open hands clenched into fists, her knuckles growing as white as the iron that began to not only soften but melt. She felt the power of her god channel through her, and she bent it all to her indomitable will. As quickly as it came, it all vanished from her, and Thyss collapsed in exhaustion, Keth catching her to carefully lower her to the ground.

The three Dahken stood in silent awe of the sight before them. Thyss had completely melted a large portal into the row of iron, easily wide enough to admit two people walking abreast. Jagged tips of steel, still set into the floor and ceiling, yet glowed red, but the heat was quickly abating. Shapeless pools of melted iron had formed on either side of the portal, and they already began to cool, congealing into asymmetrical metal plates. Thyss' wall of flame vanished as if it had never been, and the soldiers trapped on the far side slowly edged forward and investigated their burnt alive compatriot.

"Thyss?" Cor asked, kneeling over her.

"I am fine, my love," she said opening her eyes. "I just need rest."

She closed her eyes and fell straight into a deep sleep, and Cor stood to face the Westerners who now approached slowly but confidently. He drew Soulmourn and Ebonwing, allowing their song to fill him with rage and said to his Dahken, "Let's finish this."

Cor was vaguely aware that the first man fell to a single blow that broke through steel, flesh and bone and dumped organs and entrails onto the smoothed stone floor. He had slain or maimed three before his Dahken struck the first blow, and he waded clear into the middle of his foes, completely heedless of the Westerners' attacks. They piled around him, trying to bring him down with the weight of their strikes against his armor, and sometimes they even rent his flesh. But he ignored them as a Tigolean rhino might ignore mosquitoes, and his wounds closed of their own accord as Soulmourn whistled through the air, severing limbs and ripping flesh. When he could no longer find a foe, he turned to face his Dahken who stood silently, their swords hanging limply by their sides. The floor was slick with spilled Western blood as Cor brushed past them to Thyss, who snored softly on the floor.

Cor picked her limp and supple form up from the ground, cradling her in his arms as she slept. Stepping through the ruined bars, he carefully slid down the sloped side into the trench, expending all his effort not to choke on the noxious air. Human waste, mostly feces, urine, and the remains of meals, flowed slightly downhill to the south and into a tunnel, and it was this direction Cor chose. All the waste of Byrverus must eventually exit the system, more than likely somewhere outside of the city. He thought briefly of his palomino,

Kelli, but somehow, he doubted the Westerners would execute a horse for the actions of her master.

The sewer system was a maze of tunnels, small and massive, and at times the flow was several feet deep. They endeavored to stay as far up the sides of the rounded tunnels as possible, but occasionally someone would slip on the disgustingly slick stone into the muck. Usually, several minutes of hacking, vomiting, and dry heaving would follow this, and it seemed that they could never get used to it. Regardless, Cor followed the flow and chose larger passages every time they came to one.

Eventually, Cor spotted a pinpoint of orange light ahead of them as they trudged through the largest tunnel yet. As they approached, it became obvious that the light shone into the tunnel was that of the warm, afternoon sun. Marya and Keth tossed their torches aside, and the Dahken increased their pace, Cor still carrying his sleeping Thyss.

The tunnel opened into sweet, fresh air, hanging several yards over a south flowing river. The river, easily fifty feet across at this point, already carried waste and detritus, no doubt dumped there by other tunnels. The riverbanks were tall and steep, sloping dangerously on either side. This was Byrver, a great old river that fed life to the city, and they paid it by dumping the shit of thousands into it. To the north, Cor could just barely see the tops of the towers and spires of Byrverus peaking out above the riverbanks.

"What do we do now, Lord Dahken?" Marya asked.

"What do you think? We need Thyss to wake, and then we jump."

"Our armor will make us sink like a stone," she replied.

"Mine won't, but you'd better take yours off and leave it here," Cor said as he gently sat Thyss up against the tunnel wall. "We can always get you new armor."

"I'm not leaving my sword," Marya said defensively. "No way."

"Fair enough."

"Lord Dahken," Keth said, interrupting the exchange, "have you ever seen anything like this before? The stone of this tunnel, and of all the others I think, is one solid piece, not blocks of masonry."

"What's the point, Keth?"

"Nothing I suppose. It just doesn't seem like anything the Westerners could build," he said as he removed his glove and ran his hand over the rough surface. "It makes me think of the building in the mountains, where you found Ebonwing."

"Its not important right now," Cor said dismissively, and he slumped against the wall next to Thyss as he suddenly realized just how exhausted was his body.

Epilogue

Aidan fumed, and his anger boiled over, as he left the palace for the temple just across the plaza in the early morning light. Though he'd never cared for Palius, as the man always seemed to block his moves, he never would have wished such a death upon the old man, but the blatant murder of Queen Erella was a whole other matter. The Dahken made it very clear that he and his people were a danger to all the Shining West, and they must be stamped out. Aidan would have liked nothing more than to take command of the armies, hunt the renegades and slaughter the other Dahken at Fort Haldon. Kill the children now, before they learn of what they are.

Unfortunately, even Aidan could not circumvent protocol in this matter. The queen was dead, and certain things must take place.

At his command, the great bronze and copper bells at the top of the tower began to ring, a ring that could be heard for miles. The smaller temples across the city took up the call, for it could mean only one thing – the death of the High Priestess of Garod, the ruler of Aquis. Miles away, the pealing of the bells was heard by priests of the smaller towns and villages, and they rang their own in answer. It carried across the land to every temple in every village or hamlet, and it was even heard across the borders of Aquis, into the other kingdoms of the Shining West.

Four, who traveled across the countryside, avoiding the roads and not far from the great city of Byrverus, also heard it. They were a motley, disheveled lot that looked terribly exhausted and smelled worse.

Away from the stench of the sewers, hunger had set in, but putting as much distance between themselves and the city as possible was their only thought. They stopped and turned toward Byrverus at the tolling of the bells.

"What is it?" Marya asked.

"It's a sign of the queen's death," Cor answered, remembering the boyhood teachings of so long ago. "When the ruler of Aquis dies, the priests ring the bells atop the temple. They say that the power of Garod carries the sound across Aquis to every other temple bell. When the ringing ends, every priest and priestess in Aquis will travel to Byrverus."

"What for?"

"To elect a new High Priest or Priestess, a new ruler."

"What is e-lect?" Thyss asked in tired confusion.

She had awakened a few hours after they reached the sewer outlet into the river. Once she had regained some of her strength, they contrived an escape from the tunnel by looping her rope around Marya and lowering her down to the river. She then caused herself to swing back and forth until her feet could touch the slimy riverbank. Each of them did it in turn, leaving Cor for last. He threw one end of the rope to them below, tied the other tightly about his torso and jumped right into the river. It was difficult work, but they pulled him to safety.

"They all come and cast a vote," he explained, "voice their choice to lead. He or she with the majority of votes will rule."

"Politics," Thyss said the word as if it was a curse, and she spat to the side. "The powerful should simply take what is theirs."

"Westerners don't believe that. They believe that selecting the most wise to rule will prevent the abuse of power."

"And after what we've just been through, what do you believe, Dahken Cor?" she asked. When it became obvious that he had no intention to answer, she asked him something different. "How much time do you think we have?"

"I'd say at least a couple weeks for them to assemble," Cor answered, mentally picturing a map of Aquis. "I don't know how long the process is, but even if it only takes a day, at least another two weeks after that to send anyone to Fort Haldon."

"Not enough time," Thyss said softly, and she turned to continue her exhausted trudging.

"I know," Cor said as the three Dahken followed suit. "We need to reach Fort Haldon. Quickly."

"I'd kill for a horse," Thyss mumbled.

"Perhaps we should just buy one at our first opportunity. I'm through with killing for at a few days at least."

"Tell me one thing, Dahken Cor," Thyss said. "How does it feel to slay your first ruler? I hope you enjoyed it, for I wonder if Queen Erella will be the last to which you deal death."

Cor had no response, but her question gave him something to think about as they plodded through the warm Aquis countryside. He thought he should feel something for the queen he slayed so thoughtlessly, but nothing filled his heart or the pit of his stomach. He knew then he'd do it again if he had to, if it meant saving any of the three in his company.

Sovereign Nadav sat in his favorite chair, a huge claw footed throne made from one enormous piece of ebony. He no longer remembered where the ebony came from, only that he rewarded greatly the man who had made it. The back of the chair was over nine feet tall, dwarfing everyone who saw it, even Nadav. In fact, the damnable thing wasn't very comfortable, but it appealed to his grandiose affectations. Nadav sat leaning to one side, his narrow form filling only half of the uncomfortably solid ebony seat, leaning the side of his head on his palm.

He looked over a map that had been superimposed over the floor. It wasn't really there of course; it was an enchantment. The map showed topographical features to scale, all major cities, and the roads between them across the entire western continent – all of the Loszian Empire and the lands of the Shining West, which would soon belong to Losz again. Carved figures of purple stone, also enchantments that weren't really there depicted armies all over the Loszian Empire. The figures were about two inches tall with a rod that rose from the head up to another three inches. Bands of color wrapped the rods in varying degrees of thickness to indicate the type of forces and quantity of those forces of which each army consisted. Some of the figures stood stationary, while others moved almost imperceptibly across the map of their own accord.

Nadav required every lord in Losz to raise an army, the expected size of which varied with the richness of the lord, because the Sovereign was fair after all, and those armies marched across the empire to one rally point. He would invade Aquis through the same pass in which this Dahken Cor had entered Losz. Many of the forces en route would not arrive in time of course, so Nadav intended them to protect the empire from counterattack and support the main force. The Shining West had grown too sure of their security, just as the Loszians had grown decadent, and it was now time to end that.

Aquis worked to reinforce Fort Haldon on their side of the pass daily. The wooden palisade was completely replaced with a solid granite curtain wall and ground had been broken on a keep. No doubt the

Westerners would put up an impressive fight, but there was no way they could withstand the combined might of Nadav's lords. He would encounter the Dahken there, Cor and his band of children. But Nadav now had his own Lord Dahken, and he had a power unmatched by anyone of whom Nadav had ever seen or heard. He would destroy Lord Dahken Cor.

The Loszian emperor diverted his attention from the map to gaze at the Dahken across the room. Geoff slept in the arms of two slave girls slightly younger than himself. Nadav allowed the young Dahken, barely more than a boy, to abuse the girls in any way he desired, so long that he allowed Nadav to watch. Nadav smiled sickly as he looked at Geoff's contented face. He had not yet introduced Geoff to his own sexual appetites, but that time would come.

Nadav promised the boy wealth and power, a prominent place in the Loszian Empire as it again spread its purple towers across the western continent. Nadav hadn't yet decided to what extent he would keep this promise. More than likely, he would have Geoff raped repeatedly while being skinned alive the moment both Dahken Cor and Queen Erella were dead. Nadav himself may even take part in both activities. On the other hand, maybe he would reward Dahken Geoff for his aid and loyalty; it was so hard to tell.

Nadav drugged a glass of wine and prepared to become one with nothingness.

END OF VOLUME II.

TO BE CONTINUED IN *DARKNESS AND STEEL*

Who is Martin Parece?

I'd really rather you not ask me questions like this! Well, are you asking who I am or "Who am I?", because the latter is a completely different question that forces one to look deep into the heart and mind. It is the question humankind has been asking since there was humankind.

Who I am, on the other hand, is just some guy who loves to read and tell stories. As I look back, I have always been a storyteller, from my first short stories to my first faltering attempts at playing Dungeon Master. I still love TTRPGs, all sorts of fiction, heavy metal, and horror movies. In fact, this last will be readily apparent should you read my anthology Tendrils in the Dark. A lot of shout outs, homages and influences there...

I returned to my creative endeavors around 2009 as my business of seven years began to burn down around me during the recession. I suppose adversity causes growth, and though I shelved my projects for a few years, I returned to them with the publication of Blood and Steel in 2011. Regardless, people seemed to enjoy the world of Rumedia, and I returned to it with five more novels.

In the end, I'm just a guy who loves to tell stories, read other persons' stories and head bang in the car. I have so much more to come, and I hope you'll join me on the journey!

Turn the page for an excerpt from

DARKNESS AND STEEL

THE COR CHRONICLES
VOL. III

Available Now!

"We already grow short of arrows, Lord Dahken," Thom said grimly. "We scavenge from the dead, and I've told the men to make every arrow count."

"Already? How many did we start with?"

"About forty thousand total."

"Forty thousand?" Cor asked absently, and he looked out over the pass.

It grew hard to see, as the sun was low in the sky behind them, and the granite wall created a long shadow on the ground below. Squinting in the gloom, Cor could barely make out forms lying still below, hundreds even thousands. He even thought he saw blood flowing through the pass in streams, pooling at low points, and for just a brief moment, Cor felt the oddest of sensations. It was similar to the pulls he'd felt in his blood to find his weapons and armor but without the tugging strings. It gave him pause, but only for a moment as he returned his mind to the task at hand.

The Loszian host had been reduced greatly, perhaps even by half, but it meant little if his men were almost out of arrows. Even with a small opening through which to pass, the press of twenty thousand or more would crush two thousand in personal combat. The Loszians seemed to have quieted temporarily, regrouping and waiting.

"Tell the men to cease fire," Cor said, and he paused while Thom spread the order. "We must save every arrow possible. I want the archers below to give their quivers to those on the wall. They will join the soldiers.

"What have they done down there?" he asked, motioning toward the burning gate.

"I don't quite understand it, Lord Dahken," Thom said as he looked down confusedly. "Those doors are easily three feet thick of solid oak and banded with heavy iron. They doused them with some type of oil and set it ablaze. I'm not sure how long, but I think it will be a long time before they burn down enough for their battering ram to break through. And even then, they'll have to charge through a burning wreck."

Cor nodded and flinched as a Loszian crossbow bolt *dinked* right off his helm. "Perhaps we should keep our heads down a bit. I don't know what they're up to, but if they want our gates on fire, we don't. Perhaps we could throw water down onto the flames? Set up some runners to bring buckets of water, throw it down upon the wall. Have more douse the inside of the gate. Maybe we can slow whatever the Loszians are trying to do."

Thom busied himself with carrying out the orders, meanwhile archers ran here and there collecting any ammunition they could find. A few enterprising Loszians peered over the edge of the north face and fired crossbows or threw other missiles at the defenders. True to Thom's word, they were largely ineffective and easily repulsed by just a few well-placed shots from longbows. Cor saw Keth and Marya with the infantry below and waved them up the steps.

"Dahken Marya, I left Thyss in your care," he said quietly, angrily.

"She would have none of it, Lord Dahken," Marya said with a subservient nod of her head.

"It's true, Lord Dahken," chimed in Keth. "We took her back to your quarters, and she seemed well enough, only tired. She told us to tell you that she needed no nurse. She would be back in the fray shortly."

Cor smiled, though no one saw it through his black helm. "Of course. Return to your posts and stay ready."

"What is that?" Marya gasped, pointing past Cor's right shoulder.

Cor turned to see a small, black cloud approaching from the Loszian horde, which parted wide to allow its passage. No, cloud was not the correct word; the thing that had killed Prad and some others was a cloud. This was more of a dark force, completely transparent, yet somehow hard to see through. As it came close to the wall, all nearby felt an extreme unnatural cold, quite unlike the chills of the deepest winter. It enveloped the blazing doors that made Fort Haldon's gate, extinguishing the flames almost immediately. Sick realization stuck in Cor's stomach.

"Marya, Keth, prepare the men to fight," he shouted. "Thom, the men must hold their arrows, hold until we have no choice but to fire lest we be overrun."

"What is it?" Thom shouted as Cor made his way down the steps.

"Have you ever seen ice, how hard it is?" Cor asked, receiving a nod in answer. "Then you also know how easy it is to shatter with a hammer!"

By the time Cor reached the men on the ground, the great doors had already frozen. The oak, wet from the Westerners' buckets, had begun to expand as the water froze in its cracks. At the same time, the iron bands shrank ever so slightly from the cold of the spell, and Cor could hear it complain as it strained against the expanding ice. Rivets holding the bands in place began to *pop*, and then came the great boom of the battering ram. On the first impact, the entirety of the great oak doors creaked. On the second, boards that were frozen solid, once immensely strong and now brittle, cracked and broke inward, and the metal bands began to break free.

Cor drew his steel, and he heard all the rest of the men behind him do so as well. He stood at the front of his fighting men, with his Dahken at his sides, and Soulmourn and Ebonwing began to sing, a great song of war that crescendoed to drown out the sounds of the anxious men around him. Cor had killed many men in the short few years since the murder of his parents, yet rarely did battle come without a sense of fear. It was with him now, a slight nervousness in his limbs and a sick feeling in the pit of his stomach. Naran had once told him that it was fear that allowed men to be brave. It seemed odd, but Cor hoped all those behind him felt the same thing in their stomachs.

He had lost count of how many times the battering ram struck the doors, but it seemed only to be a matter of minutes before it shattered inward with a great cracking sound like the felling of a tree. The great timbers used to brace the gate's doors fell uselessly to the ground as they had no more doors to support. The forms that rushed through ragged opening were not the black armored soldiers that Cor expected, but the lumbering forms of corpses, pushed onward by Loszian magic. They poured through the open portal in scores with no end of them in sight.

The Westerners hesitated, having never faced the walking dead before today, but they shook off their fright quickly as the four Dahken at their head waded into the army of the dead, cutting them down like blades of grass.

Turn the page for an excerpt from

BOUND BY FLAME
THE CHRONICLE OF THYSS

Coming July 2024!

"I do not understand. How have you yet to find her? I have paid you well. You are the best tracker in my lands, and yet you have no news?" the priest questioned angrily as he stared down at the man who stood before him.

Mon'El eagerly awaited news for weeks, and so had no qualms about interrupting breakfast with his wife, demanding his servants bring the tracker up to their suite atop the palace straight away. As King, High Priest and Chosen of Aeyu, He whom ruled the air and winds, Mon'El could have commanded the man to locate his daughter without any compensation at all, so the priest felt extraordinarily generous in offering a sum of gold that would buy the tracker an estate on the river itself.

Much depended on Thyssalia's safe return. Thyss, he reminded himself.

The suite sat atop Mon'El's massive pyramid that stood in the center of his city and consisted of a large, central room with four open archways that led to others at each point of the compass. These all had grand balconies to allow Mon'El to look down on his people and to allow the currents of his god to pass freely through his abode. He and his wife maintained separate bedrooms to the north and the south, though they seldom slept alone, and the room to the east comprised Mon'El's private temple to Aeyu. His wife Ilia kept the room to the west, there indulging in whatever her heart desired.

Standing three or four inches taller than Mon'El, the ranger known as Guribda had smartly dropped to his knees upon being brought before the priest and king. It would have done him no good to physically overshadow a man who could send him to his death with a mere flip of a hand, but even kneeling, he felt himself shrink before Mon'El's ire even as the king seemed to grow and darken.

Guribda feebly replied, "Well, Highness, I have some news, and I will find her. I swear it."

"What news, then?" Mon'El demanded impatiently.

"Your daughter recently was seen in a village to the north, bordering on the great jungle there. I tracked her to the edge of it where she was joined by at least six other people before they entered the jungle," he explained, leaving out the part where he was sure Thyss had been accosted and taken prisoner.

"And what of the jungle?" Mon'El pressed, idly adjusting his robes. He had been told that Guribda returned to the city alone, so he opted for more blue in his robes than white, hoping that the calm wisdom of Nykeema would embrace him in the face of bad news.

"I... I did not pursue them."

"What?!" Mon'El's voice smashed the interior walls, carried by a gust of wind as thunder cracked in a cloudless sky. Silk tapestries blew from the walls to the floor, and the plates of food on the table behind him rattled and moved about. One fell to the floor with a shatter, causing his wife to sigh. He lowered his voice to a dangerous growl as he pressed on, "Explain carefully."

The tracker's eyes shot quickly around, lolling almost like that of a panicked animal as he assessed his chance of escape should he choose to run. There were four very large, heavily muscled men at each corner, excluding the one who had moved up to be but six feet behind him. All were armed with the best scimitars the city of Kaimpur could produce, and while the tracker was no stranger to swordplay, he doubted he could take out one before the others were upon him. And then he had the priest-god's magic to contend with. No, escape was not an option.

With hands open before him, almost in supplication, he responded meekly with a bowed head, "That jungle is well known to be cursed, Highness.

There are monsters in that place that defy time, that predate the rise of men, and I admit to being a coward. Surely, you would have no fear with your immense power. You are blessed of the gods, but I am but a man. I beg your forgiveness.

"Highness, I have other taken steps, however. The jungle borders the sea to the north, and a vast, lifeless desert stretches from its southern edge all the way to your lands. If she doesn't return to the village, she has little choice but to travel to King Chofir's city on the other side. I have paid for eyes in both places. She will not escape me."

Mon'El's anger seemed to abate as the man spoke, for the priest did remind himself that most men were in fact weak and powerless. So few of Dulkur's people wielded the power of the gods, and Mon'El was one of those Chosen few, arguably the greatest of them all. The tracker's words placated him enough, and he nodded at the mention of Chofir. He knew the king well, and a smile touched the corners of his mouth at the thought that the fat merchant-king might try to impose his will on Thyss.

"Very well," Mon'El replied calmly after a moment. "See to it that she does not. She has been gone too long, this time, and I demand her presence. She must be at my side in one month or much may be lost. Go."

The tracker turned to leave, just as the guard returned to his post in the corner, and as Guribda made his way down the steps that would lead him down the outer wall of the pyramid shaped palace, Mon'El surely heard the tracker issue a relieved sigh. Mon'El clenched his fists, anger brewing again, but not aimed toward the man who had just left. No. Yet again, his daughter tested his patience and his will, as she had for the last ten years or more, and it could no longer be allowed. What was soon to happen would have repercussions throughout all of Dulkur, and she was the integral piece on the gameboard.

"Must you scheme so?" Ilia, called from behind him as he began to pace.

Turn the page for an excerpt from

The Oathbreaker's Daughter
The Dragonknight Trilogy
Book 1

Coming March 12th, 2024!

Every time the swords struck each other, the ringing of steel carried on the subtle wind currents of the warm summer day. Training for one to two hours per day, three days a week for the last two years had wrought tough, lean sinews in Jenna's arms and legs. While other girls her age mooned and obsessed over boys, many of whom noticed certain differences between the genders, Jenna crossed swords with the one armed teacher of the village's children. She was the only one among them Brasalla took the time to mentor in swordsmanship and, to a lesser extent because she left it to Jenna's mother, archery, and Jenna swelled with silent pride even as the other girls jeered at her. Two years of training to help her gain strength and then learn the basic forms of fencing had finally led to sparring with real swords, though with dull edges and blunted points. Brasalla had several of these weapons in her cottage, as well as a number of wooden practice swords and other such weapons, so as to avoid any real wound besides bruises and damaged pride. The one armed woman had taught Jenna so much, and yet every time a new lesson was unveiled, Jenna found herself bested once again. She had never once defeated the former Protectress, despite the woman having but one arm, or even landed a single point. But still she fought, knowing that one day…

Brasalla attacked with a downward stroke meant to slash down and across Jenna's body starting at her right shoulder, and Jenna knew her opportunity when it presented itself. Bringing her own sword around, she easily parried the blade to her left, and scraping steel on steel, thrust her blade forward in such a way that it would skewer her opponent, if not for the spherical mound of steel that made the weapon's point. But her sword met nothing, and in her hurry to take advantage of Brasalla's careless attack, Jenna stood suddenly off balance as her arms extended well forward. Brasalla's weight came to bear on her parried blade, forcing the point of Jenna's sword down to the ground as she could contest neither the woman's weight nor strength, to say nothing of leverage.

"You over extended your thrust, little dear. You're dead, I'm afraid."

"I know. Damn it all," Jenna swore angrily.

With a disapproving glare, Brasalla eased her weight and lifted her sword from Jenna's, allowing the girl to recover her blade, and she said, "If I were your mother I'd likely tell you to watch your language."

"Then, it's a good thing you're not, huh?" Jenna shot back, but the tone held more playfulness than challenge.

"I suppose."

"Just once, I want to kill you. Just once," Jenna complained.

Brasalla chided, "Don't do that."

"What?"

"Whine," Brasalla explained. "It's unbecoming of you. You're strong and brave, and you're growing into a beautiful woman. Such bellyaching is unacceptable, especially among the Protectresses."

Jenna's eyes narrowed, and she immediately returned, "I don't want to be a Protectress."

"Is there something wrong with being a Protectress? Something wrong with being a trusted defender of Abrea and our way of life?"

"No," Jenna replied quickly, noting her teacher's suddenly solemn tone and emotionless face. She chose her next words carefully so as not to give further offense, "It's just not what I want to do."

"You cannot do what you want to do, Little Dear," Brasalla gently reminded the girl, and it was now Jenna's turn to grow silent. "Anyway, do you know what your mistake was?"

Jenna sighed quickly, puffing a snort of air out of her nostrils in annoyance as she clenched her draw and turned her head from side to side, looking at nothing. After a moment, she answered, "I assumed."

"Assumed what?" Brasalla asked with slightly raised eyebrows.

"I assumed that you, a trained warrior, someone who has killed people far more skilled than me, made a basic mistake."

Brasalla prodded, "And?"

"And I tried to capitalize on it."

"As you well should've, but that wasn't the fatal mistake."

"No?" Jenna asked, looking up at her mentor, and her face betrayed a mix of impatience at the drawing out of the lesson and aggravation at her own ineptitude.

"You did the right thing, but you're right in that you assumed. Never assume your enemy has made a mistake, but be ready to take advantage of it if they did."

The impatience turned to more annoyance as Jenna worked to unravel the riddle in her mind. "How does that work?"

"Even the best trained warriors make mistakes," Brasalla explained calmly, indicating her missing arm with a pointed look, "and you must take advantage when they do. You parried my poor attack perfectly, but you were so certain of victory that you telegraphed your thrust badly."

"What does that mean?"

"I knew the attack was coming because I was testing you, but most trained warriors would have seen it coming, too. You pulled your sword arm back just a few inches to give more force to your thrust."

Jenna breathed in a slight hiss of air between her teeth as understanding dawned on her. "So," she reasoned, "by doing that, you saw the attack coming and had more time to react to avoid it."

"Exactly! We're fighting with swords, not clubs or staves or some other weapon that we have to bash each other's brains in with. Your father's sword came from Vulgesch. It is so strong, can hold such an edge that it can easily punch through most armor, except maybe Vulgesch plate. Fight with grace, finesse, dexterity, not force."

"I..." Jenna began, but she suddenly wasn't sure what she wanted to say, so she nodded and replied softly, "I understand."

"Maybe a little, but I think you'll understand more in time. There's one more thing I'd like you to consider, just keep it in mind. As a woman and not particularly tall, people, especially men, will underestimate you. Take advantage of that. Lure them in, and do something they don't expect. Remember what I told you before – fair fights are for suckers."

Jenna nodded idly at this, her eyes downcast as she mulled it over. Without warning, she shot her left foot out, hooking her soft leather boot right behind Brasalla's right knee while giving the woman a sudden push with both hands. Caught completely unaware, Brasalla's legs bent as she tumbled backward and landed hard on her back, only the thick grass behind her cottage slightly cushioning her impact. Even so, she felt the wind painfully knocked from her lungs as she struck the ground.

"You mean like that?" Jenna asked with a wide, proud grin. She pointed her practice sword at her mentor and said one word, "Yield."

"You little shit," Brasalla spouted angrily as she struggled up to one elbow, and then she noticed the tip of the sword, blunted with a sphere of steel as it hovered only a half foot away from her. Laughter took the woman for a moment, and she tipped her head backward, answering, "Yeah, something like that. Here, Little Dear, help an old woman up."

Turn the page for an excerpt from

Wolves of War
A John Hartman Novel

Coming October 2024!

Darkness filled the ancient woodland, permeating everything around Hartman just as much as the frigid air chilled him to the bone. Nothing about his slow, quiet trek through the forest felt pleasant, and a sense of foreboding hung heavily in the air, tempting him to abandon his mission and start hoofing it back to France. It wasn't the first time he longed to be back with the regular Army, taking it to the Jerries in a straight fight, but this was different. John just couldn't shake the pervasive dread he felt as he ventured deeper into the German wood.

He shouldn't be alone out here. It was one thing to undertake a solo operation, a task he had accomplished many times in the past. But this time, he was supposed to have a guide with him who knew the woods better than he, but his contact failed to show up at the designated rendezvous. Maybe the he had gotten held up by German soldiers, or maybe he had to hunker down somewhere. After a while, John decided he couldn't wait any longer, steeled himself and went on with the operation.

For the fourth or fifth time, John wished he'd procured a heavy coat to keep the damp cold at bay. He found a tiny break in the eldritch canopy, through which shined a beam of pale light from the full moon overhead. He stood in this welcome dispeller of darkness long enough to unfold his map and become certain of his bearings. He had only a few miles left to traverse until he broke from the forest into the open where he would have little protection from watchful German eyes, and yet, he would breathe more easily once free from this place.

A shiver ran through Hartman, and he thought, *Damn, it's cold!* He began to fold the map back into itself, but his hands seemed to slow with each progressive crease. Surely, they were cold, but it wasn't the near freezing night air that made them react so. He slipped the map into a jacket pocket, and his motion slowed to a complete halt. He stood perfectly still, and the hair on his neck and arms would have stood on end were it not for his appropriated German uniform.

Narrow set, disembodied red eyes materialized out of the gloom some distance in front of him, seeming to glow with an inner, baleful light. They hovered perhaps a foot off of the ground, but Hartman couldn't for the darkness be sure if they were five feet ahead of him or twenty five. He knew only that he stood transfixed by that hellish glare, apparently frozen to inaction while they regarded him. He needed to act, draw a pistol and shoot at those eyes, ready a knife, something, but his limbs wouldn't obey his brain's commands. The entire encounter felt eerily familiar. He had been in some freezing German wood at some point before and had seen those eyes there and then as well, but this was also different. Hartman was alone, and the darkness and cold were all pervasive, not simply offensive to the senses. And there was only one set of eyes, though he remembered, on that other occasion that other attackers had come at him from the sides.

Hartman broke his paralysis just in time to see a silver and black streak from the right as it caromed off of the back of his legs. The energy from the blow knocked him off balance, and it was only his superb athleticism that kept him from tumbling to the forest floor. Just as he regained his footing, another rush of dark motion attacked from the other direction, but this one drew blood. A fierce snapping of unseen jaws severed tendons in his left leg, causing Hartman to collapse, and as he clutched the wounded limb, warm, steaming blood coated his hands.

Either out of a preternatural sense or pure luck, he managed to get his left forearm up just as a huge wolf of silver and black lunged at him. A mouth of wicked, yellowed teeth opened wide in anticipation, and Hartman wedged his arm as far into the mouth as he could. Like a dog whose chewing bone had gone too far backward, the wolf chomped its jaws trying to dislodge him. The power of those jaws wrought tremendous pain, and Hartman felt the teeth puncture the skin of his arm even through the layers of his jacket and sleeve. But it also bought him precious moments. His free hand reached for his knife, but before he could find it, another beast charged from his right. This canine minion of Hell he caught by the neck, and it took all of his might just to hold the thing at bay as it snapped at his face, rancid carrion breath caressing his face. If he could somehow manage to get his legs underneath the creature in front of him, perhaps he could launch the beast just far enough to access his knife or gun. Then, he could turn this fight around.

This glimmer of hope flickered in his mind only to be extinguished in an instant as a third monstrous wolf stood less than a foot away to his left, mouth agape and tongue hanging low out of its mouth. It panted softly, but seemingly out of anticipation rather than exhaustion, and Hartman knew he couldn't hold this one off; he was simply out of arms. It lunged toward his face, and all he could see was teeth and then darkness as the wolf's jaws clamped around his face.

Hartman bolted upright, his clothes and the bedsheets of the hospital bed soaked in sweat. As his heart and breathing gradually slowed, his head cleared so that he could regain his bearings. Two nurses moved around the room, drawing back curtains to allow in the first rays of the autumn sun, which told Hartman it was around seven in the morning. There were only six men in the score of beds in the room, and of them all, he was the only one unwounded. He was vaguely aware of a rifle toting guard that stood in a gray uniform next to the room's entrance.

One of the nurses glared his direction as he watched them, and as she made her way across the room to his bedside, he reached down and rubbed at his ankle, which was shackled to the metal frame of the bed. She stood to his right in her uniform - a dress of narrow, vertical white and blue stripes under an apron of white. Her collar, also white, contrasted against the dress, and was pinned closed severely by an emblem of the Third Reich. A black German eagle clutched a red cross in its talons, though the cross had been extended and resembled an inverted Christian cross.

"Gut morning. Nachtmares?" she asked in a hodge-podge of English and German. She wasn't pretty in the least, but she hadn't been unfriendly to him despite their nations' adversarial nature.

"*Es ist nichts,*" Hartman replied in perfect German, "*Danke.*"

"Nothing? It's nothing you say? You come into my country, my Fatherland, and kill my sons and brothers, and it is nothing?" she asked, her English becoming clearer though accented. Her eyes began to glow with an unholy red light as she continued, "You come here to fight a war that doesn't belong to you. You kill thousands of good men and deprive the Fatherland what we are owed by right. You do not know what you face, what this Old World can unleash upon you!"

She seemed to grow as she spoke, her uniform tearing at the seams as her bones popped and elongated. By the end of her tirade, her words were nearly unintelligible as her human mouth reformed to that of a wolf's toothy maw under bright red, demonic eyes. Hair, fur of silver and black had sprouted across every inch of her, and razor sharp claws extended from each of her fingers. The room grew dark, as if her very presence alone blotted out the light of the rising sun.

John shouted in alarm and leapt out of the bed as if a great spring had been compressed underneath him, except the shackle around his ankle prevented him from going too far. His back slammed hard onto the cold floor, and he would've cracked the back of his skull as well were it not for his flailing arms somehow breaking his fall. His leg remained suspended in the air, attached as it was to the bedframe, with the hospital bed acting as the only barrier between Hartman and the monstrosity.

"Captain Hartman?" a worried voice said in his ear, and cool hands cradled his sweaty face. "Captain Hartman, wake up."

John Hartman blinked his eyes and shook his head once to dispel and clear away the fading image. He indeed lay on a cool floor, but it was that of the Army field hospital in France. His left leg was propped up on his bed, his ankle wrapped up in bedsheets so twisted to be as strong as thick rope. The room was dimly lit, except for the warmth of a soft glow emanating from the hallway beyond the door. Somewhere in the next room, he heard a muffled announcer's voice calling a baseball game. It sounded like the World Series that just ended two days ago with the St. Louis Cardinals beating the St. Louis Browns.

"Captain Hartman are you all right?" the brown haired night nurse asked.

"I'm fine," he replied with a hardened face as she helped him stand and get back into bed.

"You know, I could find something to help you sleep," she offered, likely referring to whiskey or some other such spirits; being an officer had its privileges.

"No, thank you very much," he replied as he laid his head backward to stare wide awake at the ceiling. "I've slept enough."

Made in the USA
Middletown, DE
28 July 2024